N FOR NARCISSUS

FOR NARCISSUS

CHRIS HUNT

GMP

FOR RICHARD

First published in 1990 by GMP Publishers Ltd
PO Box 247, London N17 9QR, England

© *Chris Hunt 1990*

British Library Cataloguing in Publication Data

Hunt, Chris
N for Narcissus
I. Title
823.914[F]

ISBN 0 85449 136 8

Distributed in North America by Alyson Publications Inc.
40 Plympton St, Boston, MA 02118, USA

Distributed in Australia by Bulldog Books
PO Box 155, Broadway, NSW 2007, Australia

Typeset by MC Typeset Ltd, Gillingham, Kent ME8 6PL, England
Printed in the EC on environmentally-friendly paper by
Norhaven A/S, Viborg, Denmark

CHAPTER ONE

O N FEBRUARY 14th 1895 a blizzard of a startling ferocity fell upon London. From the windows of my club I watched the snowflakes gusting from a bone-coloured sky, an almost visible wind shaping the snow beneath so that the kerbstones of the pavement were completely obscured. Only the intermittent gas lamps showed where the road began. The carriages, the broughams, the hansoms passing along the broad width of Pall Mall moved cumbersome as ploughs.

I would have remembered the day for the severity of the weather alone; but, as I was to find, upon that day Fate drew a crimson line across my life with the bold stroke of a consummate artist. February 14th was the last day on which I behaved as I had always done – the dutiful husband, father, son, philanthropist, the man of property, comfortable with my associates, charming in the presence of ladies – in short, the Victorian gentleman. As I sat at my window table, lingering over luncheon, the very cutlery and tablecloth bespeaking stalwart respectability, no one could have predicted that this was the calm before the storm, the quiet before the conflict, and that henceforth I was to know a strange and chequered time, a morass of iniquity, and all the intricate steps along the devious pathway to what the moralists call Sin.

Lord Avonbury brushed past my table, pausing to enquire the state of my health.

"I would be very well," I observed languidly, "if I were not obliged to attend an opening night at the St. James' this evening, and if my wife were not becoming a Bohemian."

He laughed. "Your trouble, Algy, is that you have chosen to keep abreast of culture, and as one of culture's representatives you have a sacred duty to attend opening nights. Now had you preferred to do as I have done and remained a Philistine of the old school, tonight you could stay indoors by your own fireside with a fine St. Marceaux."

"Hugh, I would not dare. Claudia expects me to be at her side when she makes her entrance among her literary friends. I am the finishing touch."

"Ah, the fair Claudia. The now Bohemian Claudia?" he added, intrigued.

I relented; I was doing her less than justice. "Claudia knows the author's wife; this contributes to her interest in the play. We shall, however, be thoroughly entertained, I've no doubt of that, as we have been with his others."

Hugh raised a polite eyebrow. "To which literary gentleman do you refer?"

"Mr Oscar Wilde," I answered, though with a curious reticence. Justified, as I instantly observed. A slight flicker passed over Hugh's face – distaste, unease? Enough for me to notice a reaction I was half expecting. Hurriedly, as if there were a need to blur the edges of the name, I explained: "Claudia has been friendly with Constance Wilde – they like the same sort of clothes . . . Constance is a very charming woman."

"I have no doubt about it," Hugh assured me firmly, almost as if in the safety of Constance's unspotted reputation we would bask untroubled and rapidly dispel the unacknowledged ripples caused by the mention of her spouse. "And anybody graced by the friendship of your lovely wife is to be doubly blessed. I hope I may see her again before too long. And your delightful children."

"Indeed you shall." And we grumbled lightly about the dreadful weather, and he moved on his way.

Claudia, my wife since that happy day eleven years ago when I succumbed to my mother's persuasions and married, was universally acclaimed as a woman of taste and beauty. When my mother first introduced her to me Claudia was a society belle of impeccable birth and standing, and the perfect wife for a young man of quality. Everyone said as much and I saw no reason to disagree. The wedding portraits show us as an exceptionally beautiful couple: Claudia, with her wide clear eyes, firm oval chin and mass of thick corn-coloured hair intricately wound about her brow, with pretty curls at the temples and violets at her throat; the wedding dress of cream and cowslip (for even then her tastes accorded much with Constance's) admired by many; and I myself looking ridiculously young at twenty-two, my golden hair a little ruffled by the April breeze.

Our life since that day had followed its even course with no more nor less joys and discomforts than is usual. The demise of my father, an aged aristocrat whose authoritarian views had oppressed my childhood and blemished *ma jeunesse*, occasioned me little sorrow and enabled me to take control of the estate – Mortmayne in Bedfordshire – and the town house in the square where I was at present residing. Our three children, William, Sophy and Perceval, were born from a union that knew little of passion and somewhat more of obligation, without too much distaste on either part. My mother, moving from residence to residence, considered it all highly satisfactory, and no doubt congratulated herself upon the consolidation of her fondest hopes and the skilful avoidance of her darkest fears, for I know that my life just prior to my marriage caused her the gravest concern.

It was to this same highly satisfactory situation that I returned in the late afternoon, the hansom taking me slowly and laboriously through the snowy streets until we reached the square. A wretched organ grinder stood beneath the lamp post, churning out some penny ballad in the thankless air, his monkey huddled on the organ top, its tail hanging limp like old rope. I thrust a coin upon him as I passed on my way to certain warmth and sustenance, his mutter of appreciation lost in the wind's noise. Snow lay white upon the iron railings, white upon the three broad steps between the two slim pillars and in smudges on the great front door.

The fire in my study burned brightly and as Meredith poured my sherry and ministered unto me I once again regretted the need to go out that evening. Ensconced upon my bottle-green Chesterfield, my gaze moved over the dark and agreeable décor – the panelled mahogany, the burgundy wallpaper, the heavy dark red velvet curtains. Leather-bound volumes filled the bookcases. The dancing flames, the hissing gas lamps picked out light and shadow upon family photographs in gold frames; the glass of the mirror, the burnished gilt clock, the gleaming fender, the heavy old desk all radiating beyond their intrinsic value a symbolic worth important as an indication of the correct state of the world wherein I belonged. A wish to remain amongst them upon a bitterly cold evening would have been reasonable enough and needed no justification. But it was more than that, I knew.

I had always enjoyed theatre-going and with liberal tastes I had managed to find pleasure in all manner of presentations, from Mr Henry Irving's performances at the Lyceum, to the Savoy operettas, to Pinero's enormous successes and even the controversial plays of Ibsen – I had opinions on them all. A trivial farce should hold no terrors. If the previous works of Mr Wilde were any indication, I should certainly not be bored.

It would be quite untrue, quite fanciful, to relate that at this stage of it all I had any kind of prescience, any hint of connection between my own life and that of the dramatist whose play I was considering. How indeed could I upon that snowy February afternoon in any way perceive the bizarre and tortuous twists that were to lead me to a horrible conjunction with that man's miserable destiny? Anything which in the past might once have suggested that my future could be anything otherwise than untainted was long since burned out of sight, destroyed as finally as flame burns paper, forgotten.

In the early days of Oscar Wilde's success he was a sometime guest at Mortmayne. I could not help observing that on occasions such as these, he was the centre of an admiring group. It was always much the same as that scene described in *The Picture of Dorian Gray*, when Sir Henry delights the guests at Aunt Agatha's dinner. He tells them that we discover too late that the only things we never regret in life are our mistakes. He plays with an idea, he translates it to a merry dance in praise of folly, and facts flee like frightened forest things. He is all wit, charm, brilliance. His listeners are captivated. They follow his sparkling words as if a magical tune upon a Grecian pipe. And all this is done knowing that Dorian Gray is sitting there, rapt, absorbed, eager to be impressed, nay more, enchanted.

At times I caught Wilde's eye but studiously looked away. In the conservatory, when beyond the shimmering walls of glass the lawns lay white with snow, I draped myself beside an immense green fern that soared up from an ornamental urn. At the far end of the room, beneath the spidery black tracing of the delicate wrought iron, the group that followed Oscar paused. Head and shoulders above those nearest to him he was instantly distinctive. His voice carried. I did not intend to meet his eyes but I was drawn; moreover some acknowledgment of his presence was only socially polite.

"Algy, come and join us!" cooed a certain countess. "Mr Wilde is being utterly fascinating."

"How exquisite you look, Algy," added Lady Birkthorpe, a person with, until that day, no artistic pretension whatsoever, "composed against the potted fern as if upon a portrait. I venture to suggest that green is your colour."

"The colour green and Hell," said Clarissa Penhurst daringly, "is made for thieves and artists." This was certainly an observation she had heard or read, and possibly aware of the implication that she had been less than charitable to her host, she blushed and added: "And Algy is an artist."

That is the trouble with verbal posturing; you very often say more than you mean. I was, however, grateful, for the moment passed when it might have been construed that I was posing. That it could be suspected this posing was in any way for the benefit of Oscar Wilde completely discomfited me, and afterwards when I recalled the incident a feeling of disgust and loathing overcame me and it was all I could do to go in to dinner.

But why? Why did his presence so disturb me and leave me with those vile uncomfortable sensations? Gloomily I stared into the fire. I would have given much to have remained at home tonight, but it was expected that we should attend, and I had always done the expected. I would have liked to put the man completely from my thoughts, indeed I would have done so easily – but how could that be possible when at somewhat after eight tonight I would be watching his latest creation, hearing words he wrote, absorbing sentiments of his invention?

Peevishly I stood up, and in a very irritable humour sought distraction from my thoughts in the bosom of my family. I was obliged to present myself at this evening's extravaganza and I would do so; but henceforth I should put the man completely from my mind, for we had nothing binding us, no scrap in common, and the great divide of social class. For he, with all his great success in drawing room and dining room and restaurant and club, was not a gentleman and his ways were not my ways.

I doubted whether after tonight he would ever cross my mind again.

The marital bedroom of our house in the square was furnished in the style of a few years ago: cream wallpaper with roses and leaves in great profusion patterned upon it, the same pattern echoed in the window curtains, the bed hangings and valance. Upon the floor lay an oriental carpet in colours of gold, green, rose; above the fireplace hung a mirror gilt-framed. The bed was covered by a patchwork quilt in a wondrous array of silken shapes, something of a family heirloom. A dressing table flowing with lace and crowned with a coral pink bow housed Claudia's array of toiletries, a red plush chair before it. Heavily framed paintings decorated the walls. The room was warm from the fire in the hearth, and pleasantly scented from the lingering of Claudia's white heliotrope.

Amongst this most agreeable profusion sat Claudia upon a yellow chair, at a little table with a lace cloth upon it, and the remains of her tea tray, books and bric-a-brac. She wore a blue silk peignoir and she was studying her face in a hand mirror, toying with the curls at her brow, and laughing to be caught, by my entrance, in this traditional pose.

"Come in, Algy," she declared. "And kiss me for sending me such a beautiful Valentine."

Though it occurred to me briefly that the kiss should have been mine to receive, I inclined my head and kissed the intricate coiffure, while we surveyed together the floral creation she held in her hand, the Valentine, a pageant of roses and paper lace.

"It was most sweet of you," she congratulated me. "But you are always thoughtful . . ."

I always do what is expected, I agreed to myself. Life can be very easy that way.

"Now tell me," I said, sitting on the red plush chair beside the dressing table and toying with a silver-backed hairbrush, "what do you mean to wear tonight? I know you have some thrilling concoction to amaze us all. I merely hope that I can live up to it in my conventional attire."

"Oh never fear," she answered, with just a hint of sarcasm. "You will achieve your usual perfection. But," she added, determined not to ruffle the smooth texture of our marital harmony, "I will indeed favour you with a glimpse of my attire. Prepare yourself!"

She stood up, silks a-rustle, swanning over to the wardrobe. Its mirror swung as she opened the door, rotating the room's luxuries as it passed. She turned to me then, holding up a dress against herself. I admit that I groaned.

"Just as I supposed!" she challenged me before I even spoke. "You do not like it – I knew that you would not – you are so old-fashioned. Algy, come, admit it. You think that I should dress more like your mother!"

"Indeed I do not," I protested. "I have never given you to suppose so for an instant. I simply wish that your taste inclined more to those fashions which show woman as a sweet and feminine creature, a contrast to the male."

"Good Lord, Algy, you talk like a zoological lecture!" cried my wife. "I know your views – you like a woman to look as if she'd stepped from a Tissot painting – all tight-waisted, laced into unnatural slenderness, cascading at the hips to a sea of tulle and tarlatan, so many frills that she can barely move, no sign of feet beneath the frills, and every glide across the floor performing the same function as a broom and sweeping up the dirt. Admit it now," she added with a shameful pun and twinkling eyes. "'Tis so!"

"Yes," I said petulantly. "But I accept that my wife is modern – a New Woman in these days of the New Realism. I bless the day when you first joined your League of Female Philanthropists, and I am sure you will look delightful in the dress. Or, as it seems to me, blouse and skirt and waistcoat," I could not help adding with unmistakable disapproval.

"My outfit is modelled on a Roumanian peasant's dress," explained Claudia, completely unrepentant. "The blouse is silk, with voluminous sleeves, with, you will notice, the gathered leg o' mutton flounce where the sleeves meet the shoulders. The lace at the neck flatters the throat. The skirt hangs loosely in comfortable folds, allowing the legs freedom of movement. All in all I am very pleased with it, and I think you will be when you have overcome your initial narrow-mindedness."

"Roumanian peasants!" I snorted. "Your dressmaker has been no nearer to Roumania than the Kentish coast. You really think the peasants there wear silk? They wear old goatskins, smell of goat, and drink goat's curds in tents of hide and thong. Or perhaps there is a goatskin mantle which you have not shown me yet?" I looked around invitingly.

Claudia returned the garb to the wardrobe. "You'd keep women laced into outfits that caused havoc to the liver," she muttered. "Do you know what corsetry does to the internal organs?"

"Women will never leave off their whalebone," I said complacently. "It flatters the figure so. Plump damozels draw in their contours till they achieve a sylph-like shape, and thin girls force what they do possess into a passable silhouette. A woman is entirely motivated by the wish to please the man, be he friend or lover or a stranger on a train. So whales up in those Arctic seas must tremble yet."

Vastly irritated by my flippancy my spouse thrust a booklet at me, one of those slim pamphlets full of drawings of ladies in corsetry designed to sell the product in our homes. Full-bosomed nymphs with waists a double handspan smiled up from the pages.

"Look at them!" cried Claudia, jabbing with her finger. "Look at those wasp waists and jutting hips. They shift our internal organs up from where they should lie and lift them to a distorted shape, against the shape of Nature, which is this —" She slipped aside her peignoir, holding it open. She wore pretty cotton underlinen with broderie anglaise at the neck, and all that lay beneath could be quite easily supposed, the breasts that hung, the stomach which was not flat, the contours all much wider than the drawings would suggest. Her shape was womanly and it was not much like the fashion plates. I flinched in curious repulsion.

"This is unseemly, Claudia. Reclothe yourself."

"Ah, Algy," she said, drawing the garment back about herself. "You like the outward shows. It would well suit you if a woman was born clothed and coiffured, with a bonnet on her head, and gloves. The nearness of the flesh has always frightened you."

"Oh, really, I am sure this is not so."

"Then tell me," answered Claudia, still standing, awfully majestic. "Do you realise that in eleven years of marriage we have neither of us seen the other naked?"

I fidgeted at the word.

"Have we not?"

"You know it," she shrugged. "Oh, we know the shapes beneath the nightclothes; and there has been the occasional glimpse of skin.

11

But which of us has ever done so much as walk across the room without first covering ourselves? Why are we so ashamed of nakedness?"

"I've no idea," I said somewhat testily. "And really, Claudia, I fail to understand your sudden interest in the Garden of Eden. I don't find your conversation at all appropriate. I merely came in to find out how you were; and unexpectedly I am regaled with a diatribe upon the benefits of walking about in a state of undress. You used not to be like this. I blame that silly League with which you have involved yourself. They are all Modern Women, are they not? I daresay you discuss this kind of thing with them?"

"No; we discuss social issues . . ."

"Then it must be Constance Wilde. Have you been seeing her again?"

Claudia sat down in the yellow chair, and with her elbow resting on the arm of it she bit absentmindedly at her thumb. "Constance Wilde? No, I haven't seen her for – so long I barely remember."

"I thought you were close friends. I know she initiated you into the joys of Rational Dress and the casting out of mahogany and aspidistras in favour of acres of white paint and forget-me-nots on the curtains; and you were attracted to the Women's Liberal Federation in her company. Did you not attend meetings of sharp-eyed harridans urging each other to throw off the male yoke? An inexplicable fascination with nudity and a suggestion of my limitations as a husband – surely I see the influence of Constance here?"

"Indeed you do not," Claudia returned sharply. "Credit me with some thoughts of my own, if you please. If you must know, I have deemed it proper to relinquish my connection with Constance on account of the rumours concerning her husband. Since you are so devoted to the idea of seemly behaviour you cannot but approve. And besides, it was your mother's idea."

"My mother! You spoke to her about it?"

"She spoke to me. She told me it would be better if we did not invite the Wildes to Mortmayne, and she would prefer it if I did not continue my acquaintance with Constance. I have nothing against Constance; no one has. She is a sweet and agreeable person and a very good mother. But by implication . . ."

"I thought that she and Oscar lived apart now?" I said vaguely.

"It does not matter whether they do or not. She is still married to him. And therefore . . ."

"Indeed," I murmured, meaning nothing. As I digested the information I added: "Although I realised that we had had nothing to do with them socially of late I had not supposed it a matter of policy! It is rare for you to acquiesce to a suggestion of my mother's. Were you convinced by her reasoning?"

"I hardly remember," Claudia picked up the hand mirror again and idly toyed with a recalcitrant curl. "Your mother said that these days whoever invited Oscar to dine must expect to invite Lord Alfred Douglas along with him."

"Is that so terrible? I have only met him a couple of times, but as I recall, he graced the company somewhat."

"It is not his personal appearance of course, or his manners – no one would deny his good looks and breeding. Your mother gave me to understand that in some ways he was a bad influence on Oscar – or was it the other way about? – and therefore one did not encourage them."

"Did my mother specify?" I was intrigued as to how much she knew.

"I don't think so. I think the implication was that Oscar had become a womanizer."

I raised my eyebrows.

Claudia continued. "Your mother suggested that some of his activities had become unsavoury. It is not solely us, you know. Clarissa Penhurst and Lady Avonbury have come to the same conclusion. It is the proper course of action. We all have children . . ." she added with a curious righteousness that seemed irrelevant, as if to have produced offspring ranked one with the angels.

"Lord Alfred too – we are to be denied his company henceforth?"

"Your mother said – well, naturally, I did not pay too close attention to the subject. All I could suppose was that if Oscar has become a womanizer then presumably he does it in the company of Lord Alfred Douglas. To what other conclusion could I come? I suppose they womanize together . . . If Oscar chooses to jeopardise his pleasant home with its lovely wife and charming children then that is hardly our business. All we can do is show the disapproval of right-thinking people who believe in certain principles of morality."

She looked across at me, smiling, gentle, sure of my approval. She seemed so delicate suddenly, the womanly ideal that gentlemen have sought to nurture and protect across the centuries. The curious thing was that her words were cast-iron hard and intransigent, and I found that I could not reply.

"Will you go up and see the children?" she invited pleasantly.

"Indeed!" I pronounced, relieved at such a heartening prospect. "Will you accompany me?"

"No, I must arrange the evening. You go – play with them awhile; they'll be so pleased."

"You do not need to prompt me," I replied as I stood up. "You know I love to be with them."

She smiled, all affability. "You're looking well, dear, if a little tired." She studied me, a baffled frown upon her brows. She tapped her lips with some slim pencil. "What do you think – Clarissa Penhurst says that you look very similar to Lord Alfred Douglas. Personally I cannot see it. But maybe there is something?"

"What rot!" I said with well-concealed annoyance. "We are nothing like each other."

And then I wondered if my mother disagreed. I laughed at such a fancy. It was utterly inconceivable that my respected mother Lady Winterton would have become so devious as to banish Oscar Wilde from the ranks of our acquaintances from a fear that he might see in me whatever he found charming in Lord Alfred Douglas. I had lived for eleven years as a family man with wife and children and a life that shone with virtue. Posing against tropical ferns did not constitute a threat to manhood, duty and social position.

Any cause there might have been for doubt was over long ago, forgotten, buried in the past.

And besides, my mother never knew about it.

CHAPTER TWO

T HE NURSERY fire burned comfortably bright. Two night-shirts warmed upon the fire guard. The wallpaper and curtains were a daisy meadow, daisies as far as the eye could see. Two beds with painted rails stood cosily on each side of the chimney-piece, with clean white linen and delightful counterpanes, above each bed a framed sampler with birds and flowers and alphabets. A merry profusion of toys lay scattered about, for it was not yet bedtime and the great evening tidy-up had not yet taken place. William's fort had most disrespectfully been ransacked, and the heroes of Sudan and Lucknow lay in undignified disarray beside knitted rabbits and the wooden elephants and giraffes from Noah's Ark. William, securely ensconced away at school, would never know. The dappled rocking-horse nodded sagely, and the lower end of Perceval protruded from the dolls' house. The room smelt pleasantly of toys and winter medicaments.

It seemed that I had come in good time, for Sophy was in tears over some tale read to her by Emily, a dark-eyed, red-cheeked brisk young girl whom I could never bring myself to call by her proper title of Nanny. This was because the memory of the Fiend in Human Form who devastated my own nursery years had seared itself forever upon my mind, and the dread name of that creature signified to me anything as terrible as might be found in the darker reaches of the Schwarzwald so Grimmly told.

"What is it that caused us such distress?" I asked as I sat Sophy on my knees and traced away her tears with a light finger.

Emily passed me the open book with an apologetic smile. I recognised it. A swift glance reminded me of the ghastly scenario – the death of the mother, the little boys at the bedside, the unpaid rent, the threat of eviction . . .

"It was further on, sir." Emily explained. "The wasted form . . ."

This heart-tugging tale ran on through at least thirty-five verses, and I disentangled the drear tale, from the Angel Coming From the Skies, to the Crying till All Tears were Spent. Finally, the youngest boy succumbed to grim mortality, and leaving behind his Wasted

15

Form, he rose above the sleeping city, above St. Paul's, above the fog and smoke; and went to Jesus.

I closed the book and let it fall on the rug. "Now Sophy, what's all this?" I said, my arm about her. A golden-haired angel of six years old she had a heart too tender for her own good. How soft and warm her cheek was! Her large eyes looked up at me.

"Do little children die?"

I blanched. Oh how I dreaded questions that required an earnest reply! Did other children of this age lead one into the realms of Life and Death, at five o'clock, when one has come for solace and contentment?

"No!" I lied at once, and catching Emily's reproving eye I wriggled at my cowardice. "Well, sometimes. Emily will tell you – "

Emily shook her head severely; busy movement (she was tidying away the toys) betokening her view that such was the duty of Papa. "I must see about their supper," she told me firmly and left the room.

"Some little children die," I said, boldly plunging in. "But they are poor and cold, and die because they have no coat and boots, no fire to warm them, no home to live in. Like the little boy in the poem." How odd it was, I noticed, that one changed one's tone when speaking to a child. I heard my voice, an over-sweet expression lacing it. I always spoke to Sophy thus. I wondered if she noticed and observed the change when I reverted and conversed with Claudia.

"Children who are safe and warm," I continued, "need never worry. They have a loving mamma who sees that they have good food to eat and a warm bed to sleep in; and they have a loving papa who . . ." I paused. No, I did not go forth each day to earn our daily bread, toiling in some vile establishment with furrowed brow and manly perspiration. Inherited wealth had not the same purposeful associations somehow. ". . . loves them very much," I finished, conscious of inadequacy. "Here in their nursery they are safe and warm and have everything they need to grow up strong and good and useful." Just like myself in fact, I thought cynically. How often it is that one preaches to the young matters which have long since ceased to be applicable to oneself. And there was more to come. "And remember," I added, "the little boy was very glad to cast off his wasted form because he went to Jesus. He left behind all sorrow and distress, all poverty and cold. He went happily, and his brother was happy too, because he knew the little lad would find comfort in the arms of Jesus. And I've told you all about Jesus, haven't I?"

"Yes, papa."

"What have I told you?"

16

"That Jesus loves the little children and if we are good and loving and say our prayers we shall go to his Home on High and live in Ever Lasting Life."

"That's right," I said uncomfortably, hugging her. "So none of us need ever fear."

All over the land, I reflected morosely, parents must be speaking thus, parents who had long since lost the trusting faith they had as children, inculcating values which they did not believe into young unformed minds, instilling concepts which rang hollow. Were children wiser than they seemed? Could they see through the intricate façade behind which so much of our lives were built? Did my Sophy truly believe that Jesus sat on high amongst the angels, holding out his arms to little children, while a glorious sunset inflamed the clouds with crimson-amber light? Myself, since I had read the conclusions of Darwin and found them convincing, had supposed that as the beautiful Eden was a fable then all that followed from it was a charming fabrication. If our dim ancestors were fishes, who one day crawled out upon the slime and made towards the forests (those remaining in the water retaining aquatic characteristics and now victims of our rod and line) then beings in the likeness of their Creator were an idle dream – a pleasant one, I grant you, but one unable to dispel entirely that slight unease in the presence of the lively marmosets in Regent's Park.

Yet given this, I saw to it that each one of my children prayed at bedtime and was noddingly familiar with Samuel, David, Abraham, Daniel, and of course the Baby Jesus. Claudia, for all her modern views, agreed; and Emily would have expected no less from her employers. We all colluded to provide a mental world where Ever Lasting Life existed just beyond the clouds, a happy land where all was well, a kind of wondrous Nursery; with no inconsistency about the fact that Grandfather Winterton would be there, fresh as new, wine-rosy but freed from gout, along with Bimbo the aged kitchen cat, with glossy stripes and bounding energy, and all the wretched blackbirds he had mangled in his lifetime, strong of wing and golden-beaked but now at peace with Bimbo, sleeping side by side amongst the swans-down of the amber clouds. And so the myth is perpetrated, on unto the coming generation.

"Jesus loves us all," I reaffirmed.

Sophy considered this with earnest gravity. "I do say my prayers," she checked upon her fingers. "I do as Nanny tells me. But!" Alarm seized her. "Perceval does not. Will Perceval rise above the smoke?"

I blinked. Swiftly marvelling at her capacity to retain the lines of spoken verse I could not help but laugh.

"Oh, come, Sophy," I declared. "Are you afraid that Perceval will float above the clouds? Just look at him." We looked.

Perceval aged three was an astonishingly fat child. William and Sophy were faultlessly constructed and very much what one would have supposed that creatures as finely formed as Claudia and myself would have produced. In Perceval we could not but suspect a small rotund ancestor long since forgotten, each accusing the other for this tarnished secret of the family tree now reappeared in modern form. And Perceval on hands and knees protruding from the dolls' house was a sight that somehow reinforced one's previous bafflement.

"Do you know, Sophy, what it means: He left behind his wasted form?"

"Yes, papa, it means the boy was very thin. As thin as this!" She showed me with a movement of her hands.

"Quite. Now look at Perceval. Is he that thin?"

"No, papa."

"Is he even portly? Rather fat?"

"Yes, papa."

"We could try to imagine Perceval rising above the smoke if you like. A boy who was feather-light might soar upward on a little gust of wind. But a plump boy . . . the wind would huff and puff and Perceval would remain on the ground and the wind would try again – like this – and once again it would be quite defeated. Eventually, exhausted and quite out of breath, the wind would slink away to Africa and bother someone else. And Perceval would still be chortling and chuckling just like he does now."

Sensing praise, Perceval emerged and beaming came to join us. I caught him up on the other knee and there we sat, Sophy all smiles, all wasted forms forgotten, and most fortunate for me, no probing queries as to whether surely Perceval's soul was feather-light, for did not the poem talk of souls? By casuistry we thus explain away so many of the problems that would otherwise disturb our waking hours.

"We'll read a happy book," I proposed, reaching round for one that lay upon the table's edge, pocket-sized and brightly coloured, *The Alphabet of Flowers*. "Now here's a most agreeable topic."

Sophy turned up her nose. "That's Perceval's book; it's too easy for me."

"You and I will help him then." They wriggled into trouser-creasing comfortable positions, and we began.

"A for Anemones telling of Spring
And all of the joys that the warm days will bring.

B is for Bluebell that sparkles with dew
And carpets the ground with its flowers of blue.

C is for Cowslip we bind in a ball
And bunches look bright in the parlour and hall . . ."

We paused to reminisce about the cowslips in the park at Mortmayne, and then hurried on to E which Sophy liked because there was an Emily in the picture who looked like our Emily, with black hair and a white cap, teaching Eglantine to trail itself over a wooden trellis framed in pink dog-roses. We looked at Foxgloves, Gillyflowers and Heather, we passed Ivy and Jonquil, Kingcups and Lilies, each flower decorating an infant girl at play. Absentmindedly I began to count the ratio of little boys to little girls as a subject to be surrounded by flowers – six boys, eighteen girls – and more than eighteen, because many of the girls came in batches, and W showed five of them, fairies dancing on a water lily and one of them showing a coy little breast. Why was it the accepted way to show the female as the beautiful one, the one who sits among the primroses and the mignonettes? Anyone with a discerning eye knew well enough that boys were beautiful. The Café Royal was full of them, a positive *mêlée* of velvet jackets, varnished boots, carefully curled moustaches, white waistcoats, white camelias.

I began to think about *The Picture of Dorian Gray*.

It must have been about four years ago that this was published. How the newspapers raged! "An unclean book spawned from the leprous literature of the French decadents, a poisonous book, with odours of moral and spiritual putrefaction . . . a book only suitable for outlawed noblemen and perverted telegraph boys" – a reference to the Cleveland Street Scandal when a house of ill repute had been discovered by the police, where gentlemen met youths and exchanged sovereigns for sexual favours. Lord Arthur Somerset had been obliged to flee abroad, as a result. An acquaintance of mine Lord Kerwin had also judged it best to leave the country; he had now taken up abode in Paris.

We all felt obliged to read the book, if only to add our own righteous disapproval to the storm of criticism that blew up over it. My own attitude was entirely hypocritical and I venture to suggest that this may have been true of others. With supercilious laughter we kept at bay its more disturbing aspects – that one man can so influence another as to lead him down a path to degradation and evil, and that the sins he chose were sins that lurked in London, hidden behind the civilised façades of prosperous thoroughfares, down alleys and courtyards where in filth and squalor, for a price, one might gratify one's basest urges. My personal hypocrisy lay in my secret fascination with the book. While publicly decrying it I privately returned to it again and again. "Each man sees his own sin in Dorian Gray," maintained the author. This troubled me, for the sin I saw, I believed long since suppressed in me. If I could see it there amongst the gilded prose then what did that portend? I found myself mentally wandering with Dorian through the gloomy fog-bound streets of Whitechapel, the puddled grime down by the docks; or, like himself, longing to read of exquisite emperors, and gilded youths who served them wine in perfumed palaces, of kings and courtiers in golden-threaded robes who secretly caressed in bowers of roses. And just as I would shiver with a sympathetic thrill I would recall most sharply that the book was accused of hinting at sins and abominable crimes. I felt disgusted with myself; also, I hardly know why, afraid.

"L for the Lily with leaves of bright green
Wreathed round the head of our sweet Birthday Queen."

I found it perfectly possible to converse with Sophy and Perceval upon the subject of lilies and birthdays while pondering on sin and degradation. I noticed this with some alarm. What kind of monster was I, outwardly a kind papa, inwardly this mass of contradiction?

Ah, I knew far more than Claudia about the rumours concerning Oscar Wilde. Womanizing! Unhappy fellow, if only he had been so fortunate! The upper classes like a womanizer. They admire him for his flair, for his discernment if she's pretty, and for his luck. Come a year or so we'll see one on the throne of England and we'll be none the worse for it. But the Other Love is a different story . . .

Some months ago – I think it was the previous August – all the newspapers were carrying reports of a police raid on a club in Fitzroy Street. They arrested eighteen men. It occurred at midnight. How the newspapers relished it, in tones of horror telling all they knew and more beside! Taken to a police station in Tottenham Court Road the men were charged with – what? No evidence could be found. The magistrate at Marlborough Street released them, two bound over to keep the peace, two discharged unconditionally, some ordered to be of good behaviour – so much for simple fact. But there was much more to it. The house was a brothel, we were told. One Arthur Marling had been arrested dressed in "a fantastic female garb of black and gold" – he said he was a female impersonator who sang by invitation at the houses of the rich. We learned of "drag parties" held on Sunday evenings. "They are most of them *known*, your worship," said the Superintendent.

The incident raised an ugly smoke, and it was said that some of those arrested were friends of Oscar Wilde. One would have disbelieved these rumours, for what man of quality would befriend members of the lower classes? And yet Wilde did – it was painfully true, for we had seen him. At the Café Royal, at Kettner's, I had often seen him dine with boys – bright perky types with raucous laughs, the kind one saw at race tracks – and it was well known that sometimes these were taken up to private rooms to dine out of the public gaze, where tables had pink-shaded candles and one drank champagne on ice, ate candied cherries, lingered over brandy and cigars.

The Café Royal of course was highly peppered with a certain riff-raff, and these boys were not so unusual in that setting. But in connection with the rumours about Oscar Wilde there was more than merely dining boys. Why, for over a year now I had been aware of muttered hints and scandalised whispers at the mention of his name. It was said that he took rooms in certain hotels and brought his young friends back there and they remained for the duration of the night; that when he stayed in certain country houses there were adjoining rooms laid on for easy access to those youths known to be "so"; that when he visited seaside resorts he picked up lads upon the promenade; that after dark his hansom cab would prowl the streets and watch for boys that walked the pavements.

But maybe even then the rumours might have dissipated, dispersed by the prominence of some fresh *cause célèbre*, some scandal of more orthodox nature, but as it happened, in the previous September came that merry book *The Green Carnation*, the tale of Esmé Amarinth and Reggie Hastings; everybody read it; no one knew who wrote it. Patently the characters so wittily lampooned were Wilde and Alfred Douglas; and how they postured in the style of their originals! Some thought that Wilde had written it himself, and though he denied doing so he seemed to bear out in his actions the extravagant indulgences of Esmé, and in life to imitate what passed for art.

It was all because he went about with Alfred Douglas.

"N for Narcissus all white and gold
It tosses its head as it laughs at the cold . . ."

"Do you know who Narcissus was?" I said to Sophy.
"It's a flower," she replied.
"Yes; but why is it called so? Narcissus was a beautiful young man, you see, and it is his name which the flower has been given. He was the loveliest young man that ever lived. And one day in the forest he found a clear pool fringed with ferns, and sat down beside it. In the

pool he saw to his surprise a most beautiful sight – a young man exactly like himself who looked back at him from the watery depths. Of course, it was not really another young man. For what do we see when we look in water? Do you remember, at Mortmayne, when we fed the ducks, and saw the trees as clearly in the water as they were above? So what was it Narcissus saw when he looked in the pool?"

"Himself!" said Sophy.

"Yes. How clever of you! But Narcissus wasn't clever. In those days there were no mirrors and he had never seen his own face. So he hoped this youth might be his friend. He gazed and gazed; he thought the youth was very lovely, the loveliest thing he had ever seen. Indeed, he fell in love with what he saw. He did not care about anything else at all – he did not eat or sleep or talk, just lay and gazed, his face close to the pool. At last he pined away for longing, and became the flower we know by his name, which is tall and graceful as he was, with hair of fine pale gold."

Sophy was silent. I remembered then something I had heard, a charming aftermath. "When Narcissus died, the waters of the pool changed from fresh water into salt tears. Nymphs of the woodland came to sit by the pool to sing to it, thinking it was sad. They thought their songs would cheer the pool of tears.

" 'We understand,' they comforted it. 'We know that you are mourning for Narcissus because he was so beautiful.'

" 'Oh?' said the pool, surprised. 'I did not know that he was beautiful.'

" 'But of course he was! You saw him every day. You remember how he used to lie upon your banks and look into your depths, and in the mirror of your waters he could see his loveliness reflected.'

"But this is what the pool said: 'That is not why I mourn Narcissus. I loved him because when he looked down at me I could see my reflection in the mirrors of his eyes, and then I knew my own beauty.' "

Perceval wriggled. Pools and beauty did not interest him. He struggled off my lap and toddled off to push the wooden train. I tipped up Sophy's chin with my forefinger.

"What do you think?" I said.

"People don't turn into flowers," she objected.

"But it is a story," I explained. "Anything may happen in a story."

"But there were no little girls in that story."

"Why should there be?"

"There should be; that's all."

She giggled; she could not find a reason.

"I suppose you think that if there had been little girls in the story they would have brought along a picnic in a wicker basket and

22

spread a chequered tablecloth beneath the trees and tempted poor Narcissus with cream and strawberry jam and gingerbread, and then played Hide and Seek and made him laugh and teased him from the pool!"

"Yes," she nodded. "And a Punch and Judy."

"Then it would have been quite a different story!"

With all the comfortable confidence of the female, my daughter assumed that Woman's presence would have changed the outcome. I remembered Echo, sitting almost naked with her robe in disarray, gazing at Narcissus helplessly, her charms no temptation to the strange tormented lad, whose lips sought in the water an elusive beauty always out of reach, the beauty of a male, which he could gaze upon but never touch.

When Emily came back into the room I handed Sophy back to her with some relief; for I had hoped to find distraction from my thoughts. I had instead been deeper drawn into them.

CHAPTER THREE

I PAUSED on the landing, unwilling to rejoin Claudia, my hand upon the polished rail. The window curtains, swathes of sombre velvet, were drawn to keep the darkness out. A gas bracket hissed and flickered. I shivered, childhood ghosts returning – how much potential there was for shadows on a landing, in a hallway, a kind of no man's land between the noisy brilliance of the parlour where the company sat, and the secret safety of the nursery where no harm could come. Mortmayne my family home had a staircase of powerful possibility, all nooks and crannies, shadowy shapes that leapt and soared with every flicker of the moving lamp, every stair a separate creak of menace, every linen chest a goblin's home, every window flinging twisted chimeras from the dark outside.

I had not been entirely honest in my reminiscences, I must confess it. There was an incident which had disturbed me, which I had put from my mind; and now it surfaced, prompted by *The Alphabet of Flowers*, for it had been the occasion on which Oscar Wilde had recounted the story of the pool that shed salt tears and saw its own beauty reflected in the eyes of Narcissus.

It must have been the year before, when he had taken rooms at St. James' Place; I believe he was already estranged from his wife. One evening I was dining in an upstairs room at a certain hotel. It was a supper party; there were several guests. I was with Lord Heatherington whom I knew from Eton days, and young Viscount Merton, Freddy as we called him; and our party joined with Oscar's, in which there was Lord Alfred Douglas and two other lads, one of our class, one not. The one who patently was not was Charlie Parker, and I knew that all was not as it should be; the others knew it too. Young Freddy was quite pink in his unease and drank too much; Heatherington became reserved. Myself I was hideously drawn to contemplate Charles Parker.

He was at that time only twenty; he was lean, good-looking, lively. He had dark thick hair that waved across his brow, his eyebrows finely curved, his eyes set close together and his lips a curiously hard

24

and cynical line, yet monstrously appealing. He was brash and jaunty in his manner, and he fidgeted about in his stiff high collar, jerking a forefinger down his neck from time to time as if he found it most constricting. Myself having been trained from childhood to sit still in collars that circled one's neck like a clamp, I could not help observe this mannerism, wondering obscurely why it should disturb me so. The lad should never have been here in this hotel. He had no tact or social grace – why, he even boasted that he had been among the ghastly gang at Fitzroy Street, when the police had raided it and taken them away, some in their female garb!

"Not me!" Charlie assured us. "No, you wouldn't find me dressed like that. But Alfie Taylor was real pretty in his yellow taffeta – you could have took him anywhere! Ho! I don't mean *that*! I mean when he dressed like a lady you'd have sworn he was the real thing. Mincing and tripping in his high-heeled shoes, ah, he was such a laugh, you'd want to kiss him, honestly you would!"

Heatherington frowned, and Freddy coughed into his soup. But Oscar laughed and laughed – his hand half over his mouth to hide his ugly teeth – as if all Charlie said was truly proper. I had a nagging feeling that there must be some dark reason why I found the boy intriguing. Damn me, he was of the lower classes, he should not have been here at this table, in this panelled room, brocaded curtains drawn, the waiters gliding discreetly to and fro and hearing every word.

I looked at Oscar hoping for some clarification. I had not been this close to him for many a year and I wished I was not now. I should have left the room; I was too sickeningly polite, always at the mercy of my breeding. Good Lord, how vast and bloated he had become! How affluent he looked – his clothes fine quality and still as tight as ever, barely concealing the paunch of his stomach, the bulk of his thighs. His fat fingers, much in evidence with every gesture, were bare of rings save one, a big green scarab such as might have come from Egypt. His teeth were smudged with decay, and the way he had of flicking his hand across his mouth seemed a most affected and coy mannerism. He wore a green carnation. How precious of him to change nature thus! ("I have heard," the whisper went, "that the green carnation is worn openly in Paris so that all those who are 'so' may recognise each other.") Oscar's clothes did not well fit him. He was shapeless and his shoes were big and soled with cork. Of impeccable appearance myself I noted all, nursing the disgust I felt in secret, aware of the revulsion that I was experiencing, aware also that it was unnatural, even morbid, that I should be affected so.

Douglas I simply did not like. I cannot recall anyone who did; he was considered generally a spoilt brat. He was sickeningly handsome, with his golden silky hair that petulantly dropped across his brow, his limpid eyes and sulky pouting lips, his pink and white complexion. His neck was slender and his form was slight and graceful. It embarrassed me beyond description to see how Oscar fawned adoringly upon him. I wished he had had a father like mine, the little darling, simpering and declaiming, so dainty and so clean; why, if he had had a father like mine, a tyrant of the old school, he'd have soon lost all that sweetness and been made to learn – and then I paused, nonplussed, for I recalled that he did. I glanced at him then, curiously, wondering what ghastly family secrets lay behind those lovely eyes; and he returned the gaze.

"Ain't they alike?" said Charlie suddenly, who must have been observing us. "Ain't him and him alike!"

Both Douglas and myself were very discomposed and patently displeased by the comparison. We both pretended we were not, but there, we did not like each other, and we did not like to think we looked alike.

My two friends of course would not demean themselves by embarking upon a conversation which discussed our relative merits, and Oscar had no intention that they should. He said with firmness, as if he were the judge upon a grave and earnest issue: "No, Charlie; you are quite wrong. Lord Algernon is far more handsome."

It was clear to me that this was a remark made not to put an end to the ridiculous comparison, but to incite Lord Alfred for the pleasure of future sparring in more private circumstance.

"Algernon . . ." he added savouringly, his eyes turned skyward. "What a most mellifluous name. I had nevah known it till this moment . . ."

"But Winterton," said Douglas sourly, "sounds like the twittering of many birds."

I believe that Heatherington interposed then upon a different topic.

But we were not to talk of horse and hound that night, nor the latest plays, nor yet Home Rule for Ireland. Somehow all conversation glided towards matters of a risqué nature.

There was the poem Oscar read, which Lionel Johnson had written and in Latin, which Charlie had not heard, and which Oscar did not mind repeating and why not? – it was a compliment to him. Some of Oscar's party clapped, but Charlie said he did not understand it all – "Just some of it," he assured us, "even most of it; not all", and pressed for a translation. Heatherington demurred; but Douglas said that it was impolite to leave any guest in the dark, and we were all enlightened.

"He loves strange loves avidly; he gathers strange flowers of savage beauty. The more dark his spirit the more radiant his face, how false, how splendid! Here are the apples of Sodom, here is the heart of all sweet sins. In Heaven and Hell to you who perceive so much, be glory of glories."

This would have been quite indiscreet enough, but Charlie Parker, with malevolent intent I am quite sure, said: "What are they then, the apples of Sodom? Can you get them at Covent Garden?"

Douglas sniggered. "They grow in the St. James' bar, and at the back of the circle at the Alhambra."

"But I've been to both those places," Charlie said pertly. "And I haven't seen no apples."

At this point Heatherington stood up, made an apology and left the table. Freddy hesitated, and then apologised to me in a low voice, and followed. I did not leave. I should have done, I know, but I did not, and when this was observed the talk resumed on safer matters, more champagne was ordered, and we heard the pretty story of the pool of salty tears.

Charlie was as unimpressed as Sophy was to be, and yawned and fidgeted and turned to me and said: "If you don't fancy the Alhambra, them apples grow also at a little place off Shaftesbury Avenue called The Two Faces – do you know it?" Then Oscar slapped his wrist, and knowing he had gone too far the boy tucked into his *sole beaumanoir* and for a while said nothing.

Then after that, ironically, all the conversation was entirely such as might grace any dinner table. Heatherington could have participated without a blush, indeed might well have boasted about the quality, for it was very light, witty and intelligent; yet it was of the stuff of bubbles, blown and tossed as light as air, myriad shades of colour as they float, but of no substance, leaving a delightful memory of time passed pleasantly and to no purpose.

Before I left occurred the incident that had so disturbed me that I put it from my mind.

About to take my leave I made the requisite remarks, and then there was a moment when I looked at Oscar Wilde and he at me, and it was as if time paused inside a strange transparent shell. What the others were doing or saying I had no idea, yet they were there, moving, speaking; I was aware of them. He reached out with his fat and flabby hand and touched me on the knee. His gaze sought mine. He said to me, but not in the flippant social tone he had been using, which was rather high pitched and laced with affectation:

"Give *in*, Algy. In the end it's for the best."

I was as inarticulate as any first form lad before a sixth-former, the shocking aspect being that I understood exactly what he meant.

Yet such were my defences, my upbringing, social etiquette, that I could in no way respond, nor wished to, and felt monstrously insulted, hideously offended. All I could do was to pull out of the shell with all my strength and will. Reality slipped back into place, time started up again; the others had not even noticed, and I was on my feet; almost before I knew it I was in the carpeted corridor outside, moving swiftly through the dim-lit silence to where the staircase to the foyer stretched down before me.

Considering that what had happened was so trivial and slight I found myself excessively perturbed and shaking. I stood there at the stair head, my palm upon the wide flat marble surface of the balustrade. It struck me cool, hard, firm. It was composed of amber-tawny streaks, rich blended colours which with the crimson carpet of the great staircase betokened wealth and stability. I gripped its edge, because my thoughts were whirling, all stability there lacking. A tremulous confusion swept me, as if I had seen some kind of ghost. What *had* I seen? Some dark long-buried aspect of myself? I trembled then for what I might have shown unwittingly. How could he *know*? How could he guess? Did I say something, did I speak with a look unknown to myself? Ah no, much worse! It must have been that my peculiar fascination with Charles Parker had manifested itself after all, to others! I thought I had been discreet. The boy himself must have sensed it, to have made that hint to me, that Sodom's apples grew in a place off Shaftesbury Avenue. Now I was awash with dread. What had I done?

I quickly reassessed my situation. Heatherington had left before that point; he would never know. I would tell him that I had left soon afterwards. We had been foolish, straying into that situation like inquisitive boys who sneak a look into a forbidden book and do not understand all they discover. My problem was that I had understood too well. My fascination with the boy had been the result of some long suppressed memory, a time in my life when something happened – I did not wish to dwell on it – it was as if it were well hidden beneath a stone, and now the stone had tilted. Underneath were sin and fear and passion, and those old desires which I had chosen to deny. The stone must be put back, stamped down, hammered into place, and all beneath crushed out of existence.

I had not been that close to such a boy since – since that other time, a time long, long before. Oh, I had seen them in the busy streets, from the window of a hansom – but not *dining, almost knee to knee*, with someone bold and jaunty – it had unnerved me more than I could say. I must get from this place. I was quite certain that all of those who remained at the table in the panelled room would not leave the hotel tonight. I shivered; I was too close for my own comfort to the threat of living dangerously. I made my way cautiously down the staircase; one would have supposed me a little the worse for wine. The chandelier in the foyer glimmered and gleamed, its pinpoints of light swimming before my eyes. Beneath it there was a careful arrangement of leather chairs, and a monstrous display of hothouse blooms in an immense white vase. Beside the dignified dark-wood portals the plaster panels of dancing nymphs veered past my gaze. A doorman called a hansom for me.

Since that day, a year or so before, I had been more circumspect than ever before. Heatherington, Freddy and I had never referred to our supper party at the hotel and I had pushed the matter from my mind. In any social gathering my voice was as loud as anyone's in disapproving of the unacceptable.

I brought myself back to the present. On this February evening I had nothing to fear and much to be thankful for, and all that was required of me was to set off for the theatre. Meredith brought me tea. He informed me that the blizzard was still raging. The wind howled, and even in the parlour, with the curtains drawn, you could hear it, pounding at the glass.

Outside the theatre the street was choked with carriages, the more cumbersome quite jammed against each other, the hansoms always nimble, nipping in and out. The horses, silver breath'd and snorting, stamped and slid in the slippery snow. A wealth of flaring street light and the brilliance from the pillared portals of the St. James' flung a golden glow about it all in which the snowflakes danced and glittered. The wind was bitter, gusting round the houses, swaying the carriage on its springs, sending top hats flying, whipping the snowflakes into faster, wilder whirls. Amongst the tangled wheels fresh heaps of wind-blown snow impeded progress; and so broughams disgorged their passengers some way from the pavement in merry disarray, leaving shrill-voiced revellers to pick their dainty way across the drifts and hurry for the safety of the theatre steps.

Claudia rubbed at the carriage window, saying: "Algy! There are policemen outside!"

"Where?"

"Outside the theatre. Look . . . Why would that be?"

"I've no idea."

"It isn't usual . . ." she frowned.

"Perhaps they are to direct the carriages away – I have never seen King Street so congested."

"No, I think not. They are looking far too diligent and serious.

Algy, you don't think – ?" She stared at me, startled. "Those Irish people, the ones who leave dynamite in public places and post grenades in letter boxes . . . surely we are not to expect a revolutionary outrage here tonight?"

"No indeed," I assured her. "That is quite unthinkable; put it from your mind. We have enough to fear in contemplating how to make our way from the carriage to the theatre without ruining our shoes."

"You must always be flippant," Claudia complained, her Roumanian peasant silks rippling as she leaned back against the dark red plush.

We circumnavigated our way to the entrance, in weather conditions no one should be obliged to struggle through in evening wear; but even then we were not to be allowed to enter sanctuary for Claudia insisted upon stopping by one of those same minions of the law, her coat blowing about her, her hand upon her styled coiffure to hold it into place, these things of less importance than her concern about the policemen's presence.

"We are Expecting an Intruder!" explained the constable importantly.

In no way reassured my wife demanded further explanation. The constable was at first unwilling to say more, for how they love their mysteries, our defenders of the peace! But Claudia's concern – "You surely do not mean an Irishman?" she trembled – and her sweet demeanour touched the manly sensibility of our constable, and he replied in lowered tones: "No madam! The only Irishman that we expect is he who wrote the play!" He chortled at his wit; and then explained in courtroom tones: "A gentleman is attempting to gain admittance expressly to Cause a Nuisance."

We drew closer, intrigued. The constable was purple with cold but bristling with importance.

"Lord Queensberry, the Mad Marquis!" he explained. "And he has a prize fighter with him – a big bruiser I wouldn't like to take on. But I will if I have to, never fear! They first of all tried to come in through these very doors, but we was warned, and saw them off. Then they went round to the side to try to go in at the gallery, but then again they was turned back, and now he's gone to find the stage door. But don't you be afraid, for they'll not let him pass."

"What is his purpose?" I enquired.

"Beg pardon, sir, he hopes to cause a Stir. He has a bunch of – well, what ought to be flowers, sir, like a big bewkay; but they ain't flowers at all. They're turnips, sir, and carrots. He wants to throw them on the stage!"

"Astonishing . . ." murmured Claudia.

"Quite mad," I agreed.

We thanked him for his information.

"Enjoy the play, sir, madam!" I distinctly felt he thought he had the jollier prospect ahead.

Deliciously warm, the vestibule glowed after the chill without. We mingled comfortably with the rustling silks and satins and the snow-flecked velvet lapels; we shared the easy laughter and the snatches of catastrophe ("The wheel quite orf I say, the shaft split like a matchstick!" – "Quite impassable . . . three feet of snow . . . had to make a wide detour all around the park . . . amazing that we're here at all!" – "Wouldn't come! Said it would bring on her influenza. Left her reading *Woman's World*. Damn sensible girl, I say. Wish I was sitting at home by my fireside – even reading *Woman's World*!"). We exchanged greetings with our acquaintances, we protected our buttonholes of lily of the valley from the crush, we praised the ladies' dresses.

We shared a box with Clarissa Penhurst and her aunt Lady Mere, and there was also Clarissa's cousin Willoughby and his wife Elizabeth. Willoughby was a chap I knew at Eton. A big bewhiskered fellow, an authority upon Cliquot vin rosé and Château le Tertre, little else, more at home beside a race track than in present circumstances, he accompanied Elizabeth like an affable St. Bernard, always ready to offer a cigar or a smutty anecdote. In far off days he had been a brilliant cricketer, but now he had gone to seed, his once red windswept cheeks sunk to plum-coloured jowls, his youthful musculature to paunch. Elizabeth looked very smart in white and black satin; Aunt Penhurst was in blue; and though, as Claudia assured me it would be, her Roumanian attire was stunningly attractive, I preferred Clarissa Penhurst's, which, of palest pink with many frills and bows, was very like a Tissot painting.

I had been to many opening nights, but this one had a flavour of its own. Maybe it was simply the elation shared by well-dressed elegant people, who had made the voyage from their own luxurious havens through snow and blizzard and were now ensconced in warmth and gaiety, bound by an eagerness to be entertained. The atmosphere was one of peculiarly festive joy. The theatre was packed, and, superficially at least, everyone seemed beautiful – tiers of floral sprays, of feathered plumes, of velvet ribbons, lace and fur; smudges of satins and silks, the gleam of jewellery, white gloves, white shirt fronts, lit up in the new electric light. From the very first moment of the play the audience was entranced. They loved it. They, I say – for once again I noticed that as usual these days, I had grown detached from my surroundings and found that I was more an observer than a participant. I do not know why this was so; I thought it was a feature of the age we lived in. If you could not share the excitement of the New (for we had the New Hedonism, the New Woman, the New Voluptuousness and so forth) which I could not – then you sank into *Fin de Siècle* langour, and I found this far less strain than striving for the New. So, I noticed how the audience loved the play; they rippled like a field of corn with billow after billow of ecstatic laughter; I had seen nothing like it.

And to be sure the play was witty, one amusing gem after another tumbling into the perfumed air. "Pleasure – what else should bring one anywhere?" – how well that set the tone of the occasion! Willoughby, however, was not enrapt. He never could sit still for long; at school he only sprung to life upon the playing field. While Miss Rose LeClerq declaimed about the carelessness of losing both parents he muttered to me:

"You know he was kicked out of the Savoy for mucking about with a boy in his bedroom?"

"I had not heard," I coughed discreetly.

"Oh yes," he said confidently. "And the Albemarle. At the Albemarle he kept a boy there all the time. For personal use, you know, like the hotel writing paper!" The guffaw at his own wit merged into a general one at the author's. I winced. I rarely thought much about Willoughby, but here he was beside me and I was obliged so to do. *How was it possible . . .?* I marvelled. How could we be such hypocrites? Here we sat, in evening suits, each wealthy, fashionable, married; yet what we shared beyond the fine façade were memories of a shockingly sordid nature to which neither one of us would ever in a million years refer.

As a quivering golden-haired juvenile I had been slung before the hefty tree-trunk thighs of Willoughby; a voice over my head drawled: "This one's yours, you lucky pig." The pig in question was not alas myself.

"Lots were drawn," said the youthful Willoughby majestically. He was some six years older than me. In adult life this counts for nothing; in the cold corridors of the school hierarchy it has all the fine distinction of the army ranks. "And you have been allotted to me. Several of the fellows want you. Do you know why?"

"No, Willoughby."

"Little liar. I suppose you own a mirror? They wanted you because you are a pretty little thing. I don't know why it is, but yellow hair is very popular. The eternal choirboy, I suppose. And rumour has it that as well as having yellow hair, which everyone can see, you have a perfect arse, which is not so obviously apparent. And therefore several fellows wanted you, but chance has made you mine."

I do remember I had some idea what would be required of me, for other boys had whispered it at night. I was afraid, an habitual state with me; but even in my fear I weighed up whether I had landed well. I thought I had, for Willoughby was strong and popular and good at games and had no particular reputation for cruelty, as Farquhar had. Willoughby also quite patently believed I was in luck. He stood there, legs apart, secure in manliness and strength, with bulbous rugby players' thighs and ruddy cheeks, and hard, cricket bat-gripping hands.

"The first thing you can do now that you have become my bitch – for that is what you are, you little madam – is to change your name. I might well call you Alice. Alice it shall be. The next thing I expect is to survey my new possession properly, and for that reason you may take your trousers down and let me see what I have heard such tales about. What are you waiting for? Do as I say."

"Must I?"

"Indeed you must. You know what will happen if you do not."

"No. What?"

"A couple of broken ribs on the playing field. Or maybe you would like that kind of rest? You would not? Very well then; take them down."

He circled about me. "Hold your shirt tails higher. Yes! Congratulations, Alice, for you do indeed possess a perfect arse. This day is fortuitous for us both."

Fortuitous it was for me in that to have Willoughby as my protector put an instant end to the unpleasantness which I had been enduring up till then. I was his bitch, which gave me status and a certain freedom. My duties were quite light, because Willougby was not an imaginative lover. His activities on the playing field exhausted him far more than his adoring public realised, and I was more valued for my rubbing of his throbbing limbs, for sponging him down like a sweating post horse, for procuring him illicit brandy. That was why it was fortuitous in one respect; but not in others. I often envied Burley, who was the bitch of Farquhar, who called him Belinda and gave him a more inventive love life.

Did Willoughby ever think back? Above that bull neck, within that great square head, between those ugly ears tufted with sandy hair, did there lurk ever some vague memory of myself those twenty years ago, a tremulous and quivering faun who always did as he was told and bought protection with obliging ways? Yet I had been in Willoughby's presence countless times since without ever myself remembering it. Why tonight?

"Wonder what goes on backstage," hissed Willoughby to me. "I've heard it's devilish cramped, can't move without tripping over a female thigh in those black stockings with the frilly garters. All actresses wear them, you know, however demure they look on stage. And black lace corsets . . . they have them specially sent over from Paree!"

I daresay I was proving a dull companion, for I did not mutter in reply. It did not trouble Willoughby, who whispered in Clarissa's ear; she tapped him sharply with her fan. Jack became Ernest and all was resolved. The audience rose to its feet, clapping, cheering – yes, it was a fantastic success. We had seen an exceptionally brilliant play, a fountain of cascading sophistication flecked with shimmering sparkles of wit.

Outside the air struck bitter chill. Men in top hats and overcoats were lighting up cigars and pulling mufflers round their necks. The women gathered up their long skirts under their coats and fur wraps and picked their dainty way to waiting carriages. The gas lights were white blurs in the purple-grey gloom. A loose poster flapped in the wind, rattling on the wall. The hansoms jostled, with restless horses. A woman beside us fixed the rose which had come loose back into the twining of her hair. Doormen in uniform with gold buttons and trimming ushered the emerging throng to carriages and broughams. The double lights of hansoms gleamed, creating pools of golden snow flecks. A policeman in a long coat and helmet stood amongst it all, directing traffic. I handed Claudia into our carriage. All was as it should be.

Through the city streets we made our way, the main thoroughfares well sprinkled with eruptions from the theatres, music halls and clubs whence gushed bright lights and laughter. I noticed, as one always does, the ladies of the night about their work, the carriages that hugged the kerb, the policemen curiously powerless against the relentless tide of the pleasure trade. As we crossed Piccadilly Circus Eros did indeed reign supreme. Shaftesbury Avenue was quite passable now, a clear way through the centre of the street made by the wheels of carriages and the work of shovels. We turned up Charing Cross Road, we crossed St. Giles, and turned off toward the Square. It nurtured its own particular silence, abetted by the snow here still deep in places, smudged with horse dung, each house front a wall of privacy.

The social event so pleasantly concluded, I felt some release of tension. The mood was inexplicable; I knew I had been edgy and morose; I did not understand it; but I knew now it was over. My uneasiness had gone, quite dissipated, blown away. My social obligation had been fulfilled; I had attended the damned play, I had enjoyed it. I could talk about it now at any gathering, my duty done, my reputation as a playgoer intact. Claudia was pleased; I had proved a decorative accessory to her dress which, contrary to my criticisms, had been praised by many. We smiled warmly at one another as we entered the hall. Claudia began to walk upstairs.

Meredith handed me the little silver tray upon which letters were presented. I frowned to see a dirty folded scrap of paper, black with thumbprints, crumpled at the edges. I hardly liked to touch it. The fingers of my white gloves picked it up; it left a smudge upon a finger tip.

I stood there in the hall, the casement clock a slow and measured ticking in the background. I read the note, a ghastly scrawl in almost indecipherable writing.

Algy – come at once! Desperately urgent. No one else I can ask . . . An awful thing has happened. Dearest boy, don't let me down.

It was signed with a name that I could barely read which upon close perusal I saw to be Sebastian Charles. The address he gave I did not know. I had not thought of him in years. Now from beyond the ages he had written this, this intimacy without preamble or apology, as if we knew each other well, as if we had but seen each other yesterday.

In this instance I had every premonition of disaster. I feared the worst; I knew that it would lead me into trouble of the worst kind. I knew I would be sorry.

I also knew that I would answer this strange summons. I did not even hesitate. I looked towards Claudia, who turned and waited enquiringly on the stairs.

I stood there apologetically, with the letter in my hand.

"It seems I must go out . . ."

CHAPTER FOUR

I RREVERENTLY THE thought uppermost in my mind, as the carriage made its way north along Tottenham Court Road and I leaned back against the red plush, breathing the enclosed air still redolent of Claudia's white heliotrope, was that in all the time I had known him I had never known his forename was Sebastian.

Charles we always called him. And as my mind went back to the time when I knew him and I realised with a jolt that this time was twelve, thirteen years ago, my next thought was *why me? why now?* In all the intervening years we had not kept in touch. Surely he had other friends on whom he could rely in whatever crisis had now come upon him? Men of the artistic world, of which he was such a vibrant part?

A surge of unexpected pleasure overtook me. I had been happy then! A curtain lifted in my mind – a heavy curtain made up of marriage, parenthood, responsibility, Mortmayne with all its economic problems – and revealed as on a stage the carefree days of irresponsible youth. I was then twenty, with artistic leanings. A friend of mine named Madeleine – I met her at a ball in Grosvenor Square – said she would introduce me to some artists. Within a month or so the house in Kensington where they resided was a vital part of my life. I was at home there; they indulged and pampered me as they did all their protégés, and in their warmth I blossomed with the eagerness of a bud in Spring. That my mother did not approve of this new influence upon me only added charm and spice to the situation.

Was it truly always Summer there? It seemed so. There was a high-walled garden lush with blooms – poppies, wallflowers, great purple irises, and honeysuckle dripping from the ornamental latticework, and daisies, banks of daisies. Beneath the trees upon a verdant lawn the ladies sat with paint and easel dressed not in the constricting fashion of the day but in loose gowns, like Grecian nymphs. The house belonged to William Franklin – with its indoor pool full of Japanese goldfish, the black and gold tiled hall, the staircase with the alabaster statue of Antinous the youthful favourite of Emperor Hadrian, and the vast studio streaming with light that ran the length of the house on the top floor. In those days, those glorious days of perpetual Summer laced with the scent of lilacs, his house was full of people.

There was Charles of course, disturbing, lean and rangy, with wicked worldly eyes, sleek black hair and a very fine moustache. Of course he spoke a lot of gibberish, saying that we lived in grim prosaic days and we must fashion our own world guided by the beacon of the soul. Charles certainly created his own world. He covered canvas after canvas with golden dreams of Byzantium – purple sunsets, pillars of ivory, tangled ivy stems, and wonderful boiling seas with amber waves caught in the dazzling brilliance from the skies. Between painting, Charles prowled about like the Wolf looking for Red Riding Hood, twirling in his long slim fingers a silver goblet which he swore was once the property of Cesare Borgia, and so closely acquainted with *Les Fleurs du Mal* that one never knew if it was he who spoke or Baudelaire through him. At night he sprawled beside the fountain smoking hashish, while through the open casement windows the moon rose over the lilac trees in a quivering turquoise twilight.

Although some of the Grecian maidens found him sinister – and he did indeed cultivate a dark and brooding manner – I never heard of any particular scandal attached to his name and Lord knows there was opportunity enough. The girls who came ostensibly to paint adored the artists and, if perhaps unable to burn always with the hard gem-like flame, were not averse to a smoulder in the azaleas. But Charles possessed a certain taut asceticism reminiscent of a monk in some gaunt medieval monastery whose turbulent desires are ringed about with the iron of the will. Like Chorus in a Jacobean drama he knew every detail of the plot, he saw the skull beneath the skin, the flesh also, but stalked the stage apart, commentating, sneering, posturing, never partaking.

Franklin partook. In art entirely dedicated, he was in life the Knave who liked the Tarts. Serious at his work he would continue well into the night, his canvases in those days medieval scenes. But when he put the paintbrush down, if the model might be prevailed upon to stay for longer he would happily oblige with bed and bawd. He was incredibly discreet; I doubt if anyone knew much of his little follies. He had that peculiar skill of seeming utterly respectable. He was a good-looking man in a conventionally good-looking way, rather like a Romantic poet that against all odds survived to middle age: well built, with unruly hair, he strode about, his falcon eye at fifty paces picking out a beauty for his tournament or banquet scenes, that same eye instantly becoming hooded if it saw a problem, pain or anything that smacked of ugliness.

There was a young couple living there then, Maurice and Clara, quite devoted to each other, though unmarried out of principle. They said their love was stronger than the paltry law of Church, their souls bound in more unity than ever priest could give them. They were a quaint pair, very self-contained and inward-looking. She was a potter. Untypically for a potter she had long tawny hair and soulful eyes; she was in great demand for studies of Mary awaiting the Angel Gabriel. She was always baking bread and gathering herbs; a great patch of the radiant wilderness of garden was given over to her thyme, parsley, lemon balm and sage.

Artistically Maurice was old-fashioned, in the style of the Pre-Raphaelites, but like that famous brotherhood from time to time he glowed forth with a masterpiece. There was one in particular, called *Parsifal and Galahad*; it hung for a time in one of the London galleries.

Then there was Victor Strode.

What could have become of such a man! Could such indeed exist except within the portals of that strange aesthetic place? Was he not some peculiar bloom that needed for its growth that most specific hothouse, where he flourished as a plant does without natural light and water, nurtured in an artificial glow, its twisted roots in absinthe-rich soil?

He was a poet in his early forties, a most unhappy man. His melancholy turn of mind was aggravated by the characteristic which dominated his nature – love for his own kind; I do not mean philanthropy. He walked as one with earthly sorrows, head bowed down, with stooping shoulders and a downcast gaze. Yet his head was finely shaped, with a broad brow, aquiline nose and a small moustache; his hair was black and streaked with grey. You see him many times on Franklin's paintings – the apothecary, the magician, schoolmaster, the noble beggar, an early Christian martyr. He could have been successful at some branch of learning, but his burden, as he called it, so overruled his life that he was quite unfit to go forth in the common world. He felt that life had played him false, thrown him a wayward card, and therefore he was doomed to suffer. He turned his sadness inward. His gloom was so excessive as to forfeit natural sympathy. His conversation was laced with transports of despair – "For such as I . . . if you were as I am . . . you do not understand; my suffering is above common . . ." – until sometimes one could not take this serious matter seriously.

I knew that Charles and Franklin made him worse, encouraged him to further misery, because his presence added colour and variety. With so much white and crimson, peacock blue and gold, the need for grey, for black, for monochrome was evident. And so they asked him to talk more about his disability, they begged for him to write it down in verse and read it aloud beside the fountain; and worse and wickedly, they strewed his path with pretty youths whose tantalisingly conventional tendencies made his grief the more poignant – and all done in the name of art, of friendship. Charles and Franklin were immoral in more subtle ways than the mere flaunting of unconventional tastes.

It has to be said that society made this more possible. A dozen years ago, before a certain act was passed which made it illegal for two men to love each other privately, there was a different atmosphere. The Suffering Sodomite might add a perverted glamour to poetry and painting. Of course, he must not be happy, as the Greeks were prone to be, a healthy living human being delighting in fresh air and sport – oh no, for sodomites were not like that, as medical books told us. They lived in darkened rooms, their faces pale, their eyes tinged with bruise-coloured shadows, their mien uncertain, twitching, nervous. They shunned the light, the sun. They cursed their troubled life and thought extensively about decay and putrefaction. Their favourite season was Autumn. They liked to wander beside wooded streams where black lilies and ivy grew in ghastly profusion round the roots of twisted trees. Failing that, they liked to sit in cemeteries.

And so in Kensington amongst the peacock plumes and rose petals, the Japanese plates and trickling fountain, there was a welcome place for Mr Strode, just as the rollicking lordlings in the Forest of Arden welcomed melancholy Jacques. His poetry was of a morbid turn, and while in Swinburne this can be exquisite, it was not so in Strode.

> "He walks in amarinthine fields
> The boy beloved of Jove
> Beneath a purple sky he yields
> To Love.
>
> The tainted touch of those all-mastering hands
> Quiver his panting breath;
> Now will he fly to passion-haunted lands
> Or death."

I was hailed with cries of ecstasy when first I came to Franklin's house, for I was palpably a thing of beauty, and though perhaps not entirely a joy for ever, I was certainly a joy to artists wanting models. I posed as Young Lancelot and Young Saint George, and then as my particularly golden well bred qualities came to the fore, I was most often Galahad. I knelt by antique coffers and a portable stained glass window, a silver chalice in my hand or to my lips. All Franklin's famous series of the Life of Galahad is based on me.

Mr Strode used to sit nearby and watch me pose. I could not help but notice that he was attracted to me. It embarrassed me enormously. Once, indeed, he did attempt to further our acquaintance. I was sitting in the garden upon a rustic bench beneath a lilac tree, idly sketching. Everybody sketched. My spirits sank as I saw him approach. Heavily he sat down beside me, fingering the old straw hat he wore when out of doors. The edge was very frayed, the band quite twisted.

"Algernon . . ." he acknowledged, as a form of Good Afternoon.

I sketched busily. A ghastly Gothic impression of the back of the house was materializing at my pencil's point. Nobody who drew that poorly should have been allowed near art material.

"You are drawing . . ." he observed, far too refined to criticise my dreadful little oeuvre.

"It isn't very good," I acknowledged.

He looked at it but did not see; his eyes as usual inward looking.

"Algernon . . ." this time the word a preamble to his purpose. "I am sure that you are aware of my feelings towards you."

A statement, his passion tightly controlled.

"Mr Strode?" I said pleasantly, shading in the shape of the open back door.

"Algernon!" He put his hand on my wrist. It was thin and white with spidery black hairs upon it. "Algernon, I must have an answer. I am becoming distracted. Is there any possibility that we might come to the kind of arrangement whereby you permit me a closer kind of contact with you than I now enjoy?"

"I am not sure that I understand you correctly," I said, putting my sketch and pencil down in the grass to give him my proper attention.

"You must surely be aware that I am not immune to your charms. Charms which have been much in evidence of late. May I ask whether, Algernon, you are likely to be kind, now or at some future date?"

"Indeed Mr Strode, I had no idea of your sentiments towards me. I am most distressed to have disturbed the equanimity of your composure."

"I see," he said, tight-lipped. "Well. It is the answer I expected. So am I to understand that there is no chance of my hoping for intimacy between us?"

"That is so – no chance whatsoever."

"Then I will trouble you no further," he said stiffly, rose and withdrew.

I had been brusque and heartless, I knew it. But the elegant languor I presented to the world hid a state of seething turbulence few could suspect. My brief dismissal of Mr Strode's proposal was because I saw in him a hideous mirror of myself. I had known since I was very young that I was strongly attracted to my own kind – and again, I do not talk of philanthropy. Debauched by older boys at school I was a willing victim, and found it no hardship to be kind to older boys, providing that the boy was pleasing to me. When I was old enough to have picked out a young bitch of my own I did not; I refrained because I knew my feelings were more deep than the transitory romping which took place because there were no females accessible to us. My sentiments were too important and too precious to be so degraded; I carried them about with me as one might hold a fragile shell; I dreaded it might shatter from a careless word, a thoughtless touch.

Only too well was I aware what such secret thoughts would mean if they ever saw the light of day. The idea that my father might suspect – who I felt sure despised me enough already – filled me with fear and dread; my mother too would show no understanding. Although I knew the ancient Greeks valued this kind of love, gave names to different aspects of it, praised it even, my own society called it unspeakable vice, a form of madness, or at best a frightful illness, a puzzle to the medical profession. I did not wish to ally myself with perverts, lunatics and the mentally deformed. So I preserved my cool exterior and floated through a sea of glittering occasions, soirées, concerts, smiling at the ladies with a curious desperation, seeking all the time that secret – how could one love women? Where did that skill lie?

On the evening after Mr Strode made me his proposition I became quite ill – I had a fever which kept me in bed for several days. My mother thought I needed a change of air. She suggested Italy. I mentioned this to Charles, and he with inexplicable perspicacity told me to visit Rome, and in Rome the writer Mordington Fulmer, whose works on Leonardo da Vinci and Alexander the Great are well known.

And so, aged twenty, I journeyed south, arrived at Rome, and visited the great man at his home. Although I had read his works I knew little about the man himself, and naturally nothing about his private life. I knew that he now lived abroad but I understood it was for reasons of health. In some ways this was so, but as it transpired, the main reason for his exodus from our shores and his settling in Italy was the abundance and availability of doe-eyed boys whose services he could buy cheaply in the shabby picturesque streets

41

around the Colosseum.

He was then about fifty-eight years old, gaunt, bronzed, thin, with grey-black hair worn rather long, and a thick moustache. His cheeks were lined with marks of sensuality. It only took an evening in his company to prise my secret from me. In the purple twilight, at his window, which overlooked a quaint and peeling courtyard, we talked much about the foibles of society in England; and within the week I had met several young men of his acquaintance, all brown-eyed and raven-haired, suntanned of limb, with names like Giorgio, Mario, Angelo, all of a delightful disposition, and willing to be very friendly, for a pittance.

"In the days of emperors and gladiators," said the literary gentleman, leaning on his balcony and waving nonchalantly to the urchins playing in the gutter below, "young boys used to wait among the pillars of the Colosseum offering their services. Pretty little things I've no doubt, from all corners of the Mediterranean, each with a tale of strange romance to tell. The gentlemen in cloaks and togas stood and paused, on their way in to the games. They made their assignations. Coins changed hands. The chosen boy would wait, kohl-blackened eyelids all a-flutter, olive skin a-gleam with oil of sandalwood . . . at night there would be kisses, promises . . . but none of this is mentioned in *Ben Hur*!"

I returned from Italy much refreshed, and for a while much cheered in spirit. Warm memories assailed me of the touch of hot sweet skins and pleasant laughter – all Fulmer's boys had beautiful teeth – and everybody commented upon how well I was looking.

My sweet euphoria lasted for a month or so, and gradually it occurred to me that these Italian boys, so beautiful to look at, so obliging, were all bought with money, and though I had managed to overlook this fact at the time I now found it intrusive to my memories. What good was bought love, lust one paid for with a handful of coins? Where were honesty and self respect? It shamed me to think that one as attractive as myself had been reduced to buying satisfaction, just as an old and ugly rich man might. Why could I not be loved for my own self?

I flung myself into my studies, and I thought no more about the search for love. At least, not much. And when the following Spring and Summer came I hungered for those bought delights again, and with a friend of my own age from Oxford, Lord Blaine, I went to Greece, this time more skilful and aware than I had been in Rome, a little more experienced. We went of course to see the Parthenon, the wine-dark sea, the serious museums; but I went hoping for more.

What an opportunity that might have been, to pursue a relationship alone, abroad, upon those barren hillsides! But it was not to be so. If there had been the slightest suspicion attached to Blaine my mother would not have permitted me to go. His reputation was impeccable and I admired him for it. I had nothing but scorn for those gentlemen who overstepped the mark and caused idle tongues to wag. One must be secret; everything is lost if anyone guesses. Once one's reputation is tarnished one might as well give up. And so all the time we were in Greece we never mentioned our sexuality. We smiled patronizingly at the men and boys upon the Greek vases, and averted our eyes.

But at one point we separated for three days. Blaine wanted longer in Athens. I hired a guide and a donkey, adopted a peasant image, with my floppy hat and open shirt. There was a place called Sounion, like the end of the known world. The track stopped at the sea. There was a temple, ruined, with pure white columns against a peacock blue sky. The sea turquoise, the rocks hot to the touch, there I stood, looking out to infinity. The guide procured a boy for me from a village we passed. The boy spoke not a word of English but he understood sucking cock and handling money. But it upset me to pay him. It made me feel pathetic. One cannot be sure whether one is loved or despised, one's demands endured for money, and afterwards a welcome return to the girl they prefer. I longed for the impossible, a boy who would come to me openly, loving, no money involved, where we could meet as equals in sexuality, equal in need, equal in beauty.

Ah, little did I know then the pain that such could cause.

As always when I thought about those days I spent with the artists in Kensington I stopped short with my return from Greece. Something happened to me then, an experience which I had driven underground. I found true love and lost it; that is all that can be said.

Suffice to say that shortly afterwards I turned my back upon them all – Franklin, Charles and Strode, the ladies with their long hair and their flowing robes, as artificial as myself, rich women seeking a diversion while they were still young, before they committed themselves as I was to do, to the duties that awaited them in life. And the intriguing riff raff from the streets who came in in their rags and tatters to pose for the artists and were transformed on canvas into medieval maidens, knights and pages, Roman slaves, lost gods and shepherds, Sappho, Echo, Parsifal . . . but I said I would not think of that.

And it was true, I had not. I put it from me as cleanly as if it were detachable, as one might cut a sheet of paper, crumpling one half, casting it away. It was not so difficult, having been brought up as I was, trained to overcome sentimentality, to deny feelings, to pretend, to walk amongst others who did likewise, each a conspirator in the same shared plot.

I took my mother's advice, I married, I took seriously the business of my estate, land economics; I became a parent. Eleven years passed. There was much to fill my life; there was no reason to think back to one brief episode already folded fast away.

Now, with this odd communication dropping into my world on a wretched scrap of paper, everything had changed. I was beginning to remember things I had put from my mind years ago. I was curiously receptive to the flood of jumbled incidents that suddenly I started to recall. I experienced a strange fear, a strange excitement. There would be pain for me if I allowed the past to raise its head. My life was so secure, so comfortable, so ordered. What madness was I now embarked upon tonight, the carriage bearing me toward a street I did not know, at dead of night, the snowflakes whirling and the wind a bitter blizzard battering on the window glass? Suddenly I felt as helpless as one of those same snowflakes, whirling where the wind would take me, through the cold and snowy air.

And then I smiled; it was not so. I was in no way helpless; that was a mere fanciful notion. I was following a path that I had chosen for myself and I was curious to see where it would lead.

I rubbed a clear smudge on the misty window to see exactly where I was.

CHAPTER FIVE

TURNING WEST along Euston Road the carriage made its way slowly, as my coachman followed the directions I had given him. I was conscious of the fact that, to my left, amongst the closely packed streets beyond the gaslight glow, lay places that had made an ugly name for themselves – Fitzroy Street where occurred the notorious police raid; Cleveland Street where the discovery of a brothel for young men had brought disgrace and ruin upon famous names and loss of income to assorted telegraph boys; and ahead of us along the edge of Regent's Park curved Albany Street, where young soldiers supplemented their low pay by asking gentlemen who passed if they might offer them a light. So near beneath the surface of this sleeping, thriving city, with its bright lights, its rich hotels and theatres, its solid banks and shops and decorous gentlemen's clubs, its striving workers struggling to live within their means, lay the dark and sullen world of those that lived outside the law, who, even as I passed, were risking all for satisfaction of their hunger, or for simple greed, unseen, unknown and unsuspected.

And now we veered to the right, turning off the main thoroughfare, down one scarce wide enough to take the carriage. Carefully we progressed. I had some sympathy for my driver, but he was a good man and would see us through. He drew up at the kerb, beneath a flaring lamp which sputtered in the gusting wind. Upon the pavement's edge we shared a murmured conversation.

"My lord, the house we seek is just nearby. I dare not take the carriage further, for do you see, the street is very narrow and the way impeded. I believe that they are barrels, my lord. I would say it was the back yard of a public house."

"I would agree with you. Be good enough to wait here; I will walk the final steps."

"I shall accompany you, my lord," said the stout fellow.

"No need. I would rather you stayed with the carriage."

"Very good, my lord."

I peered ahead into the dimly lit alley. The one gas lamp jutting unsteadily from a metal bracket in the brickwork lit up a vile rubbish heap of a vegetable nature; the wind blew sudden beer-drenched gusts and whirled the scattered pages of a newspaper. The alley was deserted and in the house walls several storeys high, smudges of light showed at the windows. Sordid though the general tenor seemed I did not feel concern as yet, for with those images of Summer still inside my head – the poppies, daisies, lilies – and the dazzling décor of Charles' previous dwelling fresh in my remembrance, I half expected that a door would open and a flood of light reveal a wondrous chamber hid from the world's eye by this mean exterior, an Aladdin's cave of strange delights, with Charles a beckoning sultan.

Skirting the stack of beer barrels, shivering and pulling my coat about me, I knocked at the door which lay beyond in shadow. A thin hard cat more skeleton than fur rubbed at my ankle. The door was opened by a woman, tall and gaunt. I asked if this was where I would find Mr Charles. Mr Sebastian Charles. She told me no.

"It's *there* you want, sir." She gestured further down the alley, indicating with her thumb. "Round the back." She sniffed and frowned. "You ain't the police?"

I thanked her for her help. She did not shut the door, but pulled her shawl about her, watching me as I continued further down the alley.

"We're all decent folk here," she called after me, apropos of nothing.

If I had thought the alley dark and squalid there was worse to come, for in order to reach the place to which I had been directed I had to enter a low tunnel-like passage. A foul stench filled my nostrils and as I put my handkerchief to my nose I now felt some alarm, for there was nothing of the quaintly picturesque in this. I could suspect Charles of an interest in the vile and sordid if it could be seen from a position of security and comfort; but this sad alley spoke of nothing but misfortune. I emerged into a small yard, a single beam of light from an upper window showing me a wooden lean-to structure up against a wall, a rickety framework with steps. The hand rail teetered and each stair creaked ponderously, giving in the middle. At the top I knocked upon the door hurriedly, desirous to be quit of the unstable platform where I stood.

Instantly, as if I have been looked for, the door was opened, not by Charles but by a woman. She was youngish, dark, her hair a wild and tangled bush; and in her hand an oil lamp which she raised to see my face.

"*Monsieur Algie?*" she asked me eagerly.

Startled to be thus addressed by a stranger I replied in the affirmative and was then shown in.

"This is where Mr Charles lives?" Her murmured response was in French, so I spoke to her in her native tongue and elicited from her an eloquent groan: "Ah monsieur Algie, you will save him! It is not for himself that he asks help; but I, I see that he is not long for this world, and the other matter is of no concern to me. But now that you are here all will be well. I know it."

We were in darkness save for the wavering glow of her lamp which led us down a hall disintegrating with damp and slime, chill as stone, the woodwork underfoot a mass of creaking, shifting boards. We entered a room of low proportions dimly lit by a gas bracket. Shadowy shapes there seemed to be – a sofa, a bed against the wall, a curtained recess. One of these shadows now detached itself and Charles rose from the sofa.

Because I was expecting to see him I recognised this man as Charles, but he was sadly changed. His spare and rangy frame was almost skeletal and even in the gloom I thought his face much altered. He flung his hand in mine and grasped me firmly enough, clasping his other hand upon my shoulder.

"Algy!" he said warmly. "Wonderful! A genie, conjured with the lamp of times gone by!"

"Indeed I am no genie," I protested, much conscious of my stiff and formal attire, "but all too sadly mortal. I came by carriage and I am blue with cold. Have you no fire? And this dim gloom – come, let us have some light."

I strode about and turned the gaslights up. They shed a flickering glow upon the scene in all its poverty and squalor. I saw this at a glance and wished I had left us in the dark, but it was too late now and I felt better in this clarity than amongst shapes and shadows.

I saw now that Charles looked gaunt and ill. His eyes were red-rimmed, mauve-ringed; his hair was still as dark as ever, his moustache thick and black, but his skin was of a translucent pallor. There seemed a nervous intensity about him which I found disturbing for it did not seem born of natural causes.

"Algy, you'll have a drink . . ." Upon a packing case I saw some empty bottles. Charles began to rummage there to no effect.

"Polette – can't you do something? – find the man a drink," he snapped irritably. "Surely we are not completely without drink?"

"Oh!" she remonstrated. "Monsieur knows well enough . . ."

They faced each other like those who share a knowledge neither wishes to admit; then Charles shrugged, and laughed, half amused, and half self-deprecating. "I am afraid the only drink that I can offer you is absinthe," he apologised. "It's the only thing we have in the house. We seem to have run out of the more mediocre forms of

47

beverage. Can I tempt you, Algy? I know it's the brew of Satan and speaks of nameless iniquities and it embarrasses me to seem so self-consciously depraved as to possess the stuff – I do assure you it's not for effect, but simply that I like it. What's good enough for Paul Verlaine is good enough for me, eh!"

His forced joviality grated. As he spoke he found the bottle and Polette darted forward with an earthenware jug.

"Not for me, Charles. I've never been able to develop a taste for it. It's fortunate I am no Decadent, with a reputation to maintain."

"Yes, Algy," Charles observed a little caustically. "You never were decadent."

Polette poured icy water upon the green liquid in the glass, slowly, till it grew cloudy. She moved back into the shadows silently but she watched Charles with great dark anxious eyes and all the time I was aware of her presence. Now that the room was brighter I took in more details of her appearance. She was quite young, perhaps twenty-four or -five, attractive in a way, sallow-skinned with high cheek bones, brown eyes, heavy brows, her lips full and sensuous, her neck long and graceful. Her hair was thick and stood out from her narrow face in unkempt abandon. Her dress was black and edged with coffee-coloured lace. Curiously disturbing to me was the fact that it was of very good quality, such as Claudia and her friends might wear, a rustling satin with large puffed sleeves; but it had the look of being worn day in day out for any menial task, and therefore it was stained and torn and raggedly patched. She would have looked well in fine clothes, bathed and perfumed. Yet she was here.

"Oh sit down, Algy," Charles snapped, swigging down a mouthful of his drink as if it were lemonade. "I had forgotten what a prig you were. If the sofa is not too vile for you I suggest you sit there."

I placed myself upon the tattered horsehair, crossed one leg over the other and waited. Charles kicked a strange stuffed leather bolster forward and squatted down on that, cross-legged, as I have seen on Indian paintings. To my disgust I caught sight of his legs and with a shock I realised that beneath his dressing gown he was unclothed. The impropriety made me uneasy, but more than that, the room was very cold and yet he did not seem to feel it.

"I was surprised to hear from you after all these years . . ." I said. "I am ashamed to think I did not keep in touch."

"Why should you take the blame?" shrugged Charles indifferently. "I had no wish to see you. I kept half an eye upon your glittering career – I could not help it. Of course I knew about your marriage, though I own I could not bring myself to accept your kind invitation to the ceremony. I heard you sired a crop of infants. They are well,

I hope? I saw that you had gone the way of your type. I read that at your country estate you grow figs and nectarines, indeed are rather famed for it. My congratulations. I read that you attended Tennyson's funeral and were present at the opening of Franklin's gallery, at which Lord Leighton was amongst the throng of worthies. I see you keep good company; you have done well. Do guard against complacency. It is an unattractive offshoot of your class."

"I have sometimes thought about you, Charles, and wondered what had become of you. Franklin of course I knew about . . ."

"A knighthood, eh! Who would have thought it when we sat upon the floor together by the fountain, lost in hashish dreams?"

"Do you think back much to those days?" I wondered cautiously, unwilling to comment upon how his circumstances seemed to have worsened.

"Never," he said contemptuously, throwing down his glass. "Polette!" he barked. "Get me another glass." Dog-like she obeyed, moving behind the curtain which seemed to hide some alcove. "Those days?" Charles sneered. "They were nothing. We thought we were so bold, so daring. Up to our necks in creature comforts, spoiled and pampered, how we did pontificate! So free thinking – so naughty! We smoked a little herbal weed and thought ourselves a wild and wicked crew . . . We took our clothes off! We said men might love other men, and women other women, it was all right by us. We thought we were delightfully outrageous. Well. Since then I've done a thing or two, and let me tell you – those days – we were children sucking barley sugars. Barley sugars!"

Polette handed him a big cracked cup; he seized it greedily and drank the brew within. He breathed deeply and smiled. "Nectar," he explained, but Polette shook her head. "You know," said Charles, like one about to lecture, "I always hated our material existence, the chains of our conventions. I swore long ago that I would spend my time on earth in fullest relish of sensation. Sensation is the only thing – not religion, not philosophy, and certainly not love. We must experiment. Be curious, Be insatiable. If that means be perverted, so be it. If that means giving offence, offend. We live in a hypocritical society. We worship money, class. And now I sound political, but no, this is above mere politics. I am no Socialist, nor anarchist – I cannot waste my days trying to change society – it is beneath my contempt, let it fester in its own slime. But let us act against it." Charles paused to take another sip. "You have chaos inside you – look into it – deny it not or it will devour you, all in its own time. Experiment – live passionately – paint your moments crimson." Abandoning the mystic tone in which he had declaimed, he looked across at me suddenly, concerned. "You have of course read Huysmans?"

"Yes."

"And *Dorian Gray* you will certainly know?"

I felt that I should be shaking hands here, as at an introduction. I admitted that I had met the youth in question.

"Good; there is some hope for you. That chap has something to say, Algy – not the frivolous stuff at the Haymarket, no, his darker side. There's a soul there, Algy, a soul who knows . . ."

"Well, maybe," I mumbled.

"Good Lord," Charles declared. "You've hardly changed at all since you came to us so white and gold and lovely as a lily. Just look at you – it's practically immoral. Do you remember that Greek soirée we created and you came in just a belt of sapphires and a cloak of peacock blue and all your limbs and torso nude! What a shameless little hussy you were then, you and that other brat. I say, what a pair of exquisites you both were! They were good days, so innocent . . ." Charles seemed to drift into a reverie. I thought at first that the remembrance of old times had caused his sudden preoccupation. But then I saw his gaze was curiously distant, indeed quite glazed over in a way not totally consistent with mere nostalgia. I thought he did not see me at all, and I could not help but feel that this was some narcotic stupor. I looked across at Polette.

"Monsieur," she whispered. "What can I do? These dreadful days the laudanum is his only joy. He takes it as if it were water. At first it was for his sickness, but now he takes it all the time. And then he drifts away. But he is better for it, he is happy and he tells his thoughts. Without it he is tears and gibbering. I do him service to procure it for him. Alas, but it takes all our money."

"It isn't good for him . . ."

"There is no alternative," she stated. "I prefer this way. Without it he saw a very ugly world. Now he lives in beautiful dreams. This is better."

Polette moved forward and began to massage Charles' head. He jerked back into actuality and I saw with some distaste that as he did so his hand strayed to his crotch and for a moment then stroked himself as if he were quite unobserved. I looked away. When he was in full possession of his faculties again he sat upright and smiled and seemed to wish us to proceed as if there had been no such bizarre interruption. I judged it best to do so.

The reference he had made to soirées and sapphires had troubled me somewhat. "We outgrew all those things," I said firmly, "that Walter Pater ecstasy, that catching at exquisite passion. There is no place for it in the real world."

"What do you know of the real world?" Charles said, with

condescension bordering on amazement.

"What do you?" I retorted, for certainly I had enough of trials and difficulties within the sphere in which I moved, and his world I suspected now to be something of a laudanum-induced hinterland.

"Deny it not – your world was Olympus no less. How you graced us with your divinity! I can still see you as you were then, immaculate in your nakedness, so pure, so of the upper classes. I would even imagine that beneath those pompous clothes – a long way beneath, it being Winter – there still resides that very comely form as lithe and trim as ever. Have you lived so purely then in all these years, or am I to suppose you have a portrait in your attic?" He chuckled sardonically. "No, I know that you have not. You have sacrificed yourself upon the connubial altar and devoted your life to perpetuating the status quo. Those both are strenuous pursuits and will have taken all your energy and zest. Yet there was hope for you once. I remember. A little timorous seed of possibility. You almost fled to Paris with that boy; but you did not. And yet you almost did. One never loses that potential, you know. To almost means that at another time you might."

"What rot you talk," I muttered.

"Do you ever see him?" wondered Charles dreamily. "That boy – what was his name?"

"Of course I do not," I cried angrily. "There is no need. All that is long since over."

"What became of him? You do know that much, I presume?" Charles enquired mildly, not a whit affected by my outburst.

"I do. If you must know, he lives in Shoreditch. But it will do no good to me nor to you to probe into a situation which is long since past and best forgotten."

"My, how vexed you are," purred Charles. "How very intriguing."

"Nothing of the kind!" Swiftly but clumsily changing the subject I said: "Are you still painting, Charles? I hope so – are they not canvases I see stacked there?"

"You do indeed see canvases, but they are about as relevant to my circumstance as any museum object is to life. I brought them all from Franklin's house when I left. I used to think that art was meaningful. I know now it is merely economic. Would you like to see what earns such daily bread as now I eat?"

As Charles stood up he teetered on his feet and clutched his forehead. That he was ill I had supposed; I half rose to support him; but he regained his balance, swigged the dregs that lay within his cup, and handed me a folder. I opened it with interest, but when I saw what it contained my previous unease returned.

It was a series of drawings instantly apparent as the kind of illustration that one found upon the covers of the Penny Dreadfuls. Disreputable as these publications were – with ghosts and ghouls, murderers and wicked squires, fainting ladies and bloodstained corpses upon every tattered page – Charles' drawings went one step beyond in what was most vulgar and unedifying. The mean and sordid terrain round Holywell Street contains the kind of bookshop which a man of reputation does not visit. Naturally then, in my youth, I had made the occasional foray there. They sell the dregs of literature – stories of seduction, rape and shame; medical treatises upon the intimate diseases of the female form lavishly illustrated; confessions wrung from prostitutes describing every detail of their life. These books are garishly decorated with appropriate pictures, and here I found the source of some.

With sinking heart I turned the pages.

"Beauties, aren't they?" Charles remarked.

"I only see a fine talent wasted," I observed sadly.

"My God," groaned Charles. "You really are a holy little swine. What do you think of *these*?"

Before I knew it there was in my hands a second folder. Beneath my gaze a stack of drawings tumbled, a hundred times worse than those which had appalled me. I could not bring myself to study them. I saw at a glance that they were drawings of the act of lust, not tastefully portrayed, but lurid and obscene, the clear intention obviously to titillate and arouse. And neither were they simple couplings but ghastly scenes of orgy. The effect of so many rampant phalli, bared buttocks, wide-splayed thighs, so many slobbering lips clamped upon the glaring orifices of the body, so much naked flesh and dark smudges of hair was nauseating to my senses and I put them from me. Somehow it was worse that such monstrosities were so finely drawn – an artist's skilful hand had penned them, and this made it more horrific.

As I turned to Charles, perhaps to remonstrate, he twisted from me, overcome by a great fit of coughing so debilitating that he could not speak, and for a startling length of time I feared his breathing was to be impaired, for ghastly sounds were issuing from his throat and lungs.

"Is there nothing we can do?" I asked Polette alarmed. She seemed unmoved, as if all this were no surprise. She gave him more from that same cup which he had drunk before; he gulped it down and gradually the coughing eased.

"My apologies, dear boy," croaked Charles. "While you were growing nectarines and figs, my chosen path was elsewhere. All that Dorian Gray did I have done and more, and sometimes in the wretched backstreets of foreign climes. I've plumbed the depths of fascinating squalor in the company of fellows whose like you would not believe existed on this earth. I could tell you tales of Cairo . . . But now I'm paying for it – those old ghosts return with beckoning fingers to remind me that all pleasure takes its toll."

"Call it what you like," I cried in great perturbation. "To me it looks like mortal sickness."

"What if it is?" shrugged Charles with an indifference that seemed genuine enough to me. "The end of life is only to be regretted if one has wasted time. Otherwise it matters not a jot."

"Oh God!" I said somewhat wearily. "I hardly know which is to be more pitied – your recklessness as regards your fate, or your attempt to translate it to the stuff of high drama and thus justify your situation. I am most distressed to see you so. You always spoke such balderdash but then it fitted in with oriental rugs and blue porcelain. Now it seems grotesque." I eyed him sharply. "Tell me, have you a good doctor? Are you attended? What is your circumstance?"

"Damn me, Algy," Charles snapped angrily. "I did not bring you here to talk about my state of health."

There was a pause, and we both seemed to recall at once that I had been summoned here, and yet, straying amongst reminiscences and accusations, no reference had been made as to wherefore.

"Why did you send for me?" I asked.

"How curiously ironic," Charles observed. His look became vacant, vague. "When I hastily scribbled that note to you I felt in desperate straits, as if the matter in question was of a terrible importance. Of course, I still feel so, but in seeing you again it went completely from my mind."

"I would be glad to hear it. It's very late and I was out this evening, and my carriage waits."

"How petulant you sound – just as you used to . . ." Charles began to pace about. "The point is this: I have just heard that Victor Strode has been arrested."

"My God! Is it a mistake?" I cried.

"Unfortunately no," Charles murmured, pacing still. "He was arrested in the act of sodomy no less. You would think, would you not, that with his earnest pretension to poetry, he might have chosen to be arrested in the act of bestowing a kiss – presenting a flower or a sonnet – perhaps in Regent's Park beside the lake, or in a garden thick with lilies. But no. The thing occurred in the public lavatories at Piccadilly Circus."

I could scarce form words. "How – could it happen?"

"I will tell you what I think," said Charles, his hand upon the sofa back, taking his weight as he leaned there. "I believe that certain policemen who patrol the streets watch out for types whom they suspect are likely to prove guilty of this offence. I fear that Victor has become more careless of late. There have been narrow escapes in the bushes of Hyde Park. I think he may have been observed and followed. A lamentable practice has arisen, dearest boy, of which you may be ignorant, which involves the policemen lurking in the shadows by our public lavatories, and at great personal cost as regards *ennui*, cold, and loss of moral fibre, simply lying in wait. To pounce, Algy. To pounce on men who touch each others privities in the privacy of the privy, that unsavoury underground world of the chipped tile and the sound of rushing water. I believe the atmosphere can be quite poetic."

"Your flippancy is unbecoming," I muttered. "If what you say is true, Mr Strode is in great trouble. It was good of you to inform me, but . . ." I shrugged.

"Inform you? Yes, but what are we to do?" said Charles.

"Do?" I blanched. "Well, nothing. What can we do?"

"Well, at the moment I can do nothing, since I have no money and no social standing," said Charles with perfect reasonableness. "But you –"

"I!" I said in terror.

"Why, yes. He is at Bow Street Police Station. Go stand him bail; speak up for him and say he is a poet. I'll take him in if he needs a place to stay. But first of all he needs it to be seen that he is no poor Simeon Solomon but a man of standing, with friends in high places."

"He is no friend of mine," I gulped. "I hardly knew him. Good Lord, I have not seen him these eleven years. Come, Charles, this is unfair of you. In Kensington, at Franklin's house, it was the three of you, and Maurice – where is he, by the way? – I was not part of it, and it is shameful of you to include me in this vile affair. Have you asked Franklin for his help?"

"I have not. Franklin became a pillar of the establishment years ago, and since his knighthood he is somewhere up with the gods. I doubt if I would even get an audience! But you, Algy . . ." he frowned. I realised that it had not occurred to him that I might wish to keep my distance too.

"Maurice lives in Cornwall," he answered. "For all I know, he's found the Holy Grail. Algy, do you mean that you refuse to help?"

"Of course I do." I jumped to my feet. "I am appalled that you should trade on my good nature. You know that I have children – a wife – I dare not take the risk. You know nothing of my life and my responsibilities. I am not the silly lad you used to praise with overelaborate compliments, and Galahad I never was except in what you made of me. You spoke of the real world. I live in that real world and must continue to do so. If that wretched man has so disgraced himself he only has himself to blame. Why was he not more careful? And if police entrapment is a common procedure, why did he act so stupidly? No, Charles, I am sorry, but I cannot help."

Suddenly the contrast was too great. I had come here in good faith on the apex of a roseate glow composed of summertime and careless youth, recalling days of lilies, poppies, lilacs. I had expected Charles to be as he was then – sardonic, masterful and strange. I felt betrayed. The squalor of the surroundings, Charles' personal degradation, his illness and his drug-induced abberations, this unkempt woman, and the ghastly doom of Mr Strode – all filled me with abhorrence. I could face no more. I could not tell if I were cowardly or prudent but I would not take recriminations now. I reached for my wallet. I emptied every sovereign therefrom and pressed the heap in Charles' palms till his fingers closed upon them, some none the less dropping between us and careering drunkenly across the floorboards.

"For God's sake get yourself some reputable practitioner," I moaned. "Seek medical advice . . . I will send more . . ."

I waved him from me with a gesture, almost running from the room. If I looked like one in flight I daresay it was no illusion. Somehow I retraced my steps, somehow I regained the waiting carriage and conveyed instructions to my patient coachman, sinking back into the safe familiar-scented plush, pulling the window curtains to, shutting out the street and all that I had seen and heard, but with the dreadful certainty that it would follow me.

CHAPTER SIX

WHILE MANY of the upper classes wintered abroad, taking far more with them for the journey than ever swallows do, my mother the Marchioness of Turleigh, with all her typical perversity, wintered in Scotland. She stayed at some baronial hall near Inverary, all oaken panelling and coats of arms and draughts, with cronies of her rank and inclination. Tall and stately, with dark hair and sharp brown eyes, she was a frustrated pioneer. Apart from a stint in India in the 'sixties, she had devoted her energies to supporting my father's political career and to improving the estate at Mortmayne. Insanitary old villages with cottages dating back to Gothic times were pulled down, and the villagers rehoused in modern terraces. Untroubled by an interest in literature or art she now spent much time travelling. She loved pageantry and state occasions; and as a young girl she had met the Emperor Napoleon III. She considered health and duty as of prime importance; health in order to make the best of one's opportunities on earth, and duty as an example to the lower classes, who as everyone knows, learn by example.

I found a communication from my mother awaiting me one morning, a week or so after my summons from Sebastian Charles. I looked at Claudia across the breakfast table, the letter in my hand.

"This one concerns you."

"Indeed? What now?"

In spite of the warm tone of the red damask walls and heavy folds of curtain, and the spluttering fire in the tiled fireplace, I always found the room a chilly place at breakfast time. The sun made its appearance late, and not at all this morning.

"So then, Claudia," I said with mock severity. "In what wickedness have you and your disciples been indulging on your Afternoons?"

"What are you talking about, Algy?" said Claudia wearily.

"Mother has been informed that you hold Bohemian gatherings. She fears you may be misunderstood. She requests me to look into it."

"Oh what a bore," groaned Claudia, her white and gold tea cup clattering to its saucer with some force. "And what an interfering old termagant she is! Which beastly friend of hers can have been telling tales?"

"But is there anything to tell?" I marvelled.

"Of course there is not," said Claudia, visibly vexed. "As you know very well, it is simply a group of people with artistic interests who come here and talk. Some of them read their poems. Oh! It sounds so feeble. It really is quite monstrous of your mother to suppose it more serious, when it is merely my attempt to brighten life and promote culture."

"But surely there must be some grounds for the very slightest frisson of alarm if some well-meaning dowager has made some kind of complaint. Undesirable, says the letter."

"Some of them wear unusual clothes," Claudia admitted. "But they are perfectly clean. And respectable also."

"I must say that the idea of you fomenting an anarchist cell is strikingly ludicrous," I agreed. "Do you talk at all of political issues?"

"Sometimes, if they arise. But mostly people like to express their thoughts. About Life. I really am embarrassed at what your mother must be making of it. Do you mean to say that she wants you to sit there with us and make sure we are all proper?"

"How would you feel about that?"

"Vastly irritated. But you always do as your mother suggests. I hope that you will find the experience perfectly dull, and will therefore not be tempted to repeat it."

"I know that if I were to attend for whatever reason, I would not find it dull."

"Come if you wish." She lightly shrugged and drew her dark red Paisley shawl about her. "Our subject is the Revival of Interest in Celtic Folklore. If you discomfit any of my guests with unbecoming cynicism I shall not forgive you."

The prospect of Claudia's Bohemian Afternoon intrigued me. Truth to tell I was very glad of a diversion to distract my thoughts from what was certainly uppermost in my mind, my meeting with Charles. So it was with benevolent pleasure that I settled upstairs in the drawing room to meet these Undesirables that so disquieted my mother away in the far north.

A little wintry sunlight played upon the primrose yellow wallpaper with its leaf-green whorls, the pale gold stripes of the curtains, the green ruched valance along the mantelpiece. The furniture was rearranged to form a circle revealing the well-varnished wood and the patterned rugs. Upon the wall in gilt-edged frames hung scenes of rural idyll – a row of cottages beneath leafy elms, a child with a bouquet of mignonettes.

Claudia sat upon the corner of the chaise longue, in a dress of brown velvet, looking very comfortable. Were it not that I knew how much the brown velvet creation had cost I would have praised it for its apparent simplicity. Beside her sat Louisa Millbourne, whom I knew, a gentle girl who sang exquisitely. If she had set the tenor of the occasion I would have been a little disappointed, but Claudia's Bohemians did not let me down, and from my chair against the piano I had ample leisure to observe the gathering. Once the initial surprise occasioned by my presence had been overcome, the little group took readily enough to the situation. They seemed happily untroubled by the niceties of class – an attitude in itself which would have shocked my mother – and treated me much as one of themselves.

The meeting was led by one Thaddeus O'Shea, a youth of Irish origin, who stood up, coughed and rustled a paper. His hair was wild and sandy-coloured, frizzy and flowing, in the Swinburne manner. At his neck he wore a hugely knotted tie in purple silk, his jacket a well-worn dark corduroy.

"I would like to speak upon the Celtic Twilight . . ."

There were two other young women, a forthright square-chinned poetess named Helena, with wayward chestnut hair and a severe black dress enlivened by a silver pendant with a cumbersome amber stone. Her friend Maria, doe-eyed and dressed in grey was, I was told, an artist. From time to time their fingers intertwined.

A youth named Ernest sat upon the floor. Already – such is fame and fashion – he had become the good-humoured victim of pleasantries upon his name ("Ernest did not realise until the other day how important it was for him to be himself"). In case I had begun to think that flowing manes of hair were obligatory to the artistic pretender, Ernest was exceptionally neat, his hair well combed and short, his check cloth trousers finely pressed. He wore a white carnation in his buttonhole – perhaps having no access to green dye. His nose was large, his chin receded, and he spoke with an affected lisp which came and went without any logical sequence. When offered a chair he shook his head and said: "I truly prefer thitting on floorth. Particularly one as beautiful as yourth."

I was tempted to congratulate him on his poetry but did not, understanding that Ernest was an especially sensitive person.

Then there was Hubert, an elegant blond boy dressed somewhat in the style of the Fleshly Poets so caricatured a decade or so ago, with a slim-waisted, hip-hugging black velveteen jacket and black knee-breeches, a great black floppy hat to match. He wore shoes with buckles and two limp anemones in his buttonhole, his hair was

58

collar-length and he grew a sparse moustache. His outfit was carefully modelled upon what Oscar Wilde wore when he brought aestheticism to America. Oscar was his hero.

Finally there were two lads who arrived together. Ronald was perhaps the least elaborate of the group, a pleasant-faced boy with straight brown hair who wore a cream bow tie upon an outfit otherwise unremarkable. The name of his friend was Arthur Hughes.

"Arthur Hughes?" enquired Louisa brightly. She had not met him before. "Is not that the name of the sickly boy in *Tom Brown's Schooldays* who prayed excessively and caught fever?"

While it was explained to Louisa that Hughes had written the book and Arthur was a surname and at public schools one called another by his surname and that Arthur's name was George, I studied Arthur Hughes.

Indeed I could not take my eyes off him, and I was drawn so obstinately to stare at him that I was obliged to force my gaze elsewhere in order not to seem ridiculous. I could not remember ever having seen a more beautiful apparition in such unexpected circumstances. One noticed the eyes first. His lashes were so long, so dark, they made little shadows on his cheeks; the eyes were blue. And his hair – so very thick, so black, it made me want to slide my fingers into all that richness. Each feature seemed exactly as it should be for perfection – the well-shaped nose, the wide mouth, the square tilted chin and high cheek bones. He was slender – but broad – pale of skin. He moved with a boyish diffidence, hesitantly. He wore a black corduroy jacket, everything he wore was dark. He seemed withdrawn, he looked down at his hands, and those black feathery lashes rested lightly on the pale skin of his cheek. I longed to touch them with my finger tip.

"Who are the Little People?" Thaddeus asked us – rhetorically I think, for he was holding forth with vigour now. "Are they fallen angels? Or are they a forgotten race driven into the hills and secret places by the advent of our cold and callous society where money and machine are gods? Are they a part of the earth and therefore are they thus accessible to us, lurking in the innermost recesses of our minds? For we too are of Nature. Who, alone in the solitude of desolate places has not felt the stirring of some great primeval heartbeat, hidden from us in the city street and in the throng of men?"

If any of us had not felt this vast primeval stir we did not admit it, and Thaddeus proceeded.

"The word they use in Ireland for the Fairy Folk is Deenee Shee. I will spell that for you both in English and in Irish." There was a long and complicated break from his monologue here, for Hubert wished to write it down and it was not so easy in the Irish. "They live in Tir na n Og, which means the Land of the Young. Tir na n Og is in the hollow hills. It is the earthly paradise. There, happiness is commonplace, the grass is always green, and every day is spent in feasting, listening to music and," he coughed, "excuse me, making love. There is no death. It is a verdant place, with trees and summer fields and leafy bowers . . ."

Upon a low side table we had a tall glass dome containing quite a little forest of foliage and fern. Inconsequentially I found my eyes had strayed towards it and for a moment, mesmerised, I pictured Arthur like a doll inside it, miniature, with every gleaming leaf a portion of a mighty plant, some exotic forest of primordial times. I moved him, solitary, Adam-like amongst the monstrous ferns, a wide-eyed traveller in a world of green. I had to be there with him. What if we were alone there, protected from the cold by that thick dome of glass, free to roam at will amongst the luxuriant leaves? There is no death . . . and happiness is commonplace. It would be warm in there, so we would remove our clothes. Against the dark and glistening green our bodies would be clearly defined, pale, lissome. Our hands would touch, our breathing quicken, we would move closer till we saw the sparkle of each other's eyes, the brilliant desire therein. Our lips would touch and I would take him in my arms. To my complete astonishment, that afternoon, in the company of those intense young people, in the presence of my wife, I fell in love with Arthur Hughes.

"Tir na n Og is ever with us," Thaddeus explained. "For though it be in actuality the deepest lake or on the far horizon yet we in dreams may move amongst it. For do not make the mistake of believing that the spirituality of the Faery Folk is any the less holy than the faiths of more widely acceptable religions." Thaddeus grew mystic. "And the world of the occult is ever present and walks hand in hand with us."

"The dark places of the mind," said Arthur thoughtfully.

I smiled fondly. What could he at his age know of those?

Thaddeus spoke of visions which had been recorded, noted, proved; I studied Arthur's eyelashes. I believed that in a room of a hundred youths with lowered lids I could now instantly identify his – though who could have provided me with such a room and such a group I could not exactly tell.

Claudia on our behalf thanked Thaddeus for his trouble and was sure that we had all learnt much from what he said and I wondered whether I should applaud, for I had learnt a little more than most.

"Your poem, Helena," Maria prompted. "It is upon a Celtic

theme," she added for my benefit.

We sat expectantly, and the softest hint of sunlight touched Arthur's hand, where it lay on his knee.

Helena stood up, needing no persuasion.

> "The Lady of the Holly Bough
> Flitted by my rusting plough
> And I can see her gleaming now
> And nothing is the same.
>
> We came here treading painfully
> The furrows blackened frozenly,
> But where she goes ahead of me
> She leaves a wisping flame.
>
> The holly berries, which before
> Were shivering peasants red and raw,
> Spark into fearless men of war
> Roaring when she came.
>
> Felled in the rout the blood red sun
> Dripped on the green leaves one by one.
> The glistening rustling girl is gone
> And nothing is the same."

We liked it, and Helena sat down gratified.

"It's beautiful," said Hubert. He looked very pink and warm in all that velveteen, but kept his hat on for full effect.

"I see it – I see it!" Thaddeus declared. "I have been somewhere just like that – it was in Oxfordshire."

"It feels medieval," Ronald said.

"It feelth violent," observed Ernest firmly.

Helena stared. "Does it? I had not meant it to."

"It ith about death, ithn't it?" Ernest said triumphantly.

"Well – no –" said Helena blinking.

"They killed the girl," Ernest nodded.

"Who did? There are no other persons present."

"The roaring peasants. She wath a thacrifice!"

"Indeed she was not," Helena protested. "The roaring peasants are symbolic. They are the holly berries."

"What did you perthieve ath happening to the girl?" Ernest persisted. "Was she thimply dethpoiled?"

"Simply –?" squeaked Louisa, suddenly aware of what he was implying.

"Nothing of the kind!" cried Helena. "She simply went away. And

61

then the sun set."

"But the blood?"

"The blood is symbolic."

"Felled in the rout?"

"The rout is symbolic also," said Helena. "You have completely missed the point."

"No," said Ernest aggravatingly. "You have written a deeply violent poem without realithing it."

"I have not," sulked Helena. "Really – I should know what I wrote."

"A thientist would tell you, Helena, that there is violence in you and it hath come out in your poem. The poem ith about your feelingth ath regardth the pothition of women in a patriarchal sothiety."

"But you know my feelings about that subject!" Helena declared.

"Exactly!" Ernest smirked as though the point was proved.

"Not exactly at all," snapped Helena. "If you know my views already then you did not find them in the poem. You brought your own preconceived ideas to bear upon an independent work of art. You were not objective."

"Ernest never is objective," Louisa soothed. "We all know that."

Claudia rang for tea. I had supposed that now we might all relax and forget about discussion and sidle up to anyone that interested us to ask as many pertinent questions as we dared. But no, for even over tea there was a topic to be probed.

"Our tea-time talk is How to Live!"

My heart sank; but I should have known that in this gathering that did not mean the best way to make money. For the sake of argument Maria undertook to speak upon behalf of our present day society and made a passable case for materialism and the accumulation of wealth as long as it went hand in hand with social reform and the betterment of all. When Maria's argument weakened for lack of fact at her disposal I stepped in to support her case. Ernest and Hubert spoke for the other side.

"Down with commerce and industry!" Hubert said. "The important thing is to satisfy the hungry searching soul."

"If you mention anything about burning with a hard gem-like flame I shall dismiss your theory as second-hand," I warned him.

"Well, I was about to," he admitted. "But I happen to agree with that philosophy of Pater's. I think the emotions have long been played down as a reason for existence. I believe it is the duty of each one to fashion each day afresh, to make each day a sweet perfection. We live in an unusual time, the last years of the nineteenth century. We are part of the *Fin de Siècle*. We have a certain duty to our times."

"Every moment should be perfumed," agreed Maria.

"With the scent of heliotrope," Louisa murmured.

"No," said Helena. "The perfume was symbolic."

"Life ith brief, and the only thing we can be sure of," said Ernest, "ith death. Therefore we mutht live as passionately ath we may."

"How do you propose to do that?" I enquired politely.

Ernest looked a little shifty. "Thertain bookth which I have read have given me thome inthpirathion."

"I take it that you do not mean *The Pilgrim's Progress?*"

"It is no secret what we read," said Thaddeus. "We have all read Huysmans – Baudelaire – *Dorian Gray* – Verlaine – certain poems which we feel express the spirit of our times –"

"Its essence and its brevity," Maria said. "Its artificiality. Its excitement. The need to find out for oneself and not let others tell one what to think. Sometimes what we discover would very much shock our neighbours and the little minds of those about us." She smiled at Helena.

"*Epater le bourgeois,*" agreed Hubert. "Do the unexpected. Live life utterly! This may seem strange to you, sir," he said, suddenly turning to me with shining eyes. "But all of us have been brought up in homes of suffocating respectability – long rows of neat houses where curtains twitch whenever anyone passes. Our fathers are dull and hardworking and forbid us any deviation from convention. Why, Helena is forbidden to own a bicycle!"

"I intend to thtudy every refinement of the thenthes," Ernest told us, fluttering his long white hands. "However," he smiled modestly, "this ith a little difficult when one hath no money!"

"Turn to crime," said Hubert pleasantly.

"What do you suggest? Can you think of anything of that nature where the pothibility of being apprehended is only minimal? I have often wondered about safe-cracking. I wondered whether one might go to some public house in Bethnal Green and strike up acquaintance with a thkilled houthbreaker, going into partnership, becoming something of a legend in the underworld – I rather fanthy that."

"Forgery is cleaner," said Helena briskly.

"But they all take precious time," groaned Hubert. "All one's energies would be taken up with the work involved. One needs every moment of the day to penetrate the essence of sensation – to see the dawn rise over Covent Garden when on cabbages and rose petals alike the morning dew lies glistening, to lift the stopper of a bottle of white heliotrope and sniff the scent till one is drunk on perfume as a bee inside a foxglove, to spread one's hands in the folds of a heavy velvet curtain, to lift it to one's cheeks . . ."

"And – Arthur?" I said his name out loud for the first time and looked at him. "What do you think?"

"I don't think there is any point in anything," said Arthur morosely.

"Nor is there!" Hubert cried. "How right he is! And that is why we must satiate our senses with each passing pleasure – the strange perfume of incense or the soft down on the neck of a sweet maiden, or the purple taste of Sin."

"What do you mean – Sin?" I said with growing irritation. I felt middle-aged all of a sudden, and a lack of patience. Claudia shook her head at me. I understood: He doesn't mean anything, Algy, be tolerant; this is how they are . . .

"Sin – well – anything," said Hubert vaguely. "You know, sir, opium, and, well – vice."

Presumably Hubert also suddenly felt the discrepancy in our ages, slipping half unnoticed from the flamboyant to the deferential as he did.

"You mustn't pick on Hubert," Thaddeus cried warmly. "We often talk about those things. We talk about the opium dens; we talk of love and the ladies of the street and how we'd feel if – you know," he twitched coyly, "if we went with one. And we talk about unnatural vice."

"I hope that it is merely talk," I said severely. Claudia looked skyward most expressively; Louisa giggled.

"Yes sir!" I was assured from all sides eagerly.

"I don't wish to probe into your privacy," I said, like any kindly uncle. "And certainly it is perfectly proper to question anything that you are told and find out for yourselves the subtleties of certain aspects of life. But this should not include a romp around Whitechapel or the Ratcliffe Highway where you will be very much out of your depth. Those places are not peepshows or magic lantern slides to view and come away from. They are the lives of people who have gone wrong. It is immoral to see them as picturesque and dangerous to be there at all."

I could not refrain from this homily. Any one of these young people was a potential Mr Charles; they spoke the same precious language, struck a similar pose. The intervening years were all that separated them, for it was a fine line between revelling in sensation with the carefree abandonment of liberating novelty and the grim conclusion of a life devoted to self-gratification.

"My father thaid it wath a man'th duty to go with a Haymarket tart," said Ernest boldly. "Tho he knowth what to do."

"So did mine," I answered. "But I do not agree with him. Do

you?"

"No," grinned Ernest, looking for a moment ordinary and sheepish. Then he remembered his poetic pose and added: "My inclinathionth are elthwhere."

"Do not be so serious, Algy," said Louisa. "Ernest is merely posing. You *are* an old fogey this afternoon. Unnatural vice is quite romantic, and Ernest likes to play at it."

"Presumably Ernest understands that there are no facilities for play in Pentonville," I frowned. God – what a hypocrite I was! Just as with my children I had preached about Jesus while I hid my own consuming doubt, now here I was selling conventional morality directly after having pursued Arthur Hughes around Tir na n Og. I was all façade. It was astonishing that no one guessed. I then remembered Oscar Wilde had guessed, and the recollection disturbed me mightily.

"More tea?" said Claudia firmly. "My, we are being serious today. I think I enjoyed the Irish folklore better. What is our topic for next week, I wonder?"

"We were going to talk about the colour white," said Thaddeus.

"Ah yes . . ." said Claudia, a little discomposed.

"We were to discuss the essence of the words White Nights and the significance of shades of white as an expression of both innocence and rapture," Maria added.

"Who will write the poem?" Claudia asked.

"I will," Louisa volunteered.

"Sir – " said Ronald suddenly. "Hashish is all right, isn't it?"

"No," I told him firmly. "I do not believe that it is known for any good effect."

"It has," muttered Arthur. "You forget things."

I looked at him startled.

"My mother takes laudanum," said Maria. "Any chemist shop will sell it to you."

"And that's the liquid form of opium," said Helena. "The doctors tip it down the sink after a patient dies, in case the relatives drink up the laudanum for pleasure!"

I dreaded then that some more daring aesthete (I suspected Ernest of harbouring the notion) would ask me whether I had ever taken hashish, but fortunately Louisa noticed it was time to go, and everybody made their preparations to depart.

But Ronald lingered.

"Sir," he murmured. "May I call again tomorrow for a moment and talk to you and Lady Winterton about a problem?"

I hesitated.

"It concerns Arthur," he whispered.

"Of course you may," I told him.

When my wife and I were once again alone, the drawing room door closed, and Sarah the maid quietly cleaning up the cake crumbs, Claudia said defensively: "And so? What did you think of my Bohemians? Subversive, are they not?"

"I shall assure my mother that she need have no fear. Just as you observed, they are all very clean and tolerably respectable."

"You have no need to play the moral orator," she added. "They talk much, but if any kind of vice were to raise its head at them each one would flee. Ernest is all pose. He lives with his parents and would be far too frightened to share any close proximity with ladies of the Haymarket. Hubert may well have seen the dawn rise over Covent Garden – but where is the harm in that?"

Neither of us referred to unnatural vice – why dwell on unpleasant subjects?

"But keep an eye on them, Claudia," I said. "You have some responsibility here, I think, simply by virtue of who you are. I happen to know that too close an identification with the various movements loosely known as *Fin de Siècle*, in which these young people are so languidly indulging, may sometimes lead to tragedy. The Narcissus effect. And it begins with conversations such as we have heard today, a social and light-hearted interest in so-called Sin and the more romantic aspects of the Underworld."

"At least you have witnessed our gathering," Claudia smiled. "I hope you do not find it incumbent upon yourself to sit in upon our questioning of the colour white. I found your presence most inhibiting. And by the way, what does Ronald want to speak to us about tomorrow?"

I looked at her with studied blankness, incredibly vexed. I had hoped to see Ronald on my own. There was nothing I more fancied than a long discussion upon Arthur and I saw no reason for the inclusion of my wife in what was to be a private pleasure. Glumly I accepted that this was to be denied me; Ronald himself would probably tell Claudia when next they met.

"Arthur Hughes," I answered, savouring his name like a cherry on my tongue.

"How very odd," said Claudia. "I wonder why."

Eager to tell us, Ronald took tea with us next day. The three of us sat there in the drawing room, Claudia and I together on the chaise longue in a pose obscurely reminiscent of a painting I once saw entitled *Arthur and Guinevere At Home*, a couple in medieval costume looking entirely of our day and age. Ronald sat opposite us, on the

66

low green button-back. He was uncomfortable, but the knowledge that what he had to say was for the best gave him strength.

"Arthur does not know that I am here," he began.

"Excuse me – but then should you be?" said Claudia carefully.

"I know what you mean," Ronald blurted out. "But I don't think it can be sneaking when my being here is caused by concern on his behalf."

"What is the trouble?" I asked.

"Oh! I believe that Arthur keeps bad company!"

"What makes you think so?" I enquired.

"He is not as he was. He has become preoccupied and strange and very gloomy. His mother does not always know where she can find him. It is not like him to cause his mother worry. They were very close. That is not all. He has employment, but sometimes he absents himself at irregular hours, and I fear if this continues he will be dismissed."

"But why do you suppose this has to do with bad company?" said Claudia. "Maybe he has some personal trouble, known only to himself."

"Sometims he mentions names," said Ronald. "It was a foreign name. And twice now I have seen him in the street with a person. A person of what I would call a Disreputable Sort. And when he saw me – the other youth, I mean – he fled. And Arthur would not tell me who he was. Whereas once he often confided in me, now he does not."

"Have you known him long?" I wondered.

"About six months now, my lord." (Ah, so this was a formal visit.) "We both work in Holborn, and sometimes we eat together."

"What is his work?"

"He is assistant to a wood engraver. For the illustration of books."

"What kind of books?" I said, alarmed.

"Nature books," replied Ronald, surprised.

Too close proximity to Charles' pornography had obviously unsettled me.

"What is his family situation?" I enquired.

"He lives with his widowed mother in rented rooms off Gray's Inn Road," answered Ronald. "They are Welsh; you can hear it in his tone. His mother speaks with far more of an intonation; her natural tongue is Welsh. I believe he only spoke Welsh as a child."

"I wonder what you think we can do," said Claudia. "It seems to me that this is a personal matter which Arthur would not thank you for revealing to us."

I leaned forward. "Is it your fear that Arthur, in mingling with foreigners and disreputable characters, is perhaps putting into practice what was generally advised here yesterday – to live life utterly? To – er – make each moment exquisite?"

"Yes, I believe so," Ronald declared. "And because you spoke up against it, my lord, I knew that I could turn to you."

"I will make enquiries," I said importantly.

Ronald stood up and thanked me, shook my hand, was grateful. He and Claudia murmured some exchanges about colours. Was yellow the true colour of Sin after all? Ronald thought it was.

"And remember," Claudia said earnestly. "The Welsh are known for a certain gloominess of character. A melancholy. It is in their nature. It is what makes them bards and seers and why their music is always so melodious. It may simply be the characteristics of the race you see in Arthur."

Willing to be convinced, Ronald supposed so. Within a few moments he was gone, leaving Claudia and I to disagree.

We were still disagreeing as we lay in bed that night.

"No, Algy, I insist, we must not interfere."

"We must. The lad could be in serious trouble."

"We do not really know him. It would be paternalistic and presumptuous."

"It would be an act of charity."

"You are just like your mother. You probe into the lives of all the workers down at Mortmayne and tell them how to live, just as your types have always done for centuries, the benevolent squire who cares for all – a Christmas hamper for the children and a Bible for the prizewinners. But Arthur does not live on your estate. He is a slight acquaintance, I do not know him well, and you do not know him at all. You will do more harm than good to poke around his haunts asking questions, you who are so obviously a gentleman. Whatever will they think? His mother will be more worried than she is already and his employer will begin to think that Arthur has a secret and will thus grow most suspicious. You will make matters worse."

"We cannot simply do nothing."

"True. But we will move with caution," said my wife. "Next week when he comes here and in the weeks that follow I will watch him and talk to him a little – there are ways of doing things . . . Algy, you have grown very quiet . . . Algy, you will make me very displeased indeed if you secretly set about probing into the private life of that young man."

Thus we lay there, rigid and separate, each thinking our own thoughts about Arthur Hughes, staring ahead into the unfathomable darkness.

CHAPTER SEVEN

HAVING AT that stage more than a vestige of belief in the accepted bounds of propriety and convention I allowed Claudia her way, and though my instinct and desire was to stride purposefully into Arthur's life and save him from this nameless threat, I let the matter be, supposing that within a week we would see him again. A problem of a somewhat more tangible nature concerned me more – guilt at my behaviour in connection with Sebastian Charles – and having mulled the situation over I decided that his friends should help him, and if he had not spoken to Sir William Franklin himself, then I would do so. The poverty and squalor into which he had fallen might well have prevented Charles from seeking aid, but if as was suspected Franklin valued privilege and status, then maybe he would listen to me and together we might alleviate poor Charles' burden.

Thus it was I found myself one afternoon towards the end of February at the portals of the house in Kensington where as a youth I had spent such wondrous langorous days, and because the memories were more sweet than bitter I experienced a sudden surge of joy to be there.

The façade of Franklin's house was never prepossessing, was shabby even, fronting as it did a narrow street where flattened cobbles of a previous age gave it an old-world charm; there was a country air about it, a feeling of a century ago, when life was slower, more refined. Franklin himself I had not seen since the previous year at his knighthood, and prior to that the funeral of Lord Tennyson three years before was the last occasion on which we met. I remembered it well – that melancholy October day which wove itself so perfectly into the awesome splendour of the ceremony. The whole of London seemed to be in mourning, silent and bareheaded outside the walls of Westminster Abbey. I saw the laurels laid upon the coffin and the great man placed to rest among the poets of our nation. Uneasily I understood that such an occasion – the gathering of the famous and dignified in worthy settings – was Franklin's element now, but yet I persevered, hoping against hope.

Well into his fifties now, this mentor of my youth received me welcomingly. He had always been good-looking, and he was so now, though the fine lines of his youthful Romantic features had thickened to a florid well fed glossiness. Whereas before he radiated energy and confidence he now gave off a certain bristling complacency, the look of one who lived well and was universally approved. His clothes were so conventional he might have been a banker, and the once wayward hair was neatly cut and flattened with Macassar oil. His surging confidence now seemed more like that sense of satisfaction experienced by one who knows his life is running on a smooth and meritorious course. My heart sank further, but I would not be discouraged.

As I stood once more in that black and gold tiled hall I felt greatly disturbed. The curve of the wide staircase took the eye upward, past peacock-blue walls with their gilt-framed paintings and Japanese plates that seemed to hover like perching butterflies with no visible means of support. I was moved beyond belief to be here, because it seemed as if I stood within a bubble of time, the youth that I was then, before the mediocrity of ordinary life set around me, shaping me to fit itself. Entirely foolish was this notion, because of course I could have visited Franklin at any time, if I had so chosen, and the contrast would not have been so sharp – the house had always been here, Franklin glad enough to welcome me. But to have come here, so to speak, via Mr Charles, and knowing what I knew of Victor Strode, I felt most unsettled.

I saw the naked alabaster statue of young Antinous – it seemed greyer, smaller than I remembered – and I even stupidly looked down at the statue's feet where we had made a votive offering, but there were no heaps of daisies, poppies, lilies there now, upon that well swept floor. The door that led to the room with the fountain was shut.

Franklin led us past this to a room at the back of the house, which for a moment I half thought I had not seen before. But that was nonsense – simply it was that then it had been exotically furnished. Strings of peacock feathers used to hang suspended in the breeze and urns that looked as if they had been pillaged from the Elgin treasures had held tall bouquets of snowy plumes, while scattered on the floor were massive velvet cushions, low divans all slung about with Indian rugs and heaps of fur. The wallpaper had been indigo and gold – pagodas, orchids. All that was gone; and now in its place was smooth dark panelling, the wallpaper white, curiously Puritan after so much remembered excess. The whole tenor of the room was so much changed that I felt quite disorientated. A hearty fire burned in the grate, the sofa and chairs were covered in floral cloth, there was a buff carpet and all the usual accoutrements of a parlour – fringed valances along the mantel shelves and a profusion of ornaments above, fire screens, tilt-top tables, wicker chairs, side tables, potted plants, the serried ranks of little photographs in silver frames, the windows misted over with a sea of hanging lace.

We sat each side of the fireplace, and pleasantries completed, we embarked upon the business in hand.

"Sebastian Charles," I said. "I am sure that you are aware of his circumstances."

Franklin shrugged a little. "I believe he has had some bad luck lately."

"Oh it is more than that," I assured him. "He lives in squalor in a vile and sordid room attended only by a female of disreputable sort. The laudanum which once relieved the symptoms of his illness now quite possesses him. He has degenerated from the man we knew into a pitiable wreck. It shocked me utterly to see it."

"I cannot say that it surprises me," said Franklin ponderously. "Charles was always wayward. He pursued his questionable philosophy to the limits, and this is where it lands him. It was inevitable, I suppose. No, I am not surprised."

"I don't think Charles was any worse than you or Mr Strode. Why, the whole house was dedicated to the pursuit of art and pleasure and the gratification of the senses. We all indulged to a greater or lesser degree in the wonders that lay to hand."

"Ah, there you have it," said Franklin, serious as a medical man. "A greater or lesser degree. With Charles it was greater, and he pays the penalty. One must know when to stop. You and I understood that. Charles did not."

It nettled me to be bracketed with Franklin as the possessors of wisdom.

"I wonder which of us has experienced most of what life has to offer," I remarked.

"It depends upon what one's palate requires – feasting at a banquet or slobbering in the dregs. I have no complaint with my own life, nor would I have thought you had any grounds for dissatisfaction."

"I am not dissatisfied . . ." I began. "But there are times when one looks at one's situation and wonders what exactly one has done with one's allotted time – where has it gone? Has it been wasted?"

"I never wonder that," said Franklin firmly. "My life has been a steady path, through apprenticeship, to maturity, to success. I can show you well enough what I have achieved. Come with me."

He stood up, and I followed him through the panelled door into a long white hallway at the end of which was a glass door leading to the garden. Paintings hung on both sides of the hallway, paintings large and small – little portraits of ladies amongst roses, a small boy with a spaniel, a serious matron in a lace-edged cap.

"But *these* are my latest ones," said Franklin. "Mythical subjects as you see and very much in demand. I must admit," he laughed in a perplexity which was affected, "I can barely paint them swiftly enough. Soon I shall have to delegate hands and feet to students, as Michelangelo did."

Mythical subjects! They were all of naked women, big, langorous, inviting. *Daphne Pursued – The Abduction of Proserpine – Clytie and Leucothea – Danaë Imprisoned –* What was the matter with me? A month ago I would have looked at Franklin's paintings with a superficial eye, wandering from one to another as in any gallery, noticing the marble pillars and the flowing folds of cloth, the vibrant motion of the fleeing figures, the remarkable tones of living flesh. And still, at one level, I behaved so, and was able to make observations on the quality of the work and certainly my host expected this. Yet secretly as I passed painting after painting all I saw were Charles' book illustrations lurking demon-like beside each representation as if to say: But turn these paintings round and at the back, the other side of art is this.

"The Duke of Cranford's after this one," Franklin tapped the frame around Daphne. "I will not tell you what he's offering me! I only wish I could turn them out at a faster rate, like Alma Tadema does. But I've always been meticulous. It costs me pain and perspiration just to work the petals of a flower."

"Your interest, I see, no longer centres upon the medieval. Have you still your canvases of knights and minstrels?"

"Oh yes," smiled Franklin. "I've thrown nothing away. They're all up in my studio. I still have many studies of yourself – do you remember that young man with the exquisite auburn hair who was so regrettably of the street in his private life? You must do – you posed together countless times – I have some studies of you both – David and Jonathan, Herakles and Hylas, Apollo and Hyacinthus – I was very pleased with them at the time and I'm still very fond of them . . ."

While my heart unaccountably turned over at the recollections which Franklin's nonchalant remarks provoked in me, Franklin added: "I saw him at Lord Tennyson's funeral, you know." I stared. Why had not I? "I thought it odd to see him there, but then one forgets sometimes what a widespread appeal Tennyson had among the masses. Of course," he laughed, "I didn't speak to him."

I winced as I agreed. One would not, in a group of the nobility and the famous, descend so much as to acknowledge someone so patently of the lower order.

"So, as you see," said Franklin pleasantly, "I do fulfil my early promise. Life has been kind to me and I am fortunate to have friends in high places. I am not dissatisfied."

Our promenade had brought us to the end of the hallway and we faced the garden door, where the uncurtained glass showed us the wintry scene beyond. I gasped. True it was winter, but the bitter season itself could not entirely explain the strange bleakness of the garden. I saw a level lawn that stretched across to the far wall. I saw no sign of bush and shrub.

"I see that you have had the garden altered," I could not help but remark. "I seem to remember that it was – different."

"Oh it's been flattened for many a year now," said Franklin easily. "If you recall, it was a tangled wilderness, a riot of small plants that tripped your feet and spoiled the ladies' dresses. I had to have it neatened off. These days all summertime I entertain – we have foreign dignitaries visiting as well as luminaries of our own shores – tables on the lawns, musicians. And I need the space to display some sculptures which I mean to set in stone. You do not approve, I think?" he added in benevolent tolerance.

"There were some lilac trees . . ."

"They had grown wild and bushy." Franklin clapped a hand on my shoulder. "What's this? A lingering *nostalgie*? There is no place for that in a practical world. Well! Let us return within – it grows remarkably chilly in here at this time of year. I was having an interesting discussion with Edward Poynter about the most productive way to heat or not to heat any exhibition of paintings for maximum enjoyment – that was just after he became Director of the National Gallery . . ."

We returned to what I must now call the parlour, and reseated ourselves by the fire.

"I daresay that you have some reservations about this room also," Franklin wagged his finger at me like a reproving uncle who understands what's best. "It doesn't do, Algy, it doesn't do. You cannot live in the past. That way of life was proper for that particular time. But I am married now, established. You shall meet Patience before you leave. She likes this room. She receives the wives in here. They feel at home in all this frippery. I thank whatever deity arranges these things that art is now respectable. We live in marvellous days. Marvellous days!"

"But not for all," I interrupted carefully. "I should remind you of the purpose of my visit. I must admit I had not heard from Charles for many years and was surprised when I received a summons from him. That summons was to reveal some news to me of hideous import. He tells me Mr Strode has been arrested. In a public lavatory in Piccadilly. He committed a gross act. He was taken to Bow Street Police Station. Franklin! Charles recounts that policemen lie in wait in order to entrap unfortunates. I find this revelation shocking. When our streets abound with crime, to think the officers of the law have time to spare for such underhand behaviour!"

"But Algy," Franklin began slowly. "The gross act you refer to is a crime also."

"But in comparison with murder –" I cried contemptuously.

"Surely you do not condone it?" he said gently.

"Condone it – no –" I hesitated. Damn me, he knew well enough if he chose to recall it, that I had made no secret of my love for Willie Smith when he lived here as a model eleven years ago. Everyone condoned it! They encouraged it! Why, it was Franklin who gave the bizarre Greek banquet that brought us two together. "Algy, there is the divinest boy," he had told me. "Common as a shoe black, but as beautiful as anything that Moreau paints and I swear he has no interest in the female kind . . . he could be just what you are looking for."

"I know we played with silly notions," Franklin told me, radiating great good humour which could barely conceal the sharp alarm that I perceived beneath the surface. "Young men *do* . . . public schools, the army . . . it does go on . . . but everyone understands its place . . . one experiments a little . . . one is foolish . . . and then comes maturity and one sees those things for what they are. I know that we agree. I was absolutely delighted when you married and had children. Now you have your family to think of. Nobody would expect you to involve yourself with an old acquaintanceship that happened years ago when you were still unformed. You did not know Charles well, Strode not at all. You would have nothing with which to reproach yourself if you did not speak of either ever again."

This was exactly what I had previously told myself. Why then did I find it now offensive, bland, insulting?

"But *you* did, I believe?" said I, and I admit to mischief-making here. "You knew both well,"

Franklin twitched. "You are quite mistaken, Algy," he said. "It may have seemed so to an outsider. But Mr Charles and I were merely professionally and superficially connected. I rented rooms to him. I know nothing of his background and I knew he was politically unsound. Like you, I have not seen him this many a year. One is not responsible for every lame dog which one encounters on life's journey. And as for Victor Strode – he was an embarrassment in every way. A sponger and a wastrel, contributing nothing, writing stuff that passed for verse, and every kind of nuisance to the young male models. I remember one Italian boy – if I had not given out a large sum of money for him to hold his tongue I believe we would not have avoided a scandal of monstrous proportions. And that was in the days before the law was made more stringent."

"So you will not help Mr Strode then?"

"My God, Algy, what can you possibly expect –?" the great man spluttered. "I believe I am as Christian as the next man, and it is no secret that I contribute heavily to innumerable benevolent funds. But Mr Strode is nothing to me. I feel no obligation there. If he had not the sense to keep within our country's laws, then what can I do? He must have known the likelihood of his arrest when he embarked upon his criminal course. And that particular crime is, as you know, abhorrent to a normal man. You and I, Algy, are well clear of him."

"But Charles," I pointed out, "is another matter."

"Is he? I don't see it." Franklin frowned.

"Yes, and you know it," I replied. "In friendship there are duties and one of these is not to abandon one who was a friend, however long ago."

"What do you mean? Do you suggest I send him money?"

"I do; and better still, go visit him and show him he is not forgotten."

"Shall you?" said Franklin cautiously.

"I will. I fought the impulse, just as you do. I was horrified to see the pit into which he had fallen. But this revulsion is unworthy in me, and in you also if I may say so. We should put it right at once by showing him that we remain his friends."

"Listen Algy . . ." Franklin said uneasily. "I don't think you know everything. Charles has been in with a very bad crowd for some time now. By associating with him, one's good name would be tarnished. It's as well to stay clear."

I felt an upsurge of anger. "It doesn't matter what kind of company Charles keeps. He seems to be quite ill and not long for this world. He needs us."

"Ah . . ." murmured Franklin. "Well, that will be a blessing in disguise, then, if he is *in extremis*. That would solve the whole unfortunate situation."

I stood up. "Am I to understand that you refuse to help him?"

"No," cried Franklin, in a mild placatory tone. "No, I'll send him money. Just as you say, in the name of a bygone acquaintance. Never let it be said that I do not know my obligations. But I shall not visit him and he would not expect it. I daresay he would be embarrassed that I should see him in his straightened circumstances. I would be doing him a kindness to stay away."

Franklin stood up and put a hand on my arm. It was an intimacy I shrank from. I stood tense and fuming.

"You and I, Algy," said Sir William in that same avuncular and vastly irritating manner, "have been wise. We mingle in society – why, we have had the honour to have met Her Gracious Majesty. We are men of culture, manners, privilege. This places us in a position of responsibility. *To ourselves*. To become involved with Charles as he is now would be to risk it all. He isn't worth it, Algy. Think about it. You know that what I say is sound."

"I know that what you say appals me!" I exclaimed. I freed myself from his conciliatory touch. "I am ashamed that you should think I feel the same as you. I am not wise at all. If I have wealth and privilege it is because I was born to it, and I am afraid that these same privileges sometimes blind one to the course of humane action. Much has changed in your house, Franklin, but you have not. I remember well enough how you brought ragged people off the streets and used them for your portraits – 'city types' you called them – brought them in and painted them but did not feed them, and then threw them back. You thought them fodder for your art, with no conception of their rights as people."

"Ah. Now you sound just like your little auburn-headed friend," said Franklin smiling, aiming to insult.

"I do?" I blinked.

"You do. And since he came from Whitechapel and had the manners of a guttersnipe I wonder whether you should find yourself best pleased by the comparison."

"Spitalfields," I answered, unaccountably amused.

"I beg your pardon?"

"He came from Spitalfields; not Whitechapel."

"Those slums are all the same."

"I think we have no more to say to one another," I replied. "But be convinced, when I next visit Mr Charles I shall assure him of your continuing affection."

Franklin bowed. At that moment we were suddenly disturbed. The garden door in the adjoining hallway opened with a grinding creak, and then the panelled door into the parlour. A young girl entered. She was exceptionally comely, with large dark eyes and curls of chestnut hair beneath the wide fringed shawl she clutched about her person. She was so obviously Daphne Pursued that I did not need an introduction.

"Oh I am so sorry, Sir William," she said in an accent hardly consistent with Sir William's insistence upon us all remaining in our proper spheres. "I thought you'd be alone, and I came in as usual.

I'll go back."

"No, no, Annie, sit you down," said Franklin, not at all perturbed. "My model, Annie," he explained. "She is so timid she will not use the front door but creeps in like a servant. Silly girl. Well. We shall begin our new masterpiece this evening, shall we not?"

Annie sat down by the fire, the shawl unwinding from her shoulders. Franklin escorted me into the entrance hall.

Lady Franklin had descended the staircase unobserved, a plain unprepossessing woman in mauve silk, somewhat of Franklin's age, and having nothing visible with which to combat the succession of alluring girls that posed without clothes before her husband. She engaged me in light conversation to which I responded with politeness. We discussed the unusually severe climatic conditions. She had seen a photograph of the Thames below Limehouse taken earlier this month which had profoundly shocked her. Up against the wharf the mud and water alike had been frozen into sculptured billows, so hard and fast that boats had been thrust upward, jutting above the clumps of ice like jagged teeth. Beyond this icy waste the river itself lay frozen like a road.

"It's unnatural," she said, as one who foresees doom. "It's all unnatural. One ought to be able to depend upon Nature. A frost like that in February! Why, it should be almost Spring. You can depend on nothing nowadays – everything just seems to alter all the time."

"Oh really," murmured Sir William testily. "A heavy frost in February is not so rare. Snow at Easter has not been unknown."

Susceptible myself upon that day to the subtle nuances of transience I understood that Lady Franklin was not speaking of the climate. Her eyes were puffy and red-rimmed, and her manner dejected. I could not help but feel her life was not an easy one.

Beyond her, I could see the door into the fountain room was now ajar, indeed the wind had blown it open. I saw the wondrous richness within – the lapis lazuli tiles, the bottle green marble, the ebony and gilt. I saw clearly now that the room within was quite unchanged. Amongst so much that since had been destroyed, denied, or suffered time's decay, this heart-room remained just as it used to be.

It was not until I heard the words that sprang from Sir William's lips that I saw the mirror image of myself as I had been in all my previous fastidiousness and prejudice. Just as from Charles' insalubrious backstreet I had fled to seek the reassurance of the world I knew, I now could hardly wait to rid myself of all association with the sphere of culture and respectability as represented by the house in Kensington. I knew well enough that I needed a strong antidote, more, I knew where I could find it. As I stepped into my waiting hansom I was desperate to ally myself with everything opposite to what I had encountered in that house. In short, I looked for degradation.

I told the cabman to take me to Piccadilly Circus and, my mind a blank, I watched the changing panorama of the streets. The snow was gone now, but the weather remained bitterly cold, and it was almost March. The sky was grey, as were the streets. The afternoon hung on the verge of evening. A dirty mist hovered in the air, tasting of soot.

Alighting from the hansom I stood upon the pavement and watched the scene before me. I had stood here many times before but now I saw it in a different kind of way.

Opposite me, the Shaftesbury Memorial Fountain stood upon its little island; at its base the flower-sellers sat and shivered, making nosegays of snowdrops. A throng of people moved in all directions. The omnibuses trundled past, shiny carriages mingling with the cumbersome commercial conveyances, the horses' breath white in the cold air. Lights showed in the Piccadilly Restaurant, a line of hansoms waiting at the kerb. The iron railings of the public urinal on its opposing smaller island assumed a new significance. *There* it was that policemen made arrests – *down there* the reckless met and risked discovery. The whole scenario now had changed for me – I saw it as a battleground. Opposing forces moved across the streets, manoeuvring their way between the flower-sellers, lamp posts, newsboys, shoe blacks. Some would be in disguise – that man, for instance, smartly dressed, his walking cane now tapping on the cobbles, he might be "so" and looking for a youth to ease his secret needs; and that one, standing still, his hands behind his back, perhaps was even yet surveying the landscape for his prize; and he with the umbrella, looking round about him – what did he search for? That policeman now, on the opposing side, the threat, was plain enough and one could well avoid him, but what if the foe wore mufti and was such a one as he, the burly smiling fellow chatting with a flower-girl, yet watching others pass about him? Where would one hide? The roads away from Piccadilly Circus led in all directions, and from them small side streets snaked off to nameless haunts known only to the initiated. Was he one – that boy who stood beside the lamp post? No, too obvious, surely. Was *he*, the youth with the jaunty gait and slim-fitting trousers, so tight that the two halves of his ample buttocks showed – was he too obvious again? Thoughtfully my eyes were upward drawn then, to that sweet aluminium boy above upon the pyramidal mound, his wings outspread, his naked form poised in the act of letting fly his arrow. I remembered the furore caused when Gilbert's fair creation first took to the streets. And yet how very fine he was, this boy, how very beautiful his arse!

"Light, sir?" said someone at my elbow.

"No, thank you," I replied, and he was gone.

I spun round stupidly. The young man who had spoken was quite disappeared, merged into the crowd. So much for my reflections as to who was what and why! I laughed, amazed at my obtuseness; then I hesitated, chastened. If this was indeed a battleground I was a mere beginner, and I could not but feel doubtful of my chances of survival.

When by a quirk of circumstance I had shared supper in that elegant hotel with Oscar Wilde and his companions and there had been discussion as to where the Apples of Sodom might be found, I remembered Charlie Parker mentioning a place off Shaftesbury Avenue. Propelled by a curious heedlessness I now set off in that direction, walking briskly. I turned down Rupert Street and into Soho, not particularly troubled to be strolling out alone in these meaner streets, for the hour was yet a civilised one and there were many folk about. Some of these were ladies of doubtful reputation, for twice I gallantly quitted the pavement to let pass a group of brightly dressed exquisites, coiffures high as bee skeps, with perfumes heady as a summer meadow and faces caked in paint and powder, lips as crimson as a sunset.

I believe I had it in mind merely to partake of liquid refreshment as I entered the public house to which Charlie Parker referred. Certainly I had no particular intention to involve myself in anything that I might find hard to explain to anybody, most of all myself. I do suspect that the anonymous offer of a light, unseen at my elbow, was the spark that set off the curious excitement which now pulsed within my veins, and as I entered the place my heart was beating with an unaccustomed vigour.

The Two Faces was the name of this intriguing den, and I had noticed that there hung a sign above the door, of the old-fashioned kind, with those two masks portraying comedy and tragedy depicted; and after all we were not far from every kind of theatre. Yet how apt a name, I thought, as I breathed in the smoky warmth within – two faces, one the public one, and one the hidden. I looked about me.

The room was small, the windows misted glass, the counter pewter-topped, the handles of the beer pumps jutting up like painted truncheons. Marble table tops, brass-edged partitions to give privacy to those engaged in conversation, there was nothing much of the unusual here. Yet it was not a gentleman's drinking place, and I was plainly the object of many a glance as I sat down with a glass of Amontillado. There were few people here, and no women or children. A guardsman leaned against the counter, belching horribly over a tankard of stout. Two young men, by their conversation and dress of the theatrical profession, murmured in a fug of smoke at one of the partitioned tables. An older man, of curiously reputable appearance, seemed to doze, cigar between his fingertips. Two shabbily dressed youths lounged at the bar; both turned and stared, then turned back to their drinks, arguing in whispers. A stocky barman in brown waistcoat and rolled up shirtsleeves thoughtfully and slowly wiped a tankard with a stiff white cloth. The sense of anticipation I experienced was as strong as if the curtain was about to rise upon a drama.

I watched the two youths toss a coin on the counter top, slamming it down with the slap of a palm. They were laughing in low voices – "best of three!" – and they started up again. The guardsman slid his empty tankard from his elbow and walked out. The conversation of the actors rose into the air, indignant suddenly, and loud.

"He told me he was working at the Tivoli, and I went along to watch him. Do you know what he was there employed to do? They had a ship at sea upon the stage, and a great green cloth to represent the mighty billow. And underneath the cloth were ranks of rolling boys – yes! Rolling boys! They rolled in unison to and fro, which caused the cloth to simulate the waves of the Atlantic! Herbert," came the doleful, disbelieving voice, "was a billow!"

One of the youths detached himself and came over to my table.

"Mind if I sit here?" he enquired.

I indicated that I made no objection. What devil was within me I know not; it was plain enough to me that at this point I should have stood up and left. By remaining I knew I was committed – but to what?

The youth was good-looking, in a common sort of way, with curly black hair and a pale impish face with a very wide grin, which he would turn on and off as swiftly as a switch, without any reference to amusement or joy; his eyes did not smile at all. He wore a loose jacket with well padded shoulders, check trousers and a bright waistcoat of yellow and cream stripes. He apologised but he was temporarily without money in his pocket and his glass was empty. I organized the filling of it, and finished my own.

"I don't think I've had the pleasure of having seen you in here before sir," he remarked.

"Do you spend much time in here then?" I enquired.

"Oh yes. I'm often to be found here. Not that I'm not in

hemployment. I am in hemployment. But a person must 'ave 'is recreation, mustn't he? And one meets a very nice class of person in here, sir. And I think that widens the mind, sir, meetin' a nice class of person."

"I'm sure it must do," I agreed.

"May I ask who was it told you this was a nice place to come?"

"I think not," I replied discreetly.

"Oh very well," he said, put out but undeterred. "I understand. Tell me then, sir, are you a gentleman what likes to partake of a nice game of pool?"

"I beg your pardon?"

"We have a billiard room upstairs, sir, which is available at any time and is usually adjudged to provide a very pleasant way of whiling away a couple of ahs."

"As long as that!" I raised my eyebrows.

He giggled. "Or a few minutes. I should be honest. Very often that would depend on what the gentleman was willing to pay. It's disgustin', ain't it sir, how these days it's heconomical considerations what dictates the pace!"

"In all spheres," I agreed.

"What'd'you say then, sir?" He downed the dregs of his brandy. "Will you be pleased to come upstairs with me for a mo? We can give each other a game and be finished soon and no one'll know where you've been." He stood up invitingly, the crotch of his trousers much in evidence, and I stood up also.

I followed him through a door at the back of the room. Chill air struck suddenly from innumerable sources of draught; a door to a backyard thudded on its hinges, an entrance to a kitchen wafted up a cloud of cooking smells, a dingy window showed a pile of barrels stacked. Dark stairs wound upward and each creaking step took us into dim upper regions, a honeycomb of narrow passages. We did indeed pass a door that was marked "Billiard Room" and I had no doubt that therein was a pool table, balls and cues; but we did not enter. I had the impression that we were now inside a different building, for the passageways had been so contrived to link up with those of other houses, small sections of the walls knocked out, the brick edges showing jaggedly in places, shreds of plaster hanging down, the whole effect a complicated network suggesting an escape route like a rabbit warren. Such decrepit windows as we passed revealed only nameless shabby courts far below.

"Here we are," said my companion and opened a low door. "Anyone at home?"

At first the room was in complete darkness, and for a moment as I stood there it was like the moment of awakening from sleep when the mind lies poised awaiting the return of conscious thought, a strange suspension. A candle flame sprang into life, then another, then another.

"This is Heloise's room," the youth explained, repocketing his matches. "She don't like ordinary light, just candles. Pretty, ain't it?"

I marvelled. It was certainly the room of some female prostitute. But harsh reality quite paled into obscurity before the shimmering glow of the strange romance this place exuded. Small, low-ceilinged, the entire room was draped in veils and shawls and curtain cloth. I suspected that by the light of day it would seem bleak and sordid, but the candlelight's theatrical effect induced a world of dream and magic. The candles all were green, thick, scented. Each one, much burned, had sculptured itself into a turreted pinnacle, the solid wax draped down the sides in splendid rivulets, and at the base an open flower of green wax petals with the living flame its nectar. The hanging shawls dispensed with any hint of wall or structure, recreating whorls much like the inside of a rose. Fringed, translucent, they seemed rich and beautiful — black silk with purple flowers and amber butterflies and golden birds with curved white wings and fringes fine as eyelashes; pale green linen with crimson buds and clumps of hyacinthine blue bouquets; peach-coloured silk daubed extravagantly with mauve orchids and leaves of lapis lazuli, tassles lush as ostrich plumes. Upon a small low bed one such shawl, cream, a mass of finely woven lilies, draped its tangled fringes on the floor. A tiny dressing table bloomed in this profusion, its gilt-edged mirror portraying another world of equal mystery in its dark depths. Tall perfume bottles with cut glass domes, a mass of powder puffs, a slim vase full of hat pins, and a wealth of little tubes and pots and lids and creams disguised the surface, and upon a stool lay petticoats, long mesh gloves, black stockings. In this confined space the scented candles made a strange and over-sweet aroma, not like any flower, nor incense, nothing natural at all.

"Edward is my name." The youth carefully steadied each candle and adjusted them clear of the hanging draperies. "She'll set fire to us all one day!" he observed with a grin. He turned to me, put both hands on my shoulders and kissed me on the lips. Thus, suddenly and without preamble, ended those eleven chaste years of my life. I felt a curious peacefulness and no regret at all. "You may call me Eddy," he continued. "Many do."

We kissed, slowly, tentatively, savouring whether there was to be pleasure as well as satisfaction. He was attractive. There was a fine stubble about his face. Close to, his eyes were dark and hard, bead-black, devoid of tenderness. He licked me hungrily, opening

82

his mouth to me, and I responded, sensing well enough that whether I were beautiful or no, his talent was his trade and would be sold to *n'importe qui*. His fingers worked at the buttons of my coat. We sat down on the bed.

"You're nice, sir, very nice," he said. We did not take off our clothes but unloosed and unbuttoned all that made for the desired effect, and strangely enough, to do so little seemed to me delightfully erotic. The shape of his dark head, his black unruly curls against my starched white shirt which hung half open; then his warm hands on my cock, and then his lips upon it as he sank between my thighs – all this caused an arousal startling me with its intensity. The street boy, with a touch, a lick, had shown me the extent of my starvation. I badly needed him to bring me to release. His lips worked on my prick, slavering till it grew slippery and wet and bucked like some excited primitive thing. I pressed him to me, my fingers clenched in the rough cloth of his coat. I groaned in ecstasy and doubled over him. My hair fell forward covering my face and suddenly I heard it singe upon a candleflame. I drew back in alarm and lay amongst the hanging silks, breathless, gasping. He straightened up and came to sit beside me, thigh to thigh.

"You have not got burned, sir?" said he in concern.

"Not at all, no, just a hair lock singed."

"Those who play with fire, sir . . ." he teased. "You know what they say!"

"Well, they are wrong. If I have played with fire I found it . . . most warming."

"And you'll feel better for it, sir," he said, patting my knee.

"I think I will."

He looked down at his watch. "We'd best be moving, sir, now if you're ready. There'll be others waiting."

This hint of a busy vibrant world, that gathered even now to use the room where I had acted so unusually, grated upon my quivering senses.

"How much do I owe you?"

"We'll say two guineas."

"Two!" I blanched. Maybe I was out of date. I had a vague recollection that the going rate was a guinea; but of course, that was some time ago.

"A guinea for the services," replied the youth unblushingly, "and a guinea for," his wide grin came into play, his eyes unsmiling as a judge's, "not ever telling what we did." He shrugged apologetically. "That's how it goes, I'm afraid. But you can trust me, sir; I'm honest."

I handed over the amount reflectively. So that was the difference.

The passing of the Blackmailers' Charter some ten years ago, its implications reaching to street level, as firm an economic issue as any Corn Law or Property Tax.

"Tell you what," said Eddy, slipping his hand inside his jacket. "Take this address. I know you'll want to do this sort of thing again. Well, this way makes it easy."

I took the scrap of paper I was offered, unfolded it and read it. In a surprisingly well lettered hand was written the address of a house in Chelsea; I vaguely knew the road.

"You might say that's a kind of post-box," explained Eddy. "Someone who knows about this sort of thing has left a certain box there which is being looked after. Interested parties go along and there they can find whoever on that list is free and suitable, and contact can be made."

"Do you mean others like yourself?"

"Well," he said thoughtfully. "Some are. Some aren't. See, some lads make a living only this way. And others take on work, but being as the work is poorly paid, like groom work for instance, or being a waiter, well, they fall into this kind of life to top up what they make in honest toil. I don't know if you've noticed, sir," he grinned, "how honest toil don't seem to bring in high reward for a person's endeavour! Myself I'm of the honest kind. I'm what you might call an honest tart. I pride myself on it. I take what you might call high wages but that's for not snitchin'. There's some – and you was lucky not to fall in with such as they – who'll take a small remuneration, and then *bother* you, sir – know what I mean? You're never free of 'em. They come back for more and more and bleed you dry. All for one little fling, eh, that's hardly fair. Or they'll take it in a lump sum and you pay it just for them to leave you alone. Why, Freddie Atkins can make fifty quid a time. You have to admire him in a way. Don't go with him, sir, if you see his name on a list. Take it from me. He's a bad lot and will do you no good. Not that he won't give you a good time, sir, he will! But ooh my Lor', afterwards you pay for it – and again – and again!"

We swiftly restored ourselves to decency, and Eddy carefully blew out the candles.

"I worry myself silly about all this lot catchin' fire," he remarked. "You hear such stories, don't you?"

We made our way back along the twisty passageways, he leading. I experienced a marvellous sense of well-being. How curiously convenient that once the step had been made into seeking this kind of satisfaction, there should be the means to continue. I was intrigued by the notion of this secret post-box with the names of the initiated. A surge of pleasure rose within me. The immediate future seemed

84

an interesting prospect.

Eddy paused as we reached the door that led into the public house. "Here we part, sir." We shook hands. When we re-entered the tap-room Eddy slipped away without a word and disappeared into the street. I judged it best to wait a while before making my own departure and I leaned against the counter. The barman caught my eye. "I trust we shall be seeing you again, sir?" he remarked. With a somewhat unpleasant archness to his tone he added: "I believe Eddy plays a good game of pool."

I considered that the observation smacked of impudence and I did not reply. Shortly afterwards I left that place and made my way smartly back towards Piccadilly.

Now it was evening; everywhere was ablaze with lights. I paused amongst the hurrying throng, my hand upon the cold iron of a lamp post. The die was cast. Within this vibrant jungle I had now my chosen part. I did not know what it meant for me and whether I was courting danger, but I felt invigorated and alive, a secret agent in possession of forbidden knowledge. Because of what I had just done this teeming thoroughfare was now composed of allies and of foes and I would thus be predator and prey. As yet I could not tell who would be friend, who enemy, but I would learn the code.

I crossed the road to where a line of hansoms waited, gave the Euston Road address and climbed into the leading cab. I smirked with child-like satisfaction as I settled back into the leather. Here was I, that kind of reprobate that decent folk were warned against, riding through the evening streets, a deferential cab driver to take me where I wished to go. All over London -- now my fancy raced – gentlemen climbed into cabs, gave an address, and were transported to some little room known only to the initiated, there to find pleasure and relief; then returned, their action swathed in mystery, none knowing what they did. Almost a brotherhood, a far reaching secret society; and I would know more of it.

When we drew near to the narrow turn off Euston Road where Charles lived I quitted the cab, and walked down the dark alley which I found upon second acquaintance every morsel as vile as I remembered. I passed the dingy public house whose window was well lit now and whose door ajar, a pungent smell of ale and smoke surrounding it. I climbed the trembling slatted wooden structure and I rapped upon the door.

It was Polette who answered, as before, and showing some astonishment as well she might. "*Monsieur Algie* . . . we did not expect you . . ."

"Take me to Mr Charles," I said magnificently.

I found him standing by an easel, paintbrush in hand and all the signs of an artist at work about him. He looked ghastly, pale and drawn and wore the same old dressing gown. On a table by his elbow stood the cracked cup from which he took his absinthe, and he paused to drink as he observed my entrance. There were two distinct improvements in his circumstance – the lights were brighter and a fire burned in the grate. The room was almost warm.

"Charles!" I cried, throwing down hat and cane, magnanimous as any lad who has left home to seek his fortune and returns with all the treasures of the Ind. "I have come to take you out to dine. I thought we might go to the Café Royal. What do you say?"

CHAPTER EIGHT

THIS GESTURE being of such monumental importance to myself, both actually and symbolically, I had expected some slight reaction on the part of Charles but there was none.

"Since you are here, dear boy," he answered, "I wonder whether you would do me a favour."

"Yes. What?"

"I need a model for a kneeling pose, to go just here. I am painting this from memory and your limbs may jolt what threatens to fail."

"What is the picture?" I enquired. I should have guessed. The scene was of an orgy, where some hint of pillar, archway, urn gave one to understand a Roman setting, but the centre of the canvas was a sprawling mass of naked males. And though my heart sank to find that Charles continued to degrade his talent yet I must confess the picture as a whole excited me. An honesty I would not previously accept permitted me now, since my experience with Eddy, to gaze upon the painting free from the constraints of the social *mores* of our day which had so encumbered me before.

"Are all these drawn from life?" I murmured, my imagination quivering to contemplate each individual scenario. "Did this boy pose like that?"

"Indeed he did. For money. What a strong persuader that turns out to be! And yet I will get it back a hundredfold from the recipient of this masterpiece."

"You are commissioned? Someone ordered this?"

"Oh yes. A member of the House of Lords. He must have quite a gallery by now. So be a dear now, Algy, for I can't believe you've lost your pristine beauty and you'll be quite warm enough beside the fire. For which, by the way, much thanks. I would have frittered away the money you sent, but Polette was severe with me and made me order coal."

Polette was now directed to fetch Charles' clothes from the pawnbrokers. Sullenly she obeyed, murmuring that no good would come of this night's venture.

"Enough!" Charles said. "Let me be the judge of what I do. Be off with you and fetch my bundle."

Marvelling at the strange turns my life was taking, as the door closed after Polette I divested myself of my garments, and submitted to Charles' directions for a pose that involved kneeling upon the floor.

"I daresay that you did not think to see my return, after my hurriedly shameful departure."

"Keep your arms raised – remember you are grasping the thigh of a Hercules."

"Do you mean to say you know somebody with thighs like that!"

"All my characters are drawn from life. The thighs belong to a circus strongman. He can lift a pyramid composed entirely of his relatives all standing upon a series of boards. It is astonishing to see."

"I do not doubt it. But Charles, let me explain . . . Where do you think I was, just prior to our meeting?"

Charles painted stolidly on.

"There is a little public house in a street off Shaftesbury Avenue," I began, self consciously narrative, for I was expounding a drama full of revelations. "I heard about it in most unusual circumstances – at a supper in the company of Oscar Wilde and some of his . . . young acquaintances. Today a need that I had long and carefully suppressed burst forth, and from the depths of hidden thoughts came the memory of that occasion – the youth who spoke the words – the implication of what I would find there – the chance that my need would be satisfied. I did not give a thought to consequence, to reputation or respectability. I hardly understood myself. Spontaneously, as if impelled by a Mysterious Inner Force I entered that little hitherto-unknown place. It has a name which very much signifies the condition of those who enter there . . ."

"The Two Faeces," Charles remarked blandly. "I know it well."

I dropped my pose with a groan, both at the deflation of my story and at Charles' hideous pun.

"I have not been there recently," said Charles in a more conciliatory tone. "Oh do put your hands back, Algy. Tiredness creeps upon me and I need to finish you before it completes its work. I'm glad to hear the place is still 'so'. It seems to me that no sooner one such place begins to thrive, the police hear of it and it closes down. A few discreet arrests then follow in the city and the boys go underground. But then another one sparks up. And so the world goes . . ."

"It was important to me," I said, "as a gesture. Do you understand? It may well mean that I begin a different way of life today. My friends and my associates will see no change, but secretly, beneath the surface, I foresee a strange exciting time, and London a rich hothouse for a certain kind of bloom."

"You mean that you will visit that place regularly?" Charles said doubtfully. "I hardly see it in the exotic terms that you describe. Perhaps it has changed."

"Ah, there is more to come!" I cried eagerly. "I was given an address, a house in Chelsea. Here it seems I can be put in touch with many others – of the kind that frequent The Two Faces. It seems to me a gateway to a fascinating world, where I stand poised, excited, apprehensive . . ."

"Was it the one in Chapel Street?" said Charles severely, his paintbrush never leaving off its swift and urgent strokes.

"Why, yes it was," I said, completely floored.

"Don't ever go there," said Charles.

"Why not?" I wailed, abandoning the pose in every kind of sulk.

"The police are on to it, that's all."

"Oh – how can you know a thing like that?" I scowled.

"You know nothing about me, Algy," Charles replied. "Do you suppose my life is spent entirely in a drug-induced stupor splattered with intervening absinthe dreams? It is, of course!" he laughed cynically. "But in between I happen to be blessed or cursed with remnants of my wanderings that turn up unannounced, particularly when the news gets out that I am in the money. I sell a naughty painting to a duke, and lo, the shekels flow. A swarm of blight descends on me from the darkest corners of this *ville brumeuse, nuit sans fin*, and life grows most intriguing, for they're fascinating lads for all they're as vile as northern chimneys, and every one's in touch with what goes on. It was some whore of the female kind, apparently, down on her luck, who gave the place away. I know no more than that, and the implication is that the police are sitting on it, hoping they can draw a wider net. So I repeat, dear boy, do not put yourself among those mackerel. And by the way, you may now hide away your stunning nudity; you have been very helpful."

I stood up gloomily. "At one blow you have demolished all my glowing prospects. I was counting on that house in Chelsea."

"Nonsense." Charles observed, wiping his paintbrush. "I can furnish you with any number of willing lads. You can still have your bright future. But you will have to learn to be more careful – test the water with your toe before venturing your more intimate parts."

Charles eased himself down upon the sofa as I dressed.

"Poor Strode," he said, "that *enfant voué au noir*, has paid his penalty for carelessness. Section Eleven has gobbled up another victim. Two years with hard labour. What a farce, eh! He'll not last six months. An interesting way to murder someone, legally, with proper ceremony. I suspect a plot – an elaborate way to prevent his further desecration of the English tongue with ghastly verse."

"Can we do nothing?" I murmured uneasily, knotting my tie, and palpably wishing to do nothing.

"Don't pretend humanitarianism; sham does not become you. Drink?" I refused, but Charles concocted another brew. "I'd like a further favour of you, dearest boy," he said, mellifluous as the drink took effect.

"What is it?" I said warily, straightening my finished outfit.

"A full-length picture, as Narcissus."

"Oh," I said relieved. "Something so simple. Yes, of course – whenever you like."

"As I have not much time left to me," said Charles lugubriously, looking into his cup, "it had better be soon. The subject of Narcissus has always fascinated me."

"It has? It is an interesting tale."

"Tale be damned. It is a piece of flagrant symbolism and a delightful statement of a criminal act made cherishable in the disguise of art."

"Oh really?"

Charles leaned back and stretched. He was startlingly thin, his body angular and full of hollows. "The beautiful young man who gazes at himself in a pool that mirrors his own reflection. No, it's nothing to do with vanity and self love, a silly boy who faded away because he loved his own good looks. It is a pictorial representation of the man who loves his own kind, there for all the world to see, amongst paintings of Persephone and Daphne and the overblown nymphettes of Arcadia. I love to think of the art critics and the supercilious gang of high class painters squabbling for their knighthoods talking about interpretations of the classical and never seeing that if young Narcissus were alive today he'd be lounging in the bar at the St. James', looking for trade. It's even closer when the artist paints an Echo sitting by the pool. There sits luxuriant womankind, draped in thin cloth, one coy breast sweetly visible, a look of anguish, and an arm extended hopefully, and all to no purpose. There before her a lush expanse of ripe young manhood all to waste and never to be hers. What irony! What truth! I am surprised that no one sees it and the decree goes forth that, spindle-like, all paintings of Narcissus are to be destroyed for fear that they corrupt the young! I am surprised . . ."

Charles' cup dropped from his hand and his head slumped to one side. I looked around, only now aware of the necessity of Polette. What was she – servant, mistress, both? I made inadequate attempts to revive him, sitting beside him on the sofa. Some five or ten minutes passed at this crawling pace, then to my relief he spluttered into consciousness.

"Where were we?" he enquired, as pleasantly as one who has been for a stroll in summer meadows.

"I agreed to pose for you – for Narcissus."

"That's right. I'm pleased that you've turned up again, dear boy, because there's something else that you can help me with. It may well be that with your influence – it seems ridiculous to think that you have influence. You look so young. Without your clothes you are scarcely different from the youth we knew in Kensington. And yet I suppose by virtue of your family and birth you must against all odds be influential. I am concerned about a *boy* . . ."

I had a vision of his intention to spring some street arab on me, some poor urchin needing nurture and an education. I pictured leading the child to Claudia, its little unwashed face a stylised picture from those paintings Franklin thrust upon the art world – *The Flower Girl – Without a Friend – Looking at a Star*. I need not have troubled.

"This boy," continued Charles, blinking away the mists of his strange eclipse, "is one who has been known to visit me. His background, I believe, is quite respectable; but through some flaw of character he became attracted to bad company. This motley crew of thieves and renters – you shall meet them; some of them you'll like enormously – are the company I mean and many an evening we have spent in drink and dreams to no particular ill effect. I would not be concerned about him if that were all."

"And that sounds quite enough, for one whose background is respectable!"

"How deliciously severe you sound now! And that is exactly what I want from you, Lord Algernon, philanthropist and civic dignitary. The boy has met a bad angel. I want you to be his good!"

"Charles, what in Heaven's name do you mean?"

"In Heaven's name!" Charles noted gleefully. "You see – you are the part already. Have you heard of The Great Zabarov?"

"Who?" I marvelled, quite out of my depth.

"Zabarov. Some kind of magician who performs from time to time at the Hyperion."

"I rarely visit the variety theatre. I take my children to see *Puss in Boots*; but there the connection ends."

"Zabarov – I have never seen his act, but I believe it is to do with the occult in some way. A wayward count from some lost Balkan state who trades on people's gullibility and swears his grandfather was a vampire. He used to live somewhere down by Goodge Street where everyone's an anarchist and plotting to restore some petty duke to some forgotten throne. I once thought him amusing and admired his nerve and his panache. He swirls his past around him like a vast mysterious cloak. It delighted me to hope he was a vampire. I caught myself squinting at his teeth but found no sign of fangs. I love a man who's different from the common, even if his difference is bizarre. Then I began to suspect his influence was, in a word, malign. It is one thing for him to practise his odd arts on me – I welcome every new sensation – and since I received my death warrant in the shape of physical decay I trouble even less about the world's effects on me. But when I see a boy of seventeen – for he can be no more than that – fall victim to the same kinds of devilment I need to take a hand. I feel responsible; after all, I introduced the two. But what can I do – burdened down and ailing as I am?"

Nothing about my old companion inspired the kind of sentimental sympathy that his remark should have provoked.

"In other words, you thought that someone else should fight the devil," I observed.

"Oh, Algy," Charles protested. "Did I say devil? No, I said vampire. And *that* on his father's side two generations removed. And vampires don't exist, everyone knows that. So what is there to fear?"

"The gentleman's extreme displeasure! Oh really, Charles – a stage magician! What would you have me do? I never go to the music hall – your idea is quite inappropriate."

"Algy," frowned Charles. "A young boy is in the clutches of this stage magician and I can tell you that it is not in his best interest."

"Who is this boy?" I wondered languidly.

"You've seen his picture."

"I have? Where?"

"Do you remember the folder of my drawings that so affronted you? Orgies of a Bacchanalian nature?"

"But do you mean that this innocent boy is to be found within? It hardly seems the proper place for this lad of respectable background. It suggests that he was already mildly depraved before he encountered your Transylvanian, does it not?"

Charles gave me a dry, one-sided glance.

"Do you suppose I held an orgy here and painted couples in the act of fornication? Most of the poses were created in isolation, much as yours just now. However, the boy in question certainly took off his clothes once or twice and posed to my direction. He has a lovely body."

My interest quickened. "Well. Show me."

Charles reached for the folder, and we sat and earnestly surveyed the debauchery before us. Although the pictures were exactly as I remembered them I was freed this time from my hypocrisy. I found them exciting. The males particularly, with their taut muscles and straining thighs, the dripping phalli and the luscious buttocks – I was almost tempted to enquire the price.

"This is the boy," Charles indicated a youth that leaned against a pillar, one arm around a rampant Hercules. The circus strongman, no less!

I laughed, blinking. "That's odd. The face is very similar to someone I know."

"I was very pleased with the face," Charles admitted modestly.

"Is it true to life?"

"Very. I have another one of him here, close to, the head only. Brace yourself; this one is obscene."

Strange torment indeed! Arthur Hughes had not been in my mind this day. I would even go so far as to say that I had practically ceased to think of him at all. He had been a delightful fancy. A way of enlivening a rather stuffy little speech by that pompous young man with ginger hair. We had romped naked amongst the potted ferns, as I recall – I smiled at the memory. And now there he was, exquisitely drawn, his lips around some nameless penis – some nameless *large* penis moreover, and here again I suspected the circus strongman!

"And this?" I croaked. "Is this from life?"

"It is, yes. Harold and he were both here together, and neither objected. What about those eyelashes, Algy? Have you ever seen any so thick, so long – the jaw so fine and square, the lips truly sensuous . . ."

"The hair so lush, so – don't you long to spread your hands in it?" I breathed.

Charles shrugged, indifferent to the suggestion. "Painting it suffices."

"And he agreed to pose – for this?" I blanched.

"He put up no resistance, none whatsoever. He is a curiously malleable boy. Sometimes I suspect that he is a little stupid."

"Nonsense. What do you mean?"

"I mean stupid, as I say."

"In what way?"

"I am not sure. An impression, that's all." Charles said vaguely. "It's not important. Am I to understand that you believe you know this boy already? I am astonished."

"Tell me his name," I prompted.

"It's Arthur Hughes – the same name as the artist who painted *The Knight of the Sun*, which I have always rather liked, all gloom and symbolism; and *The Long Engagement* which is mawkish and detestable."

"And neither of any relevance to the boy in question! A beautiful and, I thought, troubled being, who, as in this instance also, was presented to me as in need of guidance. His friend suspected that he had fallen in bad company. Yourself and your acquaintances would seem bad company enough – and adequately justify the suspicion – but now you hint that there is worse!"

"I do not consider myself bad company," said Charles thoughtfully, "for though I do not act with socially appropriate finesse yet I am open to reason and aware of aspects of morality. The man of whom I spoke, Count Zabarov, possesses a morality of his own, which I fear in no way accords with any principles which you or I might set down for a guiding light. I think that you should meet the man."

"I am inclined to agree. You think he has some malign influence over the boy. I find this most disturbing."

"Well, Algy, I am pleased to hear you say so," Charles remarked. "It accords most pleasingly with your suggestion of our dining at the Café Royal. For Zabarov dines there every evening with the young adoring satellites that orbit round him, and by going there tonight there is the strongest possibility that we may encounter them."

Our hansom took us through the rain-streaked darkness, from the shapeless huddles of streets unknown to any but their shabby inhabitants, to the peach-rose brilliances of the well lit thoroughfares, past the immaculate satisfying curves of Regent Street, its symmetrical ranks of windows peppered with lights.

The Café Royal blazed. The lamps above the four great pillars glowed, the warmth within invited. As we mounted the staircase to the restaurant a waft of wondrous scents came floating from a passage to the kitchens, with the clink of dishes and a bellowed vigorous rendition in fine tenor of "Au Fond du Temple Saint" from *Les Pêcheurs de Perles*.

In a private panelled room I feasted Charles; for whatever curious expectations we may have hoped the place this evening might fulfil, I was determined he should eat, and this he did. We had some fine steaks and Burgundy, and in satisfying the dues of hunger which the unusual events of the day seemed to have provoked, I found that small conversation ensued. It was afterwards, down in the Domino Room where we loitered over coffee and brandy, that all sociability occurred.

Our table commanded a fine view of all who entered through the green swing doors. We leaned back in the red plush, a glittering vision of ourselves repeated in the mirrors opposite; a dark marble pillar slung about with golden wreaths like any maypole soaring up behind us. The myriad lights illumined the cobalt-gilt extravaganza

94

of the ecstatic pantheistic ceiling, and the ranks of naked caryatids arched their torsos skyward down the length of every wall. Below these Hellenistic fancies hung distinctly unmythical top hats and overcoats.

Among those drinking here I noticed in particular a young girl with a mass of thick dark hair and haunted eyes, so like Jane Morris that you could not but suppose the effect intentional. A man in black sat alone and shivered, thin and grey-skinned, with a dyed red beard; three women with elaborate coils of hair, one knitting, one reading, one toying with a pencil, each with serene ivory features, and shamelessly recalling the Three Fates who spin our Destiny or cut its thread.

Verlaine and Rimbaud had drunk here, and Gustave Doré with his dark and bitter portfolio. The well known of our own day were much to be observed moreover, for we witnessed an amusing scene.

I had supposed we would be likely to see Oscar Wilde here and I would have noticed him even if he had not waved to me across the room. How grossly corpulent he looked – like one who had not shaken off the excesses of the Christmas season. A curly-haired young man sat beside him, and an older gentleman with a cigar between his lips; also a fellow with a handle-bar moustache, and a youngish boy leaning forward, elbows on the table. Some serious discussion seemed underway between them, but it ceased when Lord Alfred Douglas entered suddenly, accompanied by a youth with yellow hair. Immaculate and lightly glistening with raindrops Lord Alfred paused, saw Oscar, glared, tilted his chin and turned about, the youthful charmer trooping after him and plucking at his sleeve with an aggrieved expression. Out they went, the doors swung to, and Oscar's party turned back to their drinks with not a little sniggering, and calling loudly for more yellow wine.

"Oh? Have Wilde and Douglas fallen out?" asked Charles with interest. "I am so out of touch."

At our adjoining table a game of dominoes was in progress, three men hunched over it with all the appearance of a life and death involvement, which it may well have been, for the piles of money showed the stakes were high. Each domino clicked down upon the chipped-edged marble table top with menacing precision. If the ensuing tension had not been enough to catch at our attention it was well caught in a moment, for a dark swarthy fellow appeared beside them, sprung from nowhere, handsome and malevolent. His hair was gipsy black, his features strongly marked, his outfit dazzling – his jacket was a saffron velvet and his neckerchief purple silk.

"Ha – Jakey, Parviss, so this is where you are," he said in a low voice with his hands upon two of the players' shoulders. "I never believed it when 'e said you was 'ere. You mahfs – you mutchers – you gonophs – ahtside wiv yer."

"Let us finish the game, Harry," one whinged. "I knew he'd be after us. I knew it was just a matter of time. But see now, I stand to win a fortune – and it's half yours, Harry, I swear it."

Their visitor swept the dominoes from the table carelessly.

"That's bad luck," he told him. "You can explain it all to 'im; 'e's waitin' for yer ahtside an' I'm ter see yer hurries."

Aware of interest around them, the two became self conscious, shifty. They got up and went out, the gaudy stranger with them, to their nameless fate. The one who was left at the table looked about him swiftly and then pocketed the money, afterwards tidying up the dominoes, as docile and circumspect as any child obedient at bedtime.

"There's our man," Charles murmured, looking to the door. "Zabarov – and Arthur with him!"

We watched the incoming group weave its way between the tables, between the garlanded pillars. I wondered what I was about to see. From Charles' hints I half supposed that Zabarov – The Great Zabarov, who had a turn at the Hyperion Theatre – was every inch a stage magician and would enter in a swirling cloak awash with mystic symbols and all would turn to stare; it was not so. Arthur I recognised, with a thrill of pleasure, and there was another young man whom I did not know. The man whom they accompanied might have been some guardian, uncle, schoolmaster – of average height, a little stooped, bearded, elderly – I think I would not have looked at him twice.

"We shall be bold and blatant," said Charles standing up.

"Perhaps not . . ." I murmured, most uneasy.

"Yes," said he. "I have not time for niceties and hesitation."

He was gone. He stood in conversation with Zabarov, who gave all appearance of polite affability. All looked in my direction. Before I knew it they were sitting down about me, drawing up chairs, and, in a mass of introductions, procuring drinks.

"And Arthur I believe you already know," said Charles.

"You know Arthur?" said Zabarov.

"Slightly." I looked at Arthur, half expecting some remark of recognition, but he scowled and looked down at his knees.

"He visited my house," I said, and hoping to sting him into some sort of response I added: "To talk about the Otherworld."

Zabarov laughed, as if he found that of intense amusement. The other boy laughed also, and I looked at him.

He was frankly stunning. He had sleek fair hair and an open good-looking countenance. Into this was set a most wicked pair of eyes that faced me appraisingly and which I found quite irresistible. Whoever was he? What had Zabarov said? "My assistant. The Fine Orlando."

"Your assistant," I said. "Charles tells me that you perform sometimes upon the stage."

"A man must live," Zabarov answered, and then he laughed, as if we all should understand that he was comfortable enough. "No, Lord Algernon, I jest. The work I do on stage is simply for amusement. I am not so vain as to hope that you have ever seen my act?"

"I hardly ever venture . . ." I said vaguely.

"Of course not," he agreed. "Why should you? It is not for you, the masses and the noise, the foolish magic of illusion. There are important things for you to do, eh – politics perhaps, the management of land?"

"These do concern me, yes," I answered. "However, I have no reason to think anything but highly of the way of life you choose to lead . . ."

"As *yet*," said Charles, his tone excessively laden with meaning.

"Ah!" said Zabarov pointing his finger severely. "So you brought me to your table to be shocking? I supposed as much. A tame magician who will entertain your friend. And you perhaps, Lord Algernon, a dilettante in the realm of the occult? A little harmless divination? A séance once or twice? A spot of dealing out the tarot cards with ladies who read ghost stories on Hallowe'en?"

I found him irritating, as no doubt he so intended. Close to, the image of the schoolmaster dispersed. He was broad of brow, the forehead heavily furrowed, and this framed in white bushy hair. His gaunt cheekbones made shadows about his mouth. His greyish beard and moustache half hid that grim and firm-set line. The stoop in his bearing caused his head to lean forward a little, so that his manner of attending to one was with an upward stare from beneath an overhang of eyebrow; this was disconcerting. While both boys and myself drank brandy, and Charles, his mission well accomplished, degenerated unrepentently to absinthe, Zabarov drank only water. He was sitting opposite me, and idly, with his long gnarled fingers, moved the tall carafe and brandy glasses slightly, as if a pattern was composed thereby. His voice was foreign, with a faint Germanic intonation, but not being familiar with central European nuances I could not place exactly whence he came.

"Lord Algernon," he smiled. "So you want to hear about the Devil?"

I suspected ostentation here; returned the smile a little superciliously and enquired: "Why not?"

"Perhaps you would be so good," he invited, "as to let me know your own religious beliefs."

"I hardly think this is the time or place . . ." I said.

He moved a brandy glass back into its position on the table, and the effect, I noticed, was to form a zigzag path between us. He looked down that path, and up to me.

"You have no religious beliefs," he observed.

My senses doubted most acutely that a collection of glass containers might lead anyone to see inside another's mind; but so forceful did the supposition seem just then, that I moved my glass out of line as if to thwart his purpose. But he laughed, as if my action only proved his point.

"Good," he said. "For now I know that anything I say shall not offend."

Orlando shifted closer to me, and beneath the table his thigh brushed mine. He took from his jacket pocket a pack of cards no bigger than an inch across and dealt them out slowly in patterns without sequence. Charles sank back into a stupor; Arthur stared ahead. I noticed Oscar Wilde's party leave.

"In the beginning," said Zabarov, "where is the Devil to be found? Who brings the evil, pain and death that come to those in the Old Testament? Who makes Adam and Eve to suffer – who sends the plagues to Egypt – who sent the evil spirit which tormented Saul? Who therefore is the Devil?"

"We are told he was a fallen angel," I said politely, as if humouring him by obliging him with a response. "In his rage at being cast from aery regions he dedicated his existence to opposing the Almighty, luring humankind to sin, in order to achieve their souls. This being, sometimes seen as cloven-hooved and ugly has held a curious fascination in his other forms, as poor Milton found when he made Satan noble. One admires an angel bold enough to challenge Heaven."

"Ah, you are purposefully unperceiving," answered Zabarov. "You understand my meaning well enough. I do not talk of little horned demons with pointed tails; nor of a beautful Son of the Morning who makes the darkness seem acceptable. No, I imply the revolution of our concept of the world, and what must follow if this truth holds good."

"What must follow? Nothing is inevitable."

"Yes," said he. "If God the Father is the Devil, there is much that is inevitable."

I switched my gaze away from his, surprised as I did so by how physically difficult this was to do. I thought he was a crank, an exhibitionist, a man who liked to startle those who sought an assuaging calm from after dinner conversation. Before I knew it I was looking at him once again as if the others were not there, as well indeed they might not have been, for all their participation in the exchange of conversation.

"The world is evil," said Zabarov. "Who can deny it? Humankind is corrupt, and the mind of Man a pit of darkness. To venture into those unfathomable depths is to embark on strange voyages; no one knows how strange. We think we are so civilised, so rational. We lay down laws, make statements. We are wrong. Society is merely a net, a fine drawn net stretched taut about a sea, a turbulent sea abounding with riches, treacherous riches, dangerous darkness. What net can ever contain a sea? We make these rules, we say I Control – we fool ourselves – the sea is still there. Primordial memory is within us, when we prowled in the swamps of the forests and feared the storms and stars. The secret is to control the sea."

His voice was mesmeric. I let it wash over me. The brandy made me sleepy, and the events of the day had caused in me a suspension of reality. I had visited a male street whore – had it truly happened? I who lived an ordered life and dreaded loss of reputation. I thought of Claudia and my children, and a great weight of uneasiness possessed me. What was I doing sitting here and letting this man spout his cloudy nonsense which he seemed to think was a philosophy of life? Could he be serious in his intentions? Was this all part of his performance?

"We were not put into this world sphere to conform to long outdated notions," he said, looking at me with his unsettling upward-slanting gaze. "The neatness of Apollo whose bright rays illumine the dark corners is not our answer, for there is a wilderness beneath, the chaos of Dionysus. Reach out your hand – that is how far away that chaos is. It is accessible. We brush against it in the street. A doorway opens to us. For some, like Charles, the door is drugs, but there are other doors, and each man has his own path to fulfilment."

The unreality I had experienced now held me, and into my mind the image of a white bird floated, above a silver sea, some kind of furrow in the surface of the water, like the trail a finger tip leaves through wet oil paint.

Zabarov said: "If the world is evil, then he who made it is a deity of harm. Isaiah, Samuel, all of them are wicked, and the adversaries of the evil god are heroes – Cain, for instance, the Sodomites, the drunken worshippers of Baal . . . That serpent in the Garden was a voice of liberation and of hope who warned the hapless couple of their creator's true identity. Now if this god is an evil god, then all morality which derives from his is evil also. Those rigid rules he made for us on Sinai are laws of bondage. Therefore they must be broken. Thus we will understand the world and better still, ourselves. You know that it is so, Lord Algernon. You long to break the bonds yourself. You have been docile long enough. But in your heart you do not subscribe to those constrictions. Now you have seen the truth you need no longer fear the wrath of the Almighty. His laws are wrong, and in disobeying them you set yourself free." He smiled, the reassuring smile of any trusted physician declaring that the diagnosis is benign. "I tell you nothing which you have not suspected for yourself. What I tell you is the truth, and as we know, the truth shall set us free. By implication then, all that society considers wrong we know not to be so. And certain crimes, perversions, weaknesses, considered by society and by the scriptures of the evil god as most abhorrent, now become the right way to behave. All this must be apparent to you. Any thinking man would tell you so."

"Yes . . . I see . . ." I said. I felt that Charles' fears about Zabarov were quite unfounded. The viewpoint which he had just put forward had had the effect on me of complete well-being, of a rather charming gift. I did not think that there was anything to fear from him, an elderly foreigner with the interests of his fellow man at heart. Myself I certainly felt reassured by what he said, and any doubts I may have had about my actions of the day were quite dispelled. I felt good-humoured, comfortable, and dozy from the wisping cigarette smoke and the mellowing effects of brandy.

Orlando, at my elbow, slid his brandy glass out of alignment to fit in the line of playing cards extending paving-like across the table. I sat back, reminded of where I was. I blinked. I looked at Arthur.

"What do you think?" I enquired.

"Arthur has no thoughts about the matter," Zabarov snapped, so sharply that it struck a cold contrast to the soporific tone which he had used with me.

"Is that so, Arthur?" I asked, confused now as to why for so long I had ignored his presence when he had been so consistently in my thoughts and now was in my company.

"I have no thoughts," he shrugged, and I wondered briefly whether Charles was right in supposing him not altogether bright. I cast a glance towards Charles, who jerked back into life and looked about him blearily.

Orlando gestured to his pack of cards. "Want me to cast your future?" he enquired.

"No thank you," I said, suddenly concerned for Charles who did not look at ease.

"Pity," said Orlando. "But I'll tell you one thing for nothing, which I know already. About your future."

"What is that?"

"I am in it." He said so with a smirk. My interest quickened. I stared at him, his invitation blatant. Was he like Eddy? Was he one of those? Was I to be so fortunate?

"Why not come and see our little act?" Zabarov suggested pleasantly. "We perform next week. I think we shall surprise you. If you wish, come afterwards backstage and talk to us. It can be enlightening."

"Arthur . . . do you intend to be there?" I asked.

Arthur faced me suddenly. "I wish you'd leave me alone," he said sulkily. "I want nothing to do with you. I don't need your protection."

"Oh, steady on, old chap," said Zabarov patting him possessively. The phrase he used sought further to emphasise his foreign character and it did not suit him. "I must apologise for young Arthur's behaviour," he added. "It was most impolite."

"Why should you?" I said nettled. "You did not cause it; nor are you responsible."

Orlando grinned, and gathered up his cards. Charles stood, his hand across his mouth. "I believe I need to leave," he told me, and when he hurried out I went with him.

While Charles knelt down in Glasshouse Street and systematically brought up each morsel of the wondrous dinner with interspersed asides of: "What a waste!" I stood nearby, my thoughts in disarray.

In that cold air, and the undeniable reality of the scene – the somewhat inevitable outcome of Charles' encounter with rich fare and many kinds of liquor – the mesmeric presence of Zabarov rapidly lost its hold on me. I thought him now a charlatan, and I resented having passed the time with him and having paid the compliment to his undoubted vanity of listening to him for so long, not querying his wild hypothesis. I was left with the impression that he had in some way tricked me and I could not grasp how or what indeed I meant by that; I felt manipulated, patronized, and not a little piqued thereby.

"What do you make of it?" said I to Charles as a hansom carried us toward his lodging.

"Of what?" he groaned, his mind on other matters.

"Of the primordial swamp and all that quasi-Gnostic rambling from Zabarov."

"I heard none of it. And please don't speak of swamps."

"And Arthur," I continued, frowning. "Why did he say that? Why did he tell me that he did not need protection?"

"He is deranged," shrugged Charles. "If anybody needed protec-

101

tion it is he – anyone can see that."

"But why talk of protection at all? I had not offered it. Why should it occur to him?"

"I don't know. How can we guess what is in the poor boy's mind?"

"We don't need to guess. He supposes that I think he needs protection. Why should he suppose that, unless he knows that there is something he should fear?"

I saw Charles to his lodgings and stood penitently by while Polette raged at us. Charles made me take a sheaf of papers with me, wrapped up in brown paper, which he said that I should read as I had been starved too long of that kind of literature. I took it without paying much attention.

"Be sure to hide it from your wife," he warned me.

I marvelled that the same city could hold scenes so different one from another. My wife! How real the world she represented seemed to me as I returned! A world of old-established values and of sentiments portrayed in parlour songs, a way of life that did not recognise magicians who spoke intimately of Satan, and boys with wicked eyes.

In order not to disturb Claudia I spent the remainder of the night in the narrow bed in my dressing room, a not infrequent occurrence, and I idly flicked the leaves of Charles' manuscript. It was entitled *Certain Confessions from Various Rent Boys, collected and edited by Henry Cleaver*. It was handwritten on foolscap, presumably by several authors, for the calligraphy varied. I could tell fairly rapidly that this was in no way the social document it purported to be, but was in fact a series of pornographic cameos written at gathering fever pitch with the intention to excite both writer and reader. The pages were well thumbed and I wondered whether any of my acquaintance – some baronet or justice of the peace, recipient of Charles' more outrageous paintings – had handled them before me. Sitting there alone in that small room, the house a tenement of silence in the silent night, I felt part of a secret brotherhood. I imagined them, gentlemen like myself, men with a public face and a private torment, alone at the end of the day in the awful solitude of self-denial; the mixture of shame, embarrassment, amusement, to sit here with this foolish stuff, to read it, more, to write one's own addition – what a thrill – so sinful in the darkness! Just for a moment, guilty as a naughty schoolboy I looked over my shoulder, half expecting to be caught and punished. I locked the bulging folder in a drawer and slept, exceptionally tired.

I was not hampered by a troubled sleep; my conscience slept as well as I. The two worlds were so separate, did not impinge the one upon the other. I had every confidence that I would have no difficulty moving between the two, and for that reason I could not regret my abberation into what of necessity would be a path of secrecy and deception. So firmly were my feet entrenched in the established order that I was untroubled by uneasiness or dread or even guilt, but was possessed by a stupendous ingenuousness of unbelievable proportion. I believe that I convinced myself that Charles' world and all that it contained did not exist when I was out of it.

Next morning the events of the preceding day took on an even more unreal sensation than they had already. Mysterious upper rooms in Soho swathed in soft embroidered shawls and lit by candle flames, enigmatic aliens who pontificated about the Devil, boys that jerked the heartstrings and the prick – these had no place in the cool morning light when over breakfast one sat upright and discussed what one found of interest in one's newspaper. And interest enough I was to find, when one day later, I read that the Marquis of Queensberry, that demented old fellow who was Lord Alfred Douglas' father, had been arrested.

He was charged with calling Oscar Wilde a sodomite.

CHAPTER NINE

C ERTAIN CONFESSIONS *from Various Rent Boys, collected and edited by Henry Cleaver B.A. PhD. D.Litt.*
"It is with the object solely of research into a phenomenon of our times that I make known these subsequent accounts. It is my earnest hope that these now reformed boys have purged their troubled souls by their confessions, made to me without coercion and entirely for the furtherance of our understanding of the human condition. These case histories may startle and disturb, but all who seek to comprehend our many-faceted society must never flinch from harsh reality. Each boy I questioned bitterly regrets the life he led and fervently desires that his unfortunate revelations will lead others to shun those paths which lead to shame and sin, and it is with this firm intent that I now offer their sad stories:

Archie Bilger, aged twenty-two, now a clerk in a shipping office.

In the brothel where I worked I was often called upon to punish my customers with a cane. One gentleman had been a army man and needed punishment for letting down the regiment. I wore a scarlet jacket with gold braid and shiny buttons. I think its origins were theatrical rather than regimental. It was very smart. This gent would stand before me very straight and upright while I paced about expressing my displeasure, flexing my cane, cracking it down on to a chair arm. I told him he was a disgrace to the regiment, that his conduct was unworthy – we never specified what he had done. I could slap him across the face if I wanted and shut him up if he tried to speak. Finally he had to lower his trousers. If he grovelled I ordered him to get up and take his punishment like a man. Then he'd bend over and I'd cane him. I was quite a competent thrasher. Caning makes welts but it doesn't bleed unless you criss-cross the ridges and then only a thin red line, so appropriate in this case. Throughout he called me sir, and I called him all the beastly names I could think of – posh words, like cur, scoundrel, blackguard, reprobate – he loved it. I covered his big bare arse with stripes. Since I was never the sort who lost control of myself I would always judge when he was ready to come and redouble my abuse till I had him toppling forward, grunting and howling, pitching over. I ended up with my own crotch bulging. It's amazing what you learn about yourself.

When the gents in the upstairs bar heard it was my birthday they sent a message down, saying that if I would take off my clothes for them nicely they would give me a bottle of champagne and a shiny sovereign in the glass I drank it from. I agreed. The upstairs room was dimly lit and crowded. A cheer went up as I came in and the atmosphere grew lewd and excited. The lamps were extinguished all but two and the gents settled down in the dark with their drinks and cigars to watch me perform. I was very cheeky. I blew kisses and pouted and stroked my body and slowly undid the buttons of my shirt. I took my shoes off, winding my body about like a snake, and sighing like I was desperate. I wriggled out of my shirt and hesitated like I was bashful. I toyed with my buttons and looked nonchalant. They yelled at me to show them everything. Slowly I unpeeled my trousers and revealed my bum and I showed it to them and they whistled; they were real coarse; you would never think that they were gentlemen. I eased my trousers slowly down, bending so my cock was obscured and I stepped carefully out of my trousers. Then I straightened up slowly and put my arms behind my neck. The impact of my revelation made them silent. Then they bellowed their approval and clapped. I was elated at their lust for me. My cock leapt up, excited by so much flagrant desire and stuck out like a unicorn's horn, and I thrust out my loins and touched myself and strutted. All the lights were then turned up.

"How old is he?" someone asked in a very meaningful way.

"Seventeen."

Then with great guffaws of laughter they all closed in on me and seized me. Some who reached me first kissed me on the mouth. My arms and legs were gripped and spreadeagled and I was lifted off my feet, held by arms and ankles, and bumped.

Oh! I wished that I was three, six, seven, something small, for seventeen seemed such a big number in this noisy painful ceremony. I was surrounded by laughing faces, jacket cloth which brushed my bare shoulders, and my loins split as opposing sides pulled my legs at different angles. "One – two – three – four – five," they yelled, slamming my bum down on the carpet and lifting me shoulder high. "Ow – Oo – Ow!" I howled with every bump. "Fourteen – fifteen – sixteen – seventeen," they bellowed and dropped me in an aching, groaning heap and all stood back to watch me where I lay. Then I heard a cork pop and the bubbly gush and a streaming bottle of champagne was put down beside me and then a glass, glinting with the gold of a coin. Next moment I was drinking champagne and they helped to me my feet and slapped me on the back – and on the bum also. I shall not forget that birthday.

Percy Wade, aged twenty-five, now a baker's assistant:

I will recount the kind of thing that happened on an ordinary night when I used to walk the streets. I used to charge five bob a time, which may seem steep, but no one quibbled, as I recall. This is how I got my gents. Well, sometimes one would tap me on the shoulder and say, "Excuse me – are you *so*?" and I would answer yes and take him to an alley. Under cover of his coat I gently took his cock and eased him to his satisfaction. My other hand felt his arse and with low breathing I conveyed my own excitement. Yet from afar you might have thought that we were simply talking. Another gent I took fell into step beside me and I offered him a light. I took him to a place I knew, a yard stacked full of tea chests so cunningly arranged they made little private places in between. We kissed and I played with his cock. He kissed me hungrily. We kept our mouths one on another, pressing front to front until our juices came. A third that I took was very merry.

"Have you time to pass, my angel?" he said to me. "How I love you common types. Take me anywhere you like – have you some filthy den, some foul hovel, some gin-stained mattress we could lie upon?"

"We could stand behind some packing cases," I replied.

"Oh you poet! Lead me on!"

Behind the packing cases he said, "Kiss me, darling!" So I put my arms around him and kissed him very nice. His hands clamped on my buttocks and I wriggled on his palms. Our mouths moistly welded and I loosened his cock from his trousers. It was very firm and big. "Oh you adorable little guttersnipe," he murmured. So we moved against each other in delight. His hands were all over my arse, feeling me through my trousers. Impatiently he tugged at my buttons and undid them, rolling my trousers down at the back so my arse was all bare. I gasped with excitement. I kept my hold on his cock which was as hard as a broom. He gripped my buttocks, his fingers digging in between. My own cock was now painfully hard, pressed between our bellies. Feverishly I worked on him. He came against my belly. His juice spread out all over my skin. "You lovely little raggamuffin," he said, and he gave me ten shillings, so he must have liked me a lot.

106

Archie Bilger once more:

When I first came to work in the brothel I was very shy and timid. You would not think that to look at me now or to hear me talk, but it was so. There were three other boys working there at that time and they decided that I needed shaping up. So they decided to give me a lesson, which as you will see was not too hard or difficult to learn. They seized me in the bedroom and they held me down upon the bed. Although I struggled weakly I was overpowered and lay limp upon my back. Oliver hung over my face and kissed me upside down. It was wonderful. I shut my eyes and felt I was all mouth, all throat and lips, wide open to receive his tongue and his sensuous kisses. But even as I half expired with that pleasure my stretched-out arms each side were kissed by Tim and Walter, up and down the sensitive inner part, their tongues moving over my palms till my fingers clenched and unclenched. Then warm lips closed on my cock. Down at my crotch Tim was beginning to suck me off. My cock felt enormous and his throat so hot, so sweet. From the moans I made one would have supposed that I was in some kind of pain, and yet I was in a state of such pleasure as I had never known before. I pressed my hands upon Tim's head, crushing him against me, feeling my juice surge up exploding into his mouth, and my whole body shuddered; I was left gasping.

"Good," said they, immensely gratified. "Now you are one of us."

Thomas Broughton, aged twenty-eight; now a missionary.

A friend of mine once took me to a place in Grays Inn Road where he said we would have Quite a Night. It was a beery chop house in a basement and all the way down the stairway we passed brightly painted boards which advertised us of the delights below and the wonderful cheap prices of the food. The room was a fog of smoke, lights and mirrors making it seem larger, and gentlemen lounged at tables, females also, smirking on the fellows' knees. We had steak and claret. Some of the women came up to us and asked if we would like to buy them a drink. Then my friend, whose tastes were for the female kind, went off with one of these and left me with the other. I thought that this was fairly shabby of him as he knew to where my own interests inclined. So I was left with the woman, who began to make advances to me. I felt most uncomfortable and did not know what to do, but I was saved by the arrival of a man who seemed to have some kind of authority here, for he said to my unwelcome companion, "Off with you, baggage," and she flounced away into the smoky gloom without a murmur. The man placed a drink on the table in front of me and sat down. I found myself face to face with a very well dressed (though flashy) gent of about forty years of age. The drink he gave me burned my throat and set my insides on fire. The gent leaned back and looked at me. His face was lined and hard. He had black-grey hair and side whiskers. He was well built as if he frequented a gymnasium. We had a brief conversation in which he established that I was as he supposed, and offering me three guineas for my time he told me to go upstairs and wait for him in room fifteen. I did so. Within the room a single lamp burned on a small table, illuminating the shabby scene. I saw a chest of drawers, a spindly bed, a low upholstered chair. Hot from the drink I took off my jacket and looked out of the window. Far below were the street lamps and the traffic of night. My gent came in and locked the door. He was panting a little from the climb and from excitement. He handed me the money he had promised, his hands trembling. He looked at me, his eyes greedy with desire. He told me to strip off. But he would not take off his own clothes. He told me that if I was naked and he was not, he stayed master. I was used to all these funny notions. When I was undressed I walked over to him and ran my hands over his body under the jacket of his suit, then undoing his flap. His cock was hard and bulging. I rubbed it for a moment while he stood breathing heavily, drinking in the sight of me.

"Ah," he said. "Such a waste of beauty . . ."

"What do you mean?" I asked him.

He replied: "Girls *ad nauseum*, girls everywhere, girls at the bar cadging drinks, while boys like you are accounted a sin. We who love the Cities of the Plain are obliged to keep it secret . . . such a waste . . ."

Time, however, he did not waste, and straightaway he ordered me over the chair and I bent over the back of it. I watched him fix one of those sheaths on to himself. He stood behind me. His hands grasped each buttock, laying bare my arsehole, touching up my balls, like I was holy. And then his fingers slid inside me. His cock began to enter. He leaned on me, thrusting. I was made to gasp. He pushed harder till suddenly he erupted, his sheath filling up. He drew himself out, and straightened up his clothes.

"You're a very beautiful young man," he told me. "It breaks my heart that you're illegal."

"It doesn't stop people who want it," I replied.

"Ah. But I mean that I would like you down in the bar, on show, like the girls. Back stairs, cubby holes, as long as we behave like rats we manage. But let any one of us dare to emerge into the light of day and it's another story."

What could I say? It was all too true.

I later learnt that this man was a well known villain of the Underworld whose victims would be found dredged up from the Thames. But he was quite all right with me, although he told me never to come back, because he could not risk a scandal."

That first week of March the subject matter of those so-called confessions was much in my mind as I sat naked on a rug in Charles' lodging.

Insisting that he was not long for this world and time was running out for him, he wasted none of it and set about the painting of Narcissus which was to be the culmination of his artistic outpouring. I was only too happy to oblige, stipulating only that Polette should be furnished with the wherewithal to see that we had heat and light and basketfuls of food and drink such as would grace the most sophisticated of picnics.

"This is most pleasing," Charles said often. "What better way to end one's days? My brush in hand, a tolerable enough effect emerging on my canvas, fine wine as well as absinthe, and the presence of a naked male as finely formed as any Hylas; one, moreover, who brings back interesting memories to me, and who has begun to drop his prudish posturing . . ."

"Prudish posturing," I grumbled. "In the society of our time there is no other way to be. One hint of deviation of the Greek Love sort and all is over. Reputation gone, decent society closed to you, a pointless life remaining. How else could I behave? I must protect myself – it is the only way."

"Yet it denies life, does it not?" suggested Charles. "If you were an artist, or a writer, how could you express your ethics, one half of you denied? And similarly, for a living human being, how can it function, only half alive?"

"But I am not denying it, am I?" I cried. "I am here with you. I am open to your influences. All it means is that my life must be divided into two. I think that I can deal with that. It isn't easy; but it's possible."

"I wonder," Charles replied. "Two halves make a whole, I know, but two halves separately remain two halves, each lacking, each incomplete."

"Well," said I. "Then it must be so. It can be no other way."

Engaged in conversation with Polette I learnt a little of her history.

"We came originally from Spain," she said. "My mother was a gipsy, a dancer. My father, a soldier. They were not happy. She took many lovers. He wasted all his money at the gambling tables. He fought a duel with one of my mother's lovers; he was killed.

Overcome with guilt my mother made us children go into the woods and pick enough primroses to lay about his body. There were the three of us, my sister, brother and myself. We picked for hours and brought back armfuls and we practically covered his corpse. A big coarse man he was, in death as in life, and entirely inappropriate to the primrose . . . My mother remarried, this time for respectability, to a baker in Ste Marie de Chignac – you will not have heard of it, a little village in the Dordogne – but naturally she grew restless. However, she bided her time, and when she had saved up enough money she simply walked away, or rather, took a train, and took us three to Paris and told us to make our own way. Louis stayed with her to look after her – I believe he took a steady occupation – waiter, something like that – but Giselle and I stood more chance of developing ourselves, for we were pretty, and Paris, monsieur, is the city of the woman. A woman with looks and talent who does not flourish there does not deserve to, for the opportunities abound. Regard the Comtesse de Chevigné, with her Afternoons in the Rue de Miromesnil, her elegance, her black cigarettes. And the Comtesse Greffulhe, so beautiful, with her mauve orchids – and Jane Avril the dancer, and La Goulue – and on the stage the divine Sarah – and of course La Belle Otero. What was she but a dancer with black hair? Yet dukes, *vicomtes* and princes flung themselves at her feet. Oh, yes, the world has much to offer to the woman who arrives . . . Giselle became a singer. She's famous now – she calls herself La Belle Zizine. I too was successful at first. I had a very fine apartment near the Boulevard des Italiens . . . but my baron lost his money . . . I had to live in straightened circumstances for a while. A certain German count became my good friend, but he was obliged to flee the country. I was unlucky in my men. I became a singer at a *café-con*. I lived a dreadful life; always I chose the man who'd let me down. It seems I attract failures, misery. Into my café one day walked Monsieur Charles. We moved to England. As you see," she shrugged elegantly, "I attract failures, misery. My life with Charles has not been easy; but yet our love is true."

True to his promise, boast or threat, Charles saw to it that what he called Obliging Boys appeared, to furnish me with what it now transpired would be too dangerous to seek at the address in Chelsea. Thus I met Francis – a merry robin of a boy whose bright Christmas card face was a very affirmation of life, whose cheeks were red, lips large, eyes big and chirpy, hair a mass of chestnut curls; you half expected him to have left a sled outside the door piled high with holly. And Jeremy, called Jem, who was lean and laconic and spoke little and wore a corduroy cap low over his brow and was reputed to have connections with the sporting world, namely the buying and selling of rats and the training of terriers and ferrets for use in rat pits; we did not talk about it. Both these boys were perfectly content to do a little whoring on the side, though neither was by nature a lover of men.

When Charles had grown too tired to paint he would gather up Polette and disappear down to the public house below, where they were believed to be a married couple who had met abroad; and I would share the room with whichever of the boys had turned up. I mention it with cynicism, for it was a cynical arrangement. Each boy was affable, unshockable, experienced, comfortable without his clothes, and I relished the physical release which our encounters produced. It left me, however, with the same uneasiness that I had felt when I had gone with prostitutes in Italy and Greece, a certain feeling of humiliation that one should have to pay for what should have been an act of love, and the inevitable resentment towards a society so shaped that payment entered into it at all, natural open communication being denied and classed as criminal.

Yet what other course could there be? One could not ask brazenly for love among the people of one's class; and if by miracle one found that kind of love, one could not then pursue it and keep one's reputation in society. I knew that. I had contemplated such a course once and it had brought me pain and sorrow.

I was often reminded of that time when I was in Charles' company, for not only did he belong to that idyllic time when I first met the boy in question, but because innumerable portraits of the object of my love lay stacked in corners of the sordid room. I was prompted first by mere curiosity to root through Charles' ancient artwork which he had kept with him throughout the intervening years, and I had ample leisure between poses to prowl about and brood and gaze at what I saw.

Willie was a boy with auburn hair whose startling beauty and disreputable past combined to make him thoroughly at ease in posing naked, and the artists eagerly devoured him, regurgitating him as Saint Sebastian, Hylas, Ganymede. Here he was, stuck full of arrows, as nonchalant as Saint Sebastian always is, to the amazement of the thoughtful spectator; and here he reached his arms to Jove, all eager to be borne aloft and savour the delights of Elysium. That I had not seen Willie for ten years or so, that he was as far as I knew perfectly happy in the life that he had chosen, none of this prevented me from suffering a bitter pang as I surveyed his picture, the boy that I knew then, before I so badly let him down; and half the bitterness, I knew, was due to the half-formed realisation in my mind that if only I had been different then, braver, truer, maybe now my life would be much other than it was and I would be a happier man. He and I might be together, living, say, in Paris or in Rome, the fortunate possessors of true love. For we did know love, yes, I was sure of that. True love had been once offered to me and I had spurned it. One did not have a second chance in life, not that kind of chance.

"I always thought it was a shame you did not stay with him," said Charles. "Such beauty, both of you – a joy to gaze upon. I would have liked you for my book ends!"

"How could we have stayed together?" I said morosely. "He came from Spitalfields, and in moments of excitability he spoke like a costermonger."

"Indeed, and was he not a whore before he came to us?" Charles pleasantly agreed. "I wonder how we deigned to let him cross our threshold."

I scowled at Charles. "I cannot help my character. I acted badly. I was weak. I tried to put the matter right. It is my funds which keep the place where he works solvent."

"Is he still beautiful?" Charles asked.

"I don't know. We never meet. There was no need. Transactions all occur through bankers."

"As you know," said Charles laconically, "I am not long for this world. How pleasant it would be for me before I die to see you in his company. What reminiscences we might share ... perhaps a painting might be inspired?"

"Ganymede in middle years?" I scoffed. "I think not. And let us hear no more of your not being long for this world. You know that you may go at my expense to Italy if you but say the word, or to a Swiss retreat, as Symonds did. Your curious *nostalgie de la boue* is self-induced and need not be so."

"I own it," Charles agreed. "Nor am I complaining, am I? Merely stating facts. Do you enjoy the gathered recollections from the learned Henry Cleaver? You would be surprised to learn the names of some of the contributors. Feel free to add your own."

That evening I told my first outright lie to Claudia, who for no reason asked me where I had been. A little lie it was; I said that I was at the club, and so I had been earlier; but I followed it with more.

"That boy Arthur Hughes," she told me frowning. "He never has been back here. Do you remember, we discussed whether we should intervene, because his friend was anxious?"

"I do remember, yes."

"Do you still think it would be interfering? I must confess I feel some responsibility now, considering that he was at my house and Ronald came to us especially. I wonder if we should make enquiries after all?"

"I think not," I replied. "I think it would be presumptuous. We should let the matter be. Did you discuss the colour white?"

"Yes," she smiled wrily. "I know you find it all amusing; but you would be surprised how fascinating white can be!"

I sat up late into the night, again sleeping in the dressing room. I stood for a moment at the window, before I drew the curtain. All London seemed asleep. I turned back to the room. I unlocked the drawer of the little writing desk and took out Charles' manuscript, rereading the accounts therein. I wondered about Willie. I never liked to hear him talk about his days of whoring. I always wished that he had come to me untouched. He had been so exquisite as a lover. Never before had I known such passion and pleasure as I had found in his arms; and certainly never since. I began to think about his body – his long back, slim chest, his wonderful arse, the red-gold curly hair about his prick – thoughts I had not allowed myself for years. I felt a pain about my heart.

I took a pen and ink and half before I knew that I was doing it I started writing, on the remaining pages of the secret portfolio. After Thomas Broughton's entry finished I wrote:

"Willie Brown, aged twenty-eight, now a teacher:

I was taken to the house of a certain young lord. He was very rich and spoilt and all his life he had had everything he wanted, but he had not had a boy to love his body and so he was unhappy at heart. But I understood his needs. I remember very well. I'd suck him off so nicely down there between his taut clean golden-haired thighs. I'd take his lordly juice down my throat, fine white wine, sophisticated spunk, and there he'd lie, this Honourable, his cock lost between my wet lips, his cultured voice a shattered croak as I brought him to fulfilment with my tart's tricks. And he would love me in return.

Upon an Indian rug behind a silk screen embroidered with bronze flowers he traced the contours of my body with a peacock feather tip. Every hair on my skin rose at his touch. He kissed the nape of my neck, parting my hair with sensuous fingers and he stroked my shoulder blades with the feather till I was a sea of goose pimples, wave upon wave of pleasure. He kissed me all down my spine and all over my behind, cupping my arse in his hands, kissing the slope of my thighs and the backs of my knees and all down my legs till he was kissing the soles of my feet – and he a lord! He rubbed his soft blond hair against the hairs on my thighs. He kissed my balls and he sucked my crotch hair. Then he took pity on my bursting cock

113

and closed his lips around it and sweetly sucked me to coming. He eased himself up to lie beside me, the cream juice of my come smeared on his chin and glistening on his lips.

"Willie," he murmured. "You taught me how to love – I never had that gift before."

"With you and me," I said, "it's hard to tell who gives and who receives. We're timeless, aren't we, when we're naked."

Sometimes we were naughty and played around like children, chasing each other up and down the stairs. We didn't care who saw us. Once I dragged him down to the fountain and his howls were horrible to hear. I had his arm pulled up behind him; he was quite helpless. I was as erect as a beanpole at his wriggling nakedness struggling in my grip, his round white buttocks bending and his long golden hair dishevelled and rippling over his face. I forced him to his knees by the fountain's edge and we struggled in a heap of lascivious limbs. I pressed his head into the water. I put it right underneath till all his hair was wet and then I let him go. He came up spluttering and furious and grabbed me by the hair. We fought and rolled – right over the edge. Splash – into the tepid water, scattering arrows of startled Japanese goldfish and wrecking an expensive lily. We crawled to our knees gasping and shaking. Then we began to laugh and reached out for each other. Dripping and trailing lily leaves we kissed. We had a long and passionate embrace and the fountain trickled and the goldfish trembled."

I laughed out loud remembering that. Charles and Franklin had come running, Franklin petrified that somebody would see us like that – some homely Italian housewife modelling Penelope – or that his blue and white porcelain might be broken.

"Oh my Ophelias, be warned," cried Charles. "The King of the Rushy River is upon you!" – for Franklin was enraged.

Mr Strode then joined us, gazing rapturously at our wet nudity, and Charles began to laugh. Narcissus was never quite like this, he quivered. Franklin was like an ogre. Giggling stupidly and holding hands Willie and I stood shivering in ever-increasing puddles of water while Franklin berated us for our immorality, vandalism, selfishness. We looked too ridiculous to be properly contrite. Our teeth chattered, our hair hung down flat, plastered to our shoulders, and lily tendrils clung to our legs. We squelched away, sniggering. I heard Franklin say darkly: "The sooner those two go off to Paris and leave us in peace the better . . ."

"Upon another occasion," I began, and then I stopped, and stared unseeing straight ahead. I put the pen down, consumed by indescribable sadness.

CHAPTER TEN

WHETHER IN the sweet and melancholy reflections on the subject of my former passion I had recognised at last some long denied yearning for the possibility of love, or whether the bitter knowledge that this love was irrevocably over now urged me to assert myself within the present moment I know not, but the following day I went to Holborn to seek out Arthur Hughes.

The city streets were crowded with all kinds of jostling vehicles – country carts unloading wares against the kerb, blocking the passage of the lumbering omnibuses, neat hansoms, shiny carriages with restless horses, plodding drays, the struggling pedestrians between, awash with mud and slush flung up by churning wheels. The day was cold, the sky above St Paul's a smoky grey, the wind whirling sudden gusts of sleet.

I had no logical excuse for my visit; my reasons were buried in the mind, and not so very deeply at that; therefore I was reduced to a deception of a not particularly convincing kind in order to explain my presence at the shop where Arthur worked – the purchase of a print.

Alighting from my cab near Fetter Lane I entered a wide alley where shop front faced shop front across the miry cobbles. At my elbow an unwieldy stack of books and chairs and birdcages half blocked a doorway; next door, bunches of woven baskets hung in jumbled profusion, with cradles such as might have housed the Infant Moses obscuring every inch of window. And now my destination was upon me: "Simmons – Fine Prints, Engraving, and Picture Frames". Here the window was quite taken up with images of the natural world – print after print of thoughtful robins, field mice swaying upon corn stems, fallow deer, a myriad owls, hedgerow plants and butterflies. They hung like lines of linen at the back, pegged upon string; they lay in ranks within the window glass and stood in columns each side of the door.

For a moment my reflection paused alongside them, gilt-haired, tall-hatted, well-tailored; the high collar looking exceptionally white, a pearl-grey tie pin gleaming, the image one of shameless elegance. I dreaded to seem condescending.

A dark-toned bell announced my entrance and I shut the door behind me. Those endless field voles, inexhaustible owls stared up afresh from prints upon the counter, and a proud notice boasted that each print was carved by hand in the traditional method – no mechanised process involved. Indeed, this truth was borne out by the open doorway at the back of the shop, where a heavy curtain had been specially roped back to show a scene of industry – Mr Simmons and (ah, wonderful!) Arthur both sitting at a table, each working at a block, an open book in front of them, a welter of small pointed instruments to hand and on the wall behind them, unfinished pictures clamped on thread.

Mr Simmons was a small dapper man who carefully unwound himself and hurried to attend. Arthur stared at me with those wide beautiful eyes and then slipped into his habitual dark-browed scowl. I spoke to Mr Simmons earnestly and perused the owls and robins; but I added pleasantly: "I see that you are busy; why do I not discuss it further with your young assistant whom I am sure will help me." Though Mr Simmons was surprised, he was not displeased, as if he saw a chance here for his protegé to shine, and, beaming, he encouraged Arthur forward. He then retired to the back room returning to his work, but not with his entire attention, I suspected.

"What are you doing here?" Arthur muttered, his face close to mine, his eyelashes even thicker and darker than I recollected. Sulkily he added: "It is unfair of you to find me here."

"I suppose that you are allowed time for a meal? It's nearly noon. I came on purpose at this hour to take you out to eat."

"Oh I could not," said Arthur quickly.

"Why not? Are you meeting Ronald?"

"No. No, it's – it would look so odd."

"Why would it?"

"Well – I am not dressed right for the kind of places you are used to."

"Then we will go wherever you feel comfortable."

"But then you would look out of place."

"But that would not concern me. Unless you have in mind some sordid dockland den?"

"No indeed I haven't." Arthur shuffled a handful of swaying fieldmice, curiously and most delightfully flustered.

"I'll speak to Mr Simmons if you like."

"No. Please don't. That would only make it worse."

"How so?" I wondered. "I am a perfectly reputable person, you know. It's quite socially acceptable that I should take you out for a meal."

"You make it very difficult for me," he said in a low voice. "Your wife and you have both been very kind. It so happens Mr Simmons thinks I have some odd acquaintances, and he watches me. It would only add fuel to his suspicions if I swept out with a gentleman. Which, Lord Algernon, you very obviously are."

Meticulously I examined a wood mouse in a wreath of berries.

"Apart from that, you have no other objection to eating out with me?"

"Why do you make it so difficult for me?" he whispered harshly. "I think it will cause trouble, that's all."

"You put up a wall of resistance to me every time we meet," I murmured.

"There are things that you don't know. It would be better if you left me alone."

I suppose I should have bowed out gracefully then; but entirely selfish reasons prompted me to persevere. I had never stood so close to him before. The effect was enchanting. That he was not at ease intrigued me. When his nervous fingers shifted little heaps of field voles and owls I contrived to brush my hand on his; the warm touch lingered for an instant, and a round-eyed owl stared up at me, all knowing.

"If I leave now," I said, "and wait outside, will you join me in the street?"

"I can't think why you want me," he resisted. "I'm very dull to talk to."

"I'll take that chance," I answered amused.

"No, it isn't humorous," he told me dolefully. "I know I should not go with you. I know it will bring trouble, for you and for me, I know that."

"How can it?" I said kindly. "I only wish you well."

"It doesn't matter what you wish. That has nothing to do with anything. You won't be able to deal with what is wrong. So I am bound to cause you trouble. Why don't you see that and leave me alone?"

His urgent voice caused Mr Simmons to look across at us and cough. We studiously moved the prints about.

"Will you take any?" Arthur wondered disbelievingly.

"Of course I will. What do you think? Not the owl – he looks too wise and might make me feel uncomfortable."

"Oh? Have you things to hide?"

I laughed lightly. "We all do, don't we? I'll take a robin, and the mouse amongst the rose hips. And I'll wait for you outside, beyond the baskets."

He gave me an odd sideways look and did not answer. I wondered whether he would come.

I felt – and surely was – conspicuous there on the street corner patently without a purpose, while passers by leafed through the old books on display, and tested out the chairs.

He came. I watched him with a surge of fondness. He had on a corduroy cap that made me think of Willie; and a most pleasing ancient chord struck as I realised that not since then had I made this kind of street assignation with a pretty lad with whom I hoped to start a friendship. A swift despondency soon came over me. What kind of friendship was available to us – of different ages, different classes, different paths in life?

"I usually eat at The Gordon Arms," said Arthur conversationally. "But I don't suppose you will want to eat there."

"Why not?"

"Because Ronald dines there, and Thaddeus sometimes, and I daresay they would tell your wife."

I would have liked to protest cheerfully and answer that it did not matter. The fact remained – I did not wish that Claudia should hear of this encounter, and that Arthur guessed as much and stated it so baldly caused a little stab of guilt, a most uncomfortable sensation, for it made me feel as if my conduct in this matter was shabby and underhand. I did not think it was; for whatever might be my secret thoughts concerning Arthur I had not the slightest intention of revealing them to him. My intentions were, as they say, strictly honourable. Never in a thousand years would I confess to him that I had imagined us together naked, embracing in a copse of tropical greenery underneath a great glass dome.

"Then where shall we go?" I enquired meekly.

"There are several possibilities, each only a short walk away. Will you be guided by me?"

"With pleasure. But do you mean," I looked down with distaste at the mud-stained cobblestones, "that we should go on foot?"

"Yes I do," he said and laughed.

Winding our way through a series of narrow streets among the jostling throng we reached eventually a gap in the wall between high buildings of a rambling sort left over from the previous century. A little alley led away to further streets and here above some iron railings hung an inn sign creaking in the wind: The Jolly Jug. Two well-worn steps led to the door and whorled glass leaded windows hid from sight all that lay within. We entered. It was a dark and timbered place, all nooks and crannies, with a lively fire in the hearth that now and then blew forth a murky cloud of smoke. We dined on bottled stout and sizzling chops, and though there certainly were others round about and a landlord who attended us, and a large dog dozing by the fire, they were as shadows on the periphery of my vision, which concerned itself solely with my companion.

"You did not feel inspired then," I remarked, "to return with the others to discuss the colour white?"

"Is that why you've asked me out?" said he suspiciously. "You think I should have done so?"

"Not at all," I shrugged. "To me it seemed an unproductive exercise. As far as I am concerned white is white and there's an end to it. Presumably you felt the same?"

"Well, no, I did not," answered Arthur seriously. "White is ivory and pallor and purity, and snow and cloud; and there is fear and ghostliness; and certain skies, and petals, blackthorn you know, and lilies. And so on," he added lamely, "as you know."

"Very well then, since you have some views upon the subject, why did you not rejoin the others? Ronald, it seems, is concerned about you?"

"Oh not really," Arthur shrugged. "Only through duty. I am a sort of trophy to them. I am not like them. You can tell, can't you? I don't speak the same, and their circumstances are more secure."

"What do you mean, a trophy?"

"Well, you heard them, didn't you?" he said. "They love to talk about the Celtic Twilight. They are all very English, see, and live in nice houses, all their lives, and so the mountains seem a strange and wondrous place to them, unreal, like dreams and memories. I suppose at first I found it flattering for they all seemed very interested in me. But they were not really. They don't mind where you come from as long as it is primitive. Ireland would have done, or Scotland – anywhere with what they call Romance. Thaddeus suggested I should talk to them upon the subject of 'The Land Of Merlin'. I said I would not. They thought I was a spoilsport and have never shown the same interest in me since. But I could hardly talk about the wonder of the mountains when I could not wait to get away from them. Not that they are not wondrous; they are; but I did not want to live by them."

"Where is it that you come from?" I enquired.

"You will not have heard of it," he said, reverting to the dark defensiveness to which I had become accustomed.

"I daresay you have not heard of the village where I spent my childhood either," I remarked. That made him laugh.

"Really a village?" he challenged. "An inn, a shop, a little street, and your house in it?"

"All those things," I answered stoutly. "But I must admit the house was further off. In many acres of parkland."

"What was it called?"

"Mortmayne."

"No, I don't know it," he said, pondering the matter. "What is it like?"

"The land is rather flat; the house is rather old," I answered diffidently.

"And large, I suppose?"

"Not really."

"We could not be more different then in our beginnings," said he thoughtfully. "My house was small and in a valley. All around were mountains. Moel Hebog, and Cerrig Llan, which is steep and black. They say it is like the Pyrenees. Those are mountains in Spain," he added. "A visitor told me this."

"A visitor! I was imagining a place unknown to the world, to hear you talk."

"Well," he said sheepishly. "No, we had visitors all summer long. Because of the legend. The dog, see, whose name was Gelert, and they say that he is buried there."

"Bedd Gelert! I know of it. I know about the legend."

"You do?" he marvelled doubtfully. "How is that then? And, by the way, you don't say Bed; you say Beth."

We paused awhile to speak of pronunciation.

"It's a famous tale, you know," I said. "I read about it as a child. The king who slew his faithful hound, believing it had devoured his baby son, when it had fought a wolf instead and saved the child. And did it not die licking its master's hand? I was most moved. And what do you think the book was entitled? *Legends of the Land of Merlin!*"

Arthur smiled. "Oh well, you probably know more about it than I do then. I used to earn myself some handy money taking visitors to the tomb. It's down beside the river. There's a weeping willow hanging over three stone slabs, a little railing round it, in the meadow under Cerrig Llan. It's very pretty. All the visitors are most affected. Some ladies have been known to weep. It's true. I used to think that was very silly."

"Why so? Have you no heart? It's a very sad story."

"Why so? Because it may not be a tomb at all. Everyone in the village knows that. It may just be three slabs of stone. There is nothing under it, only grass; I've looked. But many books have now been written telling people what to visit when they travel. And they come to Llyn Cwellyn and Mynydd Mawr and so on to Bedd Gelert, and you see them in all weathers plodding up and down the path beside the river and their shoes all spoiled – the path is always very muddy. There is nothing to do in that village except look after visitors – unless you are a shepherd – so the inn does very well, and

120

the visitors liked to stare at us and hear us talking Welsh; we seemed more savage and they liked that."

"You spoke in Welsh!"

"And nothing else, until we moved to Swansea."

"How did you come to make such a change?"

"No work. And we had uncles there. So all of us went south – parents, three brothers, three sisters, and we lived in poor conditions near the harbour. All my brothers went to sea; my father also; there he died. My eldest brother's travelling took him to the port of London where he settled. He sent for us to join him, which we did; but now he is away at sea again; my sisters are all married; I am still with mam. And now you know my history, or some of it."

"I hope you do not plan to go to sea!" I told him severely.

"Of course I don't. I am, as you have seen, set up in some employment. It was discovered that I had some skill in drawing. Mr Simmons, who met my mother at a chapel tea party, offered to find me work."

A chapel tea party! I shuddered at this further proof of rumoured respectability. I felt my shoulders bowed down with a weight of guilt, which swiftly turned to irritation. There was no reason to feel guilty. I was not a wicked seducer twirling my moustaches, however it might superficially seem. My thoughts were lewd, I grant it, but they were well under control and at this stage all I wanted was to reassure myself that this youth who had so touched my burgeoning sensibilities was happy and secure, for I suspected he was neither.

"That was kind of Mr Simmons," I observed, a little sanctimoniously, wishing to seem righteous and benign.

Arthur shrugged. "He fancies my mother."

I raised an eyebrow. I had imagined an ancient white-haired matron at a spinning wheel. "Is there likelihood of – marriage?" I enquired.

"I hope not," he replied. "For then I'd certainly leave home."

"You do not like him?"

"Not much, no. He is always quoting Scriptures at me. Day in, day out. He thinks I am a trouble to my mother. Which if I am," he muttered, "is nobody else's business. So if this interest you are taking in me is along those kind of lines I warn you it is of no use at all. I don't respond to well-meaning meddling. It only makes me worse."

I wondered inconsequentially whether it betokened signs of growing old if one were seized with sudden urges to spank the person opposite; then I remembered Swinburne and decided age had nothing to do with it.

"Worse?" I enquired languidly. "What exactly is it that you do which is so shocking?"

He looked blank. "Isn't that why you invited me out? Have you not been asked to keep an eye on me? In case I'm going wrong?"

"*Are* you going wrong?" I asked him. Our eyes met. Those briliant blue orbs melted me. Arthur fidgeted and scowled.

"It's true I have been . . . rather discontented."

"You do not like your work," I guessed. "Excess of owls and robins."

He smiled wanly. "It is not simply that. It is my troubled thoughts."

I was not accustomed to this recurrent sensation of feeling elderly. Dammit, I was merely thirty-three. I had a monstrous estate to manage, which a series of disastrous harvests and the import of American grain had made no easier; I lived a life of vacuous sterility and I did not love my wife; I was submitting to those secret desires I had so long suppressed, which if discovered could send me to trial; and this boy had troubled thoughts.

"Can I help, perhaps?" I asked him, leaning forward, all but taking hold of his slim wrist, refraining.

"No one can," he responded gloomily.

"But – why not? Believe me, Arthur, I would like you to think of me as a friend."

I winced to hear my soft cajoling words, the long accepted language of seducers and manipulators. I felt a fraud, for though I yearned to ease his mind and cheer him, my vehemently good intentions were shamelessly coloured by a powerful desire to take him in my arms, to look at him undressed, to watch his eyelids closed in sleep, those glorious lashes lightly resting on his cheek.

"It is too late," he answered darkly.

"It never is!" I told him fervently.

"It's very well for you to speak like that," said Arthur. "You can do whatever you like. Rich people may. But my life has been lacking. My mother has sought consolation in religion. But though I went again and again to hear the holy words they went over my head. The troubled thoughts were always stronger. And they drove me from what I suppose could be called the Path of Good, because the other path seemed to care about me more, and offer something nearer to the kinds of things I want."

"Are we talking now of Zabarov?" I suggested.

"What if we are?" he sullenly replied.

"What is he to you?" I said, most uneasily.

"I told you, leave me alone!" said Arthur angrily.

"No," I said. "Because whatever you are sharing with that man it does not make you happy . . ."

"It does, it does," he insisted like a sulky child.

"How did you come first to encounter him?"

"Orlando came into the shop one day. He took me to places and we met people. Then once we went to Mr Charles' lodgings and then again." He smirked. "It was more entertaining than religion."

A swift remembrance of the pictures I had seen passed through my mind – Arthur posing for those obscene drawings – the rampant phalli and the sprawling limbs. Even obliquely I did not dare refer to this, allowing him to realise that I knew these secrets of his life. I could not meet his eyes; the truth was that I longed to see him naked and I feared that my desires would show.

"I have to go now," he said. "I have to be back at work."

A searing void rose up before me, the potential of loss. I bitterly regretted the lack of that power my ancestors were reputed to possess. But we are civilised now, and a title gave me no prerogative in this instance.

"I think that we should meet again," I said polite and pleasant, with an underlying firmness.

Arthur shook his head. "Count Zabarov would not like it."

"His likes and dislikes are not my concern. However, if the man is important to you in some way perhaps you'd care to accompany me when I go to watch his performance on the stage. This should be an interesting experience for all."

"Yes," said Arthur nodding. "Yes, I will do that."

I was astonished at this capitulation; I had obviously said the right thing. I was baffled and annoyed and heartily resented the weird foreigner.

Arthur stood up. We parted in the doorway. Unfortunately, since he was no tender female there was no need for me to accompany him to his place of work. I had to let him disappear into the crowd.

For the rest of the day I could settle to nothing. I thought only of him. The object of my desire had been with me, talking, eating, looking at me. I recalled each gesture. I saw again the dark and sullen brows, the clear blue eyes, the lush black hair that flopped across his forehead; his long fingers, inkstained cuffs, his black corduroy jacket and his low-brimmed cap. I recalled the way he spoke, and I cherished the memory of his lilting voice. I realised that our encounter had left me most disturbed. I had throughout the meal, I hoped, behaved impeccably; and now I felt the strain. My whole body ached with the suppression of desire.

Leafing through the newspapers at the club I could not focus on the world's events. There was still much discussion of the Dreyfus case, the Irish Question, and the ill health of Lord Rosebery the prime minister. I noticed references to the Queensberry affair, the marquis having been arrested for his unexpected and bizarre attempt to libel Oscar Wilde, an object of some speculation by the press. I read that the adjourned hearing of the case against him was now fixed to take place in a few days' time upon the 9th, at Great Marlborough Street; and indeed if I had not read as much I would have heard about it, for the subject was discussed by those in the smoking room on that occasion.

"What it all boils down to," Willoughby remarked, his legs apart, his ample posterior warming at the fireside, "is whether Oscar *is* a sodomite or not. If he is, then Queensberry will get off; and if he is not, then he won't."

"And how do you go about proving a thing like that?" Avonbury asked him scornfully, and this, adjudged to be rhetorical because of course it was assumed such things beyond the scope of law courts, remained unanswered.

An elderly peer Lord Barkworth looked up from his armchair to observe with feeling: "I have never understood, you know, the way the public took to Oscar Wilde. He can go anywhere, you know, received in all the best society, and foolish women fawn on him. But he's an Irishman! And an adventurer!"

"You know him slightly, Algy, don't you?" Willoughby said pleasantly, with every intention to make gentle mischief.

"No, I don't," I answered curtly, moving to the window, looking out upon the wide sweep of Pall Mall.

"I have two nephews newly come to London," said Lord Barkworth. "Both of them expressed a wish to meet with Oscar Wilde. I warned them off him. They are silly fellows both of them; I blame their mother. You keep away from him, I told them, he's a bad influence. Neither of them valued my advice. I don't understand it; I don't understand what people see in him but I'm damned if I'll stand by and see my nephews join the sycophants who follow him about."

Merton murmured something soothing. I turned back into the room and sat down at a writing desk. I took a piece of paper and I wrote:

My darling boy,

It is only a few moments since I quitted your sweet company. If only I might tell you how I feel. If only I might speak of the turbulent and exquisite sensations which consume me. I think now of your lips that spoke so sweetly to me of your life and which I now imagine put to other uses. I am tormented. How I long to be with you again. But soon, if the Fates are willing.

Algernon

It was a letter which I dared not ever send. To have written it at all and to have written it here, amongst this company, showed something of insanity, and I realised that I had best be leaving while this fit was upon me. What I had written, moreover, was potentially explosive as an anarchist bomb: I dared not even tear it up and leave the segments in a waste paper basket nor cross the room to toss it in the fire – one mere charred fragment would condemn me. So I folded it, and put it in my wallet and withdrew.

I took a cab to Charles' place – early evening it was now – hoping Jem or Francis was available to serve my needs, for I knew well enough that what I longed to have with Arthur I must have wherever I could find it. But unaccountably Charles was from home, the place deserted, and I left, frustrated in my intent and very agitated.

This desperation took me in the direction of The Two Faces, a haunt I'd swore I'd never visit further, for the notion that I had been given a dangerous address alarmed me. But half an hour with Eddy, I maintained, would ease this dreadful need and permit me to return home at night in calm.

I sat there, as before, in that vile public house. Yes, vile! For what before had once seemed thrilling, novel, bold, I now found uncomfortable and degrading. The name of the place, which I had thought startlingly symbolic, now embarrassed me, for I remembered Charles' ghastly pun. This time the Amontillado tasted sour to me and I suspected it of being watered. The barman of the previous occasion was still there, still wiping tankards with his cloth, and he had observed me, recognised me, understood why I was here. I felt humiliated by this knowledge, the more so because this time there were no boys lounging against the counter; merely customers, who sat and drank, morose and shabby. But I was desperate, all for the love of Arthur. The clock above the counter ticked the minutes by; my restlessness must have been most apparent for I was not myself – habitual self-restraint had left me, and I ran my forefinger around the wet rim of the glass, tugged irritably at my tie and nibbled at my thumb. My eyes strayed constantly towards the doorway that led backward to those sordid upper regions where I had been satisfied amongst the silken shawls. Eventually I could stand no more – the fruitless waiting and the barman's understanding stare contrived to make the situation quite intolerable. I stepped over to the counter.

"Yes sir?" smiled the barman with a whiff of triumph, as if it were some victory to him to find my nerve had cracked, as if for all the world he had been making bets to ascertain how long before I weakened and came over to him, to ask for what I wanted, to betray my craving.

"Excuse me – " I began. "I wonder could you tell me –"

"Sir?" he prompted most obligingly.

"Will – is it likely Eddy may be here tonight?" I looked down at the counter to disguise the urgency of my demand. I was bitterly ashamed that any hint of private anguish might be guessed at, and I knew, of course, it was. We spoke in lowered voices.

"Eddy?" answered he implacably, the stiff white cloth in motion all the while. "These boys are, as they say, a law unto themselves. Coming and going." He paused, the implications of his words intended to be sexual; I winced. "I never know from one day to another where they'll be."

I wondered if he was expecting me to bribe him for the information. I did not know the formula for this kind of encounter. The whole transaction sickened me. I took a breath. "Well," I said, defeated, "I can wait no longer."

"Steady on, sir," he replied, as one who has been jesting and repented. "It's true I don't know whether Eddy will be in tonight, or out." He chuckled lewdly. "I would tell you if I knew. But none of our boys seem to be about just at the moment. You was just unlucky in the time you picked. Another time and they'd be here in droves. Up and down from the Dilly all night long . . ."

"What do you suggest?" I asked him tersely.

"Two things you could do, sir, at a time like this," he answered. "One is, wait. Like the omnibuses sir, there'll always be another one along in a minute! Alternatively . . ." and he savoured a little silence like one who has a nice surprise in store. "I could tell you somewhere else where your requirements can be seen to, some- where very nice and not too far away."

"Yes please," I murmured, "if you are sure that it is safe."

"What'll I say, sir?" he answered with a helpless shrug. "You know the score. You know how it is. All I can say is the place is a gem. Very agreeable people. I know it, 'cause I've been there. Everyone you meet there is just like yourself; they understand, know what I mean? It's good there – like a little world all of its own. They keep the curtains drawn and burn sweet-smelling sticks, and all the boys are perfect peaches. *Peaches*, sir, know what I mean? It's worth a try tonight, sir, and you won't be disappointed."

"Give me the address," I breathed. I longed to get away. My mind was in a turmoil, fear and lust at odds and raging through my being like a fever.

The barman put his tankard down, hung up his cloth on a hook, and wrote in pencil on a notepad, handing me the torn-off page.

"You know who goes there," said he, from the corner of his mouth, "the likes of Oscar Wilde. And," he added, as if perhaps suspecting that this might not entirely tip the balance for me, "many gentlemen much like yourself."

"Thank you," I said, with a mouth as dry as paper, and I pocketed the note and fled.

Reason and common sense played no part in my behaviour on that night, desperation all. I took a cab from Piccadilly Circus down to Westminster Bridge in the bright lamp-lit darkness. I alighted at this most civilised of destinations, and paid my fare with every appearance of a gentleman engaged on the business of our nation.

I walked along Millbank, much oppressed by the proximity of the Houses of Parliament. Within those walls had been passed the very law that now obliged me to prowl secretly about, my conscience and my lusts at war. It stood there like a fortress and thus it seemed to me then, hostile and impenetrable as any medieval castle to the hapless stones that peasants slung, a place where laws were passed, not for the common man, but against his interest by those in power who thought that they knew best and did not. Some half forgotten lines of Blake came to my mind, concerning Church and State and walls. If I, with all my so-called advantages and wealth could feel like this, what of the deprived, the poor? So, there lay the symbol of the State, and now the symbol of that other ruler of our lives, the Church. The dark bulk of Westminster Abbey blackened the already fast-encroaching night. I found its presence sinister. I felt as far away from that occasion when I had attended Tennyson's funeral as if an actual chasm separated me from it. I had then been a member of what the newspapers are prone to call "the glittering throng". Now I felt more like an outcast, walking in the shadows. The god personified within that massive gloomy edifice was in every aspect as threatening to those like me as was the State. It was impossible to walk these streets without an awareness of those mighty enemies. I smiled weakly. What irony, that the address I sought should be placed here.

It was not difficult to find. Beyond the abbey lay a group of interjecting streets and Little College Street amongst them. It was small and quiet, the houses nondescript, three storeys high, the kind of road where people take lodgers who might come and go unnoticed. Number thirteen seemed no different. I stood opposite it and looked across. The top floor – Mr Alfred Taylor – this was written on the paper I had just received, and in the top floor

127

window was a light. I hesitated, the impetus that had propelled me here receding. How I longed for Arthur. How I needed to embrace . . . anybody, somebody, and lose this wretched craving in the sweet flesh of another. The images inside my head tormented me. Across that great divide – the width of the little street – lay something almost heavenly – a curtained room, scented with burning incense, with boys who for a little payment could give me what I needed. *Sell* me what I needed, I corrected myself. It made no difference. There would be beds there, low divans and rugs, and boys would sprawl about them, half undressed, with lovely bodies, yielding lips, provocative and pleasing ways, no questions asked, and I could make believe that they were Arthur. And there I could forget myself and lose myself in love. In lust, my conscience said. It felt like love to me. It waited for me in that upstairs room and all I had to do was cross the road.

I did so. Yes, I put my hand upon the door. Then I withdrew. I dared not. I despised myself for cowardice – give in, give in, I told myself. Oh! What if I met Oscar there engaged upon similar business! I would expire from shame. That somebody I knew might see me, guess my secret . . . I could not risk it. But nobody frequenting that place would ever tell – how could he, without implicating himself? So I would be safe. I had nothing to fear. But personal integrity – I must keep that intact – I must not ever be encountered in a sordid den where boys sold favours to the desperate – my limbs were racked with longing, my stomach knotted with frustration, the pounding in my loins insufferable. I must go in . . .

I dared not and I knew that I would not. Although I paced the street, pretending I might change my mind, my resolution weakened with each passing minute. And that was how I was, I told myself in fierce despair, weak-natured, just as I had always been. I would reject the chance of Heaven. Then I controlled myself, as I would always do. Heaven? It would have been a loathsome squalid stew, I knew it. I would return to earth where one lived by rules and reputation and correct behaviour.

Self-loathing now suffused my every fibre. I was like Mr Strode. I was no better than that wretched fellow whom I had so despised when I was young. For he had been ridiculous, everybody thought so, and we mocked him behind his back for his melancholic ugliness, his inability to disguise his cravings. I understood him now; I understood how it was that he had been driven to his sordid fate, trapped by those prowling constables instructed to be on the watch for such as he – for such as I. What could my future hold?

Cloaked in despondency I walked aimlessly about. I saw the river, black and gleaming, with ranks of lights strung glittering the length of it. I wondered that the abbey bells did not ring out, that Parliament's meticulous time-keeper did not chime deridingly; but no, both Church and State were for the moment silent, comfortable in the knowledge that for most of us our own fears did their work for them.

The night air tasted bitter – soot and waterdrops. Beside the solid cast iron bridge some hansoms waited at the kerb. I settled into one and gave directions. The cab driver suggested it was chilly for the time of year. I said I thought it was.

CHAPTER ELEVEN

THAT COUNT Zabarov was exerting some devious influence over Arthur I did not doubt, and my avowed intention was now to release the boy from that man's hold. A crusade of such worthiness, however, was not without some passing pleasure to myself.

So determined was I to tread carefully in my pursuit of Arthur that my behaviour resembled little short of courtship; and as I set off one evening a few days later, well aware that in time-honoured tradition of suitors I would be obliged to meet his mother, it was all I could do not to indulge the amusement and exhilaration that I felt and purchase him an orchid.

Arthur and his mother lived in rooms, the house of modest appearance, the street not far from Grays Inn Road; and Arthur's mother was delightful, as I knew she would be. She sat within the parlour, a dark-haired woman of some fifty years, dressed in brown and looking younger than her age, her hair looped up in plaited coils, her eyes pale blue.

The room was small and so contained with furniture that it was scarce possible to move about. A fire burned in the grate, the mantelpiece a mass of photographs and much of the wall also, along with many dusky paintings of Eryri. There were two tall chairs beside the hearth, a sideboard thick with ornaments – nor did I miss the great bound Bible as its centrepiece. A corner cupboard gleamed with china. Low tables, work baskets and wicker stools filled the remaining spaces, and a tabby cat blinked up from the patterned rug. The heavy curtains and the turned-down gaslight made the room a dim, warm pleasant place, but I could understand that Arthur living here would sometimes find its sweetness and its clutter cloying and constricting.

The photographs of his family showed dark-eyed girls and sailor youths with serious faces. I wanted to know everything about him, and his mother needed no encouragement, her pride in all the portraits most apparent. She spoke as one to whom the English language was not the natural tongue. She said it was kind of me to

130

take an interest in her son; and Arthur fidgeted beside the open door. Soon we were in the street, where urchins scrapped around the waiting hansom wheels.

"Ooh, travelling in style!" said Arthur as we climbed inside. "Well," he added. "You had a good look at the family then."

"I hope you did not mind."

Arthur shrugged. "You pleased my mother. I still don't know why you find us so interesting. You'll soon know all about me, won't you!"

"If it would make you feel any better you shall see my family album at any time you choose. There are portraits of me that go back to childhood. Many studies of my fearsome parents. My father was a military man; my mother should have been!"

"Really?" Arthur said. "Is she so bad?"

"Frightening. Not at all as sweet as yours."

Arthur looked through the window thoughtfully. "And you also have a wife and children."

"Yes," I answered lightly. "And they were delighted with the robin and the mouse."

"What are your children's names?"

"Perceval and Sophy; and William is away at school."

I behaved as though the references to my family had not caused me some irritation. Why it should have been so I was not entirely sure, except it seemed to put me in my place. *You have a wife and children* – with the implication following: *then why are you with this young man who is no nephew, ward, associate, and of another class besides?* It was my guilty conscience speaking, in a voice uncomfortably loud. The questions that I longed to ask I dared not, and it nettled me to have to sink to inconsequential chatter; and so we both fell silent. I was with Arthur, knee to knee, and with the speed of Faustus's last hour the hansom cab was spinning us too quickly to our destination.

The theatre, in the area of Drury Lane, must in its heyday certainly have been familiar with the elegance of Regency society, but now had long since gone to seed. Its exterior was most unprepossessing even in the gaslit gloom, and all the length of it a shuffling tail of people edged their way towards the doors. Above the pillared portico two garish statues of a painted fairground type, one male, one female, loosely classical in pose, beckoned us to enter. Placards in the smoky vestibule blared out the thrills in store – Zabarov's name was there ("The Great Zabarov, Mysteries of the East") – but I found my attention was distracted by the others: LIVE HORSES! A HUNDRED FAIRIES SUSPENDED IN MID AIR! A GENUINE SHIPWRECK! REAL WATER! JANEY JONES, FEMALE WEIGHT LIFTER! And much as I might wonder what I was about in entering this palace of delights I could not help but ask myself what Zabarov was doing here; his moral standpoint I might query but I knew that in his way he was a man of culture.

We sat up in the circle, and, to either side, between us and the stage three tiers of balconies stretched forward, packed with people, while above it all was a painted dome much decorated with cupids, stars and trumpets. Cigar smoke from the bar at the back of the stalls wisped upward in blue coils, and all the time there was an intermittent stream of traffic to the bar for whisky and champagne. At no time was there possibility of conversation of an intimate nature with my companion.

We saw the Genuine Shipwreck. The great hulk of an old-time vessel filled the stage. The side of the hull then slid back to show the passengers within, eating and drinking, the room all lit up. The orchestra played menacing music, the ship began to roll to and fro with much creaking and straining till it lay almost horizontal, and the passengers slid up and down. Tables and crockery teetered and smashed, lights flickered, passengers now hurtling through the air, suspended, one supposed, on wire threads, for they somersaulted most artistically in poses of anguish. Then came a cascade of water – Real Water – on the side of the ship, and one saw that the stage was all geared up to receive it, as on a great tray; and afterwards thunderous billowy sounds on the drums hid the gushing away as it drained. To quieten our nerves as the curtains were drawn a conjuror next entertained at the front of the stage, with card tricks, rabbits and doves. When he had retired we saw some kind of ballet with fairy-tale music and girls in taffeta skirts who danced in a glimmering glade. So full did the stage then become we suspected that these were the one hundred fairies; this proved to be so, for at the soar of one final crescendo up they rose, every one, the metallic wires that lifted them glinting momentarily in the lights; and over the heads of the audience in the stalls they hung and swayed, to cheers of delight and to blatant attempts by the eager to look up their skirts. While this marvel was tidied away, the female weight lifter showed off her skills; and next came The Mysterious Bedroom: all unsuspecting, young honeymooners were shown into their hotel room by a sinister innkeeper. During the course of the night they were much harassed, giving the wife ample opportunity to scream piercingly with every fresh alarm. Wardrobe doors swung open, mirrors became doorways, a dressing table glided inwards – and every form of horror lay behind them, from gibbering skeletons to devils with horns, and shaggy little creatures with fangs, till finally the demon king himself arose majestically from a trap door in the floor, with a great splutter of fireworks, much turning

132

on and off of lights, and near hysteria from the drums and cymbals. As the curtain came down we were soothed by a selection of parlour songs by a stout female and a pianist; and after these came Zabarov.

No interim performance this before the curtain; no, he possessed the centre stage which had the look of oriental splendour, with a painted backcloth of minarets and palm trees. He was got up in every Englishman's idea of the inscrutable desert potentate complete with flowing robe and turban, a glamorous jumble of exotica about him, from tigers' head rugs upon the floor to a lacquered black and silver cabinet. From this, Orlando appeared, dressed in an outfit that caused the first thrill for me of that entire evening's miracles – white tights flecked with spangled stars, his chest and arms all bare except for some fine glittering dust that the light caught in a myriad sparkles.

Zabarov made him vanish and return via that strange cabinet. I experienced a certain disappointment that he seemed to be no better than a conjuror and I thought scornfully that I should have brought Perceval and Sophy with me, not Arthur. I had once seen a genie very similar and with a marvellous array of pink and purple smoke. But I was dubious too readily – there were wonders still to come.

Drawing near to the front of the stage, where the eerie glow of light from underneath lit up his face from below and made its hollows a mass of shadows, Zabarov spoke. Who would have thought the restless watchers who had shouted their enthusiasm for the buxom nymphs would have sat silent and absorbed? And yet they did. Zabarov talked about an Austrian doctor, Frederick Mesmer, "a man much misunderstood in his own lifetime. He believed in Animal Magnetism. The waters of our bodies give off a glow which can be manipulated in harmony with universal fluids, the pull of the moon's influence, the wanderings of the planets. Metals can be magnetised in the service of mankind. Patients can be cured of illnesses simply by grasping a handle that leads directly to a source of magnetism. The magnetic flow darts to the place of pain. By touching a plant or tree that has been so magnetised a patient can be completely restored to health. But Doctor Mesmer was not at all the first to use his art for good," Zabarov told us. "Throughout history man has understood that health comes from the mind. The god within! We call this state of strong suggestion Hypnosis. Hypnosis! It has always been with us! The Druids used it at Stonehenge, the Celts in secret groves, the Africans in their deep jungles, and the wise Chinese in their pagodas – Hypnosis! the use of Mind for betterment, for understanding, and for self-improvement!"

133

However, if we assumed some kind of mass healing process was to follow we were wrong. The stage was not transformed into Bethesda Pool. To prove how harmless hypnotism was, Zabarov showed us with Orlando. He sat him in a chair; he moved about him, making passes through the air, his arms a zigzag of gestures in their long exotic sleeves. He told us that Orlando's Organ of Individuality lay between the eyebrows. Then he began to speak to him. The patter sounded eerie:

"I want you to listen to what I am saying to you – your eyes are closed – you are relaxed and at ease – you think of nothing, you think of nothing but what I say to you – your arms and legs feel heavy, very heavy, your whole body is so heavy now – you sink backward into darkness – you are sleepy now – your sleep is growing deeper . . ."

There was absolute silence. No one jumped up and cried it was a sham, all prearranged; no, everyone seemed spellbound. Eventually Zabarov proved his victim was entranced; he lifted Orlando's limp arm up and dropped it and moved his head about.

"Perception of reality," Zabarov explained, "is changed when the subject is in a state of relaxed consciousness. For instance, here is a citrus fruit, in fact a lemon, upon a plate, cut into quarters – you!" he beckoned to a young man in the stalls. "Verify for me that this in indeed a lemon."

This was done.

"My young assistant," said Zabarov, "will now eat it, thinking that it is an orange. Orlando," he turned to the inert youth who sat sprawled there, those delicious white tights clinging to his lean and muscular thighs, spread wide apart, so much so that I for one doubted whether Orlando's Organ of Individuality lay between the eyebrows. "Here is an orange for you, a sweet and luscious fruit and I want you to eat it; eat it for me now . . ." He put into Orlando's hand each fragment of the lemon, and we watched him eat it, slowly, even the peel.

"There is a cockerel on the stage!" Zabarov snapped. "Catch it, Orlando – it is there – and there – and there!"

It was amazing to behold, for the boy leapt up and ran about the stage as if he thought that he was in a farmyard, grasping at nothing, while Zabarov told him where the cockerel was until it perched upon the arm of the chair and was caught. The people laughed; it had been droll, and now they felt more comfortable, for the boy was his assistant, and of course he knew there was no cockerel; it was all a trick.

Zabarov sat Orlando down. "I bring him back to us now," he said, and with a similar series of gestures and the murmured invitations to relax, to wake, he did so. Orlando bowed and strolled about. The people clapped, Zabarov bowed. Standing at the front of the stage he said: "It is a trick, yes? The boy was shamming. It was all a game."

"It'd never work with me!" one bright spark boasted.

"Let us see," suggested the conjurer. "Who would like to try? Who is so bold? But then – it is nothing, eh? For if it is a trick then you may laugh at me and say, 'You see, it did not work'. And if it is not a trick, you will have nothing to fear, for you are among friends, and afterwards I bring you back unharmed, just as I brought Orlando."

A positive flood of volunteers gushed forward. From these some six were chosen – diverse and ordinary enough to seem a random group who had not previously made an arrangement. Who could say? If it was trickery it was entertaining trickery, and that was all the audience required.

Those six, at first sniggering and fidgeting and grinning at the stalls, were set in chairs and subjected to the same process as Orlando. I stole a glance at Arthur; he was silent and enrapt.

On the stage the six sat entranced, immobile. Gone the jaunty airs, the disbelief. Unless they were indeed in some collusion and had been taught to act the part they now showed every appearance of complete malleability. Orlando, to Zabarov's directions, lifted their limp arms, let their heads sink forward. Zabarov told them now their arms were leaden and they could not raise them. Raise your arms, he told them, and no one could, though several weakly tried. Orlando brought six brooms on to the stage, and introduced them to his six guests. He told them these were lovely maidens, rosy-cheeked and graceful, with hair like rippling corn. He told them to stand up and dance, dance with the maidens. And they did, most solemnly, each one with a besom in his arms, around the stage, till Zabarov said the dance was over. Then he had them catching chickens. Here is one, he said, and here – a little squawking chicken and it's running away – now catch it – bend and clutch it in your hands – now here – now there. And round the stage they lolloped, bending down and jumping up, and grabbing at the air. It was a strange, quaint sight, so funny that the audience was laughing, rocking in their seats. So, all the chickens caught, the six were settled back into their chairs, and slowly, carefully, Zabarov brought them up from trance.

"You will remember nothing. But as you leave the stage I want you to tweak your own ears. This will be the last thing I ask you to do. After that you will behave as usual, and you will remember nothing of this."

We watched intrigued. They stretched and blinked and smiled; they thanked Zabarov; he thanked them; they left the stage, and each one tweaked his ear as he went by. The audience clapped and cheered; it had been most amusing, and before they had time to wonder more about it the mysterious Orient left the stage, the orchestra played swirling music, and the Genuine Horses ran across; a most dramatic spectacle, and one which I felt did not bode well for the survival of the theatre, for the floorboards shook, the backcloth quivered and the vibrations could be felt up in the circle. These leaping horses were the climax of our evening's entertainment. Dull would indeed have been the soul who was unsatisfied with such rich fare; and the folk who streamed forth into the chilly night were patently delighted and impressed.

"Was he not wonderful!" cried Arthur, shining-eyed. We must see him – we must tell him so."

"We must?" I answered dubiously. For myself I found that in the presence of Zabarov, even so far distant as I had been from him in the theatre, I was to some extent – I use his own language – mesmerised; but once away from him I found his influence receded, as it now did. Not so with Arthur. So entranced was he that I do not believe I could have taken him home and achieved a coherent conversation. There was nothing for it but to do as Zabarov had suggested at the Café Royal and go to visit him behind the scenes.

Arthur led the way. It was apparent that he had been before to pay court to the master, and his blind-eyed obedience disturbed me. We traversed the outer wall of the theatre, turning into a puddled yard, where carts from a nearby inn stood, their iron-rimmed wheels glinting wet in the light of a flaring gas jet that hung above an entrance marked "Stage Door". I was embarrassed to be acting so, as if I had been marvellously impressed and must tell of my rapture, when in cold fact I felt exactly as I did before, suspicious and dubious. It struck me now that I was rather surprised Zabarov's act had been so droll. Like Faustus he had seemed to boast excess of cunning, access to some superhuman power, and yet with all the wealth at his disposal he had merely indulged in foolish romps about the stage, in farcical clowning, ludicrous display – like Faustus, who had most majestic dreams, yet took his pleasure tweaking the Pope's beard and playing tricks on cardinals.

We entered a cold narrow passage, climbed twisty steps, pressed ourselves back against the brickwork to let pass in overcoats and hats those visions who had once been fairies, demons. I was bewildered, eyeing Arthur with extreme misgiving. What was going on? He was hurrying to Zabarov with a curious urgency, as if time mattered and was in short supply. His eyes were glazed, and his demeanour purposeful quite out of all proportion to the situation. I followed him with gathering uneasiness.

Zabarov's dressing room was small and warm and glamorous. A rich array of shimmering robes hung from a rail, a feathered turban sat upon a hatstand, an amber gem glowing therein like a great owl's unblinking eye. Zabarov sat in front of a mirror, and I met his eyes in that glassy surface before he turned around and greeted us profusely.

"So welcome a surprise . . ." he purred, and yet I knew that he expected us. He wore an oriental dressing gown of dark silk, a gold embroidered dragon on the back, a sash about his waist. Beside him, lounging against his chair stood the fair Orlando, heart-stoppingly attractive in the outfit he had worn on stage. I found him dazzling. His hair was liberally streaked with gold dust, and his eyelids also, and upon his naked chest a mass of glittering spangles caught the light. His white tights clung to him like a skin, revealing every aspect of his shape, indeed one's eye could not help being drawn to contemplate the luscious crotch. Was this what Dr Mesmer meant by Animal Magnetism?

I murmured niceties to Zabarov which I did not mean and which he knew I did not. Arthur meanwhile was behaving very oddly. He sat at Zabarov's feet and gazed up at him for all the world like some endearing puppy. When I pulled at his shoulder, mortified at his inexplicable servility, he shook me off with an intensity that startled me.

"There, Arthur," Zabarov reassured him, touching Arthur's head with a possessiveness I heartily resented. "You had to come here; I know it. You have been away and now you are returned."

"Arthur – " I began severely. He ignored me.

"I was so confused," said Arthur to Zabarov. "I knew I must get back. I need direction once again."

"And you shall have it," said Zabarov, magnanimous as a monarch with his favours. "Now, stay still, be silent; wait."

I interposed. "Excuse me. Arthur came here with me tonight. I shall return him to his home."

Zabarov turned from Arthur to his former position facing the mirror. He caught my gaze within the glass. He remained with his back to me, attending to his face, which had been smeared with colour and which now he cleaned with ointment from a small dark jar. Our conversation took place through the mirror, the words and glances darting back and forth as if they touched the glass and jaggedly richocheted off the surface.

"There is no need," Zabarov told me carefully. "Arthur will stay with me now. This is where he wishes to remain. I will look after him, as I have done before. Lord Algernon, your task is finished.

Arthur has no more need of you."

"However, I still believe . . ." I answered ineffectually. With crass stupidity, in the light of what I had just witnessed on the stage, I continued to look at Zabarov in the mirror, fascinated by the fact that his eyes and the amber jewel set in the turban looked all of the same transluscent substance.

"No, you are wrong," he told me firmly. "You have been kind and you have performed your duty. And now you may take your reward; you can relax, and you can go away with what it is you really want."

"What do I really want?" I wondered, simple as a child.

"Orlando," said Zabarov.

Orlando moved, turning to the mirror. I could see nothing but him. Sparkling, irridescent as sunlight in water, he stood there gleaming at me, half nude and very splendid. Zabarov blinked, and it was as if a curtain had come down, terminating one act, setting the scene for the one that followed. Suddenly all was movement.

"I must get dressed," Orlando laughed, and bent and pulled the tights from off his hips. I could not keep my eyes from him. He wore a posing pouch such as models sometimes wear, but I could see the golden crotch hair in his groin, and his thighs gleamed gold as he unpeeled. I watched dry-mouthed as he moved about, pulling on his trousers, shoes and stockings, tucking in his shirt, a jacket now about his gorgeous nudity, depressing as a cloud about the sun.

"You will come home with me, Lord Algy?" he coaxed. "I'd be awfully pleased." There was a boyish eagerness in his manner which I found irresistible.

"Why, yes, I'd like to," I replied.

"Well, good," he beamed. "We'll take ourselves off, then, shall we? Waste no time. I never believe in saving treats for later, do you? Have the best first, I always say, and then you know you've had it. After all, you could drop dead between the second cherry and the cream."

"A fine philosophy!" Zabarov told us heartily, as jovial as any wolf in Grandmother's bedroom. With his approval then, I and Orlando left the room, and I retraced the path whereby I had entered, the cold air startling as we trod through the wet yard and found the street.

"I have a room in Count Zabarov's house," Orlando confided. "We'll go there; it'll be quite all right."

"Where does he live?"

"Fitzroy Street."

I was surprised; it was not where I had expected. That was where the famous police raid had occurred last year, when members of a

138

brothel for male prostitutes had been carted off to answer questions at the police station.

As if reading my thoughts Orlando giggled: "At the opposite end from where the scandal was!"

"Well then, let us acquire ourselves a cab."

We found one near the colonnades of Covent Garden and sped north west. My mental state seemed unaccountably vague but not unpleasant, and I certainly was well aware that I was sitting thigh to thigh with Orlando, who smelt of greasepaint and a pungent perfume, a combination of a most delicious decadence. Every lamp we passed by touched his face with gold and made his eyelids shimmer.

"So?" he asked. "Did you enjoy the show?"

The pleasant banality of our ensuing talk was reassuring. It was not so strange at all that I should be here with Orlando, delightfulness personified, a sweet obliging boy, a friend of Mr Charles. We chatted comfortably of stage productions, theatres, entertainers; time passed quickly; and it was not long before we reached a house in Fitzroy Street, an elegant white building with a fine Adam façade where we were let in by a French-speaking butler with every appearance of respectability.

The downstairs room where Orlando poured us drinks was similarly acceptable. If this was Zabarov's house it was a place where anyone might be received and feel no qualm; I certainly felt none, as I admired the general tenor of the room: the high ceiling with its central ornamental rose, the towering classical-style fireplace beneath a gilt-edged mirror, the heavy curtains and the paintings in their elaborately embossed frames – scenes of English rural life, as if to reassure the wary who might be expecting pentacles. Orlando seemed at ease here, comfortable as a young lord, sprawling on an arm chair, boasting – he had been *this close* to Henry Irving; he had lent his coat to Mrs Langtry one wet afternoon in Charlotte Street; and at least a dozen girls from the Gaiety Theatre were desperate for his affection. He had much to tell, and told it. Then he laughed.

"Well, Lord Algy then," he said. "So much for entertaining you while you drink. But that's enough of that, now that I see you've finished. Shall we go upstairs?"

I needed no persuasion. I followed him up the thickly carpeted staircase, along a landing, and into a small room at the back of the house. He turned on the lamps and revealed a room whose details I did not take in beyond its extravagant untidiness – an unmade bed, strewn clothes of social and theatrical nature, with sober shoes and hats entwined with cloaks with crimson lining, painted swords and ostrich plumes and great gauze fairy wings, as if the juxtaposition

139

were quite natural. He locked the door behind us and let out a rapturous sigh:

"We are alone!"

He flung himself into my arms; I held him hungrily. For a moment time stood still as our lips met; then we indulged in a long exploratory kiss. He pulled away, laughing.

"Let's undress quickly and get into bed. I'm so sticky with paint I'll mess up your clean shirt and then where will we be?"

We began to take off our clothes. The room not being particularly warm, we pulled the sheets and blankets up about us and settled into bed. Everywhere was quiet and there were no sounds from the rest of the house, only the secret stillness of the bed whereon we lay, in a house I did not know, owned by a man I did not like.

Our naked bodies pressed together. The dim lights showed the beauty of my young companion and the eerie sparkles of his yellow hair. His glittering eyelids gave the impression of some woodland elf, some Puck I had encountered in a glade. The oils on his body made him smooth and slippery to hold, the personification of illusion, seeming real and yet quick to vanish, leaving the embrace to close on emptiness. But Orlando was actual enough, no doubt of that. His back was long and slender, his shoulders lithe and strong, his arms taut with muscle. I felt his long cock pushing at me, nudging mine, and the bush of his crotch hair brushed my skin. We kissed a little, but we did not pause for tenderness; lust must be satisfied. He let me turn him over to his front; I lay upon him and his pert round buttocks moved against my belly. A little moment and the glittering elf was mine.

I dared not stay there till morning; I feared there would be some awkwardness by daylight and I could think of no more grisly prospect than to meet Zabarov over breakfast. So I took my leave at some unearthly hour; Orlando saw me out through some side entrance from the servants' quarters, and I slipped into the street.

I blessed my good fortune when I found a cab in Warren Street. I walked towards it and my feet were light as air. Visions of beauty danced before my eyes.

CHAPTER TWELVE

I N THE cold light of day – and that first week of March was cold indeed – I felt appalled at my behaviour.

My abandonment of Arthur was unforgiveable. I had received him from his mother – a woman known for regular attendance at chapel tea parties – and I had quitted him without a struggle, at the instigation of a suspect Balkan adventurer in whose questionable clutches I had left the hapless youth. I felt most deeply ashamed. I did not, however, regret Orlando, the memory of whose lovely limbs produced in me an eager pulsing of the loins and a hope to know such gratification again.

But how had that occurrred? I sat in my study the following morning, a long list of accounts before me on the desk unseen and unattended, and I pondered much on what had happened. It was true that I had wanted Orlando from the first moment I had seen him at the Café Royal when we all dined together. *Shall I tell your future?* he had asked me – *I will tell you, I am in it.* So it was not inconceivable that he experienced reciprocal emotions and intended that we should one day share lust. And yet . . . I could not help but feel that it had been at Zabarov's direction. He had thrust Orlando upon me, I had eagerly received him, and from that moment Arthur had been blanked out of my thoughts. I do not recall his presence after that; I did not say goodbye; I did not think of him at all.

There is a magic in lust and Orlando had been gold and glittering as any starry creature out of faery. Had there been other kinds of magic also?

I pushed the thought aside. I had never been obliged to analyse my thoughts on hypnotism, if indeed I ever had any. But it was not impossible that a man who had the skill so potently that he could entertain an entire theatre might use that same power to his own ends. Had Zabarov indulged himself at my expense? If so, it was abominable.

I recalled the unease that I had felt when we had dined together, how he kept my attention so that I barely noticed any of the others, the way he shifted the line of wine glasses to form a pattern seeming a direct link from me to him, and how I came away with the sense of having been manipulated. Now I thought about our eyes locked in a gaze in glass, the mirror where he sat, and where I stared, and where I turned my back on Arthur. I remembered the implication in his talk at the theatre, that hypnotism was a force for good. I assumed that this meant that the victim only performed the kind of acts of which he was capable in his normal state of mind – in other words, because I did desire Orlando it was easy to propel me in that direction; I was a willing participant. But even so – what monstrous liberty! What villainy!

Ah, now I understood his hold on Arthur. That poor boy had been subjected to the same. I saw again his dog-like gaze, his glazed expression. I began to guess at his confusion – chance remarks which had seemed odd – and would seem so, since Arthur could not understand himself. If this were so, then it was dire even beyond my initial suppositions. But why should he want Arthur? Why force his will upon that unhappy boy? What use could Arthur be to him?

As I sat over my accounts, the combination of the columns of figures, the sprawling handwriting of my tenants, the lurching recollections of my lovely lewd night with Orlando, my fear for Arthur and my growing rage towards Zabarov all conspired to produce a most unsatisfactory morning, and a headache, and a need to quit the house. I would have dearly loved a horse-ride over Mortmayne's fields, with no sight of humankind from noon till dusk; however, this was not to be, and so I went to visit Charles to talk of my suspicions and to sit and pose while he worked towards the culmination of Narcissus.

"Of course he uses hypnosis," he agreed. "He has done so for me on many occasions – of course, it was at my request. He said I was an Interesting Subject. I was Taken Back. Do you know what that means, Algy? It means he can take you back to childhood and ask questions of the child you were. Such findings can throw light upon the problems you encounter as the swine that you become later. In my case I went right back into a previous life. Do you believe in reincarnation?"

"No."

"I must. I am living proof. I was an Egyptian. Frown a little now while I paint the eyes. Look as if you understand life's sorrows. Narcissus has no hope, and yet he sits there, hoping . . ."

"Will mere confusion suffice?" I suggested. "This at least will be genuine. Tell me, Charles, what do you know about Orlando?"

"The beautiful brat? Not much. He was thrown out of his public school, you can guess what for. I wouldn't trust him. But he's a

142

winsome little tart. I like him." Charles paused contemplatively.
"You will be surprised to hear this but, to return to the subject of
Egypt, it was I who drew the two serpents on the wall of the tomb of
Seti, the goddess Nephthys and the goddess Isis. I knew the
attributes of the goddesses and I knew the way out of the tomb – in
fine detail – and I could describe the house in which I lived. I had a
wife and children. I was much respected in the community. They
say that with each successive life you show improvement. I wonder
where it was that I went wrong . . ."

"Do you suppose it likely that this man has hypnotised Arthur?" I
demanded.

"Why do you not ask him?"

About this simple approach to the problem I felt some ambiva-
lence, for I had already arranged to meet Orlando again in
Zabarov's house, during the hours when Zabarov would be dining at
the Café Royal, later that day. I felt that I could hardly take a high
moral standpoint when I had every intention of abusing his
hospitality by default, for whether I used the front door or the side,
there would seem a certain shiftiness in my behaviour.

However, in full possession of my faculties now and no longer
suffering from the vestigial effects of close proximity to Zabarov,
this time I found the house a little odder than I had the night
before. The downstairs room I now discovered, far from reassuring, possessed a too conspicuous blandness, so innocuous as to be
without character. The French-speaking butler – who possessed
such a one through choice! However had I supposed him to
personify respectability? I noticed now his sallow cheeks, dark with
the shadow of an irregular shave, his slight moustache, his hair a
touch too long, and in his narrow eyes a guarded look that did not
hold one's gaze. To be sure, he wore the suitable and sober
accoutrements of his discreet profession, and withdrew when he
had let me in. I thought I heard him moving about in an upstairs
room next to Orlando's; but I saw nothing more of him.

Not that he was uppermost in my thoughts at that time, for in the
presence of the lovely Orlando I thought almost entirely of him. I
could not believe my good fortune. Orlando was about as perfectly
made as a young man could be. Even without the glitter of his stage
make-up he had a certain otherworldliness which I found irresistible. I half expected some Elf King to reach out for him in a flash of
green fire and ask for him back. We spoke in whispers, as we made
love in his dim back bedroom. There was a tangible silence about
the little room. I could hardly believe that I was here in London,
behaving like this. The beauty of it was that Orlando seemed to love
the act for itself; he never asked for money. Could it really be so,

that this beautiful youth was like myself, no questions asked, the pleasure of what we did its own justification?

Upon Orlando's crumpled sheets we lay in warm confusion, our limbs entwined, our bodies moving till we both were satisfied. It was bliss to me to find a partner of such loveliness who seemed to find a similar joy in being close to me. "You cannot understand," I murmured, "what it means to me to be able to liberate my true desires at last."

"I think I can," he answered. "And I'm pleased to help."

Delightful, as I supposed, in every way.

"Tell me, Orlando," I said carefully, tracing my finger down the fine hairs on his neck. "If you had been hypnotised by Zabarov, would you know it?"

He chuckled noisily. "I should say so! Are you worried that I'm with you because I've been directed and not because I want to be? Not a chance! You mustn't think such things. I'm with you because you're very nice to be with. And because I always like to handle Quality – whether it's horseflesh or cloth or jewellery – or arses. And you can always tell Quality."

"Well, thank you – I think. But does Zabarov ever hypnotise you? That business on stage, for instance, when you ate a lemon?"

"Put it this way," said he confidentially, "I happen to love lemons."

"Do you mean that all that was a fraud?"

"I mustn't tell, eh?" said Orlando, his finger on the side of his nose. "You wouldn't want me to divulge state secrets! But," he relented, "I'll tell you that I am a difficult subject."

I contemplated this. "And Arthur Hughes? What about him?"

Orlando shrugged. "What of him? He isn't very interesting."

"But does Zabarov play with hypnotism there?"

"Well, I don't know," said Orlando, shifting on to his back and stretching. "Arthur Hughes is dull; he really is. He doesn't speak much and he has that silly way of talking."

"But it was you that introduced him to Charles, wasn't it, and suggested he went to Charles' place to meet a certain type of disreputable person – much like yourself, I suppose?" I added with affection: "For you are disreputable, are you not?"

"I suppose I am – and don't you enjoy it!" said Orlando comfortably. "But Arthur isn't. I found him a bit of a prude. The trouble with Arthur is that he doesn't know what he wants. He isn't happy at home because the only book they own is the Bible – in Welsh. And he isn't happy mixing with interesting people because he knows it's wrong and his mother wouldn't like it. It is a situation which makes him rather vulnerable. When Count Zabarov senses

144

that, he pounces."

"But for what? What possible use or interest can Arthur have for him? It isn't Lust, is it?" I asked uneasily. "Zabarov is not – so?"

"No, and nor is Arthur," answered Orlando bluntly.

With one blow thus Orlando quenched my hopes. Although I had not formulated all my aspirations I had dared to presume that one day maybe I might speak of my true feelings to Arthur, and in time perhaps . . .

"But are you sure?" I asked, the urgency in my voice no doubt betraying my close personal interest in the matter.

"Oh yes," Orlando said. "I tried it once with him. He was revolted. Well, I am not so ugly, am I? You'd think I had been Quasimodo."

So Arthur never could be mine? But what had I been expecting? Of course he could not. Orlando's words brought home to me the dismal truth. I could indeed make love to those of my own sex – but only if I bought the experience with sovereigns in secret, or if by chance I found a shameless minx like Orlando, a boy who liked to lie with lords for piquancy but who would give himself to whom he pleased upon a slight acquaintance.

Then if my future was to be with such as he I had best relish it and savour it. I knew that I was lucky to have found this finely sculptured Dionysus. I turned to him; I reached for him. His mischievous eyes glimmered.

"I'll tell you what," he said. "We'll go into another room. It will be more exciting."

"There is no need; to be with you excites me."

"No," he said, looking mysterious. "This is special – this is different."

Orlando flung back the sheets. "After all," he said, "this room is hardly worthy. I rarely tidy it. I should be most ashamed – I live like a pig; just look about us. No, we'll go elsewhere. Our bodies will function even more finely in a fairer setting."

I thought it odd that he did not mention servants. An establishment such as this must need a few domestics and one of these ought to be attending to Orlando's room. But I believed him when he promised us delights, and throwing on a robe I followed him.

There was no one about in the narrow corridor outside. I thought that Orlando would lead me to some darker unknown place, up a stair maybe, in some dim nook or cranny. But instead he walked – quite naked – back where we had passed at first, along the carpeted floor, the corridor still lit, our destination a large panelled door leading to a big room at the front of the house, so obviously Zabarov's bedroom that I stood still on the threshold, most unwilling to proceed.

"He keeps it locked," Orlando chuckled, bending to the keyhole. "But I've been picking locks since I was ten years old and this one's easy."

Distracted for a moment by his quivering nudity I watched him open the door.

"Come on!" Orlando beckoned me from inside the room, a demon with narcissus-coloured hair.

The curtains drawn, the room was first of all in darkness, but Orlando moved about lighting candles with a taper. I stared aghast at the sight now illumined.

A large bed faced us. Its coverlet was a huge tapestried pentagram, that five-fold symbol of occult practice; its headboard was a twisted wooden structure culminating in a figure of grotesque proportion, seemingly that devil which in popular mythology is represented as a goat with horns. The eyes were hollow and slanting, the nostrils flared, tendrils of beard hanging down below the grimace of the mouth. Two gnarled and knotted horns curved outward, and upon the brow a star was embedded, gleaming oddly in some kind of metal. Below the monster head were twined about innumerable carved serpents, their tongues out-thrust, and amongst these reptiles, strange little primeval faces in every aspect of ugliness. Even as I gazed, a light sprang up behind the hollow eyes, and this effect was fiendish, startling, for the pupils glimmered red, the star upon the brow gave off an eerie glow. I gasped; Orlando sniggered – it was he had caused the light, some hidden switch to hand.

I looked about the room. Its contrast with that bland innocuous chamber below appalled me. Each wall was covered with a painting. A mere brief glance sufficed to show the genre. One was a dancing skeleton, a scythe in hand, against a background of fire; another showed a king of sinister aspect with fangs and claws and dragon's wings, with demons round about him, beaked and horned. Another was a scene as from some Gothic manuscript, a monstrous green god on a crimson throne, devouring naked men and women who sprawled about him in subservience and fear, propelled by loathsome lizards while graves gaped underfoot. Finally, a painting of some quality from the eighteenth century depicting some strange rite, where in a forest glade women, children, men disported themselves in obscene gyration before a seated figure with a goat's head mask, beneath a crimson sky.

Against one wall there was a low table covered with purple velvet fringed with gold. A candlestick stood at each end; between them was a silver chalice and a Christian crucifix. Further, there was an ancient chest of drawers, with candlesticks upon it, and a great

146

leather book between, closed with a golden clasp.

"You should not have brought me here," I murmured.

"Are you afraid?" mocked Orlando, approaching me.

"No," I said uneasily.

"It's more exciting to make love in forbidden places," said Orlando. And he set about to rouse me. Such was his power that I am ashamed to related that he succeeded. He put his arms about my neck and pressed his naked body against mine. His kissed me slowly, lingeringly and his fingers played about my neck and shoulders, while his tongue wound round my own. My cock hardened. I clasped him to me. He moved the edges of my robe aside and kissed my chest. He glided sinuously down upon his knees before me, taking in his mouth my rampant prick. I shivered as I clutched him to my waist. He looked up at me with a provocative smile.

"Shall I go on?"

"Yes! Do it!"

He bent his head, and into his hot mouth I seemed to plunge awash in rippling pools of pleasure that made me sigh with ecstasy. How voluptuously sweet that coming was! I kneeled down beside Orlando, hugging him in gratitude. My state of bliss had blinded me to where I was, and now beyond Orlando's soft cheek and dazzling hair I saw the demons gather.

Orlando watched me closely. "Ah, you mustn't mind that," he said. "What are they but images? Look. You mustn't be afraid."

He jumped on to the bed and spread his limbs wide, lying on his back inside the pentagram, a vision of Pagan perfection that caused me awe. I moved towards him.

"Love me then," he invited. "Here, inside the symbol."

I laughed in embarrassment. "I could not. Not on Zabarov's bed."

Orlando leaned up on his elbow. "Curious . . ." he told me in amusement. "You do not fear the pentagram. What you fear is social impropriety!"

"Amongst the company I keep," I answered wryly, "it is not the done thing to make love to a naked youth upon the bed of a stranger in that stranger's house, whoever he may be, and particularly if his return is likely to be imminent – and it is, Orlando, is it not? I cannot help but feel that you were mischievously hoping that he would return while we were lost in lust's embraces?"

Orlando giggled. "Maybe," he replied. "You wish to leave then? Enjoy the paintings . . . I will go and fetch your clothes."

He sped away, like Ariel.

I moved about the room. Its atmosphere was strange, seductive. What occurred here in the secrecy of night? Did Zabarov truly worship Satan, as he had implied? Was he in touch with others of like mind? Did he invoke spirits at that little altar? More than ever now I felt his influence a dangerous one for Arthur. How I longed to prise that boy from his power!

Standing beside the chest of drawers I opened the heavy leather book. I thought to find a book of spells, a grand grimoire such as a magus of old might once have used up in some castle turret – and was not Zabarov reputed to be a Balkan count with lands in Europe? Maybe his ancestors had handed down their necromantic skills.

To my surprise the book was sharply of this century, and packed with cuttings from contemporary and recent newspapers. Most were in French. They had been chosen for their reference to incidents in England and in France involving what had come to be known as "revolutionary outrages", an incident where an incendiary device had been used in a public place by anarchists to make some grievance known. There was a large section concerning the Taverne du Bagne on the Boulevard de Clichy. "Here, the waiters wear gaol garb. Here the anarchists meet, and here in Montmartre are their printing presses. Beneath portraits of dead heroes the anarchists and their women sing their revolutionary songs and remember the days of the Commune."

Indeed, those days were enshrined in this book. "Horror in Montmartre! Government troops rush in . . . the streets of La Butte run red with blood . . . the cemetery of Père-Lachaise sees fighting amongst the graves . . . the martyrs' bodies slung into a single ditch . . . those communards who managed to escape are later caught in the Montmartre dance halls . . ." All this some ten years back, yet all these cuttings carefully kept, and others since: "December 1893 – Outrage at the Palais Bourbon – bomb thrown from public gallery causes devastation – Vaillant arrested. At his trial declares his intention was to promote justice and freedom. At the guillotine unrepentant – cries: Death to bourgeois society . . . February 1894 – Bomb in Café Terminus kills one, injures many more. Emile Henry guillotined May 21st, unregretting of his crime . . . A mass trial of at least thirty anarchists, most of them acquitted . . ." And there were photographs, with the names in handwriting scrawled beneath, some dozen of them, sullen sad-faced men, and women also, here and there a line drawn through the face. I could not help but recognise amongst them he who passed for Zabarov's butler. "Paul Picard," it said, "sought by the French police . . ."

There were extracts from, presumably, those same newspapers printed in some backstreet in Montmartre and circulated to the faithful. Their titles were extreme, subversive – "The Necessity for Violence", "Why Terror?", "The Effectiveness of Carrying the

Campaign to England." I flicked through page after page of similar accounts – incidents which I myself recalled occurring in London throughout the eighties, small explosions believed to be in connection with the Irish Question – and grim obituaries of youths who had caused their own destruction when a bomb had gone off prematurely and taken the perpetrator with it. There were long harangues about the moral dilemmas, gentler voices speaking for less use of violence, stern replies that violence was imperative. And one particularly horrific discussion upon how far it was permissible to use the innocent in the furtherance of the cause – must we each and every one be dedicated idealists or might one justify involving those that did not know what they were about? Such people were a godsend, for their innocence protected them; they could sit in a crowded omnibus carrying a lethal package – leave a parcel on a railway station unsuspected, and if questioned by the police could give nothing away, for they knew nothing and had merely thought to oblige a friend. The use of the innocent was a development yet to be exploited . . .

Thoughtfully I closed the book. I remembered when Charles had first mentioned Zabarov he had told me that he lived in Goodge Street "where everyone's an anarchist, or plotting." The information which I now had gleaned seemed far more sinister to me than Zabarov's devotion to the Devil. When Orlando returned, dressed, and with my clothes over his arm I asked him: "Have you read that book?"

"I've looked at it," he shrugged. "But it's in French. French history."

"Do you ever talk with that French butler?"

"He doesn't speak English, except little phrases. I'll tell you what, though, he has some very odd friends."

"In what way?"

"I don't know," said Orlando vaguely. "Very down at heel."

"Do they meet here?"

"Yes, but I don't know much about it. Those evenings are my nights for visiting the Gaiety or the Alhambra, and as Zabarov pays for me I don't complain."

I finished dressing; Orlando helped. We moved out of that disquieting room and left it locked behind us.

As I walked down the stairs the front door opened and Zabarov entered. Framed as he was, the street light behind him, and clad in a dark swirling cloak, his walking cane with its dragon head for all the world like a magician's wand, he seemed the personification of all that was disturbing and malign.

"Lord Algernon," he said, exaggeratedly polite. "This is indeed

an honour. You have been calling on Orlando . . . how charming . . .
must you leave?"

"Zabarov, I must speak with you," I said, unable to let pass this
opportunity to confront the man and my own uneasiness besides.

"Must?" he raised his eyebrows quizzically. "The hour is late. And
you are surely tired after your evening's work!"

Orlando gleamed behind me, sniggering. I winced.

Zabarov laughed. "Perhaps you would care to step into my
parlour where we may share the urgent converse you require in
greater comfort."

With every appearance of good humour he ushered me into the
room, turned on the lights and dismissed Orlando to the upper
regions. "I think you need your beauty sleep, my pretty one."

"Oh let me stay," Orlando wheedled.

"Certainly not – you will cause Lord Algernon embarrassment. Is
that not so, my lord? And now," he smiled, closing the door upon
the petulant youth. "Sit down and be at ease. Upon what matter did
you wish to speak to me?"

Difficult indeed was that moment for me. What if I were totally
wrong in my suspicions, suffering from a morbid dose of imagination, an overactive fancy born of my own disturbed state of mind?
How suddenly benign the wretched fellow looked, a mild-eyed
visitor to our shores with a harmless interest in the supernatural –
and a scrapbook of French anarchists wanted by the police hidden
in his bedroom. I decided I would take the risk. I must voice my
suspicions. For Arthur's sake I must dare all. I plunged in then
without preamble.

"Tell me, Zabarov, have you bound Arthur Hughes to you by
occult practices?"

"Can one man have such power?" he answered mockingly. "You
surely do not believe that? Why, that would make me terrible
indeed!"

Mild and harmless? My suspicions were entirely appropriate. The
man's eyes gleamed, becoming vibrantly alive with the flagrant
pleasure of a challenge.

"I do believe it – and if you have plans for Arthur you must know
that I intend to see they come to nothing."

"And what do you propose to do?" he sneered.

I did not answer. He found my silence amusing and he relished
his advantage. "Since you ask," he smiled, "your supposition is
correct. Arthur is my subject and at my suggestion he will perform
whatever I require. I shall deny it hereafter; but at this moment,
between ourselves, it pleases me to boast of it."

"You are an evil man!" I said. "What use can Arthur be to you?"

I knew as soon as I had asked it. The innocent who might be used for the furtherance of the cause. The ghastliness of Arthur's predicament – and my own, for more than ever now I knew that I must save him – rendered me speechless.

"*That* I do not choose to reveal," Zabarov answered. "It would be something quite beyond your comprehension. But you interest me, Lord Algernon. I thought at first that you were typical of your kind – an empty-headed landowner practising the ideals of his epoch. But it is not so. Behind your eyes I see turbulence and confusion, that same primordial chaos I talked about before. I tell you, you must find your path, and quickly, or that chaos will destroy you. The human mind is not capable of dwelling in perpetual confusion; in that situation it disintegrates, and others must pick up the pieces. I tell you this for your own good."

"My own good . . ." I gasped. "What can you know of that? Or of any good?"

"Ha! You think that I am evil!" said Zabarov, with a laugh worthy of an incandescent genie, lacking only the pall of luminous green smoke.

"I do! And I shall make it my intention to prise Arthur from your clutches."

This purpose gleamed before me like a Holy Grail. No knight of old more resolute than I, no combatant more fervent.

"Perhaps before you begin the undertaking," said Zabarov in a derisory tone, "you might examine the disinterested purity of your motives, my Sir Galahad. Is Arthur to exchange one less than noble master for another of an equally dubious nature? It is very well for you to find amusement with Orlando. That boy came into the world debauched. Orlando is a natural mischief-maker: I admire him for it. But Arthur . . . think carefully, Lord Algernon, what you can offer him. I understand your secret hopes, but if you were to be successful the very best that you could give the boy would be a life of crime. Perversion is against the law. Some call it insanity, and some a horror worse than murder. The boy as yet has no direction that way. Would you corrupt him? Would you dare to do that to an innocent? How would your conscience sleep?"

"You are quite wrong!" I told him passionately. "My motivation of necessity is honorable. I have reason to suppose that Arthur would not welcome my advances. That may distress and sadden me, but personal considerations have no bearing on the only course that I must take. I know that you are bad for Arthur and he must break free."

"He cannot do that unless I give him permission," said Zabarov. "That I will not do. The boy is mine, and so he shall remain."

"I think not," I declared, consumed with rising anger. Now I was eager to be quit of this man's presence, which suddenly seemed to exude a tainted pall of shadow. I got to my feet and moved quickly to the door. He followed. In the vestibule I paused. He opened the front door for me, stood by to let me pass and bowed ironically as he did so. I hesitated in the doorway, but there was nothing I could say that did not reek of melodrama. I will return? We shall meet again ere long? Look to it! All were appropriate, but the wet and solid pavements of Fitzroy Street that waited outside had that undeniable ring of actuality that quashed the histrionic. I merely strode away.

As the cold air wound about my inflamed senses I thought how odd it was that Zabarov had chosen Galahad to fling in my face. When I was twenty-one and posed for Charles in all the pride and gilt of youth it was as Galahad that I had made my mark. I wondered wrily whether the recollection had inspired me and whether such flagrant posing had gone to my head.

CHAPTER THIRTEEN

A KNIGHT errant I might imagine myself to be, but alone and palely loitering I was not.

The hour was not as late as I had expected. I took a cab down to Pall Mall where I believed that I would find the person that I had in mind, a fellow member of my club, a certain high-ranking officer in our most diligent police force, and there indeed did I discover him. He was dozing in the card room quite oblivious to jest and guffaw from the lively games in progress at the tables. Over a glass of port we sat and conversed, our business soon concluded.

I paused to let my household know that I intended sleeping at the club, and chatted to Lord Avonbury for a moment. The mellow and unruffled atmosphere of the place produced a calming, steadying effect. As I descended the wide staircase, between the sculptured pillars at the base into the marble-floored and well lit vestibule, I was much heartened, for I felt the weight of the establishment behind me. And after all, what use were privilege and class if they could not provide support and succour in one's hour of need?

The doorman called a cab for me and I set off for Holborn. It was late now and I feared that Arthur and his mother might be already abed; but when I reached their house I saw the parlour light and leaving the cab to wait, I knocked and waited. It was Arthur's mother who opened the door, looking surprised, as well she might. A sudden uneasiness possessed me as I asked for Arthur.

"No, Lord Algernon, I cannot help you," she replied. "He is not here. A foreign gentleman came for him, a gentleman who has been here before."

I hoped my face did not show the disquiet I felt. I thanked her and apologised for having had occasion to disturb her, assured her that my business was not urgent, and I hurried to the hansom, my obliging driver happy to set off at speed in the direction of Fitzroy Street. A socially acceptable hour it was no longer, but that had no relevance between Zabarov and myself. The streets flashed past. Soon we had crossed Tottenham Court Road and entered Charlotte Street. The hansom stopped at my direction. I told my driver to wait; I paid him well and knocked upon Zabarov's door.

It was the Count himself who opened to me. He was wearing an exotic robe, the kind one saw on stage, a brilliant shimmering green. His white bushy hair jutted up about the broad brow and his cheeks were gaunt and hollow. With that disconcerting gaze he eyed me speculatively. "Lord Algernon," he said, "I knew it would be you."

"Have you Arthur in your house?" I said.

"I have. You are too late."

"I have a proposition," I replied.

"Then come inside. I bear you no particular grudge, and will be interested in whatever you have to say. Who knows – we might find attributes in common and discuss together aspects of Gnostic philosophy. Stranger things have happened."

He was affable, composed. He ushered me within. We entered that bland parlour and sat down. A fire burned in the hearth; the curtains were drawn. The firelight flickered upon gilt frame, polished wood. The mirror above the mantelpiece glinted in that glow. I tensed, aware that glass had some mysterious effect, and swiftly changed the angle of my chair so that the glass did not reflect in my direction.

Zabarov noticed, laughed. "How you do fear me," he observed.

"You play by different rules," I murmured.

"Who makes the rules?" he shrugged.

"There are certain things one does not do. Between civilised people this is understood."

"Ah, now I am uncivilised as well as evil!" he observed, with an amusement that had something of a brittle edge.

"Where is Arthur now?" I asked.

"Upstairs. With Orlando. Like two dear children in their nursery."

It was true that I feared him. For even as he spoke I noticed that his fingers lightly moved a paperweight upon a little side table that lay between us. The paperweight was like a great glass pebble. It lay at the apex of the diagonal line from my face to his. I knew that he had at least once before affected my judgement somehow by the use of glass. I could well believe him capable of transferring dark vibrations through that heavy ornamental object, that third eye. I laid my hand across it, covering it.

"The reason I have come . . ." I said. I hesitated. I felt that I had behaved shabbily by entering his room and prying into his possessions. I wished that I had acquired my information some other way. "As you know, I wish you to relinquish your hold upon Arthur. I am aware that you have certain powers and I understand that while this gift may be of benefit in certain instances, in others it is harmful.

154

You tell me that you intend to use Arthur for some purpose of your own. I believe it has to do with anarchy, with the French political situation, and the applications of its lessons on the streets of England. I know that your butler is a man sought by the French police. I suspect that London anarchists meet here. I do not know, nor do I wish to, any details of your situation. I have mentioned my suspicions to a member of the police force and your house will now be under surveillance. The matter is not official and the man is a personal acquaintance. No other action will be taken than to watch your house. Unless you give me Arthur it is likely that investigation may proceed. There may be that within your house which you would prefer to remain undiscovered. You will remain merely an observed man under mild suspicion, but if you do not act as I require, a search could well ensue."

"You have been in the cellars," said Zabarov in a cold expressionless voice. "You have been busy in my absences."

I blinked. So there was more? More than the book of newspaper cuttings, which I had found incriminating enough.

"There is no need for you to fear beyond what I have told you," I remarked. "If you lead a blameless life henceforth, no action will be taken."

"Spare me pious advice," said Zabarov unpleasantly. "Well; this is a new development. I was not aware that you had been prowling round my house. I thought you came here only to fornicate with Orlando."

"That also," I said, emboldened as I saw the chastening effects my words had had upon him.

"Lord Algernon, I thought better of you," said he, looking upwards at me from beneath his heavy brows. "I saw us as adversaries. You liked to think that since I represented evil and you were my foe, you represented goodness. Of course we both know nothing is that simple. However, it amused. You challenged me. Sir Galahad and the Black Knight. I was intrigued. It pleased me, it savoured of romance. What, I wondered fascinated, could you do, you who had at your disposal merely your disinterested love for Arthur Hughes? I knew that I would win, of course, because Arthur is already in my power and thus allies himself with me. But I had thought there would be combat in some sphere of mutual agreement. I admired your desperate bravery and briefly thought that you would be a worthy opponent. I would have enjoyed defeating you. When I had done so, and when I had satisfied myself that you admitted failure, my vanity appeased, I may indeed have given you what you required. A gift, out of magnanimity. For I can be munificent. It is the prerogative of he who has the power. But you

155

. . . what did you do? You went to the police."

I understood his meaning very well and flinched before the contempt in his harangue. But for the most part I was unrepentant for I knew that I had chosen the most successful weapon of all, the intrusion of the ordinary and the real into a situation that was elusive and bizarre.

"The law!" he spat. "What is the law to you and I? Are we not spirits of a higher plane who have our being in the sphere of concepts, timelessness? The law represents bourgeois morality, the outward expression of the fears of the mediocre. What can it ever know of artists and of lovers?"

"Nevertheless," I ventured. "We must live by it, or anarchy ensues."

"You think that would be worse than what we have?" he cried in scorn. "Are you at one with our society? It stumbles towards the last years of the century, a clumsy blind and stupid organism and each wretched person that it drags along with it a microcosm of itself. The Church is helpless and the swarming masses swelling like a fetid sea. And you fear anarchy? A clean sweep. A new world. Upon the bones and ashes of the old."

"While I live within the old," I murmured, "I shall do my best to seek my own salvation there."

"No doubt," Zabarov said. "No doubt. What are you after all but an aristocrat with the usual methods at his disposal? If only I could believe that England would ever go the way of France, and slaughter you all."

The acrimony of his tone suggested to me that he was not now so confident of the outcome of our conflict.

"Will you release your hold on Arthur?" I reminded him.

"Arthur?" he said scornfully. "He is nothing. Yes, I will give him to you. It was a cunning step, your lordship, to seek out your policeman. I wondered why you did not rush immediately to Arthur. You passed the intervening moment wisely."

I hid my elation, answering merely: "I assure you, I did no more than express to him the vaguest hints. I told him nothing about what the house contains. Just go about your business, entertain upon the stage; no further action will be taken."

"If, as you say, I lead a blameless life henceforth," he sneered. "But what if foreign strangers visit me, or the known anarchists the police already have their fingers on – or if unaccountable packages arrive at my door? As you will see, I shall have to change some of my ways."

"That would be no bad thing," I snapped. "The civilised world has no place for your kind and you know it. As a foreigner you are welcome under our laws but not if you abuse the freedoms which they give you."

"And you?" he asked. "Are you so free?"

"Let us go to Arthur," I said tersely.

Zabarov stood up. I did so too, but warily, and kept my eyes clear of the mirror.

"I will give you Arthur," he said slowly, "for he is no great loss to me. It is perfectly true that I want no bumbling minions of the law within my house. They would not understand," he smiled crookedly, "my rather unusual religion. People are so nervous when Satan is mentioned. In our little duel, Lord Algernon, I had assumed your choice of weapon would be delicate and light, composed of skill and artistry. Instead you chose a cumbersome club. But I congratulate you on its effectiveness. I have only this to say. Our duel is not over. *Remember* this. And when I strike, I shall use the same weapon as you did."

I put his wild words down to bitterness. I waited.

"Yes, yes," he said wearily. "You await your prize. Let us go upstairs and seek it out."

As I followed him I thought he looked hunched and old, a hermit of the forest, no magician. He plodded upstairs slowly. When we reached the landing Orlando stood there, and behind him Arthur. Orlando gleamed, a predatory elf. He always looked as if he had swung down from a trapeze from somewhere in the wings. Beside him Arthur waited and my heart warmed.

Not that I received any reaction from him. He had a look of someone who did not know what he was doing here – which was certainly the case.

Zabarov made a sign that he should follow, as we made our way towards his bedroom door.

"Not you, Orlando," he said brusquely. "Later."

And so it was Arthur and I only who accompanied Zabarov into the room of demons. I made a point of looking about me in surprise, unwilling to admit that I had been here before. But now to my genuine surprise, and alarm also, we passed into a further chamber of whose existence I had hitherto been unaware. A panel in the wall creaked open at Zabarov's touch, revealing a small ante-room. Zabarov held the door open for Arthur and myself. When he closed it after us, the three of us inside the room, all presence of the outer world was at a blow extinguished.

The room was barely ten feet square in all dimensions. It contained a low seat upon the floor, much like a leather cushion with a chair's back. Every wall – the ceiling also – was made of glass. We were hemmed in by mirrors. Neither were they simple reflections, but so formed as to create a thousand images of ourselves receding further and further back, and every time we moved, the myriad other selves, disjointed and segmented, shifted also. There were no windows and the light came from no visible source – a steady glow from somewhere at the ceiling's edge, that hidden light that one associates with stage effects, unseen and startlingly effective. The closing of the door seemed eminently symbolic, as if a final step had been taken, and all retreat cut off. How could we breathe in here? We were enclosed in this small space of dread. There was no reference to any point of reality, no indication that an outer world existed. I was surrounded by glass, I who had been unsettled by a paperweight, and a ghastly panic rose within me. I was alone in a cell of mirrors with one who worked through glass, who surely hated me, who had the power to toy with others' minds; I was suffused with terror.

"It is true that you are in my power," Zabarov told me pleasantly, observing me with clinical detachment. "But did you not believe me when I said that I could be munificent?"

A fine sweat covered me; I could not answer, and my palms against the glass were moist upon its cold surface. Myself stared back at me wherever I looked, pale and vulnerable, curiously young. These quivering images merged with those of Arthur and Zabarov – I swear that, genie-like, the latter's images were monstrous and immense.

"Sit down, Arthur," said Zabarov, and Arthur sat down on the seat. Zabarov folded himself opposite upon the floor, much like an Oriental mystic, cross-legged and serene, facing Arthur, a small space between them.

"I would recommend you also sit, Lord Algernon," Zabarov said. "I have assumed you wish to witness Arthur's restoration, but I do not want the distraction of your trepidation."

I sat down in a corner trying to compose myself. And now, by reaching out his hand, Zabarov dimmed the light. We were almost in darkness except for two pinpoints of a reddish glow which hovered behind Zabarov's shoulder and at which Arthur's gaze woud be directed. Suddenly I feared for him.

"You will promise me he will come to no harm . . ."

"I promise you," Zabarov answered. He glanced at me reprovingly. "Do not, whatever you do, come between Arthur and myself as I speak to him."

I had pulled myself together now, concern for Arthur a strong antidote to personal mortification. I watched spellbound as Zabarov began.

"I want you to listen carefully to what I say to you, Arthur; I want

158

you to listen carefully to what I say. Your eyes are closed, your eyes are closed, you are comfortable, thinking of nothing, nothing but what I say, your arms and legs feel heavy, you feel sleepy now, you want to sleep . . . you are going backward into the darkness, backward into the darkness, you are listening only to my voice, only my voice, thinking of nothing . . . very drowsy, drowsy, breathing deeply, you are going into a sleep, a deep comfortable sleep . . . now as I count from one to ten your sleep will become deeper, much deeper . . . One – deeper and deeper – two – still deeper – three . . ."

I dared not move a muscle. Arthur was asleep, Zabarov murmuring over him in that strange compelling monotone. "You have been close to me, Arthur," he told him. "You were unhappy and confused when first I found you. I have helped you. I have told you that you need my guidance and I have told you that you need my protection. But now you are strong. You are strong, Arthur, and you do not need my guidance. You are strong and you do not need the protection that I once offered you. You will leave me for you no longer need me. You will not return to me for guidance. I have been your friend, but now you will find other friends. I gave you direction, but now you will find your own direction. You are strong. Now tell me that you have understood."

The voice that was both Arthur's and not Arthur's answered and told Zabarov all that he required to hear.

"Sleep now," said Zabarov. Then he inclined towards me slightly. "At this moment I could give him alternative instruction. You realise this, do you not? Do you wish that I should direct him towards you, to see yourself as his protector? *Or as his lover?*"

"No," I gulped, aghast. "Tell him nothing. God! If I thought that he ever came to me because you told him to!"

Expressionlessly Zabarov turned back to Arthur.

"Arthur, listen to me now. In a moment I will awaken you. When you awaken you will feel refreshed and wide awake. You are now beginning to awaken, your sleep is becoming lighter, much lighter . . . as I count backwards from ten to one your sleep will grow lighter and lighter, and at the count of ten you will be awake . . . ten – nine – eight – your sleep is getting lighter – you are starting to awaken – seven – six – five – you are starting to awaken – four – three – two – you are almost awake now, wide awake . . . One . . . you are now ready to awaken, you are wide awake."

Indeed it was so. Arthur looked quite fresh and cheerful. It was I who emerged from that strange room exhausted, pale and drained. We stood upon the landing. It seemed to me that Zabarov had kept his part of the bargain honourably and I could not but suppose that

159

Arthur was restored and free from that dark influence. A wonderful relief suffused me. I saw Zabarov as a gracious benefactor. He had had potential for great wrongdoing; he had not used it, and we were in his debt. I wrung his hand in a warm clasp.

"Thank you!" I said inarticulately. "Thank you."

He looked at me gravely, and with much, I thought, of pity.

"It was not a gift, Lord Algernon," he answered soberly. It sounded like a warning; but I did not understand his meaning. He remained standing by the door to his room. Orlando, shadow-like, slipped by his side to join him. But Arthur and I hurried away. Somehow we were down the stairs and in the vestibule, we had regained our hats and coats, and we were outside in the street. My faithful hansom waited, and we climbed inside.

"Where to, sir?" The cab driver, astonishingly alert, was poised for flight and certainly my directions heretofore had a ring of urgency, to which he had responded with efficiency and goodwill. I disappointed him.

"Drive anywhere," I told him. "Drive about. I will let you know in a moment."

We set off, the horses' hooves an echo on the dark night streets.

"Arthur – dear Arthur –" I murmured, turning to my companion in a state of some emotion. "Are you well? How do you feel?"

"I feel very well," he answered me. He peered out through the glass. "Is it the middle of the night?"

"It is past midnight," I answered.

"I am not exactly sure why we are here," he said. "I hope that I do not seem stupid to you. I am under an obligation to you, am I not? I understand that I should not have been at Count Zabarov's house. I am not sure why I happened to be there at all."

"Would you like now to be taken home?" I asked him. I hoped he would say no, but I was determined not to influence him, believing that if sleep was a curative for all transitory ills the boy had best be in his bed.

"Oh no, I shan't go home," he answered firmly. "My mother does not expect me back tonight, and in that house all comings and goings are heard and seen by all. It would cause me more problems to go home at this hour than to walk the streets and sleep on the Embankment."

"You certainly shall not do that!" I assured him. But where should we go? I could not take him home, nor to the club. We would have to spend the night in the rooms of an hotel. Delight and alarm were about equal within me, as this fact became obvious to me. A night in close proximity to Arthur! The heady matter of a heavenly dream . . . And yet – hotel rooms! That was what Oscar Wilde did.

We all knew it. Willoughby said he had been thrown out of the Savoy, and a boy with him. And we had no luggage – no nightshirts – how would it seem?

"I thought we might go to a hotel," I stated carelessly.

"But I have no money," Arthur protested.

"Don't be absurd, dear boy," I answered, annoyed with myself for sounding like Charles.

"I don't want to put you to trouble and expense."

"We shall not go to the ostentatious kind, but one where we shall both feel comfortable. We shall take a room each, and we shall sleep, for we have both endured a stressful evening."

"Well, if you think that's best," said Arthur gravely. "I would be lying if I said I would prefer to walk the streets. You are very kind, Lord Algernon. I hope I did not seem abusive and ungrateful, before."

"No, you didn't, and it is a pleasure to me to take care of you."

The embarrassing warmth I could not keep out of my voice betrayed me once again, and I judged it best to take refuge in silence while my emotions played so near the surface.

Although I had stipulated that we would not use one of the more resplendent hotels I did not know the names of any of inferior quality, and to be frank I had no intention of being with Arthur in circumstances of deprivation. I gave a street off Grosvenor Square, not far away, as our proposed address, where I believed I knew of a place that would answer to our requirements, and thus, a short time later, we found ourselves upon the steps of a pleasant hotel where we took a suite of rooms. In the small sitting room we ate a meal, conversing upon generalities while an obliging waiter attended to us with discreet amiability. I noticed with approval and relief that Arthur's experiences had in no way diminished his appetite. I also found that I was hungry. After we had eaten we retired to bed. Our rooms were separate, but they had adjoining doors.

The sheets were crisp and cold, and as I lay there, naked, my thoughts were of Arthur in his bed in the next room. Not that I could think clearly. I felt exhausted from the strain of my evening's exertions, but too much so to drift into easy slumber. What could the future hold? What now would Arthur be to me? I passionately hoped that we would become close. Surely I had not saved him from Zabarov merely to cast him back into the anonymity of London life, to read his Bible with his mother, and carve field mice in a little shop? Yet if I hoped for more, what did that make me? – an opportunist, using wealth and influence for my own ends.

Here we lay, separated by a door, replete and private, our secret selves till morning – which was not now so far off. I caught myself again recalling Oscar Wilde. Did he book adjoining rooms when he brought boys to the Savoy? Had he the nerve to use one bed and assume the use of *honi soit qui mal y pense* when waiters brought in the breakfast tray? What was the form? How awkward and naive I was in the world of devious living – how puzzling and fatiguing did a situation grow when one behaved outside society's well regulated dictates . . .

I thought that strain and wishing had so worked upon my faculties that I was dreaming when the door came quietly open and Arthur entered my room.

"Lord Algernon," he whispered. "Sir!"

"Yes, Arthur?" I gulped, wide awake.

"Can I come in?"

"Of course you may," I encouraged warmly.

"And into your bed?" he added, as if doubting the completeness of my generosity. "I noticed it was wide enough for two."

"Yes, it certainly is," I said, shifting my position and hurriedly pulling aside the sheets and blankets before he changed his mind.

"Thank you." A warm boy in his shirt climbed into bed beside me. "I was lonely," he admitted, snuggling down against me. I put my arm around him, and with my other hand I covered up my cock which, as I knew it would, had stiffened like a ramrod. I told myself: be calm, engrave this moment on your senses, for it may never occur again. Oh, what a moment, though! His face against my shoulder, his thick lush hair about my face, strands of that hair between my lips, his whole warm body in the crook of my arm, my fingers lying lightly on the cloth of his shirt. I listened to his breathing; I felt half sick with the intensity of my pent-up emotion.

"I feel such a fool," he blurted out. "I just feel such a fool!"

"No need . . . ." I murmured, vaguely reassuring.

"Yes!" he said urgently, his warm breath on my skin. "You must think me an idiot. You'd better tell me everything that happened tonight. I've been piecing it together and some bits are missing; but I know I've been an awful fool."

I very carefully explained all that had occurred, as far as I could understand it all myself, and we agreed that Zabarov had been arrogant and high-handed and that Arthur was well rid of him and we had been most fortunate to acquire the means to see him off.

"Oh!" said Arthur. "If you had not come along! If Mr Charles had not expressed a fear for me and if you had not rescued me! I am forever in your debt, and I know the deepest gratitude for your great kindness."

I winced. I longed to blurt out that I loved him – for I knew that that was so. I dared not, for it would be to take advantage of his

162

troubled sensibility. But to be accused of kindliness with all sincerity was greatly disturbing to me; I felt guilt-ridden, almost despicable.

"Lie still," I said. "You need to sleep. It's almost morning, I'll look after you."

He nestled close against me, like a child. Immensely moved, I stroked his hair. With Arthur in my arms I lay and watched the night fade, and the soft approach of daylight. I was rewarded in the morning by the knowledge that there was a closeness now between us, understood by both.

In our separate rooms we dressed; then breakfasted in the sitting room.

"What will you do?" I asked. "How do you feel?"

"I feel all right. I shall go home first, and then to work. All will go on much as usual." He laughed. "But I shan't go to the theatre!"

"We'll share a cab," I said. "I'll see you home, and then go home myself. But now that we have met," I added, "and grown to know each other better it would be a shame to let the friendship lapse. I will call upon you again, if I may?"

Arthur favoured me with a sideways smile. "That's curiously polite, after what has passed between us." Then he added quickly: "I mean that you have rescued me from being half stupid. I think that entitles you to call upon me, whenever you like."

"Well – do you wish it?" I demanded.

"Yes. Of course I do," he answered, equally aggressively.

That settled, we began to make our move, and set out from that pleasant haven to the street below.

Once more, we sat together in a hansom cab, now in an easterly direction, which perchance took us across Regent Street and down Great Marlborough Street. To my surprise the road was blocked with carriages and crowds and we were trapped in the ensuing muddle. A couple of hapless policemen were attempting to direct the traffic. The activity was centred about the entrance to the magistrate's court. Beyond the jostling throng, the angry drivers of the great four-wheelers and the irritable restive horses, I caught sight of a carriage and pair, containing Oscar Wilde and Bosie Douglas and Lord Alfred's brother, which was having difficulty getting near the pavement; and I recalled with some astonishment that this was the day of Lord Queensberry's adjourned hearing, and I had forgotten all about it.

"What is it?" Arthur asked, leaning across.

"That gentleman is Oscar Wilde – d'you see? The dramatist. He has accused Lord Queensberry of libel. The Marquis has to answer, and he may be brought to trial."

"Libel?" said Arthur, who was patently not conversant with the case.

I hesitated. "He called Oscar Wilde a sodomite."

"What's that?" said Arthur blankly.

"That's a man who takes other men to bed," I answered cautiously, then, recalling our shared night with its innocent sweetness, I added in some exasperation: "I mean he uses them as men should do with women. Did you really not know?" I wondered in surprise.

"I knew about *It*," said Arthur blushing. "But I didn't know it was called that."

I itched to know about his failed experience with Orlando. I hoped that he might blurt it out. He did not.

"So then," said Arthur with great interest, staring. "*Is* he a sodomite?"

I shrugged. "Who can prove a thing like that? You do not have court cases about the intimate details of what people do in bed, in private. He is not likely to admit it, and nor will anyone do so who was with him, for that would send them straight off to prison. All the same, it's most unpleasant," I said with distaste, observing how the people pushed and shoved to make their way inside. "The court is likely to be packed. How they do love a whiff of scandal . . ."

Unpleasant, yes; the whole affair left a very disagreeable taste and I was glad when we had forged a pathway through the seething street and put it well behind us. Unpleasant also, I reflected, how my path crossed Oscar Wilde's from time to time, and each time never leaving me with any other sensation than distinct unease.

Our cab took Arthur to his door and we shook hands. We agreed to meet again very soon.

"And thank you, Lord Algernon," he said to me with a glowing gaze. "With all my heart!"

"It was my pleasure," I replied, and smiled. I almost guessed he knew as much.

As I was driven homeward I felt in a great need of peace and stillness. I was content, but very tired. We turned into the square, and as we approached my own front door I saw with some surprise a cab was waiting there already, at the kerb. I emerged from mine, and as I stood upon the pavement my heart jumped with apprehension, for coming down the steps of my house was Dr Hollowell, our family physician, a serious bespectacled Scot, short of stature and grey-haired, and in general demeanour so very like one imagines a doctor that I wondered people did not stop him in the street to offer him their ailments for diagnosis.

The children! I thought, petrified, and ran to him.

"Lord Algernon!" he exclaimed, an odd expression on his face –

164

reproving, twinkling, mysterious, sympathetic – I could not place it.

"Who is it? What has happened?" I cried urgently.

"Prepare yourself." He gripped my arm. "A friend of yours has been brought to your home in a state of collapse, and even now lies there within, close to death's door."

"A friend? Who? *Here*?" I stuttered stupidly.

"Sebastian Charles. I warn you, Algy, that man has no more than a week of life, two weeks at most; you must be ready for the worst." He peered at me in some concern. "Who is he, Algy? Some old companion from a misspent youth? Your wife knew nothing of him. Yet – poor good woman – she took him in last night, ordered a bed made up, procured him food and care. I have to tell you, though, her ladyship was not best pleased by the event."

"I would assume as much," I muttered faintly.

"That is not all," said Dr Hollowell, and now I understood why he had had that twinkle I previously observed. "Your mother the marchioness returned from Scotland yesterday, as no doubt you know, and chose this morning to come calling. She has some thoughts upon the presence of the visitor. She feels that he should not have been admitted and has made her viewpoint clear. Her humanity I am sure is not in question, but it is a matter of morality: a *woman* of the meaner sort was sent for, to be with the dying man. This person makes no claim to be the fellow's wife. Her precise status is unclear. I did what I could do, Lord Algy, and I'll call again, but to be honest, I was glad to get away!"

"Yes – thank you," I said with a sinking heart.

"They will all be glad to see you returned, no doubt," the doctor told me comfortably.

"I do dare say," said I.

I would have given much to go off with him in his cab. Any grim and ghastly backstreet would have seemed more tempting than the situation that awaited me.

But I took a breath and went inside.

CHAPTER FOURTEEN

"AL-GER-NON!"

My mother, immense upon the staircase, her hand upon the balustrade, sounded so like Lady Bracknell in the majesty of her high-toned accusation that hysteria welled within me and I had to suppress a raging urge to burst out laughing.

"Yes mother?"

"I think your wife and I are owed some explanation."

Meredith scuttled forward to relieve me of my hat and coat, and just as swiftly scuttled away.

"Did you have a wonderful time in Scotland?" I enquired warmly, looking upward. What a superb ship's figurehead she would have made!

My mother, the Marchioness of Turleigh, and inappropriately christened Violet, had been a dominant influence throughout my formative years and looked very much as if she intended to continue to be so. Behind her, lurking upon the landing, Claudia, who in her own way could be almost as alarming, paled almost to insignificance, though I knew well enough this was a wished for illusion. Once my mother had gone home, Claudia would be fierce enough.

"Algy – who is this man?" my mother said in what the theatre calls *sotto voce*, a stage whisper that can be heard in the bar at the back of the stalls. "Who is this man who has thrust himself upon us in a condition of decrepitude and decay and brought with him a Female of the Vilest Kind to tend his illness at our expense and *says he is a friend of yours?*"

"He is a friend of mine, just as he says," said I, determining on a policy of limited honesty. "Unfortunately he has fallen upon hard times, and the dwelling wherein he is obliged to reside is insalubrious. If he thought to count upon my charity in his hour of need there is nothing else to be done but give him succour. To cast him back into the sordid quarters where I found him would be to hasten him to his grave. I am sure that any Christian soul would treat the man with kindness."

Such an appeal to piety softened the initial fervour of my mother's accusations. She said suspiciously: "I thought that I knew all your friends, Algy?"

"I daresay you do," I said carelessly. "And this one also, if you cast your mind back. Mr Charles was an acquaintance of Sir William Franklin and is an artist himself of no mean talent. You need feel no shame to find him beneath our roof."

As I passed my mother on the stairs and hoping I had made a case for Charles on humanitarian and artistic grounds, I encountered Claudia's frosty stare.

"Algy, how could you?" she murmured.

"How could I what?" said I uneasily.

"We will talk of it later," she answered in a low voice that I sensed promised me an uncomfortable hour to come.

"Where have you put him?" I said briskly, looking upward at the turning of the stairs.

"Up at the top of the house," answered Claudia, Wincing, she added: "Algy – he was so dirty – and there was this *woman* with him. They have adjoining rooms, since there is no pretence of wedlock. Well, Algy!" Her voice shook with hostility and indignation. "If I have not done right then you should have been here to direct matters yourself. It is all very well to sleep at the club whenever it suits you but life does go on, you know, at your home, and if you will have unsavoury friends coming here to die, then you should be here to make the arrangements."

"I'm terribly sorry," I said inadequately. "Let me go upstairs and see what is to do."

Beneath our roof, as I had declared to be a fitting place for any friend of mine, was precisely where I found that friend. The little attic, set into the eave-slope at the end of a small corridor, housed a wardrobe, with an old-fashioned iron tripod washstand with an enamel bowl and water jug. Polette sat by the bed and as I entered the room I recognised that she was reading aloud one of the poems of Baudelaire from *Les Fleurs du Mal*, a collection of images and conceits surely never before experienced by these particular walls.

"Oh! Monsieur Algie!" she declared with an expansive gesture of the hands, the pages of the book flapping like an ungainly bird's wing. "What must you think? I am so ashamed. But there was no other course for us – it was too late – what could I do?"

"Calm yourself, madame," I murmured reassuringly. "Stay seated." I was struck by the incongruity of the scene before me. Charles lay shockingly pale and wasted, looking more emaciated and cadaverous now that he was cleaned and tidied into bed than ever he had prowling his dreary abode. The wallpaper was a mass of

167

regimented orange tulips, chosen, I believe, to cheer potential housemaids on waking. Polette also became more personally emphasised, clear of her previous surroundings. She was now wearing a plain dress of grey and black striped serge, which I later learnt had been given to her by Emily, with whom she struck up a friendship. Above the dress her wild unruly hair seemed all the more luxuriant, her eyes the darker and more intense, her lips now taking on a vibrant beauty in their sensuous fullness. I understood at once my mother's apprehension. But that this scenario had been prompted by calamity now took precedence over all other thoughts. Upon the bedside cupboard was set a small tray with a jumble of labelled bottles left by Dr Hollowell, and already the curious odour of the sick room lay upon the place. I knelt down by the bed.

"Charles!" I said. "What happened?"

"Do forgive me," said Charles weakly and unconvincingly. "I do hope that I have not put you and your wife to inconvenience. What a charming woman she is, by the way – so gentle and affable. It was delightful to meet her at last."

"She is neither gentle nor affable, and she is very vexed with you," I said, severe to hide the pain I felt to see him brought to this extremity.

"Yes, I know," he answered petulantly. "But since, as we both know, I am not long for this world, I was smitten with a fancy not to die in squalor. And so when I was taken ill . . ."

"He collapsed in the Burlington Arcade," Polette explained.

"How tasteful!" I murmured.

"A gentleman," added Polette, "gave him the money for a cab."

"What were you doing in the Burlington Arcade?"

"Picking up a boy." At the flicker in my expression Charles said irritably: "For his head, dear boy, not for his arse. I wanted him for a thoughtful shepherd. Not everyone has your proclivities, Algy."

"My God – don't ever mention that here!" I blanched, looking round at the listening tulips. I turned to Polette. "Not a word must ever be spoken here of what you know about me from elsewhere. You will see to it that he's discreet?"

"What do you think I am?" demanded Charles. "Do you think I have no subtlety? Far from it. Besides, I intend to drift from the world on the sweet and bitter cloud of opium dreams, and none shall guess the moment of my going. Now that Polette is here we shall have the stuff at our disposal, so we shall be no trouble. You may simply carry on your lives downstairs as if we were not here. Forget about us . . ."

As if that were possible!

"Ah, Charles," I said with a rush of warmth, "I'm glad you chose

to come here – you did right. I've worried about you ever since we
first met up again. At least I'll know you're well looked after here,
for all I shall have a deuce of a task explaining to my wife . . ."

" – an angel in human form – "

"Quite. But nonetheless, you are most welcome."

I pressed his hand. His eyes glazed over and I saw that he had
begun to drift away. I stood up and Polette accompanied me to the
door.

"Ask for anything you require, anything at all." As we stood there
my old unease returned. "For God's sake keep his laudanum hidden
from Dr Hollowell. Along the landing on this attic floor some of the
servants live. Please don't give them cause to be inquisitive . . . at
least," I added gloomily, "no more than can be helped . . ."

"Ah monsieur," reproached Polette. "With him as he is?"

We looked back at the bed. Against all odds, I still credited
Charles with the power to cause me mischief.

Fortunately my mother did not stay for dinner, but after expressing her opinion upon the subject of Charles with icy dignity and
utter disapproval, she took herself off to her own delightful
dwelling in Belgravia with many direst promises to return. I
contrived to steer clear of Claudia throughout the remainder of the
day and passed a very happy hour with Perceval and Sophy at their
bedtime, with plans to take them to see all the animals that Regent's
Park could offer on the first fine day that showed itself. But at bed
time there was no escape and stoically refusing to take refuge in my
dressing room I presented myself for the brunt of her attack.

With rigid self-control she waited until we were both in bed. Then
in the darkness she began.

"I did not speak of this before your mother. But you were not at
your club last night. When your peculiar friend arrived I sent a
message to Pall Mall. You had just left. I naturally assumed that you
would shortly be returning home. You did not."

"No. I had to go out."

"Where did you go?"

A horrible little silence hovered in the air between us.

"I've never asked exactly where you are," said Claudia. "You go
out, you come back, and you have never given me tangible reason to
mistrust you. I have always considered you, Algy, an honourable
person. And I have always despised the kind of wife who asks
concise accounts of every movement when her husband is from
her."

"I know. I have often admired you for it."

"But even Reason itself must question whether it is right that you
should tell me that you intended to sleep at the club and then at

dead of night go secretly to somewhere else. You left no message. No one knew where you were. I would never have found out . . . What if the children had been taken ill? I think an explanation is long overdue. So – where were you last night?"

"Claudia, you are quite right to feel as you do. Everything you say is justified. Of course I would have told you if it had been possible . . ."

"I know we have not been intimate for many months," she interrupted in an urgent whisper. "But I had supposed that was your nature – cool, reserved – you have always been so. But now I begin to wonder, and I have to ask you: Algy – have you a mistress?"

I was astonished. I had never guessed that her line of questioning was tending this way. Relief suffused me and I laughed out loud.

"No! I have not. Good Lord, indeed no!"

"Truly?" she asked doubtfully.

"I swear it!" I assured her heartily.

"I long to believe you."

"Then please believe me. I never have, nor ever will, engage in that particular deception. Ugh!" I added with an unwise fervency. "The idea is distasteful."

"Then where were you last night?"

"I believe that this is true of all women," I said sanctimoniously. "They think that if a husband strays he strays to other women. It is not so. There are so many things that lead a man from home – adventure, trade and commerce, the pursuit of some unusual interest –"

"So much for the masses, Algy. What of you?"

"Claudia, I was helping a friend. I cannot explain to you what that help entailed because it is a matter of some secrecy. To him. It was, however, nothing of a sordid nature, and I did nothing of which I should feel ashamed. It's over now; the business is finished and the friend is very grateful. As for not letting my whereabouts be known, I did not know where I would be myself. But I am now returned, and I assure you once again that I am keeping no mistress, nor, perish the thought, was I with any woman of the meaner kind. You are the only woman for whom I have any sentimental feeling, and this will always be so."

I waited cautiously. My explanation had not been so far from the truth.

"Well," said Claudia. "I suppose I shall have to be satisfied with that. Very well, dear, thank you. It does relieve me. And now we come to Mr Charles."

"We do?"

She paused. I could almost hear the ticking of her thoughts.

"Like your mother," she began. "I also understood that you had long since ceased to have connection with those old friends of yours I only heard about and never met. But this cannot be, can it? Else why would this man come to you as he has done, sure of his reception?"

I explained to her the very recent renewal of my friendship with Charles, the sympathy I felt to see an old friend in reduced circumstances, the sometime visits to ease his distress, the surprise I felt to find him seeking refuge here, the regret that this should happen when I was from home.

"Very well," said Claudia. "I see I have misjudged you somewhat, and in fact you have behaved with great philanthropy. While I cannot say that I like the situation which has arisen, I will do my best to tolerate it, and give you what support may be necessary."

"Thank you," I said, and patted her shoulder. Guilt I felt indeed, emerging from the tale as some disinterested humanitarian, but far stronger was my relief that nothing remotely concerning all I had been up to in the past month had been suspected. I vowed to tread extremely cautiously henceforth.

The dining room in the evening was most attractive, the table laid with starched damask, the silver-branched candelabras lit and centrally placed, reflecting myriad pinpoints of mirrored light in gleaming ranks of cutlery, the tall-stemmed wine glasses and the glittering jewels of the ladies who graced our table. The heavy curtains were drawn against a vile wet night, the fire burned brightly, and the rich reds and golds in the room's furnishings blended most agreeably to provide an effect of warmth and conviviality.

Freddy Merton had managed to get into the hearing against the Marquis of Queensberry and as we dined, all those of us who had not been there were interested to hear what he had to say about it. I had met Freddy socially many times since that unfortunate supper party when we had stumbled across Oscar Wilde and Alfred Douglas with their friends and that disturbing and attractive youth Charles Parker. Freddy had left with Heatherington, also my guest this evening. Heatherington, here with his wife Elaine and his sister Lucy, was tall and upright with a fine moustache and sleek brown hair. A man, like myself, trained to sit still in tight collars as if he felt thoroughly at ease; and in Heatherington's case this rigidity extended to all his mannerisms, for he smiled as if his lips could stretch no further than a tie pin's width – one often wondered if he had teeth; one never saw them – and the movement of his limbs and hands were all of a fine economy.

171

Freddy, conversely, was a mouth of teeth, all smiles, slack-lipped and gauche, with quick little shifts of stance and a head that seemed too loosely fixed upon his skinny neck in its eagerness to turn this way and that to speak and listen. His eyes were long-lashed girlish prettiness, but the beaky nose and jutting chin saved him from any hint of effeminacy. He was slim and slight and rumoured to be desperately in love with Lucy Heatherington. To help promote this passion Claudia had seated Freddy next to the object of his love. One doubted a reciprocal *tendresse*.

"Well," said Freddy. "The court room was packed and Oscar Wilde was in very good form, very merry. When he was asked whether he was a dramatist he said indeed he thought he was believed to be so, and the magistrate reproved him much like some old schoolmaster, and said only to answer what he was asked. And then there was an awful lot of talk about some letters. There are letters written by Oscar to Lord Alfred, and there are letters which the magistrate did not want to have brought into court. He said it would be opening a door to something that ought not to take place in a court room! I daresay I was not the only one who hoped to hear some scandal. There were certainly several enigmatic remarks made and mention of 'exalted personnages' whose names should not be mentioned!"

"Oh God!" said Heatherington wearily. "What wretch in high places have they got their hooks into now? Are we in line for a new political scandal of some kind?"

"I say, I hope so!" Willoughby beamed. "We haven't had a decent one since – when was it – '89? That business in Cleveland Street when they uncovered a nest of obliging telegraph boys and Lord Arthur Somerset had to leave the country!"

"Wasn't Prince Eddy part of it?" Freddy remarked. "And Lord Kerwin, of course – but he did the decent thing and fled to France."

"Indeed; my cousin Philippe saw him only last week on one of the *grands boulevards*," I said, intending for us to talk about Paris and to lose the present highly dubious course of conversation. But Freddy would not be stopped.

"*And* the Earl of Euston," he continued. "Well! It wasn't *proved*, exactly, was it, but they said they'd seen him going in . . . into the brothel, I mean . . ."

"Steady on, now," Avonbury said severely. "Ladies present."

The ladies, who had all been listening with a ready interest, now reverted to an appearance of careless unconcern, and Freddy blushed foolishly at having been indiscreet.

"And what was the outcome of the hearing?" I asked Freddy. Regaining his composure Freddy answered: "Queensberry maintained that he wrote the offensive libel card in order to bring everything out into the open. He said his only interest was in saving his son's reputation. He stands by what he wrote. And so now he is committed for trial and let out on bail. I believe the trial is to be in about three weeks' time."

"A nasty business all round," said Avonbury thoughtfully. "I can't see there being anything but a load of muck-raking."

"We heard that Constance was in tears at the theatre the other night," Clarissa ventured.

"All Oscar has to do is prove his innocence," said Freddy warmly. Really, Freddy would have done better to have closed his mouth that evening. No doubt all of us could secretly call to mind the rumoured indiscretions committed by Oscar. Someone once told me – but it may have been a lie – that he had heard Oscar boast that he had five telegraph boys a day! It made a jolly story at the time; but now it did not seem so droll.

"Well, yes," agreed Lord Avonbury. "Indeed so." He continued sourly: "I detest trials of this nature. Personal matters. A man should keep his private life under control."

At this moment our maid entered the dining room, apologised, and drew near to me with further apologies. "If you please, sir, there is a Person in the hall."

Her manner, intended to be entirely circumspect, was so laden with a flustered kind of embarrassment as to draw all eyes upon herself.

"To see me, do you mean?" I said, perplexed by her demeanour.

"No, sir," she replied. "But Meredith thought that you may wish to see *him*. If you might come, sir . . ."

I left the table and accompanied her into the hall.

I could barely control my horror. I believe I blanched. While Meredith twitched aggressively beside him, there upon the tiled floor, dripping from a journey through the streets in heavy rain, stood Francis, that rosy-cheeked Christmas card boy who had been introduced to me by Charles for sexual release.

He grinned sheepishly.

"Lord Algy," he began. "I'm pleased to see you."

In no way could I return the compliment.

"My lord," Meredith began rather pompously. "This is a visitor for the gentleman upstairs. But being as the hour is late, and as he had not prior appointment and may not have been expected, I imagined you would wish to be informed. Am I to send him upstairs, my lord?"

I sensed in Meredith's tone a plea that I should show Francis the door. *We are not accustomed to receiving this quality of personage, my lord* . . .

"You've come to see Charles," I said in a low voice.

"Yes, my lord! I had to, sir," the youth assured me. "He owes me money."

"You should not have come here, you know," I began soberly.

"I know it. But what else could I do, sir? This is where he is!"

Francis wore an ill-fitting dark green jacket; one trouser leg had lengthened itself to become longer than the other, and his boots looked startlingly large standing upon the immaculately blended tiles. Two pools of water oozed from them. As Meredith so correctly hinted, this was not the sort of apparition we were accustomed to receive. At Charles' lodging Francis had seemed thoroughly appropriate. At Charles' lodging Francis had sucked my prick. The idea of him being here at all was freezing me to immobility. The idea of him walking up my stairs, past the door that led to my bedroom and past the door behind which my innocent children lay asleep appalled me to the core. I knew nothing of his morals – I mean I did not know whether he could be trusted not to steal what is loosely termed the silver. I could see him now, nude and inviting, positioning himself over Charles' sofa, a big round arse with interesting shadows in its curves, its teasing crevice. The smirk in his bright eyes showed well enough that he remembered our encounters also. A feeling of pure terror constricted my throat, as if a handgrip held me there. I could not speak; I stood like one in nightmare, praying to wake. A tinkle of feminine laughter wafted from the dining room. It nudged me sharply into movement.

"Meredith, if you would be so good as to escort this young man up to Mr Charles' room . . . then wait upon the landing and escort him down when his business is completed."

I returned to my guests, a vacuous smile upon my face, explaining nothing, and, well bred beings that they were, they did not ask. It was as well, for no form of the truth could have been preferred.

In the week that followed, other visitors arrived.

I myself sent for Sir William Franklin, for I felt he owed Charles the courtesy of a visit, and as I expected, he obeyed my summons, his integrity unthreatened now that Charles was housed in reputable surroundings.

We now had chairs about the bed, and under Polette's careful ministrations, anyone might sit, and watch in silence or indulge in whispered conversation, for at that time Charles seemed to have sunk into some unfathomable depth of opium stupor and debilitation.

"I believe he scarcely knows me," Franklin decided, corpulent and opulent, and making little effort to penetrate the mists of incommunication. I could not help but notice that all his attention was centred upon Polette. At first it was a mere half glance, a flicker of interest, then a smile, little acts of gallantry to do with carrying trays and lifting chairs. By the third visit he had bought her a silk scarf and even in my presence now he shamelessly pursued.

"You poor dear girl!" he told her. "Your life has not been easy. But have no fear for the future. One exists who will look after you . . ."

"Monsieur . . ." murmured Polette and looked at him from lowered lids. "You are so kind." I wished her well. But I suspected that with Franklin also her luck would run true to pattern.

Laden down with bulky parcels, cumbered with canvases, the next person to arrive was Orlando.

Unlike Francis who had fidgeted uneasily as he waited to be shown upstairs, Orlando exuded a brash and nonchalant careless-ness and faced me cheerily, as if the last time we had met had never been on the landing at Zabarov's house when Arthur was to be freed from that man's dark control.

Placid, affable, Orlando had been standing there, golden and ethereal, beside Arthur, obligingly withdrawing at Zabarov's com-mand.

"Good afternoon, Lord Algy," he remarked. "I brought the stuff Charles sent for. Here it is. Where shall I put it? And I'd be quite pleased to see the old feller if you can see your way clear."

I sent Meredith away. His silent disapproval was annoying me. I took some of the canvases from Orlando, wedged them under my arm and started up the stairs.

"Follow me," I told him.

A housemaid folding linen away into a chest on one of the upstairs landings stared at us as we went by, and then averted her gaze in a most conspicuous manner. We reached Charles' door and entered, fortunately catching a lucid phase – indeed, he was busily sketching scenes of pornographic debauch; and there we sat, with Polette, Charles and Orlando merrily swigging back the absinthe which the latter smuggled in, for all the world like naughty schoolboys at a midnight feast.

"I don't know what you did to Count Zabarov," smirked Orlando cheekily. "But he's left the country, and shut up his house."

"Me? I did nothing."

"Well! He was not best pleased with you, I can tell you that. Let me give you a warning to be on your guard. I wouldn't like him for my enemy!"

"I thought you said he'd left the country."

"So indeed he has. But he's a strange mysterious man, now, wouldn't you say? He doesn't have to be beside you to make his presence felt. He works through powers we cannot see. He sends his influence," said Orlando, gesturing theatrically, "through the ether!"

"Oh what rot!" I murmured. "That isn't possible."

"Not possible?" said Charles. "Of course it is. I knew a fakir in Cairo who could put a jinx on someone in another town, merely by sitting at a tray of sand and making mystic symbols with his fingers in the grains. Within the hour his victim would receive the deadly fluence and so much the worse for him!".

"What you may have seen in Cairo," I said firmly, "has no relevance to modern London. And besides, I happen to know something about Zabarov and his methods. It's true that he has no reason to feel kindly towards me. Indeed, he hinted, as you suggested, that he wished me ill. He told me that he saw our little conflict as a duel. He said that he would use the same weapons as I had used. He was speaking figuratively, of course – no weapons were involved."

"What then do you guess to be his plan?"

"I doubt very much that he has one. But I believe him when he speaks of using civilised methods. I have no idea what this might mean, nor shall I waste my time in wondering. I certainly have no fear of hocus pocus messages in sand. I daresay it was an empty threat born of spite and anger. Particularly since, as you say, he now has gone abroad."

"Where has he gone?" Charles asked.

"Well, Transylvania, obviously," sniggered Orlando. "Didn't you know that he slept by day in a coffin lined with white satin and spent his nights flitting round the tombstones in Highgate Cemetery?"

I asked Orlando: "And what about you, now that he has gone?"

"No change," shrugged the careless lad. "I can get work in any of the theatres. It's true I've had to move into a different lodging but that has not presented any difficulty. Just at present I'm scene-shifting at the Alhambra, but I'm hoping to get an act together, with someone I know. Look out for us!"

We had no doubt of his success.

"I like your house, Algy," he said comfortably, leaning back in the cane chair and looking about him. "Not this room, of course – this one's very dull – but I suppose old Charles has to be kept out of the way for fear of frightening the servants!" I winced. "Well," continued Orlando cheerily, "He could hardly come staggering down to dinner, could he? The spectre at the feast!"

"Don't be objectionable," I snapped.

"I am, aren't I?" he winked. "But still damned attractive to you, eh?"

"Your flaunting is in bad taste . . ."

"Isn't it just!" he chirruped. "But what this house needs is a bit of bad taste. It's too elegant here, Algy, it's too utterly exquisite. Even your staircases and landings are faultless – potted plants beside the window at exactly the right angle, matching wallpaper and drapes – why, even your housemaid blended in, her dress exactly the right shade of grey. It must be very nice to be so rich and powerful."

"It has its responsibilities as well as its joys," I answered soberly.

"You brought the Narcissus, did you not?" Charles enquired of Orlando.

Orlando jumped up and began unravelling a canvas.

"Lord! You have not brought that one!" I cried aghast.

Orlando shook the canvas out and held it up, and there I sat, beside a forest pool, naked as Adam, and for all the overhanging purple foliage and golden-bronze flesh tints, as recognisable as if I were on my way to take a bath. I stood up and stared at it.

"I say," I admitted. "It's awfully good."

Orlando laid the canvas down and darted to me, seizing me about the waist and looking into my face. "Ah, Algy! It brings back memories. It has been such a long time since we made love!"

"Desist!" I cried, attempting to break free of him. He would not let me go.

"Kiss me, Algy, kiss me with your tongue . . ."

Such was my weakness for that provocative boy that I found I had no power to resist. I ceased to pretend that I found his attention unwelcome. I put my arms around him and gave him the kiss that he required. Charles and Polette applauded. Orlando said: "I am the lust which he is trying to suppress. I am his deep desires."

"You are a nasty little brat," I muttered.

"Yes, I suppose I am," he nodded.

"I think that Algy has incipient weakness," Charles decided. "I pray that he will never have to meet a crisis. He's always been so rich and so good-looking that he's never had to struggle to achieve. By conflict we attain and grow to know ourselves. That little auburn-haired friend of yours had twenty times the character that you have, Algy, simply through having been born poor and making his own way."

"That isn't fair," I cried. "What would you have me do – go on the streets in borrowed rags to test my bravery? And as for crises, have I thrown you out? Who else of my class and acquaintance would put up with you lurking in an upstairs room like the mad wife in *Jane Eyre*, and permitting visitors which make my servants raise their eyebrows? And I sent Zabarov packing – that was not easy."

"Well, perhaps I'm wrong," admitted Charles. "But it seems to me that the rich and beautiful are rarely strong. I was thinking that about our exalted prime minister Lord Rosebery the other day . . . So fabulously rich, so well protected from the day to day decisions of the folk who have to scrimp and save, never knowing money worry, and to crown it all, so damned good-looking."

"Ah, Rosebery," I agreed. "I always liked that story about him, how he used to live in a tumbledown old castle somewhere beside the sea up there in Scotland. It was when a guest was knocked down by a wave on his way to the dining room that he judged it about time to move house!"

"Is that so?" grinned Charles. "But I maintain my initial premise. I doubt if he will ever be widely remembered somehow. I don't believe he will ever become great."

"That will be no fault of his own," said I. "He will suffer by virtue of succeeding a greater. Unless he achieve unusual recognition by an unforeseen challenge successfully overcome, he will just be remembered as the chap who followed Gladstone."

"Charles is tired now . . ." said Polette.

"I'll see our visitor out."

As we came through the door Orlando murmured: "Shan't we meet again soon? It seems a shame not to."

"It isn't easy for me just at present," I pointed out. "Perhaps . . . afterwards sometime . . ."

"All right," he said obligingly. "Always good taste, eh! I'll be in touch with you then. You'll be feeling sad when Mr Charles goes; you'll need some cheering up."

CHAPTER FIFTEEN

TO MY relief and gratitude my concerned and tactful wife decided to take the children to stay with her sister, their aunt, in Ramsgate for a month or so. The news was very welcome to me, not simply to ease the strain upon my nervous system which Charles' visitors induced – and there were others beside Orlando and Francis – but because I did not think that there was any way we could have kept a funeral and all its necessary garniture from the children's eager eyes, with the resulting probing questions that my daughter's lively mind would certainly bring forth.

I took them for their afternoon in Regent's Park, a lovely windy day when kites were flying, daffodils were blooming, birds were chirping; and the beasts in the zoological garden a piquant contrast to the English Spring. Myself I liked the parrots, but to the children monkeys would always be the favourites. I was sorry to see the merry pair off to the eastern sea coast but once they had gone, I knew it was truly for the best on all counts.

I called in at the club on my way back from the railway station to catch up on the gossip – and there was some. A little peach of a scandal was in the offing.

The deliberations of the Grand Jury, which took place in private concerning the coming trial of the Marquis of Queensberry, had seeped a leakage of information through the machinations of a French journalist, and now the continental newspapers were full of the story with all the relish which that nation shows when it uncovers or invents a scandal concerning our nation's morality.

It seemed that the "exalted personage" referred to at the hearing had been Lord Rosebery our prime minister who, although a Liberal, was generally considered to be handsome, charming, eloquent and popular. His name had been mentioned in a letter written by the Marquis of Queensberry – the contents of a very compromising nature. It was no secret that the Prime Minister had not been in the best of health – there were rumours of chronic insomnia, nervous strain and influenza; and no doubt his worries

179

would in no way be alleviated by the threat of calumny from the Mad Marquis, who was known to cherish rancour towards him.

"What *was* it about Lord Rosebery?" Freddy asked. "I remember something . . ."

Willoughby was happy to remind him. "Last Autumn, when that very pretty lad Drumlanrig shot himself . . ."

"Bosie Douglas's brother, of course, yes," said Freddy. "He was Rosebery's secretary, I believe."

"A shooting accident," corrected Heatherington severely.

"Nonsense; it was suicide," said Willoughby. "He was being blackmailed, wasn't he, over Rosebery?"

"It's beastly of you, Willoughby, to fan these old flames." said Heatherington. "You're no better than those same French newspapers whom you purport to condemn."

"Well, young Drumlanrig's redoubtable father certainly agreed with me," Willoughby stoutly maintained. "Didn't he follow Rosebery to Homburg and hang around his hotel with a dogwhip? I say, what a vicious little man he is! What a joke on him, eh, to see Bosie Douglas going the same way as his elder brother! Serves the old man right. I wonder if we'll see the dogwhip out again between the pillars of the Café Royal!"

"What an unholy mess it all is!" Heatherington grumbled. "I hate to see our dirty linen, so to speak, washed in full view of foreigners. If Rosebery has anything to hide, it must come out. We can't afford suspicion of bad character."

"At least," said Willoughby cheerfully, "if the fellow is obliged to resign we'll have some chance of getting the Tories back in!"

Although this prospect had the effect of introducing a note of optimism to the proceedings, it was not enough to alter the general opinion that a monumental scandal of one nature or another was about to burst upon society. The same French newspapers that carried the reports of an involvement with Lord Rosebery and much bizarre speculation beside, announced that Oscar Wilde and Bosie were in the south of France on holiday, and that in Monaco they had been thrown out of a hotel. They were calling attention to themselves by rollicking at the gaming tables and strolling the streets of Monte Carlo like a couple on their honeymoon. The consensus of the club was that their time would have been better spent in London being seen giving alms to the poor, inaugurating libraries, and most important of all, going about separately, each with a woman on his arm.

One evening when I sat with Charles and talked about old times he mentioned Willie Smith, my old love from the days when we all lived in artistic abandon amongst the lilacs in Franklin's garden, long since flattened to make way for visiting dignitaries. Indeed we could not help thinking about Willie, because most of the paintings which Orlando brought on that visit, and others which came later brought by lads I did not know, were of that youthful form which meant so much to me at that sweet and distant time. Late evening it was, and the overheated room was lit by firelight's glow alone, the only sound the shifting of the coals. Polette sat quietly by the hearth, a silhouette, and I sat by the bed-head, thoughtful, sipping wine, for we kept an unashamed supply of claret, absinthe – even water – ever present by the pillow.

It was Charles himself who had brought Willie to the house in Kensington. He found him at an art school sitting in a shaft of sunlight, and brought him home to model Parsifal. It was May time, and when I got back from Greece, Willie was a *fait accompli*, adored by all the artists for his brilliant auburn hair. Beautiful to look at, bold and bright, aflame with ridiculous Socialist principles, he was at heart a street urchin with a street urchin's curiously disturbing charm. Charles played the pander to us, knowing my suppressed desires and nurturing Willie's till, victims of the pink-tinted Camelot atmosphere of that place and the summer evening's fragrances, we fell in love and vowed fidelity. It was I that failed.

In all the years between, I put him from my mind; and only now, in the strange and awful circumstance of Charles' last days, did I feel that I could answer Charles' questions.

"You were going to elope to Paris," he reminded me. "We all thought the idea excellent. Obviously you could not live together openly, you with your position in society, but Paris seemed a fair solution, at least for long enough to find out whether you were certainly in love."

"We were!" I cried. "There was no doubt of that. But he had nothing to lose, had he? Whereas I . . ." There was no way round it; I had acted shabbily.

"We arranged to meet on Victoria Station," I explained. "I had the tickets, money, everything; I told him where to wait; I knew he would be there. I could not bring myself to leave the house. My trunks were packed. I sat and stared at them like one bereft of reason. An inexplicable immobility froze me to the spot. Hours went by. I got up and walked about, just to and fro, to and fro, all in the same room. I don't believe I thought as such, or weighed the various alternatives. I simply knew that I could not go through with our plan. I dared not. Oh! I who had always been afraid of things – how could I ever have supposed that I could have committed such an affirmation of life as to leave these shores to go abroad and live with a male lover! Whatever would my mother have thought – my family – my friends? How could I face them, how could I live any recognisable form of the life I knew? You cannot run away like that and find the kind of happiness known only in a children's fairy tale. The real world is a dull and workaday place, where you have an estate to manage, an economy to grapple with, responsibilities . . . I could not pass a strange half life among the boulevards, *flâneur* and refugee. It was my common sense that spoke to me and made me stay at home. Oh yes, and also fear. I was afraid; I don't deny it; I won't make a virtue of my cowardice. And so I wrote him a brief note; I took an opium draught and slept."

"And the boy . . . presumably he also did not go to France?"

"I tried to find him. You remember, I came looking for him at the house. No one knew where he'd gone. I became distraught, depressed. My mother made me go to Italy."

"Dear Algy," Charles said weakly. "Money is such a convenient thing to have. Did you feel better when you got back from Italy?"

"A little," I said defensively. "But I could not rest till I knew what had become of Willie. I remembered that he had been friendly with a model at the art school, rumoured to be a lady of the night. And she knew where he was. At first I dared not face him, I was so ashamed. Eventually I forced myself to take that step . . . I often asked myself what I was hoping for. Was it merely reconciliation, reassurance? I think not. Deep in my heart I think I hoped that we might once again be lovers . . . I think that I have told you that Willie had found himself a place as an assistant master in a school for homeless boys. You know yourself that he believed the common man had certain rights – oh, how he did go on, do you remember? He rattled his social conscience as noisily as any tinker does a load of pots and pans! And so I believed him very well suited to the employment in which I found him, for he was not ill-educated and could speak Queen's English very nicely when he chose to.

"When he received me all my old love feelings surged to the surface – I longed to take him in my arms, beg his forgiveness. I remained, I hope, controlled and calm and I was glad to see him looking so contented. He told me he was happy. He seemed so. The shabbiness of the place was only too apparent and I guessed they needed funds. This he admitted when I asked him. At once I offered them a grant – the sum that would save their finances was but little loss to me."

"Them?" said Charles. "There were other teachers there?"

"The school is run by a Mr Pearson, a very upright fellow, an altogether worthy person, who has devoted his life to the education of waifs and strays much in the style of Dr Barnardo. He comes of good class and was in the Indian Army at some stage in his career. He has the effect of making one feel useless and inadequate," I added ruefully, "as do all those who genuinely work for good, dirtying their hands while most of us merely give money. I have had some dealings with him over the years in connection with the funding of the school."

Charles' next question astonished me. "Are he and Willie lovers?"

"Good Lord, no," I replied and laughed. "Oh I am sure that Willie will have given all *that* up, just as I did."

"No doubt," murmured Charles. "And so you have not seen him since?"

"Since then I have supported their venture through my bank. But I have never visited. It seemed best to come away, with much unsaid, and my guilt was much appeased at the chance of becoming his benefactor. And there you have it. I came away from our last meeting all those years ago and turned my back on that phase of my life. Under my mother's direction I became enamoured of the lady who has since become my wife. I put Willie from my mind, successfully I think. It has only been your presence that has caused me to call up old ghosts as I have done."

"Ah," Charles interposed. "But he is not a ghost, and Algy, I would like to see him."

"See him? But how?" I answered blankly.

"Well, that's clear enough, dear boy. You go round to his school and you tell him and you bring him here."

"I could not possibly," I protested. "You do not know what you are asking – in terms of past pains long buried, and future problems which inevitably would follow."

"I was very fond of that boy. I want to see him."

"Charles, you are a mischief-maker."

"I own it. And dare you refuse a last request? Do you wish that on your conscience?"

"God, Charles, this is beastly of you." I sat upright, all the wine-induced nostalgia draining from me rapidly. "I suppose you could not be delirious?" I enquired hopefully.

"If you went *now*," suggested Charles, "you might bring him back in your cab and we could share a glass of wine together. Possibly my last," he added, with a sideways glance at me. That this remark held all the poignancy of truth made it no less apparent that the wretch was working on my finer feelings.

"Damn you, Charles," I said, stood up, and strode out of the room.

It occurred to me that I had undergone a temporary lapse of sanity. I was sitting in a hansom which was carrying me at dead of night to Shoreditch upon a mission not a whit of my own choosing. It seemed to me that since that night in February when the past had first caught up with me in the shape of Charles' summons, a good deal of my life had been spent thus, traversing London by night, racked by emotions. I was conscious of the strangeness of my sortie, a venture to the jungle of forgotten places of the mind, a journey hazardous in its way as any to the African interior.

As I alighted at the kerb of the street I sought, I was aware of a heavy odour from the brewery nearby, the pungent smell of hops in concentration hanging on the sullen air. The school for waifs and strays was a tall cumbersome building set behind a high brick wall, by daylight revealed as somewhat shabby and dilapidated. There were no gates – an opening led into a little forecourt with flower beds and bushy trees that grew behind the wall, bare-branched at this time of year and rustling brittlely. A faded notice board rammed in the gravel showed the place to be Goff Street Home for Boys, and Joseph Pearson's name beneath. Some lights showed in the windows. With one brief glance at them I crunched my way to the front door and up the steps; I rang the bell. My mind felt like a swarm of bees clamped down and rigidly contained by a skep.

Joseph Pearson opened the door to me; I felt relief and disappointment. As I had told Charles, I found the fellow daunting. He had a soldierly uprightness born no doubt of the constant battle which engages those who give their lives to doing good. Worthiness shone from him like a light. From the haven of his refuge no wretched boy was ever turned away; he took the homeless ragged from the streets and educated them and sent them forth with some chance to make their way in a world loaded against them. Now in his mid forties the man was not simply a tower of strength and forcefulness, he was also blessed with startling good looks somewhat in the style of Gordon of Khartoum. He was tall and broad, with brown hair and a neat moustache, and dark brown eyes which smouldered disconcertingly even over sterile matters like the querying of accounts. He had appalling carelessness in dress – the lining of his jackets regularly hung below the hem. The impeccably clad cannot help but notice such things.

"Yes?" he said abruptly.

That was another thing; he was never obsequious. I suspected that to owe his continuing livelihood to my generosity rankled.

"Good evening, Mr Pearson," I said suavely. "I wonder if I might speak to Willie."

"No," he answered bluntly. As I stared, a little taken aback by such a peremptory response, he seemed mentally to correct himself and added in a gentler tone: "No – I'm sorry; Willie is not here."

184

"Ah." I was vexed now. "When will he be back?"

"I don't know," said Mr Pearson unhelpfully, looking, if a hero could be said to look so, dubious and shifty. It even crossed my mind that he had no idea where Willie was.

"Well, where has he gone?" Frustration made me querulous. "Surely you have some expectation of the time of his return?"

"I haven't, no," said Mr Pearson testily. "Obviously I would tell you if I had. It is unfortunate that you should pick this time to call. I daresay he will be back. Was it an urgent matter upon which you wished to see him?"

"I believe it was, after all, a matter of no consequence," I murmured. Now that it had turned out so, I felt a curious gratitude to Willie for his absence. I had done as Mr Charles requested. Perhaps I would try again some time; tonight I could do no more.

We said goodnight; he closed the door, and I tramped back to my waiting cab.

I felt tired and drained as I was driven home, leaving behind the mean streets, alleys and warehouses of this poorer part of town, gladly watching the enveloping approach of gentility. Perversely now I felt an ache of sharp regret. My one-time love – how did he fare these days? What was he like? What had he become? I doubted I would ever make that call again; the circumstances never would be quite so right, the impetus never so strong.

Maybe it was for the best – the unseen hand of Providence ordering the ways of things. What business had we tampering with time, what right to trespass on the past?

In sober mood I arrived home. Slowly I mounted the dark stairs to the attic room beneath the eaves. There, in the warm firelit silence, I discovered that in the intervening hours of my absence Charles had breathed his last. Solitary and unfearing, Polette had done all that was required, and now sat immobile by the bedside, lost in thought, while Charles, his eyes closed and his jaw bound in place by a tight bandage which wound round his head, lay stiff beneath the quilted coverlet, with every appearance of one who had endured a bad time at the dentist's.

The following afternoon, when I was sitting at my desk and feeling much stressed from arranging details of the funeral, I received a vistor, Orlando.

I was not surprised. Polette had gone out in the morning upon various errands, one of which had been to let Charles' old acquaint-ance know the sorry state of things. Young Francis had come back with her to pay his last respects, stayed for a moment and then left. I half expected others.

185

I accompanied Orlando into Charles' room – we were alone – but I had no wish to gaze further on the corpse, which lay beneath a sheet, and I stood with my back to the room, looking out on to the rain.

"When is the funeral?" said Orlando.

"Tomorrow."

"I don't think I shall be there. I hate that sort of thing, don't you? Still, he looks peaceful enough now, don't he? Even dead he has a cynical smirk."

"Do you want any of the paintings here?"

"Ooh yes, let's have a look."

Orlando replaced the turned-down sheet corner, and we went through the drawings Charles had left, crouching on the floor.

"Not the Narcissus," I said.

"It's the rude ones I like."

Orlando sorted out half a dozen pictures and rolled them up. We stood. He darted at me and kissed me on the mouth. I drew back.

"Ah no, this is ghoulish."

"Not at all – he'd love it – he'd be laughing, to think that we were kissing with him lying there."

"Come away."

"Poor Algy," cooed Orlando. "You're looking awfully tired. It hasn't been easy for you, has it, this? Is there somewhere we can go where I can put my arms around you?"

"Yes."

We went down the two short flights of stairs. Of course I had no intention of desecrating the marriage bed; but I had no such compunction about the adjoining dressing room. Nobody saw us go in, and once inside I locked the door.

There was no escaping the sound of the rain – it coursed down the window panes, obscuring the view of the square and trees below, and the gust of the wind rattled some loose fitting outside. The room was dim, the dark and heavy furniture adding to the gloom. But Orlando gleamed. He brought his stage presence with him like a radiant aureole. His golden hair was unnaturally bright – whatever had he combed into it to give it that curious lustre? His manner was elaborately graceful. He swanned into my arms.

I hugged him to me. Ah! How I needed him – or needed the release he would provide. I was a mass of strain and tension, bitterly lonely, and terribly cut up over Charles. I was moreover much affected by the aftermath of my strange night drive to the streets of Shoreditch with all my old memories of Willie, the sharper for having been suppressed for so long. I needed to lie close to someone and to give and receive love and comfort – and Orlando was the answer. He was startlingly desirable. We tore and pulled at each other's clothes, and all the old remembered sensations of anticipated pleasure overcame me.

"Let's be naked!" he said salaciously, with a mischievous grin of promise.

We stepped out of the remnants of our clothes and stood in an embrace. I had not known how hungry I had been for him. I put my head against his neck and tasted his skin and the fine golden hairs of his chest; my hands perused the texture of his lean muscular arms, his slender back, the luscious globes of his arse; then our mouths clamped in a long warm kiss, our tongues a slippery entanglement and the activity of our loins causing difficulty in standing close together. We moved on to the bed, hurrying beneath the sheets, shivering with cold and arousal.

We wound our limbs about each other, kissing, licking, biting, and face to face we moved in eager seeking. The mingling of our body hair teased and caressed, our hands reached for each other's cock. Silent but for the gasps of our breathing – one slim door separated us from the austere world of propriety, our foe – we wreaked our passion upon each other's flesh.

"Let's make it so we come together," Orlando invited merrily. "I'll tell you when, then you . . ."

We started laughing at the secrecy, the remembrances of dormitories and prowling masters, the thrill of stolen pleasure; groans eased from our lips, and we knew that sweet happiness whereby one is a body simply, no recall of anything but lust.

"Nearly – no – yes – now!" Orlando panted, and with a sudden burst of feverish activity we strained to come together, and lay tightly pressed, the warm fluid swelling, spreading wickedly between us. We clung together, writhing in content, until what had seemed such delicious bondage grew cool and disagreeably sticky, and we ruefully smiled and moved apart, and I found cloths to clean us up.

"Tell you what," said Orlando stretching comfortably. "I'd love a drink – I'd love to drink some sherry sitting up in bed."

"Oh? Do you suggest I ring for service?" I enquired quizzically.

"You could go and fetch it – is it downstairs?"

"Oh, very well," I grumbled tolerantly, beginning to dress. A little crumpled, but clothed now, I unlocked the door, looked about and strolled down to the study. There I made us up a little tray and carried it upstairs without any embarrassing encounter. I let myself back in and placed the tray upon the dressing table.

Orland was lying where I had left him, flushed and naked, with his hair a-tangle like the fronds of an exotic flower. I poured him sherry and we sat and drank, while he chatted to me of his life upon the boards, and boasted of his off-stage conquests and told me gossip of the famous. Did I know that Mr Gladstone in his dubious crusade to save fallen women had once tried to save Lillie Langtry? Had I heard about the dancer who appeared on stage in a costume composed merely of fish net with her breasts all bare and little coins sewed into the mesh to cover up her privates, who ended up gaoled for three months on a charge of indecency? And much of similar ilk. But he diverted me, and I was grateful.

That little fling had been a bright spot in a dismal week. I had no love feelings for him, nor he for me, but he was carnal and mischievous and a most delightful contrast to the straitjacket of society.

Sir William Franklin, now that Charles was safely gone, was much in evidence and I appreciated his support. He managed to gather a surprising number of notable gentlemen who remembered Charles from better days, whose presence gave the funeral an air approaching respectability; and if a more disreputable element merged in amongst them, merge it did, and caused no apparent comment. The service over – all of us bedewed with dampness from a relentless rain that fell throughout, lugubriously apt – Sir William preferred his arm to Polette who took it gratefully; within a day or two she had quit her room in my household and took her scant belongings to wherever it was Franklin deemed should be appropriate.

The whole doleful business left me dreary and depressed – exacerbated by the regular visits I had been obliged to make to my mother in order to forestall her possible visits to me. Immensely gratified to hear that my unwelcome visitor was no more, her vigilance relaxed and she assumed that ordinary life would once again exert its pleasures and responsibilities upon me. She was pleased to hear that I was joining Claudia in Ramsgate and was generous with instructions as to how best breathe sea air for maximum benefit to the lungs.

I had not realised quite how arduous I had found the strain of the last two weeks but Claudia noticed it immediately and commented with concern upon my pallor. I found a surprising solace in her company. William my eldest was home from school now, an attractive child with fair hair and intelligent eyes and at that time an earnest desire to become a sailor. The long bare tawny beach was soothing to my mind and I spent many hours pacing the sand beneath the great expanse of sky.

During the few days I spent there we had some fine weather, chill but bright, with silver sunlight glittering on the sea and in the shallow pools. Sea birds stood in their own shadows on the cobbled sand. A smudged grey headland stretched to the horizon, its ridge topped with tufted grass. In the little harbour I leaned upon the wall with William and Sophy and we watched the bright boats on the turquoise water. I sat with Claudia in the evening reading; and wholeness settled on me, of which its strongest manifestation was a warm and urgent longing to see Arthur.

CHAPTER SIXTEEN

·

LET IT not be supposed that Arthur had not been much in my thoughts over the past three weeks; he had. Indeed, I had penned him a couple of brief affectionate letters to which he had not replied. But close proximity to death's approach and the atmosphere and general condition of a household where this occurs provokes a certain feeling of unreality, of distance from the world outside. Now it was over I felt ready and eager to return to that world. Leaving my family to continue their sojourn at Ramsgate, I departed for London and settled back into my house in the square.

The following evening, when I assumed Arthur would be home from work, I went by cab to Holborn to see how it fared with my young friend.

It was one day towards the end of March. There was rain in the air; the sky was grey. I firmly trusted that the sight of Arthur would have the effect of lifting my despondent spirits, which were already rising in the contemplation of his dear person. I walked up to the door and knocked, and shortly it was opened to me by his mother. She brightened at the sight of me and ushered me into the parlour, which smelt of beeswax and was bright with daffodils in vases. The room, however, bore its habitual atmosphere of oppressive crepuscular stillness, and I hoped that I could persuade Arthur to come out with me.

"Well, yes, Lord Algernon, Arthur is at home," his mother answered to my enquiry. "But he has been very ill, see, so you will find him in his room. Of course he surely will see you; but he has not been himself at all, and his illness has left him much weakened."

Appalled and shocked I demanded to learn all. Although it seemed to have been an attack of influenza, verified by the doctor which the solicitous Mr Simmons had procured at his own expense, I could not help but feel that such a sickness had been brought on by the boy's curious and distressing mental experience under the influence of Zabarov, and I blamed myself for not having guessed that such might ensue.

"Take me to him, please."

In the little bedroom above, Arthur was sitting up in bed in a striped nightshirt, with tousled hair and waxen cheeks, a picture of child-like vulnerability and warm boyishness that turned my heart over. I sat down on the bed and clasped his hand.

"Oh Arthur! You should have let me know!"

"But what could you have done?" he answered reasonably. "I have been well looked after."

"Yes, but I didn't *know* . . ." I complained.

"I'm better now," he assured me. "I've been downstairs these past few days and I'll be back at work in a day or two."

"Ah – no," I began. "A person needs to recover."

"A person *has* recovered, and a person needs to be earning."

"I want you to recuperate properly; I want you to –" What could I propose? The benefits to myself of bracing coastal air had been apparent, and I wished the same for him. But upon what terms? Delicious visions of myself and Arthur strolling hand in hand in Italy darted through my mind, swiftly to be overlaid with visions of Oscar Wilde and Bosie as recounted by the French newspapers – hustled out of clubs, requested to leave hotel foyers by stony-faced residents, irate managers with perspiring brows. I hesitated.

"I can't afford to go away," said Arthur, "and don't particularly want to."

"Would you consider spending some time with me at Mortmayne?" I suggested. Lord knows what prompted such a spontaneous notion; it had not been in my mind.

"Your country house?"

"In Bedfordshire. It's not far away. Why, even the prime minister has his house in that part of the world. You see – it's where all the best people live!"

"Do you mean that both of us would be there, with your wife and children and servants?" said Arthur carefully.

"No – yes – " I twitched. "Both of us would be there. And a few servants. We aren't planning to open up the house properly till early Summer, when we have a string of events lined up. But my bailiff keeps the place while I'm away, and it would be no problem to sort something out which would make it possible to spend some time there. As for my wife and children, they are in Ramsgate. On the Kentish coast," I added. "A seaside town."

"Will she not think it odd?" Arthur wondered with a little crooked grin. "I mean when you tell her."

"No!" I assured him grandly. "I am master in my own household, you know. What do you say, Arthur? It's most agreeable there, you know – woods, and a lake, fields . . . it will do you no end of good. I'll square it with your mother and Mr Simmons. I'll make it all right."

It was not, however, without misgivings, that I embarked upon this venture. I was haunted by images of Oscar Wilde and Bosie, the wealthy older man, the beautiful acolyte, the gossip that followed them, the rumours current in London. But Arthur and I could be in no way comparable, I told myself. I was his benefactor, and concern about his health had been the largest consideration behind my offer. His mother had been touchingly grateful. What stronger seal of approbation could have been demanded? And then uneasily I would remember that a gentleman had done as much for Willie in circumstances rather similar. He took him to his country house and fed and nurtured him, then took his pleasure on his body in bizarre fantasies, and having had his fill sent him back home laden down with exotic presents. The comparison sickened me. I dared not deeply delve into my motives. With a glazed smile upon my face, sitting opposite Arthur in the train that carried us to Bedford, I pointed out St. Albans and its impressive cathedral, and spoke earnestly about John Bunyan who had used the hills and fields of Bedfordshire as symbols on the route to Heaven in that great work which I had truly never very much enjoyed.

The first day of that week which Arthur and I spent together was a difficult one.

Mortmayne had daunted me when I was a child and it was my ancestral home; I had not foreseen the similar effect that it would have upon Arthur. However much I tried to reassure him by my words or attitude, he was thoroughly ill at ease, reminding me of some bright but humble scholar from a village school who, having done well in his Bible studies, earns a day at the big house as his prize.

The railway carried us into the countryside past the near-bare hedgerows of early Spring. From the windows we could see a dun grey sky – a smudge of trees on the brow of a low hill, the slim pointed spire of a church – then near at hand the ivy clustered on the trunks of a grove of oak, last year's leaves hanging there dull, dry and shrivelled. In a ditch a brown stream. Then catkins. A distant wood with charcoal-coloured trees.

"So much sky," said Arthur, marvelling.

"Yes. Bedfordshire is very flat. Compared to what you are used to." The banality of my observation embarrassed me. It was obvious enough that a person who had first seen light of day in the North Welsh mountains might find a difference in the scenery before him. Was this whole idea a ghastly mistake? A leaden dread suffused me.

The drive to Mortmayne in the covered carriage revealed little of our route – an excess of hedgerow and more sky – and therefore to emerge and find the house before him may have proved alarming to my guest. A wide drive curved around a green of ancient yews, and further tall trees hid the approach of the grounds and gardens. The house was square and solid, built of stone; the centre of the front was taken up with a massive portico reaching to the roof, with four immense pillars, up to which a wide flight of steps led from the drive. The house bore an unwelcome look, as it always seemed to do when the family was away. A large proportion of it was shut up and under dust sheets. I had never found Mortmayne appealing or friendly. My own children had brought life and humour to the grisly pile, but they were not here now, and old memories threatened to engulf me once again as, hesitant and dubious, I led Arthur up the steps, and footmen scuttled to and fro with baggage.

Our dinner that night was an awkward business alleviated only by the shared half smiles that let the other know that each was suffering the same discomfort. We sat at either end of the dining table, too far apart to converse much. The light of many candelabra flickered over walls with serried ranks of gilt-framed paintings, the ceiling very far above our heads.

"We don't have gaslight or electricity here," I explained. "It would spoil the room design and make unsightly holes. We use oil lamps mostly. Hundreds of the things. And candles, loads of candles. When we have guests here, a couple of lamp boys have their work cut out to keep them filled and trimmed."

Afterwards we retired to separate rooms, with servants hovering, and John my valet, who came by a later train, attending to us both. The idea was for Arthur to build up his strength and so I obliged him to go to bed early and sleep late in the morning.

Next day we walked about the estate. There was a grey sky full of clouds and a chill wind bringing hints of rain. I took Arthur down to the lake. This was a place I liked from boyhood, and with William and Sophy. I waxed enthusiastic.

"In April this field is a mass of cowslips . . . and here we have toads . . . they come from that ditch over there to this part of the lake; this whole path is covered with them, squeaking in high voices, some of them mating as they go! We dammed this stream up last year and changed its course – William and I – and sailed boats the whole length of it . . ."

We followed the stream down to the lake. It was wild here, with the reddish thorns of a thicket of wild rose bushes, and the tangled hedges lightly brushed with green. The little mere was covered with lime-coloured weed and slime. The path was rutted, muddy. A duck and drake pottered placidly in the deep ditch. A few shut celandines showed.

Down at the lake were bulrushes. Willows hung low with sprays of thin branches; the pewter surface of the water was pitted with rain. We stood beside a pussy willow, and Arthur rubbed his palms against its fur; the yellow pollen stained his fingers. Honking ducks flew up suddenly, and peewits called, plunging and twisting over the tawny undergrowth. The swans drew near, stately and inquisitive.

All my conversation was of the delights I'd known here with my children. "All the swans have names – Sophy christened them – she says that when they dip their heads below the water their tails are like white sundials. She took Percy out in a boat last summer and she lost the oar . . . one of the gardeners waded in and rescued them . . . it isn't very deep . . . we're planning to have a new boat house and extend the lake . . ."

I didn't mean to talk this way, but at that moment I missed Perceval and Sophy dreadfully and felt that I had nothing whatsoever in common with Arthur, who stood, hunched up and muffled, listening without comment. The awesome clouds built up above our heads, thickly grey with dark blue undertones.

"Some of my happiest boyhood days were spent here on this lake," I said. "I made a lopsided boat, stocked it with bread and apples – I made charts – I was a pirate's cabin boy – much like Jim Hawkins."

"Who?" said Arthur morosely.

"Oh!" I cried. "Don't tell me you have not read *Treasure Island*!"

"No I haven't."

"It's a lovely book; you should. I believe we have it here in the nursery . . . I'll find it."

And so I did. That afternoon, the rain now in full flow, we sat upstairs – I had a fire lit – in the nursery. What merry times I'd had here reading bedtime tales to William and Sophy as we first discovered the heroes and villains of that book and many others! Claudia had had the room freshly wallpapered in yellow stripes and I would even say that the jolly presences of my children had laughed away the ghosts and sadnesses of other childhoods and made it a happy room. Arthur waded in amongst the toys.

"Oh! What a beautiful fort!" said Arthur, darting to it.

"Isn't it! And we added soldiers to it over the years. Look – these are Scots Greys, and these are the Second Inniskillings who fought at Balaclava."

I never had such a good game of soldiers as we had then. It occurred to me that grown men do make better opponents than excited children; we take it all so much more seriously, are devious,

194

and badly wish to win. In fact my troops won and Arthur proved himself delightfully human with a little sulk; but we ended laughing.

"Do you like Upside Down Winter Pudding?" I enquired.

"What exactly is that?"

"Well, it's made with cooking pears and cherries, or other fruits in their season, and all set like a wheel into a kind of cake of syrup and treacle, cinnamon and ginger; and you eat it with cream or lemon sauce. We're having it tonight."

"And that," said Arthur cheerfully, "is another Beautiful Fort!"

The dining room had its original overawing effect upon him, though perhaps less so than the previous evening. He confided to me: "Did you know that when your servants lay the table they unroll the tablecloth like a tube, one on each side of the table, and run with it along each side?"

He ate well, and I sent him to bed laden with jolly books I thought he should be reading. He didn't read them. He said in the morning that he hadn't felt much like reading and had gone straight to sleep.

After breakfast (another silent meal) we went down to look at the gardens. The wind was rough but the sun was bright. Everywhere now there were green budding leaves and merry birdsong. Ranks of quivering daffodils were poised to flower, and beneath the trees the ground was white with snowdrops, while in sheltered places violets grew. Inside the wall of the kitchen garden we surveyed the peach and nectarine buds – on dull cold days they were bedded in a thatch of spruce and laurel till the effect was of a clumpy bush; today this had been taken off and one of the gardeners was using a furry rabbit's tail on a stick to pollenate the pink flowers.

Leaving the gardens behind we walked into the wood and there we paused by a gardener's cottage.

"Now this is nice!" said Arthur. "Who lives here?"

"At present two gardener's lads; but there are two rooms upstairs and in the summer there will be other gardeners."

"It looks so jolly," Arthur remarked wistfully.

"Does it?" I wondered.

"Yes! It is just the right size for two."

I looked at him, and then at the cottage. I knew in an instant that he was right, and that it was the answer to our distances.

Everybody in my position ought to have a Wingate. This bailiff of mine was a gem in human form. With tact and diplomacy he found other quarters for the two gardener boys, and organized all that was necessary for Arthur and myself to move in. He perfectly comprehended that my young guest was a sensitive youth recovering from influenza and nervous exhaustion, overawed by the dining hall and servants and the unaccustomed elegance of the massive bedroom where he tried to sleep in solitary splendour, restive and ill at ease. The little back room of the cottage would be far more comfortable, and I would keep him company and look after him and see he did not become lonely. I sent John my valet back to London for the time being; and thus prepared I looked toward the immediate future with agreeable anticipation.

There is a childish pleasure in playing at house, not, I am sure, confined to female children; and Arthur and I took care and pleasure in settling into the cottage on the edge of the wood for the few days that remained to us.

The cottage was a homely brick-built structure, with a low front door leading straight into the downstairs room. We had a fire burning continually in the grate to keep the house dry and aired. In that small low-ceilinged room was a sofa by the fire and a wing chair, a table with two chairs and an old casement clock that ticked with triumphant serenity – you could hear it in every room. There was a scullery, which we did not use, for Wingate saw to the meals that were brought down from the house. A door with a cumbersome latch opened upon the twisty stairs which led to two bedrooms of minuscule size, one with a narrow bed which had been made up for Arthur, the other with a wider bed deemed more fitting for myself, for my clothes were put there and my brushes and such laid out on the little dressing table. There was not much room to move about; it was Perfection.

Our time was spent in lazing, talking, and striding forth on long invigorating walks, while in the evenings I read *Treasure Island* out loud to Arthur who lay sprawled upon the sofa. I had never felt such sweet content in all my life.

On our first evening when I had seen Arthur to bed I settled to my own bed feeling mellow and avuncular. I lay, my arms folded behind my neck, looking up into the darkness, listening to the noises of the house – the ticking clock, the scurrying of mice in the woodwork, the calls of hunting owls across the fields. It would not matter, I decided, if I could never become Arthur's lover. If what Orlando said was true, that Arthur had no liking for that, well, so be it. It was enough for me to be with him and care for him. It gave me an enormous pleasure to see him looking healthier and more at ease. What a good idea this had been! We must not waste a moment of this precious interlude. And even as I turned to go to sleep, my bedroom door creaked open.

"Arthur?" Was this a wonderful dream?

"Are you asleep?" he whispered.

"No."

"Would it disturb you much if I came in with you?"

"No, not a bit!"

"After all, we have slept together once, if you remember."

"I do remember."

"So we know we do not bother each other and keep each other awake."

"Please do come in then, Arthur, and don't stand there in the cold."

The bed creaked ponderously, and he settled against me, night-shirt to nightshirt.

"I didn't sleep at all well these past two nights," he confided against my ear. "The bed was so big. I was lost in it. I dreaded the morning when your valet came in and told me about the weather."

"You get used to it."

"I prefer it this way, just the two of us, all on our own."

"So do I, Arthur; so do I."

"I won't talk much and disturb you; I'll just go to sleep."

"You won't disturb me," I lied.

"Good; I really am tired, and I'll sleep much better next to you."

I stroked his hair reflectively. I did not share Orlando's view that Arthur was in some way stupid. I had the impression that Arthur knew his own mind well enough. I began to wonder whether Orlando had been wrong about the other thing.

An urchin starling on a hawthorn branch awoke me. I could see him through the little window, the wind ruffling his tousled feathers. Within moments Arthur had nipped smartly back to his own room, for breakfast would be brought down from the house. This set the pattern for every night we spent there; Arthur's bed was never slept in.

In the morning we walked miles. We crossed open fields which in the summer were a mass of buttercups and daisies, clumpy tufted meadows now, beneath a lardy sky. Every meadow, so it seemed, had its own lark, a spiralling melodious speck that trilled overhead wherever we went. We passed culverts of brown water where teazles grew. We did not talk much, but now it was a different kind of silence, amicable, warm. I had stopped talking about my children and the fact was of no importance that these fields were mine.

We returned to our cottage where we ate and warmed ourselves and settled to the further saga of the *Hispaniola*. Arthur was like a little boy. "Don't stop," he said. "Let's have another chapter."

And, come night, we went to bed, and slept together, brother-like, companionable and warm.

Would I regret it afterwards, I wondered, that I was not devoting these night hours to the seduction of my sweet bedfellow? I would, yes; but I could not act otherwise. It is a cliché of the novel of the lending library, I know, but my love for Arthur was pure. I had accustomed myself to expecting no more than this, and Heaven knows this was bliss enough. He lay in my arms, a warm endearing bundle, with his black sleek hair spread on the pillow, the shape of him in angular proximity close against me, breathing, in that curious innocence that sleepers seem to show. I felt protective, sentimental. Well, simply I loved him. And I greatly feared that I would not be able to keep this truth from him – that I could not part from him when the week was over without telling him so.

Our conversations were of ordinary things – no politics, no social arguments, no morbid introspection. I don't think it bothered Arthur that I was rich, in the way it had bothered Willie, for instance, who believed that property was theft and that in a more sensible age I should have been obliged to flee the country with my silver in a carpet bag. Arthur found my wealth a nuisance, and was infinitely happier when we lived in two rooms. I was concerned about his patent lack of education but he said he got by without the need to know the dates of every famous battle or who wrote which celebrated literary work; though he admitted he would like to go to concerts. I assured him we would go to concerts when we were back in London – every night, if he liked.

"Your wife is going to love that!" said Arthur ruefully; and a certain gloom descended for a moment.

One evening we went walking in the dusk. As we returned, the sun was setting in a wonderful splash of amber, peach, and deep blood red. The black bare trees against it gave the illusion of a Japanese print on silk. The sky above was a grey wash over blue-silver, and full of soaring larks. We watched the dusk fall, a filmy veil, over the dark furrows. There were lights in distant cottages, and fine flecks of rain. It would have been a study in silence, but for the thrilling and melodious birdsong overhead.

Arthur suddenly took my arm and squeezed it, grinning at me like an imp.

"Wot larks!" he said.

We took the carriage and drove into Bedford the next morning – a chilly windswept day which alternated between sharp brilliant sunlight and hard pelting rain – because I wanted to buy Arthur some new clothes. I winced a little as I overcame the repugnance caused by images of Willie's rich protector buying jewellery and ornate literature, and Oscar's fabulous suppers for his boys at

Kettner's; the fact was that Arthur needed some new clothes and I would buy them. I did not think that jacket, shoes and cap could be seen by anyone as the wicked gifts of a seducer; they were eminently serviceable garments and hardly libidinous.

Upon our peregrinations up and down the High Street we encountered the two statues of the town's most famous luminaries. John Howard the philanthropist is a damned good-looking fellow and surveys the world in thoughtful pose in his elegant eighteenth century attire complete with most exquisite boots. A fine figure of a man, up whose bulging crotch one is obliged to stare when viewing the man from beneath. I believe he was designed by the same Gilbert who conceived the statue of young Eros in Piccadilly, in which connection a certain perception of beauty of the male might be expected. John Bunyan on the other hand is plump and stocky, smirking Heavenward, sure of a good reception there. Arthur had encountered *The Pilgrim's Progress* at his school – religious books he had endured to excess. He found the statue interesting.

"You can bring it to life, you know," I told him seriously. "You have to chant a little poem. It goes like this: Old John Bun-y-an, what a fun-ny 'un, if you come down I'll give you an unn-y-an. Try it – it never fails."

But there were people about, so Arthur would not.

We had luncheon at the Swan Hotel down by the river, and walked beside the Ouse to the suspension bridge where halfway across on the highest point of its gentle curve we leaned and looked towards the town to where the noble spire of St. Paul's church showed beyond the trees. At the coldest part of the Winter the Ouse had frozen over and people had come skating here and brought sledges; even horses had stood upon the ice and it withstood them. Now the water flowed grey and high, and daffodils were only just in flower; it was a late Spring this year.

We drove back to Mortmayne and toasted ourselves beside the fire, and read about the burnished sand and steaming marshes and tall pines that made the backcloth to our pirates and their plotting.

On our last morning we took a rowing boat out on the lake. The boathouse smelt of damp and the mustiness of old forgotten seat cushions. The surface of the lake was ruffled like the ridges of a wet beach. Peewits called and dipped, and partridges came flapping over from the fields. I taught Arthur to row. If anyone who knew me had observed us there they would have been astonished, I daresay, for we behaved much younger than our years, indeed we fooled about with much "ahoy theres" and "belays". There was something about the company of Arthur that induced in me a great well-being and lightheartedness, an easiness of tone not entirely explicable but very tangible and delightful. And yet I would be hard put to explain exactly what we spoke about when we were together – trivia, perhaps, exchange of knowledge on the smaller points of life, the chance recollection of an incident from our past prompted by something that we saw or thought. Nothing jarred. If I had brought my young friend here for the benefits of his health, I may only say that equal benefits were mine.

I was obliged to spend the afternoon with Wingate over matters of estate up at the house, leaving Arthur to wander where he would indoors. I wanted him to know the house, which after all was where I lived, and while I sat in deep discussion with my bailiff, Arthur rambled through the rooms and peered at portraits and the family photographs and handled ornaments and sat in chairs. When we met up again I guessed from his expression that he had had his fill of this and I suggested we return outside to walk away excess of rooms.

We did so, going as far as Odell, where the same river we had seen bordered by stone and steps and bridges now curved its quiet way through water meadows past a mill. Beside a row of cottages we found a sheltered sloping bank where a whole mass of golden celandines had opened up in brilliant display. A surge of great happiness rose in me, one of those moments when the problems of this life seem small, of no account, and the world seems full of possibilities.

Nearer to home, on our way back, we paused beside a little mere to look for frogspawn. This pond, a mossy, stagnant half forgotten hollow, ringed by willows, always reminded me of a poem from the pen of Thomas Hardy, a chilling account of a pond on a winter day and the bleak sky and the wreck of a friendship. Such a place as this, I thought with a shiver, where we are now.

A long-fallen tree, pitted with worm holes, lay to one side. A bush of pussy willow leaned stuntedly, bent from years of wind force. Larks were singing overhead. Arthur at the pond's edge turned his face and grinned.

"No frogspawn."

"Come away."

He clambered back to me. The sky was radiant and loud with the call of a lark.

"Can you see it there? Look!" I pointed.

"No I can't," said Arthur peering, squinting. "Oh yes! Now I see it."

One lark was soaring slowly, singing into a bank of white-grey clouds, wisped smokily by the wind. A vibrant speck, a pinpoint, hard to hold in a mere eye-gaze. The horizon was white, under banks of grey billows. We lost the lark, then found it, held it in sight, both of us immobile, straining, bound by that quivering thread of singing. Wings whirring, down it dropped, plummetting in stages, till the bird shape became recognisable and then disappeared.

I turned to Arthur instantly.

"You must have guessed," I said, "that I love you."

Arthur said nothing, but he stared at me in what I thought seemed sheer surprise.

I had to go on now. I said quickly: "I shan't of course compromise you in any way. But it's only fair to tell you that although I am married and have children I am one of those unfortunate people who are drawn to their own kind. Nothing of this nature was in my mind when I invited you to Mortmayne and if you wish I will say no more about it. I understand that you were once subjected to the attention of Orlando – my love is not like that. Whatever it is, all I know is that it is indeed love. These days together with you, Arthur, have been very precious to me. I hope my declaration has not too much offended you. I could not keep it secret any longer."

"I am very honoured, Lord Algernon," murmured Arthur, looking, I thought, bewildered.

"I was Algy when we were in the boat," I snapped.

"Yes I know. And that is very confusing, isn't it? You are Algy also in the cottage, but tomorrow back in London you will be Lord Algernon. And," added Arthur with a rush of accusation, "whether or not you feel this way or that with your family, that family is real and lives with you."

"In other words," I said bitterly, "I should behave myself as is proper for a married man."

"Oh no," groaned Arthur miserably. "It is merely that I think I am more practical than you."

"What do you mean?"

"Well – with money," Arthur fumbled, "you have always been able to buy whatever you want, to put things right by paying . . . but your money will not be able to make it possible for you and I to be together when we live in London. And love, I understood, is about being together, isn't it?"

"I don't know," I said gloomily. "Love *is*. You discover love. And then it's like a bomb – you carry it around looking for somewhere to put it down, afraid it will blow up on you."

Arthur smiled wanly. "It doesn't sound much fun for us."

"For us?" I clutched at these words. "What do you mean by that?"

"I love you too," said Arthur.

"Oh!" I gasped, immensely moved. And there was nothing for it but to kiss him. A little clumsy kiss it was, my fingers gripping both his arms, my self-control a dam against my desperate passion.

"What now?" said Arthur with a helpless shrug.

I had no reply. We turned to leave that place. That tree-ringed pond would jostle in me different memories from those that stirred the unhappy Wessex poet. With our hands loosely entwined we began to make our way homewards. As we approached the first cottage of Mortmayne, we drew apart.

Treasure Island lay unfinished; instead Arthur and I sat by the fireside thoughtfully, he on the sofa, I in the wing chair, as usual, while darkness thickened about us, and the wind howled louder than the cries of owls.

"I was not sure what you felt about the idea of men loving men," I said. "There are some people who find it personally revolting and loathsome. Indeed," I added gloomily, "I understand that is the common opinion."

"No; I have a simple view; I think that anybody may love anybody," Arthur answered. "In loving you, I don't love other men, or see myself as thus required to feel ashamed. I simply love you, yourself, and as you happen to be a man, it means I love a man."

"I know that Orlando made advances to you . . ."

"Yes, once he did. But I don't like Orlando, and I told him no."

"I thought that meant you found the whole idea repugnant."

"No – I just can't stand Orlando. I find him somehow slimy, like a toad. He thinks that everybody dotes on him."

I could not bring myself at this stage to admit that I was one of those.

"But all that posing for Charles – " I blurted out. "I saw the drawings."

"Oh those," grinned Arthur sheepishly. "Well, the explanation there is a foolish one. I sometimes get so sick of how it is at home. So holy, you know, always the Bible . . . I wanted to do something bad. I let Charles talk me into taking off my clothes and drawing pictures of me. And when I'd had a drink or two I didn't mind the idea of posing with the others in naughty positions. Charles told me what to do. I thought it quite wicked and it gave me quite a thrill. Then afterwards I felt so embarrassed and ashamed. I wouldn't do it any more. I was very muddled in my head. Then Count Zabarov found me and he seemed to take a fancy to me. I was very much out of my depth. I hope I shall be wiser now. I'll go back to Mr Simmons' shop and be a good boy. Always say no!" He laughed and wriggled.

"Not *always*," I said cautiously.

"Ah, well now, that depends who asks!" he said quite archly. "If a handsome lord with yellow hair was to come into the shop and ask me to a concert I would go with him."

"That is likely to occur," I said. "And so it's just as well! There isn't anybody else, is there, Arthur? No rivals for me to subdue?"

"No; there is no one else."

I knelt upon the rug and clasped his hands. "Oh listen, Arthur," I said ardently. "When we get back to London there is no need for our happiness to end. We can still see each other. Trust me. These things can be arranged."

"How? Hotel bedrooms?" Arthur said with unbecoming cynicism.

"I don't know; I haven't thought," I hedged.

"I have thought. That's why when you said you loved me I was so dull. I *wondered* if you loved me. In a way I hoped you didn't. It would be easier for us if you didn't."

"I'm not sorry!" I declared. "I've always loved you Arthur, you're so beautiful. Your eyelashes, your thick dark hair – I longed to have the right to run my hands through it. We can come back here . . ." I paused. Of course, we could not. Within a month or so the house would be thick with guests, the garden full of working lads, this cottage their home. This quiet time was a once only time, an eye-blink, almost past already.

"So you loved me from the first?" said Arthur patently amazed. "I wonder why; I was so rude and sullen."

"Then when did you first love me?" I asked.

"Although I *respected* you from the first," said Arthur solemnly, "it was respect alone when I first met you in your splendid house – with your splendid wife," he added with a flicker of mischief. "And then I felt great gratitude for all you did for me and strong affection when you brought me here and I began to understand you. I've seen your childhood photographs, the little boy you were, the house you played in, and the way it is now, all so very proper. Love came suddenly, when we were on the lake, when you were rowing, and your hair so wild and windy, and you so far forgot your lordliness to laugh out loud and grin as boys do – *all* your teeth, not just the little smile of faint amusement. And then when you called me Jim Lad, at that silly moment, then I knew it. And I've been very troubled ever since. I hoped you wouldn't say anything. Our love is like a great big statue in the room which we are walking round and climbing over, greatly in the way, and all the while pretending that it isn't there, when truthfully it blocks our view of everything and is too big to lift."

"Oh Arthur, let us go to bed," I groaned.

"It won't be the same . . . I don't know if we should."

"I won't do anything that you don't want . . ."

"I suppose we can't put it off for ever."

I smiled at Arthur's gloominess and got to my feet. Taking his hand I prised him from the sofa.

"You haven't drawn the curtains," Arthur warned me.

"Sorry; I forgot."

Now for the first time we undressed in the same bedroom, standing each side of the bed. Finished, we stood and looked at one another; just long enough to see each other's nakedness and admire it; then darted into bed, because for all the glowing of the little fire it wasn't very warm.

We lay with our arms about each other, tentative hands on unfamiliar skin. I kissed him, but I was dogged by images of Orlando's teasing petulant invitation "Kiss me with your tongue", which made the same with Arthur seem a desecration. I held him, kissing him lightly on the face, the neck.

"It isn't very warm, though, is it?" Arthur murmured.

"No it isn't. Shall we put our nightshirts back on?"

"Yes." We did so. I turned out the lamp.

We lay there close together, stupidly inept. When my hand brushed his loins I murmured "Sorry", not wanting him to think that I would take advantage of the declaration of our love, that he would be expected to yield to demands of mine now that we had admitted our true feelings. Indeed, we were less comfortable than we had been with each other on the previous nights merely sleeping, in the harmony of friendship.

If I could have described it at all I would have said that it was something akin to the discovery of a chart, a treasure map. (Blame the image on my reading matter.) The chart you have in your possession, with the cross scrawled by the ragged pines, and the treasure waits for you, you know it. But you have to travel there across an ocean, you have to fit a ship and find a crew, provisions. You are not ready to go jumping in the treasure pit, you fear to smash the jewels with your heavy boots. In plain language, there with Arthur in my arms I was as limp as a rag and I could not have pleasured him in any carnal way without a deal of flattery and seduction which he, poor soul, seemed no more up to offering than I.

"Shall we just go to sleep?" said Arthur politely.

"Yes; we had better, I think."

"Do you like to sleep on the right or on the left?"

"Well, what did we do last night?" I said irritably.

"I don't remember; we just slept."

"Suppose we try just sleeping then."

"Is anything the matter?" Arthur asked me tentatively. "I mean, would you like to do it?"

"Oh God!" I snapped. "Not like that anyway."

"I may not be very good," said Arthur apologetically. "I know you've been with other people, people who are good at it."

"For Heaven's sake, this is no competition. All I know is," I tried to qualify my exasperation, "is that it's easy with somebody you don't care about. And with somebody that you love it takes on an importance so painful that it's curiously crippling. I haven't any other explanation."

"You don't need one. I thought it might be like this."

I hugged him. "Go to sleep. There will be other times."

"You know as well as I do that it will be difficult."

"Oh damn you, don't you see that is the problem – if this is the only night that we are ever likely to have in circumstances of some privacy, some perfection, the burden is too great to get it right. I'm frightened. I don't want the memory of some hurried bungle which leaves us both dissatisfied, and then in the morning to have to separate with some shared ghastly failure to look back on. I want to do it, as you put it, knowing I can be with you again tomorrow night and always. Some devil's plaguing me and I don't feel able. Oh damn this stupid love; it always spoils things."

"No it doesn't; it only changes them."

Curiously comforted we lay together close and gradually fell asleep. In the night I woke – the wind was rattling the hawthorn branches outside the window. A lurch of my heart reminded me that this was our last morning. Prompted by this unworthy motive I moved further down the bed and lifted Arthur's nightshirt. I put my face against his warm belly and moved my cheek against his hair; my lips caught his cock; I took it in my mouth. The action excited me, and him also, for under the caresses of my tongue his cock grew hard. I licked him, kissed him, took the hardness into my throat. I moved him to a rhythm. I felt his hands clasp on my head; he pushed me close to him. Oh! now I needed him to come, I ached to taste him; I worked my wet lips along his prick, I felt the stirring of his balls, I made him come. The wetness filled my mouth, I licked it from his thigh. Then, my hand on my own cock I quickly drew myself to satisfaction; it hardly took a moment. I crawled up the bed, hot and breathing hard. He held me to him. We had had our pleasure, but it left me empty; I felt like a thief.

We overslept, and leapt apart as the vigorous thumping on the front door heralded the arrival of our breakfast. Oh! Had the night been the disaster I remembered or merely one of those things sent to try us, which time and consideration can put right?

Mid morning saw us dressed and spruce up at the house to gather the remainder of our possessions and to talk in serious tones to housekeeper and bailiff, to make statements, plans.

Arthur wandered off.

I found him in the conservatory, which led out of the drawing room. I joined him there, already in my coat, for our departure.

This place was always associated in my mind with Oscar Wilde, for he had caught my eye here, leaving me confused. How long ago those days seemed when he had been a visitor in my house and everybody hung upon his every passing epigram, and not a whiff of impropriety! I saw him once again surrounded by the adoring throng, taller than the rest, with violets in his buttonhole; and I much younger, posing by a plant.

How warm it was here! That solid fuel boiler which enabled us to keep it so must be working to bursting point. Beyond the glass, the lawns were bright with daffodils, and pale soft-blown narcissi swaying in the wind. Within, the vines climbed carefully to the roof, the lush green leaves trailed down from hanging baskets, while great urns spewed forth thick shiny tropical foliage and waves of feathery ferns, so many varied greens, so much of glass containing it.

"Arthur . . . it's time to go."

He looked so young, so darkly handsome – and last night I'd tasted him and put my mouth about his cock – was it a dream? We moved together till our hands touched; neither moved.

"I like this place," said Arthur.

"It's romantic, isn't it!"

"Like Tir na n Og?" he grinned, recalling that odd tea party when I first met him. Ginger-haired Thaddeus O'Shea had discoursed upon the world of Faery, a green and verdant place special to lovers, where there is no death, and all the time is spent in making love. Inspired and doting, I had pictured Arthur and myself there, dancing round inside the glass dome in every kind of ecstasy amongst the plants therein, Adam and Adam, in a green garden. Damn me, I thought aghast, and here we were exactly like that strange whimsy of mine – except that we were clothed, alas! – but here we were, alone together amongst leaves and ferns, in a great glass bowl, a weird fulfilment of an idle flight of fancy.

Obscured by foliage, we stood.

"You do love me, don't you?" I said urgently.

"I do love you," Arthur answered in a low voice.

"And I love you too. It's important we establish this . . . a discovery made here, which we carry with us back to London."

"Like a very heavy suitcase, with a handle each," Arthur gave a little twisted smile. "I always thought love was supposed to make you happy."

"Love makes you happy; then society takes over," I replied.

We heard the servants bustling about beyond the glass doors to the drawing room.

"They'll be wondering . . ." said Arthur, fidgeting.

"So they will, but it's guilt that makes us feel uneasy, not that they are growing suspicious. This is something we will have to guard against; I mean a guilt that's self-induced, producing problems that do not exist."

However, I knew the carriage was now ready, waiting in the drive. We went to seek it out.

We were both in sober mood as we journeyed towards London, the railway a line of fate on the palm of a hand. Arthur in his luggage had the copy of *Treasure Island* which we had not finished reading; I inscribed our names on the flyleaf – "To Arthur With Love from Algy". I reasoned as we travelled that we need not feel too apprehensive. One could not possibly predict the outcome, but if we were careful all would be well. There were ways of working these things. Trusting in the unwillingness of the casual acquaintance to seek trouble or to see vice where it did not exist, we could very well get by. We could be companions, go about together. We would not be able to meet as often as we would like, but we could meet, and sometimes chance might throw us up an opportunity for more. All we had to be was discreet, and pray that it escaped the notice of society that sometimes Greek Love did exist, deep down beneath the surface of its throbbing maelstrom, but only thought about when some fool stirred the pool.

I smiled encouragingly at Arthur as the framework of St. Pancras station closed about us and the train drew in.

We joined the teeming throng and made our way towards the portals. Six or seven newsboys selling newspapers were pestering the returning travellers, flapping like excited chickens, squawking, yelling, vying with each other in their raucous voices to be loudest, boldest, most shocking:

"Hoscar Wilde arrested!"

"Hoscar Wilde in prison!"

"Corruption of youf!"

"Scenes of Orrible Debauchery!"

"Horgies in a Den of Vice!"

"Read all abaht it!"

CHAPTER SEVENTEEN

I HAD not even realised that Oscar Wilde was back in England. A week in the country and in the heady regions of the emotions had left me entirely out of touch with the events in London and I had completely missed the Queensberry trial. It took all my resources to retain my self-composure, in the face of the hideous howling of the newsboys; and my parting from Arthur was somewhat marred, as I handed him into a cab with his luggage, mutual kind words and the promise of a meeting very soon.

This done I took a cab myself to Pall Mall and installed myself at my club. In a corner of the smoking room I met up with a collection of cronies all of whom were avidly perusing the newspaper accounts. I sat with Heatherington and Freddy, and a parley ensued half public, half private, for the gentlemen nearby in similar groups were all talking upon the same subject as ourselves, our conversations partly overlapping. In an atmosphere thick with cigar smoke and the clink of brandy glasses, with the dedication of a horde of vultures, we picked over what had happened.

Both Freddy and Heatherington had gone along to the Old Bailey for the Queensberry trial. "There in front of the dock," said Freddy, "stood the Marquis of Queensberry glowering at Oscar, and Oscar looking very smart and fashionable with a tall silk hat and a white flower in his buttonhole. Sir Edward Clarke spoke for the prosecution. He's a small stout man but very dignified, with the funniest side whiskers billowing out below his ears like something off a goat! He said it was very wrong of Queensberry to leave a wicked card like that at Oscar's club, particularly since it referred to the gravest of all offences!"

"The gravest?" I marvelled instantly. "More so than murder?"

"For myself," said Heatherington stretching in his chair, "I don't see much to choose between the two."

"Well, Queensberry's side said that the so-called libel statement was the truth," said Freddy. "And they proposed to prove it. Did you know that Oscar had been blackmailed? Clarke read out this letter which Oscar had written to Bosie – d'you know how it began:

'My Own Boy'!"

Kennington guffawed. Barkworth frowned at him. "Revolting," he said. "No cause for humour there!"

I smiled wanly. When I had written to Arthur – what had I said? Those two swift notes I penned to which he made no answer, being ill ... what had I said? Dear Arthur ... could *that* be seen as compromising? I must let him know to burn them if he had not done so already. Then I berated myself for being a fool, for my letter was in no way similar to Oscar's, as I learnt when Freddy chirpily continued, recounting with a snigger that Oscar had written about "the music of song and the madness of kisses" and "something about lips and passion" and "*signed with undying love*. Yes! And everybody burst out laughing."

I shifted uncomfortably, and my heart went out to that misguided Irishman.

"There was lots of laughing," Freddy added. "It wasn't serious at all. And Oscar was very funny and made everybody laugh the more. Poor Clarke made a mistake and called Lord Queensberry by the name of Lord Rosebery and the judge said he would clear the court if everybody kept on laughing. And then Clarke asked Oscar if there was any truth in the accusation of bad conduct and Oscar promised there wasn't. Then we went to luncheon." With a pause for more brandy he continued. "I thought that when Lord Queensberry's counsel Edward Carson started questioning Oscar he would not prove very effective on account of his suffering from a dreadfully bad cold. Have you met him, Algy? He's a tall thin man with a protruding chin, and hair scraped back to show his big forehead – and as Irish as they come."

"There followed much close questioning of Wilde by Carson," Heatherington said. "He was querying the morality of Wilde's smart phrases in the books he writes. Some of the language is embarrassing. No decent man could have written it."

"He read a passage about adoring someone madly and extravagantly and he made Oscar say whether he had ever loved a young man madly."

"What insolence!" I gasped.

"No, Algy," frowned Freddy, as if I had not properly understood. "He was merely trying to prove that Oscar's personal ideas are rather odd. Not normal. Not the normal sort of thing one thinks; not what you and I think. It was all perfectly reasonable at the time. There's this passage about being afraid that the world will get to hear about this kind of love – "

"*What* kind of love?" I said irritably.

"Corruption," answered Heatherington. "When an older man

corrupts a youth by introducing him to unnatural vice. The kind of thing we all know Wilde has been up to."

We were silent. Then Freddy burbled quickly: "He wanted Oscar to read his letters out. How dreadfully embarrassing that must be for anyone! Lord! If I had to read out loud a letter I had written in my bedroom – a private letter – I would really *die*! But my letters aren't very interesting, not like Oscar's were – all about curved lips and wine and calling Bosie Douglas the Dearest of All Boys!"

"Carson suggested it was not the kind of letter one man writes to another," said Heatherington, "and I daresay none of us would disagree."

Murmurs of assent ensued. "Hear, hear," said Kennington noisily.

"And then there came the part about the blackmailing," recounted Freddy, "and then about the," he lowered his voice as if he were in a church, "sodomy. It was Awful!"

"It sounds to have been so," I said soberly.

"All those boys!" said Freddy shaking his head. "Private hotel rooms that led through to bedrooms – whiskies and sodas – expensive dinners – gifts of money – youths of eighteen – why, he picked one up on a beach, pushing a boat! *And he bought him clothes!*"

I dared not speak. I suddenly imagined clothiers from Bedford trooping past like Banquo's descendants, identifying Arthur and myself. *He brought the boy into our shop, your honour, and he bought him clothes!*

"I think that was about all on the first day," said Heatherington. "And personally I had had enough. I did not wish to hear vile details. Whether the bedrooms communicated by a green baize door I did not wish to know. But Freddy's stomach is of stronger stuff and he went back next morning."

I looked at Freddy; thus invited he proceeded.

"It was all about a man named Alfred Taylor, who kept a Den of Vice in Little College Street."

"*Where*?" I asked appalled.

"I believe it's near the Houses of Parliament. It's shocking, isn't it, to think these things go on near the seat of our government! And who would imagine what kind of a place it was inside – the curtains were always drawn, and even in the daytime they lit candles and burned perfumes. And they dressed in women's clothing! And that was where Oscar Wilde went to meet young men. It seems the police suspected it and kept a watch. They'd had their eye upon it for some time. Are you quite well, Algy?"

"I'm tired, that's all," I murmured, feeling haggard. "Travelling, you know . . ."

I saw myself again upon that dreadful night when I had walked

210

the streets, desperate for the love of my own kind. Outside the house in Little College Street I had stood, too cowardly to enter, longing, yearning, but afraid. If I had entered – oh! would my name now be upon some bumbling policeman's list – my fate the same as Oscar's – his disgrace mine? I gave a silent prayer of thanks that fear had stayed my hand.

"Algy, you are grown quite pale."

"I tell you, I am well . . . only tired. And to be frank with you I find the matter curiously distressing."

"It's worse than that – abominable!" said Heatherington.

I gave him a withering look. "That someone has his private life laid bare – spread out for fools to gawp at – his intimate letters read – how must he feel?"

Freddy put a kindly hand upon my arm. "Dear Algy, you are so sensitive. But there is no need. Oscar Wilde is not like you, like us – he isn't normal; he's depraved and evil. He won't feel the things a finer nature feels . . . you waste your pity."

"I shouldn't go round speaking up for him," Heatherington told me meaningfully. "I advise you, as a friend. *Everyone* will drop them now; it's only common sense. I say, though," he added, sounding most aggrieved. "What a way to repay our hospitality! We take him into our homes and introduce him to the cream of society and all the time he knocks about with grooms and valets behind our backs . . ."

"Behind *their* backs!" Kennington corrected, to throaty sniggers of amusement.

"Was that all that happened at the trial?" I asked of Freddy.

"Why no. The most dramatic was yet to come!"

"Oh really?" I said weakly.

"Yes. You see, there was a deal of questioning about one of the boys in particular – Charles Parker. He was one of those that Wilde took dining at the Café Royal and Kettner's . . ."

"And any of us who have dined there at the same time will have seen the lad in question," Barkworth grumbled. "Which means of course that we have been unwittingly in the company of sodomites. It leaves a very nasty taste in the mouth."

Kennington snorted lewdly. "They have rooms upstairs, don't they?" he enquired with a salacious grin. "You bloat yourself on iced champagne, then up – you – go."

His contribution generally deemed distasteful, other sprays of conversation blossomed here and there.

Freddy told me: "Just as we were all considering the awfulness of Wilde being so friendly with young men of that type, Mr Edward Carson said that Charles Parker would be called in evidence! Well,

211

everybody gasped! Carson reminded us that Charlie Parker had been involved in that scandal in Fitzroy Street, when the police arrested all those men who dressed as women and held orgies, and so we could not believe that the young man would dare give evidence, since he would convict himself also, by implication."

"The explanation for that is obvious," said Lord Avonbury, who had not spoken before. His voice was loud, his tone bitter. "The youth has been given police protection."

"Oh surely not!" said Kennington. "What – a self-confessed sodomite? And you think they'll let him go?"

Avonbury shrugged expressively and turned back to his newspaper.

"There isn't only Parker," said Freddy. "A whole list of other youths were mentioned – one was Freddy Atkins, who is supposed to be a music hall hopeful. Wilde took *him* to *Paris*! They cannot all be in police protection, can they? Whatever would that say about the correct procedures of the police force!"

Freddy Atkins! My heart sank further. I recalled my brief flirtation with the dark life behind the façade of The Two Faces near Shaftesbury Avenue. What was his name, that curly-headed whore who had relieved me so delightfully? Eddy. What had he said? Freddy Atkins could make fifty pound a time from his sideline, blackmailing his customers. Oh God! What a fool I had been! Dancing about so carelessly on the edge of conflagration – flitting between the flames . . .

"Now let me tell you about the breakthrough!" Freddy said. "Well! There was this boy that he and Bosie knew. Have you ever kissed him, says Carson. Oh dear no, says Wilde; he was such a plain boy – really ugly! Well – he tried to cover up what he had said, but Carson fell on it quick as a flash. Is that why you didn't kiss him, he cries? And then Oscar became upset, why, almost in tears, and couldn't answer properly, and Carson kept on at him, pestering and pestering, pointing his skinny finger, leaning forward like a wraith of doom. He's had it now, I thought!"

I could not, dared not speak. Whatever Oscar had endured then, my sympathy was so great that it was myself I saw there in the pillory – indeed I could have been there with him, for my recent past had led me only too close to his hunting grounds, and chance alone had saved me and protected me, where he had fallen.

"Sir Edward Clarke then tried to soften things," said Freddy. "He pointed out that Oscar Wilde's wife had not petitioned for divorce. The implication is that if the wife stands by the man he must be innocent. I think we went to luncheon around then? Yes, that's right, and when we came back Oscar wasn't there, and everybody thought that he had fled to France."

"Fled to France?" I blinked.

"Why yes," laughed Kennington. "That's what the pederast does when they've ferreted him out. Flees to France. Or shoots himself!"

More throaty laughter. But the wretched Oscar had merely been lunching late.

"And so," continued Freddy, "Mr Carson began a spirited speech in defence of Lord Queensberry, who. had been sitting there red-faced and scowling, and he said that everything done by the marquis has been solely in the interest of saving his son from Oscar's wicked influence. We had heard evidence enough that this influence had been pretty bad – but Carson promised that he would provide more! The boys and the blackmailers would all be brought before us to tell their sordid tales! And then the court rose and we all went home. Outside on the pavement crowds of people surrounded us, screeching for details. It was all we could do to push through. I hardly slept last night, I was so excited – I could hardly wait to see what was going to happen. This morning I would not have missed it for the world. Were we going to see those wicked witnesses? But no. What happened was that Oscar Wilde was advised to drop the case, because if it continued he would surely be arrested. There was a lot of to-ing and fro-ing, and someone told me that they were going to keep it going so that Wilde could leave the country. Or shoot himself!" he added with a grin at Kennington. "But he did not go. And by withdrawing from the case, the prosecution were admitting that the marquis had been in the right, and the jury agreed that Queensberry had acted for the public good. And so the marquis was let off, and everybody cheered. Oscar sneaked out by a side door with Bosie and Robert Ross, and the marquis was the hero of the hour. When we came outside, the crowds were worse than yesterday and there were women out there too, yelling and dancing about – I'd never seen anything like it."

"Bosie Douglas?" I asked. I never liked the brat, but even he, I feared, had suffered dreadfully throughout those ghastly revelations. "He was there each day?"

"Oh yes. Looking very pale and quiet. He's awfully like you to look at, Algy. I kept thinking that when I looked at him."

"Oh, leave it, Freddy," I snapped. "I am at least ten years older than he and I hope I have more dignity."

"You are nothing like him," Heatherington said, as irritable as I had been. "Really, Freddy, that is a tasteless remark." Indeed, Heatherington was so offended on my behalf by Freddy's foolish opinion that I could not but suppose he thought there was some truth in it.

"And now Wilde is arrested," Kennington observed. "It seems they got him at the Cadogan Hotel and took him off to Bow Street. Why the fellow did not go abroad I cannot imagine. He had the opportunity. He must be every kind of fool. You get two years for sodomy; he must know that."

"So you will have another succulent trial to attend, Freddy," Lord Avonbury observed dourly. "And this one, Algy, *you* need not miss."

"The sooner the better, I say," said Lord Barkworth fiercely. "The man is evil. He has lived a life abhorrent to decent society. Ordinary sane people like ourselves cannot conceive of that kind of monstrosity, and to think it walked here in our midst! Of course, I suspected for some time that the man was outside the bounds of human compassion. We've all known it, haven't we? To think that he has spoken to my wife! My gorge rises at the very notion."

"Without wishing to excuse the man," said Kennington seriously, "I do believe that this condition occurs sometimes as a result of hereditary factors. If you recall, his mother is an odd eccentric woman, and his father, a doctor, was involved in a disgusting scandal with a female patient. Such antecedents must prejudice the fate of any offspring."

"Huh! An excess of Literature, that's what!" spat Barkworth with contempt.

"I do not think that any of us would deny that Oscar Wilde is evil," Heatherington proposed. "But my theory is that he may have suffered from a brain disease. I believe that it is possible for certain brain cells to decay and cause derangement bordering on madness. The victim does not know that he himself is affected, nor does his condition manifest itself to those about him. None of us who spoke to him experienced a sensation of instinctive dread . . . Because his crime is so abhorrent, it may be that he had no power to prevent himself – for obviously nobody would act like that through choice! Therefore I suggest it was a degenerative disorder – a curious discrepancy between the two sides of his nature, a fatal lesion. It is unthinkable of course that by suggesting this theory I mean to defend his conduct. I merely offer up an explanation."

"Yes – you mean he was much like a vampire," Kennington agreed. "By day one thing, by night another."

Startled, I waited for the smirk to show upon his face, the snigger from the listeners; but no one laughed, and Kennington had been utterly serious in volunteering that hypothesis.

Lord Avonbury slowly stood up.

"I must congratulate you all," he said. "Might I remind you that the trial which you have been discussing with such fair-minded interest has been the trial of Lord Queensberry, not of Oscar Wilde?

Might I put to you that Mr Wilde has not yet stood trial for his alleged crimes and that in this country it is understood that one is innocent until proved guilty? You have damned the man on every side, have tried and sentenced him. I hold no brief for one side or the other; I merely state the case for justice."

Red-faced he coughed, and moved away between the leather chairs towards the door.

"Well," grumbled Barkworth huffily. "I'm sure I stand by all I said."

"I don't think any of us have said anything of which we need feel ashamed," Heatherington assured us. "And if a man may not talk freely in his club, then where may he?"

I had a foolish notion that perhaps I might anonymously stand bail for Mr Wilde. Such was my innocence that I thought that I could go to Bow Street and slip in unnoticed, as if I had come there on other business. A quiet word with the inspector on duty would be all that would be required, and nobody need ever know what I had done. The odd thing was, that much later I learnt that others like myself had had the same idea, and more than one had been touched by his plight enough to make this gesture. Lord Alfred Douglas, of course, as everyone knows, went rushing down there on that selfsame errand and then all over town in a search for other sureties should they be required. All to no avail.

What none of us knew at this stage was that Whitehall had determined upon a conviction and would not allow bail under any circumstances because of letters concerning "exalted personages", namely our prime minister Lord Rosebery. Now that the letters had become public knowledge and common gossip in French newspapers, if Oscar was not sentenced it would seem that Rosebery had connived at his release to protect himself. The government must have been in a panic, scared that a scandal would come out in court; but it must go through with the trial to vindicate itself and not to be accused of covering up for Rosebery. It was true that the prime minister was unwell at this time. Whether he had anything to fear from the Drumlanrig business who can tell? We all knew that the death of his wife five years ago had hit him very hard and that he went into a decline as a result. It was reputed that he lived a very lonely life. If he had known some reciprocal tenderness with that unfortunate young man I saw no shame in that; indeed I hoped that it was so, for both their sakes. Whatever had happened, the possibility of potential political crisis was heavily to contribute towards Oscar's ultimate fate. But this I did not know as I set off for Bow Street late that evening.

As we skirted Covent Garden Market and turned up from Russell

215

Street we saw what amounted to a mob, spilling all over the road, pushing up against the walls of the police station and making such a clamour that one questioned what one was about to find. My driver certainly felt some alarm, for he enquired down at me through the cab roof: "Here we are then, guvnor – do you wish me to proceed?"

"Go as far as you may."

Our hansom proceeded slowly up the street and brought us into close proximity with the fringes of the crowd. I confess I had never seen such ugly faces. It is a fact that whatever a man's features may be like in normal circumstances, if he is bawling abuse and contorted with hatred he is not a handsome sight. And there were women also, of the street kind, painted and unkempt, in tawdry shawls and garish gowns, shaking their fists and screeching. Policemen moved amongst them, trying to exert some authority, calling on them to go home.

"The horse don't like it," warned my cabby.

Now we could hear some of the individual shouts and none were pleasant.

"Bring the bugger out here – we'll give him what for – "

"Slit 'is froat – "

"Who's goin' ter be cuddlin' 'is poor boys tonight? *He* ain't!"

Their faces seemed to me quite demented, not like human faces, and the crude rough laughter was like stage laughter, exaggerated, awful . . . it reminded me of a play I had once seen about the French Revolution. I was revolted; and I reasoned that they must have been engaged in this display for hours, since some of them were plainly hoarse, and yet they seemed to be impelled by a machine-like impetus, void of sense and civilised demeanour.

Now that we were amongst them, these same faces peered in at the windows, leering, growling, with hard empty eyes. One halfwit pointed with a yell and bellowed: "Look! It's Bosie Douglas – it's his *Own Dearest Boy*!"

This development I had not foreseen; the cloth-eared rabble, having no regular access to the famous, took the lead from this misguided cretin and gathered round us, thumping with clenched fists on the glass.

"I'll have to turn about!" my driver shouted.

"Please do!"

The expressive hooves of the cab horse proved good argument for the parting of the crowd as we circled round; but not before I had been obliged to hear a welter of insults that by rights should have been Bosie's. The nubs of splayed-out fingers pressed against the windows, grotesque and flattened; ugly mouths gaped and I heard but too well the obscenities they belched. Astonishment uppermost in my mind, I was not so much frightened at the time, but once clear of the place I found myself shaking, as much with anger as with anything.

"Bleedin' 'ell," accused my cab driver sourly. "Why didn't you tell me you was 'im?"

"You fool!" I seethed; but I was overwrought.

So, no chance was there of anybody sneaking into Bow Street on an errand of anonymity that night; and next day the celebrated prisoner was removed to Holloway Gaol.

My mother arrived next afternoon in a very flustered state. She had barely been shown into the privacy of the drawing room and seated herself on the sofa before she began upon the object of her mission.

"Algy! You used to receive this Wilde person at Mortmayne, did you not?"

To hear the frame of her sentence you would have supposed that she had been referring to a savage. "Which wild person?" I enquired.

"Don't be flippant, Algy; you know whom I mean. Of course I long ago advised Claudia to have nothing to do with Constance Wilde and I believe she did as I suggested. I know that neither of you have seen the Wildes socially for several years. But an appalling thought occurred to me last night – Algy, have you any letters in the house from that man, or did you ever write him any letter, which might be misconstrued?"

"No, I never wrote to him," I assured her patiently. "Nor are my cupboards stocked with letters about rose red lips and slim gilt souls. Be easy on that score, mother. You may sleep peacefully tonight."

"It is no laughing matter," said my mother, looking at me piercingly. "You know the kind of damage that can be done with letters if they fall into the wrong hands. Oh Algy!" she said earnestly. "If you have anything like that in your possession, burn it, burn it, no matter what! The most innocent remark can be misconstrued and manipulated in the hands of an evil person . . ."

"Truly, mamma! I have no guilty secret, no incriminating letters, nothing . . ."

"You know, Algernon," she said in a quiet voice. "Your father and I used to worry about you, before you married. When you frequented that house in Kensington . . . were familiar with those artists . . . we feared for you . . . you were always so sensitive and malleable. Your father used to say some dreadful things, things no father ought ever to say about his son. But these remarks were prompted only by his uneasiness concerning your character . . . and I too shared his deep concern. I never spoke of it. Will you assure me now, that I have no cause for concern at *this* juncture? I think you know what I mean."

I felt my face grow pale. "Of course you need not worry," I said evenly. "You have my word."

That night I was a picture of woe. I could not sleep. I lay awake in the great marital bed, shifting my position, pounding the pillow, burying myself beneath the sheets, now hot, now cold. Eventually I slung my dressing gown about myself and stood at the window looking down upon the dark square with its black trees and its deserted pavements. I was monstrously depressed about the newspapers' reportage of the trials and the righteous hysteria that accompanied it. I guessed that until Oscar's trial, and maybe beyond, the love of men for men would be very much to the fore in the minds of the populace. The secrecy and discretion that I had hoped for in the furtherance of my relations with Arthur was now impossible. I did not know, as I stood there that night, whether in the present climate I could contact him at all without compromising him. Although I was completely sure of the loyalty of the servants at Mortmayne I could not help seeing a ghastly comparison between myself and Oscar. The boy he had picked up on a beach at Worthing – I saw again the horrid newspaper accounts – *you took the lad to Brighton – you bought him a suit of blue serge – and a hat – and presents, including a book – now why did Mr Wilde do this? If he wanted to help the lad the very worst thing he could have done was to take him from his proper sphere, staying at a hotel, living in a way in which the boy could never in the future expect to live . . .*

How the points would all have been hammered home in that vile courtroom! But for me there followed hideous echoes from my own behaviour. *You took the lad to your family home – was your wife present? NO one? You bought him gifts – a jacket and a cap, a pair of shoes and –* I sniggered mirthlessly – *a copy of* Treasure Island*! You treated him in a manner in which the boy could never in the future expect to live. You gave him Upside Down Winter Pudding! And furthermore you gave your word to your mother that there was no cause for concern . . .*

I fidgeted about, walked to and fro. I knew now that when I had noticed Oscar as he went about his life that the revulsion I experienced towards him, the unnatural disgust I showed for his appearance, dress, behaviour, was the over-zealous dread of one who sees a mirror image – I use the term in its loosest sense – an image of myself distorted, emphasised, enlarged. I had sensed all along an instinctive fellowship with him, and he had known it too. Give in, Algy, he had told me, in the end it's for the best. Well, I had given in; and so had he. Did he still believe that it was for the best?

And what of me? What would it mean for me?

It seemed that London could talk of nothing other than the Oscar Wilde affair. The newspapers in heated indignation shrieked for blood. At the St. James' Theatre, where but two months ago, in a snowstorm, society in all its glamour had witnessed the opening night of *The Importance of Being Earnest*, that same play was advertised with the name of its author blocked out on placard and programme. We learnt at the club that some of Oscar's closest friends had fled to France and that the boat trains to the continent were packed with gentlemen who all of a sudden felt a pressing need to leave the country. It was sniggered that anyone who left for France had damned himself by his own action; and then those same voices became strangely quiet when it was learnt that Heatherington had gone. Heatherington! He who had told me that he saw no difference between the gravity of sodomy and murder, and then put forward the suggestion that a brain disorder caused Oscar Wilde's condition. What did it mean? Could Heatherington have been a secret participant in Uranian Love? It was not possible. But then, what did we ever know of each other, we who dealt in surface matters, social niceties? We were like country houses, where the façade was all that counted, and behind it rooms and endless rooms, some of them always locked.

When I returned home from the club I found a letter waiting for me. I did not recognise the untidy handwriting and I opened it there in the hall. A brief note it was, containing various misspellings and somewhat thumb-printed.

Dear Lord Algy,

Please meet me at Piccadilly by the statue this afternoon at four o'clock. It is an urgent matter.

Your friend Francis

Whatever could the boy want with me? I had never expected to see him again now that poor Charles was buried. I wondered whether he was in some kind of trouble. Lord! Surely he was not one of the boys involved in Oscar's scandal and coming to me for help!

Under a dull grey sky and upon an afternoon of some chilliness I joined the jostling Piccadilly throng. I crossed the road to the centre point of those streets which converged upon the island, and approached the statue of young Eros. Upon the steps at the base the flower sellers called us:

"Varlets! Lahvly varlets!"

"Fresh cut daffs, sir? Beauties!"

" 'Ave a bunch o' these, sir. Varlets!"

Absentmindedly I bought a bunch of violets from a buxom matron in a checked shawl. About her skirts were buckets of brilliant daffodils gleaming with waterdrops, and stiff scarlet tulips startlingly bright in the grey puddled street. Delicate white and gold narcissi shivered in the wind. The violets lay upon wooden trays, already bunched into small nosegays. In sudden wafts that sweet perfume rose, assailing the sleeping senses by its beauty.

I looked about me thoughtfully. So long ago it seemed now I had stood here undecided, visualising this evocative junction of roads as a wilderness where predator and prey moved round about each other in a wary dance, and secret lovers recognised each other, giving aid, providing bolt-holes to the warrens of escape from dangers. More than ever now, I surmised, we must help each other. For now I understood where my allegiance lay; I hoped that I would try to ease the path of any troubled brother, and I hoped that he would do the same for me.

Francis moved towards me from amongst the crowd. I noticed a certain shiftiness in his manner. I experienced a rush of kindliness and warmth towards him. Far apart as we may have been in social spheres we were brothers in adversity, bound by our way of loving which society had deemed a criminal offence comparable with murder, theft, brutality. I remembered with gratitude our shared hours of lust in Charles' lodgings. How much worse his life would inevitably be now that the newspapers had got their teeth into that particular moral issue . . .

"I knew you'd come," he said, from the corner of his mouth. "Did you guess what I wanted?"

"Not at all."

"Well, I think it must be obvious enough," said Francis in a low and rather ugly tone. "The plain truth is that I want money."

"I beg your pardon?"

"Money, Lord Algernon," said Francis sharply. "Do I have to spell it out?"

"I am afraid so," I replied with a certain coolness. How ill it became his rosy-red and apple-cheeked exterior, this odd and underhand manner, this hint of mystery.

He lowered his voice, speaking with an intensity the more vibrant for its hoarse whisper. "For not telling the law about what you did with me on more than one occasion. I don't suppose you'd like the truth to come out now, with all this Hoscar business. You could end up standing where he'll be standing – in the dock. I thought ten pounds for starters. What d'you say?"

It is a fact that those brought up to treat the world with dignity and a perfect belief in their own right to be where birth has placed them have no confusion in dealing with the sordid and emotionally shabby. Centuries of breeding instantly stepped in to give me no doubt whatsoever of my course.

"I am sorry, Francis, that you think to take advantage of my friendship to behave so. I suggest that since you have no proof of what you speak, neither in letter, gift nor witness, you ask yourself which of us the police will believe when you make your allegations and I firmly deny it. Since the inspector is a friend of mine you will be very likely to find yourself behind bars within the hour, for the law shows no sensitivity when dealing with a street whore. I shall forget this silly interchange between us; but if you ever attempt to pester me again, in any way whatsoever, I shall make it my business to see you into prison."

The wretched boy then behaved like villains often seem to do in certain stage productions. He wrung his hands together, twitched, pointed his feet inward, snivelled. "I didn't mean nothing, sir," he fumbled. "Honest I didn't. It just seemed like a good idea. I thought you'd give, see, 'cos of Mr Wilde. I don't mean nothing against you, sir. You won't put me in prison, will yer? I won't try it no more."

"Oh be off with you!" I said in growing irritation; and he nodded, turned about and scuttled off into the crowd. I watched him go, and stood in thought, chewing my lip in some perplexity.

I was unsettled by the encounter. What had disturbed me was the unforeseen – the fact that at this time of communal danger, instead of closing ranks and promising loyalty, the lover turned against himself, betraying his own kind, when more than ever we should stand as one. What hope was there when facing the lion of the establishment, the fleeing animals should seek to offer up one of their number to the foe for their vile advancement! If Francis had simply come to me for ten pounds and asked, he would have gone away ten pounds the richer – yet he chose so to degrade himself and me by a transaction of a sordid nature whose outcome must be unpleasantness for both; no gentleman responds to blackmail.

The flower sellers called and chorused, and above their heads the delicate dancing boy darted arrows at random into unsuspecting hearts. In great despondency I stood there, holding violets.

The eager welcome which I accorded to my wife on her return from Ramsgate was very largely prompted by relief at finding myself surrounded once more by the trappings of respectability and normality. In the pleasant personage of Claudia lay all my camouflage. With her beside me, who could ever suspect me of deviancy? I noticed as for the first time her undeniable beauty, the honest candour of her blue eyes, the soft silk of her hair. What if she had unconventional views on women's dress? Anyone may possess at least one foible. She took instant charge of the household reins, confirmed our promised attendance at Lady Girton's ball and, in her warm and vigorous care of every aspect of the children's welfare, showed herself only too apparently the perfect mother. She was the best thing that could have happened to me at this dismal juncture and I was delighted to receive her.

Some time during the second week of April, Claudia and I were dining alone; Emily had seen Sophy and Perceval to bed, and no more conversation had passed our lips than the usual comments about unseasonable weather. Suddenly Claudia put down her knife and fork and sat up straight.

"Algy, I have to tell you something."

I waited, surprised.

She sighed and made a little grimace. "I wish I did not have to tell you. I wish it were possible that I could live my own life without being accountable to you for my actions. But it isn't so. Our social position – your mother – all these curious things combine to dictate our behaviour. I have done something of which you will not approve. I am not ashamed of it, but I know that you will be displeased. And so I rather dread telling you; and I despise myself for this."

"My God . . ." I murmured not taking any of this particularly seriously. "Whatever can you have done?"

"I went to see Constance Wilde," said my wife.

"I beg your pardon? You did *what*?"

"Yes, I see that you are annoyed. I knew you would be."

"But are you crazy?" I cried, taken aback. "You do understand the nature of her husband's crime? Of the feelings of repugnance throughout the whole of society – the same people amongst whom we shall be moving at Lady Girton's ball?"

"Yes, I realise of what Oscar Wilde is accused," said Claudia carefully. "I must admit that I had not supposed it; I thought he was a womanizer. I thought the mysterious rumours were to do with the kind of female in whom Mr Gladstone was known to take an interest."

"I would like to have spared you the knowledge; but I suppose with the newspapers . . ."

"It wasn't the newspapers; I knew before. The Ladies at the League . . ." she began cautiously. "I know your feelings about my friends . . . I know you do not approve. In deference to your opinions I have not attended many meetings in the past. But lately, particularly since you and I have never been close in matters of either physical or emotional support, I have taken a growing pleasure in the society of other women. It is a great delight to me to discover that other ladies beside myself feel some discontent with mere socialising and have certain opinions which we do not share with our husbands."

"Oh Claudia," I complained. "When have I been such an ogre? I will not be bundled together as 'husbands'. When could you not tell me your opinions?"

"I chose not to, because you are very much under the influence of your mother, whose standards go back some fifty years, and you are personally rather supercilious. Life is a more agreeable prospect when one remains silent and thus avoids having one's hesitant sentiments treated with good-humoured tolerance."

I sat silent, amazed.

"But at the League," continued Claudia, heartened, leaning forward. "We have been able to discuss our thoughts and feelings. Some will seem very strange to you, rather daring. Women to have exactly the same freedoms as men . . ."

"But you have every kind of freedom!" I expostulated.

"I have certain freedoms," she agreed carefully. "But many of these are the freedoms which money and privilege buy. Some of us would like to see laws passed which enable all women to possess all kinds of freedoms, by legal right, d'you see, unhampered by wealth and tradition."

"I truly do not believe that the majority of women want any kind of freedom that counterbalances the care and protection which have always been received by right when they marry," I declared.

"Women are indeed well protected, as long as they do exactly what is required of them by men," said Claudia sharply. "But let them once step out of line . . ."

"Oh really," I laughed. "Our dinner table is not the place for a discussion of this nature."

"Exactly; and therefore you and I will never have such a discussion, will we? It is a pity, Algy," Claudia added ruefully, "that the things which I hold dear are difficult to share with he who should be closest to me. But we are not close, are we? We never have been. In truth we know nothing about each other. Not the real things. Maybe you are just as shallow as you seem. Maybe you have hidden secrets. But I will never know about them. It doesn't matter. I'm not asking you to be other than you are. I merely try in this instance to explain to you what was behind the idea of my visiting Constance at this difficult time."

"Well, yes, I think you had better explain it. I'm surprised you could get into Tite Street. I understood there was a yowling mob outside."

"She isn't at Tite Street. She's with the Napiers. Her aunt Mary and cousin Eliza. And I haven't been the only person to visit. Laura Hope was there. It was pretty horrible."

"In what way?"

"She is very much changed since I saw her last – dark shadows under her eyes and a despondent manner. I don't think the Napiers are the best people for her to be with at this stage. They talk in hushed tones and call her 'poor dear Constance'. They do not even speak of Oscar by name. I feel it only encourages her misery and she sees herself as much martyred. I am afraid that she will go under and let society trample her. Of course, it isn't easy for her . . ."

"I should say not! A masterly understatement, I think."

"You are right about Tite Street; she couldn't stay there. They've shut the house now, except for the butler. Do you know, people have spat upon her in the streets? When she went out of her front door she had to veil her face and even then she was recognised and people followed her and called out horrid things. She's terribly worried about the boys, Cyril particularly. He's nine years old and very astute and has been reading some street headlines. He is to be sent off to Dublin to stay with a cousin. I couldn't help but think about William – what *I* would do – how he would be feeling – "

"Why do you say that?" I blurted out alarmed.

She put her hand on my wrist. "I don't mean anything. As a mother one identifies. Her poor children . . . William and Cyril are of comparable ages. And I was disturbed to see her so sad and down, she who had always been so firm an advocate of the rights of women."

"What have women's right to do with it?" I said. "I begin to feel out of my depth."

"Constance is innocent, is she not? She is a person in her own right. I do not wish to see her life spoilt because her husband was foolish. I advised her not to run away. I advised her to brave it out, not to play by society's rules, not to be intimidated. By being there at all I hoped to show her that it was possible."

"Your advice to her was thoughtless. If she stays she will be made dreadfully miserable. No one will receive her, she will be forever snubbed and avoided. The same happened to Lord Henry Somerset's wife when they separated. It will be worse for Constance – how can it not?"

"Oh!" cried Claudia desperately. "Somebody has to start somewhere to break into this dreadful chain of hypocrisy and conformity!"

"This is a silly and hysterical time. We all have to tread carefully. I

224

know you meant well by your gesture; but it was inappropriate."

"As it happens I do not intend to visit Mrs Wilde again. She has not taken my advice; she leaves for Torquay on the 19th and the boys are to be taken away from their schools. You may breathe again; she is behaving exactly as one would expect."

CHAPTER EIGHTEEN

I DO not know whether you realise the fact or no," said Claudia. "But there is to be an Afternoon here after luncheon."

"That is generally the way of things," I agreed morosely.

"I mean that those young people whom you met upon a previous occasion are gathering here again this afternoon. I hope that you do not feel obliged to attend."

I jerked into awareness. "Do you know who is coming, or do they just turn up?"

"Of course I know. There will be Louisa of course, and the two rather severe young women, Helena and Maria. Thaddeus O'Shea will certainly be there – the one who looks like Swinburne – and Ernest, who almost seems as if his entire person has been in the trouser press. Hubert Vane, a name which unfortunately has always suited him terribly well – oh dear, he must be feeling rather sad to think of the straits into which his hero has fallen. He studies so hard to follow Oscar Wilde . . . and Ronald Grey who appears to me the only truly sensible one of the bunch; I often wonder why he comes at all. Oh, and Arthur Hughes, the rather gloomy Welsh boy. Do you remember how we worried about him? Well, Ronald tells me that he is much improved, and though he suffered a bout of influenza last month, in character and outlook he is a changed being. I'm so relieved to hear that, are not you? I did not wish to intervene, but I feared that we might have to do so. Time works wonders. I daresay it was simply the bad weather of the Winter that brought him low."

"Indeed," I said. "And you say he is coming here . . ."

"Yes. And the present climate being what it is I decided that aesthetic matters should be totally ignored today. And so I asked my friend Hannah Richardson from the Female Philanthropists to lecture us on Women's Rights. I think that will provoke an interesting discussion. Will you attend?"

"Oh no – " I cringed. "I find Hannah Richardson terrifying, and she will feel obliged to tear me to shreds as usual – a male, a landowner, a possessor of rights."

This was true; it had happened before. Etiquette had demanded that I meet Hannah more than once and none of the encounters had brought me pleasure. She was alarming; and her alarm lay in the fact that she was extremely intelligent, good-looking, bold and unconventional, and I could find no logical answer to her arguments. But that was not the main reason for my refusal, as can be imagined. I could not believe that Arthur had decided to bring himself here without ulterior motive, and I could not imagine sitting opposite him in a ghastly social situation that included my wife, discussing issues of the day. The idea of seeing him again filled me with ecstasy and dread.

"No, I will remain skulking in the study," I smiled. "But I would be happy to make polite conversation with them as they depart, if you think that would be appreciated."

"Yes, please do," said Claudia thoughtfully. "Algy," she added with a little frown. "Hannah visited me in Ramsgate, at my invitation. I knew that you would not object."

"Object? Of course not. I simply cannot understand why you like her so much. She's such a virago. You do not seem to me to have much in common. She is unmarried, is she not?"

"Yes; but through choice."

"Oh come now! All women seek true love, admit it. Those who pretend otherwise are indulging in a little self deception."

"Oh really Algy – I cannot talk to you when you are thus!"

All through that long dull afternoon I sat in the study at my desk, knowing that Arthur was in the house, and thinking only about him. Women's Rights – what interest could that topic have for him? Why had he come? To see me of course; but what could he hope for? We could not be alone. What pretext could we give? What could he hope to gain by this? It would only be worse, to see him but to have no loving converse . . . how could he torment me so? I struggled between despondency, elation and unease. I wrote nothing other than the date. I thought about the gardeners' cottage at Mortmayne and the scent of Arthur's hair and the sound of larks. I ached with longing.

Eventually I heard the sound of the voices of the Afternoon group as they made their way across the hall. I jumped up and opened the study door. Before I knew it I was murmuring pleasantries, for everyone seemed much disposed to chatter.

"Algy," beamed Louisa. "You should have joined us. Miss Richardson's talk was wonderful, and terribly relevant to you!"

"Hannah – how very agreeable to see you – I do hope your talk went well."

"Thank you, Lord Algernon; I think it did. When one speaks on a subject of universal relevance one tends to find a fair response in the listener."

"But Miss Richardson," I could not resist the unworthy jibe. "I understand that you were speaking upon Women's Rights!"

"The acquisition of such rights," she returned, "would at the same time liberate some gentlemen from the obligation to defend their ancient position by foolish utterances."

"How vehemently I look forward to the day when you achieve them," I shuddered.

"You should. The world will be a better place."

"You can now see why," said Claudia firmly, "I kept him well clear of our meeting. I do apologise for him, Hannah; there was a Winterton in the Ark."

"I have always believed that men and women should be considered equal before the law," said Thaddeus, obviously returned from Tir na n Og with no ill effects. "But as we supposed, the responsibility of child-rearing will always condemn women to the home, and until conception can be prevented upon a wide scale this will continue to be the case."

"I don't think Algy wants to hear about that," giggled Louisa.

"Why not?" said Hannah brusquely. "He obviously practises the notion in one form or another."

Such an indelicate remark was patently considered to be taking liberation a little too far, and in the sudden social prattle that followed, Ernest – he of the lisp and neat appearance – murmured at my elbow: "You may not recognise Hubert, thir. He hath been obliged to change hith appearanth."

"Indeed I did not recognise him. Last time we met he was an aesthete."

Hubert blushed. "I was set upon, sir. In the street."

"A crowd of louts outside a public house – they followed him and threw stones at him – it was shocking – quite unbelievable."

"They called him Oscar."

"But this is monstrous!" I said. "Where was this – in some backstreet?"

"No; it was in the Strand," said Hubert.

"But did no one come to your aid?"

"No one did. Those who saw the occurrence only laughed."

"They took his flowers and tore his velvet jacket. He barely escaped with his life!"

A tangible aura of sympathy surrounded Hubert. Certainly the velvet jacket and the complementary knee breeches which he had worn before had seemed excessive, and moreover slightly out of date, and his long blond curls had possibly been like to earn him the epithet of dandy. But unlike his one-time hero the effect had been merely a pose, and now it seemed he could not walk a broad thoroughfare without mishap. Much shaken, he had gone to have his hair cut and completely changed his style. A pleasant-looking inoffensive lad, you would not now have noticed him in a crowd, and any girl might take him home and introduce him to her parents, sure of their approval. I was sorry for the loss of his individuality. It seemed a shame, one more small incident spinning off the wheel that Oscar's troubles set in motion.

"And anyway," said Hubert with a startling fervour. "I never liked the fellow. What he has done disgusts me. I'm glad to see him caught. I think it's horrible. Horrible! I thought he was a poet, with a sensitive soul. But he's a monster."

"I think it's time I left," said Hannah pleasantly. "Next time perhaps I might be invited to speak upon the virtues of tolerance. Thank you, Claudia dear, for inviting me . . ."

Meredith had opened the door and some of them now began to leave. At last Arthur was able to move closer to me. He had said nothing all the while, though I was conscious of his every movement and his eyes upon me, burning with demand, reproach; beside him Ronald, also silent, brimming with benevolence, patently taking a personal pride in Arthur's being here at all.

"Arthur – " I said dry-mouthed, shaking his hand. "I am so pleased to see you. I understood that you had felt unable to attend some of the previous afternoons. It is most pleasant to find – to know – " I floundered stupidly.

"Thank you," said Arthur. He took a breath. "Afternoons, yes, it's an odd way to describe a meeting. Some people call them Wednesdays or Tuesdays. With my mother it's always Evenings. She goes off to an Evening. In her case it's a Bible class. But it's Thursdays, every Thursday, without fail, eight o'clock sharp."

Ronald laughed politely. Lord knows what inanity I murmured; and before I knew it Arthur was gone, and everybody disappearing down the steps and out into the square.

I knew that it had not been easy for Arthur to come seek me out. I felt much chastened by his determination. It would have been quite as painful for him as for me, to sit in Claudia's presence in the house where she and I presented a united front of civilised splendour and to smile and prattle in a group from which he surely felt divergent, nor, did I suppose with a wry smile, had he much personal involvement with the subject of the meeting. I knew that it had cost him something in embarrassment to make the little speech about his mother, and I respected him immensely in his effort to make contact, for I as usual had dealt with disaster by inactivity, my motives a confused jumble of fear and sacrifice. That way was no longer possible. The next day was Thursday and the invitation had been plain enough.

Arthur had been watching out for me. I saw the curtain twitch, and even before I knocked he had opened the door and let me in. Our meeting had the savour of the clandestine. I was extremely jumpy, and Arthur bore the air of one who has organised a careful plan whose outcome required skill and calm handling.

"Upstairs," he said, gesturing over his shoulder.

"Is that wise?" I breathed.

"We're not going in the parlour and sit opposite the Bible and a row of my relations."

So I followed him upstairs, no good thing for my vibrant nerves, for my eyes were on a level with his thighs and his behind, and here we were marching off to his bedroom. We entered, and he closed and locked the door.

It was a small, neat shabby room with dull wallpaper and dark brown paintwork. The narrow window, heavily draped in dingy net, overlooked a small yard at the back of the house. The bed was narrow, a brass bedstead with polished knobs at each corner, and a white coverlet upon it. There was an open grate with a mantelshelf upon which a couple of china shepherdesses stood in beatific attitudes, and two china high-heeled shoes which would have been quite unwearable and were stacked full of buttons and pins. Above the fireplace hung a heavily framed print of *Saul and the Witch of Endor*.

"We are safe for exactly one hour," said Arthur. "My mother will return at a quarter past nine, and Mr Simmons then comes in for cocoa. I knew you'd smile! The only other person in the house is another lodger Miss Verrinder, and she stays in her room. Now are we going to waste this time or not?"

He ran at me and flung his arms around my neck and hugged me. I held him tightly, pressing him to me, a sudden spurt of tears catching me unaware as the strength of my feelings soared.

"Why didn't you come to me?" he cried.

"I dared not!"

"Why?" he accused, almost shaking me.

"Why? – because of Oscar Wilde," I moaned.

"*What has he to do with us?*" said Arthur hoarsely.

We moved apart slightly, our hands still on each other.

"On one level, nothing," I said wearily. "On another, everything."

"Suppose you explain to me," said Arthur, and we sat down on the bed.

"You must have read the newspapers," I began. "For myself I've thought of nothing else. I knew the man, Arthur, slightly, and I've always known that he was someone who liked boys, indeed, the rough and ready kind, the kind you buy on a Piccadilly street corner. And now that he has been arrested, the matter of Greek love is uppermost in everybody's mind. People who before had never thought about it have an opinion on the subject – boys with long hair are persecuted in the street – and Oscar is for some reason seen as a monster, a corrupter of youth. An older man who preys on young boys. Somehow that jeopardizes every older man who takes a young boy out. Whereas before, a passer by might have assumed a father and son – an uncle and nephew – a schoolmaster and pupil – now, *now* it's different. I feared that if you and I were seen together we would be the subject of vile glances, whispers. Oh Arthur! I could not subject you to that!"

"Well, I think you are being over-sensitive," said Arthur seriously. "Sin is in the eye of the beholder, like beauty. Look at me now – every day I spend my time alone with Mr Simmons! Yet we still have plenty of customers!"

I smiled and squeezed his knee. "Yes. But I am prettier than Mr Simmons. Unfortunately I seem also to bear a slight resemblance to Lord Alfred Douglas, and this tends to put the matter into the minds of the stupid, if it was not there before. I've been terrified, Arthur, because of what we've already done. And for what we might do, if we met. I fear for myself, but more I fear for you. I could not be the cause of any pain. I could not bear to make life difficult for you. So taken up was I with the awfulness of Oscar's plight and the virulency of public feeling against all such as we, that fear froze my hand; I dared not come to your door; nor write to you. I hoped that you would understand."

I looked into his eyes, ardent and distressed.

"I understood up to a point," he answered. "But then, I thought, something must be done. Besides, I missed you."

"Oh," I groaned, and held him. "And I missed you. I have been a superficial shell around an ache of pain and loss."

"Have you?" he said, impressed.

"Yes!" I laughed ruefully, ruffling his hair.

"Algy," Arthur said, all eyes and eyelashes. "Let's become close now . . . as close as we can be."

My heart lurched as I understood his meaning. Swiftly we began to take off our clothes, swearing in whispers over buttons, ties and collars, tormented by the fact that ultimate ecstasy had to be contained within three quarters of an hour. Our clothes lay round about us in ragged heaps, we naked in the midst of them. We hurried into bed, a tangle of limbs, reaching for each other. A passionate kiss welded us together, the urgency of time's onrushing bringing a fierce and forceful eagerness and greed. No time for more than whispered words of love, each other's name in hurried tender sighs, the drowning thrill of hair, the smell of skin, the lovely play of tongues, the grasping hands that squeezed the firm flesh of arse, that held the warm rough handfuls between the thighs. Then slowly, carefully I moved within. We lay there silent, awed. For the first time since I had returned to London I felt peace. I could have lain there for Eternity. So this was Heaven . . .

Arthur gave a polite cough, such as are used by butlers.

"It's twenty minutes to nine," he said.

I gave him a sharp shove, and was rewarded with a charming boyish yelp.

"If we had world enough and time," I said, "I'd enjoy teaching you what is and what is not good form."

"I'd like that! But we haven't!"

I moved a little, coming easily, and clinging to him with a rush of happy sighs. "And you, my love – how about you?"

"What I wanted was that," said Arthur. We lay awhile, in a harmonious dream-like closeness. My face was in his hair, and as I moved to take him in my arms our lips touched in sleepy little kisses and whispered words of love.

Arthur shifted.

"I know," I groaned. "It's nearly nine o'clock."

"Best get dressed," he said.

We stood up, washed hurriedly from a jug and bowl, and helped each other dress.

Arthur faced me challengingly. "You said you'd take me to a concert."

"Very well," I said grimly. "We will try it, assuming, as you say, the willingness of the populace to assume innocence."

"I think you'll find that no one will give us a second glance," said Arthur. "Now I shall have to mention to my mother that you were here because a neighbour will certainly have noticed."

"Say I came to bring you a book."

Arthur smiled wanly. "No, no, you merely came to ask how I was. But we won't be able to keep doing this – you visiting me here, I mean," he added wrily. "People will notice. We'll have to find other ways."

"Let's not think that far ahead," I told him firmly. "Do you like Brahms?"

Having decided upon a policy of limited honesty I told Claudia that

232

I was taking Arthur to a concert at the Royal Albert Hall.

"He doesn't get out much," I said easily. "And he's very fond of music. I daresay his mother will come too; he's very caring of her welfare. The Welsh," I added didactically, "are a very musical nation."

Claudia looked up from her writing – I assumed it was a letter – and nodded.

"That's kind," she said approvingly. "I always felt that he was rather a sad person. Perhaps you'll cheer him. What a very sweet idea to take his mother also. I'm sure they'll both enjoy the evening immensely."

Both did; but the two in question were Arthur and myself. I need have feared nothing. We mingled with the cultured throng, unnoticed, unremarked. As the first quiet notes of the Second Symphony sounded I experienced a most tangible relief of tension. We sat there, in a loggia box, upon red plush seats, in the company of people we did not know, all of us mere faces in an audience, listeners, no one as important as the communal experience of the music. Around the huge auditorium the elegant tiered ranks soared, looking like a children's cut-out theatre, yet there was a curious intimacy for so high a dome, so wide a space, and all that ornate bubble vibrant with melody. It has been called a Pastoral Symphony, the Second, with power to transport to leafy glades and summer fields, where slow rivers curve between grey misty fields of August dawns. Serenity and gravity, excitement and happiness were in those notes that evening, and by the time the clarinets got to work for the Finale I had experienced a marvellous elation. I was here with Arthur! We had dared it. Lovers, we were sitting together, ordinary, human, our secret safe. Not pariahs, not "beasts that walked the streets", but merely he and I who loved each other and wanted to be together to share the things we liked. I smiled as I recalled how I had tried to bring the joys of music to Willie and how he'd twitched and fidgeted; our tastes were not the same. But Arthur sat enrapt; I fell in love with him all over again. My heart was lifted by the music, by his presence at my side, and by the thrill of being here at all. It *was* possible! Even now, at this precise date, with Oscar's trial imminent and the newspapers yapping like bloodhounds round our legs, it was possible. Suddenly I felt such hope. We need not fear – we did not have to hide – we could simply be ourselves – keep calm and brave – it would work out – it must, for we would make it do so. The symphony rose to its climax – *allegro con spirito* – the only way to be – and I understood true happiness.

Since we had not come here in secret, I had ordered my carriage to collect us, and we drove back through the night-lit streets so civilised, so openly. At his door we said a discreet farewell, with the little half smiles of those who share the unspoken, and I returned home upon something of a golden cloud.

While I was working in my study the next morning I was surprised to be disturbed by Meredith, who informed me that a young man had called.

"Who is it?" I enquired.

"He said to tell you that he could be found in the Forest of Arden," said Meredith in great distaste.

"Ah!" I experienced some curiosity and some pleasure. Orlando? What could he want with me?

"Show him in, please."

Within a moment the fair-haired elf was in my presence, and the door was quietly closed. I turned, still sitting, gesturing him to the sofa.

"To what do I owe – ?" I began smoothly.

"The pleasure? Don't say that. I'm afraid I'm bringing something which you won't much like."

"Whatever do you mean?

"Well," said Orlando, crossing one languid thigh over the other and lighting a cigarette. "I've come to blackmail you."

"I beg your pardon?"

"I said I've come to blackmail you," he said, inhaling.

"I suppose you're joking?"

"Not a bit of it, my lord. I see that Oscar Wilde has his trial fixed for next week. With what I've got on you I reckon that the next celebrated society trial could be yours. I daresay you know what I mean?"

I stood up angrily.

"How you have the audacity to walk in here and speak to me like this I cannot imagine. I always knew you had the cheek of the Devil but this is beyond belief. I suggest you take yourself off before I call the police."

"Ah now, wait a moment," said Orlando, budging not an inch. "I'm no Francis, a poor bungler who you can frighten off with tales of your friend the Chief Inspector. With me you deal with class – or hadn't you noticed?"

"Up till now, Orlando," I said evenly, "I would have agreed with you. But blackmail puts you down there in the dregs with Oscar's renters and the shabby half-world where the creatures roll in their own slime. You are above all that. I would have thought better of you."

234

"Oh come now. You always knew I was a rotter. They chucked me out of school, you know. I was a mean brat then, and I remain so. I always reckoned I might one day turn our friendship to advantage; but I must admit that it was Count Zabarov who gave me the final prompt."

"What in Hell's name do you mean by that?" I seethed, my fingers gripping the chair arm.

"Ah, you're worried now," smirked Orlando comfortably. "You were quite scared of him. We all were. He always planned to get even with you. See if you can fix him, Orlando, he told me. Incriminate him. Something he can't wriggle out of, with his wealth and his connections . . ."

"But there isn't anything!" I gasped, pale as a sheet. "I did not ever write to you; and I will deny most forcibly that ever there was anything between us."

"Oh yes, you were careful enough with me," Orlando conceded carelessly. "Your sort always are. Have a good time, but don't commit yourself."

"I thought that we were friends!" I cried, aggrieved. "I thought that everything we shared was for our mutual pleasure – it certainly seemed so. I know you cherish some pretension to the acting profession, but surely even you could not pretend the sighs and groans of lust?"

"No, no," he admitted. "I fancied you all right. I still do. But a man must live. And it will come as no surprise to you that scene-shifting at the Alhambra is not exactly well remunerated."

"But – how much do you need?" I asked. "Ten pounds? Twenty? Just ask me – don't degrade yourself by blackmail. We've no ill will towards each other, have we?"

"I don't want your patronage," replied Orlando. "My way is better. This way I'm in charge. It's like a profitable little business, man to man. And as for your ten pounds and your twenties, that's pittance. I'm aiming higher, because I could grow very luxury-loving if I had the chance. I now have that chance."

"Oh really," I said irritably. "Stop it. Behave yourself or go. And don't imagine that I wouldn't have you thrown out if you became a pest."

Orlando leaned back and looked at the ceiling, idly puffing smoke that stank abominably, and looking so much like a stage villain that I could half believe that he was playing to an audience.

"*Certain Confessions from Various Rent Boys*," he quoted at me. "Collected and edited by Henry Cleaver. Archie Bilger, a clerk in a shipping office . . . Percy Wade, what was he now, a baker? And then there was one at the end, in your writing. Willie Brown – a lovely episode that was, splashing in the fountain – *we're timeless, aren't we, when we're naked! I'd take his juice down my throat, his cock between my wet lips* . . . yes, I see that you remember now!"

"My God! Charles' pornography!" I blanched. "How did you get to see that?"

"I did more than see it," said Orlando. "I nabbed it. I snitched it from your dressing table drawer that time we made love upstairs here and you went down for the sherry. I can pick any lock, easy as pie."

"You little swine . . ." This is serious, said a voice in my head – my God this is serious . . . "What have you done with it?" I asked uneasily.

"Kept it. I haven't brought it with me. I'm not that stupid. It was a good read. I liked yours best. I thought it was very tasteful."

"I don't know what you mean," I hedged. "I didn't write any of it. I only borrowed it from Charles. You can't prove any of it is mine."

"Oh yes I can." said Orlando. He looked at me, eyes glinting, narrowed in a leer. "There was a letter with it, in the same writing. And you signed that."

"What letter?" I said blankly.

"You wrote it from your club in Pall Mall. It had the address all over the top of the page. How did it go? 'My darling boy – it is only a few moments since I quitted your sweet company – I want to tell you how I feel – turbulent and exquisite sensations – your sweet lips which I want to put to other uses – soon, if the Fates are willing – signed, Algernon!"

"But – that was all fancy – I did not ever send it – " I stammered. Christ! I had completely forgotten about that stupid little episode. I had penned the airy extravaganza heady with elation, full of love. I brought it home and stuffed it in the drawer, with Charles' offerings – I'd locked the drawer – I'd thought no more about it.

"But who's to know?" said Orlando sweetly. "Compares quite favourably with Oscar's, doesn't it? Of course, his is more poetic. But I don't think a jury would be in any doubt as to the intention behind yours, do you, any more than his? I'd even go so far as to say I could hazard a guess as to who the darling boy is!"

I put my hand across my eyes. "If you so much as hint that you intend to involve that person I will have the police here for you and damn the consequences . . ."

"Steady, Algy," said Orlando mildly. "I'm not after him – he hasn't any money. Don't be so noble. I don't want sacrifices. I just want a nice little arrangement where I can get my money on tap. You've got the money. And I think you'll agree that I have you in the kind of position whereby you would be reckless to disagree. I mean, a court case can be so public, and the newspapers don't seem to understand Christian charity. And the police might want to talk to your Darling Boy and ask him questions. Prison suits are so unbecoming, even if one has beautiful eyelashes. And then there's your wife and children to consider . . ."

My head swam. I could hear Zabarov speaking to me, clear as if he stood there in the room. *Our duel is not over; remember this. And when I strike I shall use the same weapon as you did. The cumbersome club of the Law . . .*

I pulled myself together rapidly. "I had no idea that you were such an unspeakable rat," I said evenly. "And naturally I will pay you whatever you require for the return of the papers in your possession."

"Yes," said Orlando. "I rather thought you would. I have to warn you, Algy dear, the price is going to be rather high."

CHAPTER NINETEEN

THE TRIAL of Oscar Wilde began on the 26th of April at the Old Bailey, and I attended.

I could not help but feel that the majority of those who crammed themselves into the crowded court room had come with a salacious desire to be entertained and to savour the thrill of righteous horror, that unworthy emotion so enthusiastically enjoyed by the consciously respectable. Some would be there clothed in a cloak of morality, genuinely believing that by this legal means an odious influence was to be removed, for some peculiar collective good, a cathartic process by which we would all emerge somehow purified. Indeed I suspected that these included the jury. I only hoped that amongst the hot and empty-faced rabble against which I found myself pressed, there stood another like myself, who came to offer silent sympathy and sorrow, and even – yes, I would admit as much – love.

Mr Charles Gill for the prosecution, a plump stocky figure with a propensity to lean his fat thigh upon his desk, described the brothel in Little College Street where Oscar had been introduced by Alfred Taylor to young men. I stole a glance at Oscar. He looked gaunt and weary, indifferent even, and he lacked the old impeccable panache. The phrases followed swiftly – "young men – selling their bodies – this abominable traffic – favourite vice – filthy practices." Then in came Charlie Parker.

I shrank amongst the crowd, suddenly petrified that this treacherous youth would recognise me; but he was far too busy saving his skin by presenting himself as a hapless victim. He explained how he had met Oscar at Taylor's instigation and they had all dined at the Solferino and Oscar had said: "This is the boy for me!" I had never witnessed such a cynical display as this youth's testimony. My own dismal forays into the illicit flashed before me as Parker continued with his tales of sleeping at Wilde's house and sneaking out at dawn, of sexual encounters carefully described, of dining at Kettner's, of presents.

Sir Edward Clarke, Oscar's counsel, then made a very decent job of proving Charlie Parker was a thoroughly bad lot, knew exactly what was required of him when he met up with Oscar, was a willing participant and a blackmailer to boot. It seemed that £300 or £400 was the going rate for blackmailing a gentleman. I was interested to hear this from such an independent source. I might discuss it with Orlando later.

A series of landladies followed. They verified the darkened rooms, the exotic lighting, the strong perfume, the locked doors and the whispering and laughing behind them, the cabs that drove up late at night and disappeared soon after. Then came the blackmailer Alfred Wood, looking neat, clean-shaven and smart, with a slightly aggrieved expression – but then, blackmailers came in all shapes and sizes, as well I knew. This man had slept with Taylor and was introduced to Oscar at the Café Royal; he then dined royally with Oscar at the Florence in Rupert Street. During the meal – those about me buzzed with interest – the two of them put their hands inside each other's trousers under the table! Later, the "act of indecency" took place – how arch our language – and the blackmail. The first day of the trial closed with this witness's evidence; and we struggled out. I made immediately for the tobacconist's to buy Orlando's Turkish cigarettes.

The singular subjugation in which Orlando had kept me during the past week had taken on a distinct pattern, to which already I was habituated, nor could I envisage any likelihood of its termination in the immediate future.

A large payment in return for the incriminating evidence which he possessed was not what Orlando had in mind. I was to be treated more like a bank from which money could be drawn whenever necessary, a solution which changed his circumstances very much for the better and reduced me to a grimly philosophical acquiescence. I was entirely at his mercy. I had the living example before me of what happened to the man of society who sought the company of renters, wrote letters and gave presents. As was soon to be apparent, in the hands of the law, even Oscar's gentler friendships appeared crude and tarnished. Orlando knew my contacts and, most damaging of all, he knew Arthur. For this reason alone I would have done whatever he required; and the fear of the ghastly revelation to my wife and family came a very close second.

"You are to visit me every day," Orlando told me. Where? In the elegant flat in Half Moon Street in which I was obliged to set him up, and whose rent I was to pay indefinitely. The initial down payment to him of £100 for "expenses" I accepted; and the £20 to both Francis and Jem I considered suitable penance for my stupidity in having anything to do with them in the first place. "And when you visit me you must always bring a little gift." Hence the Turkish cigarettes, of which the little monster was inordinately fond. I understood the thrill it gave him to play the sultan – I assumed that he would tire of it in time. He had certainly relished his new found wealth for the furnishing of his rooms, and with complete and cheerful lack of taste he filled them with a theatrical hotchpotch of whatever caught his fancy, mostly what is termed Exotica. His rooms now contained a flamboyant melange of tigers' head rugs, elephants' foot hallstands, mirrors framed by Gothic canopies, lurid paintings, heavy velvet drapes, huge urns. This decor was topped with a final touch which I particularly disliked – a large and garish poster of Zabarov in his stage pose, in a cloak of stars and moons – "Zabarov! Nights of Magic!"

Orlando lived now almost entirely on champagne and dined at Kettner's – seemingly the certain path to ruin. Each evening he indulged his passion for the girls at the Gaiety Theatre, at last able to treat them to the extravagant existence he felt the world had owed him throughout all the lean time before he hit upon the notion of the life of a blackmailer. There was a curious innocence in his mastery of me – at first. I, meanwhile, like a rather superb lackey, brought him cigarettes.

Would it sound bizarre to say that to begin with I did not too much mind? The money he had so far asked for I could well afford; it was no more than many of my peers were dishing out on the sly to luscious nymphs of which their wives knew nothing. The peculiar bondage in which he held me (for his monetary demands were not the only tribute he required) was not offensive to me – unusual, but not especially distasteful; after all, we had been lovers, and I used to find his body had the power to excite me. When I brought him his cigarettes he liked me to light them for him while he sprawled upon the bed, and pour him drinks and pass him the clothes that he intended to wear when he went out. He was very discreet, and never brought anybody to the place while I was there, no one who might have recognised or compromised me later; only those who knew our strange arrangement, Jem and Francis. He began to demand favours of a more personal nature. Once the cigarette was lit he he would expect to spread his legs for me to suck his prick – on the first occasion to his direction, but after that it was to be a part of the act of bringing and lighting his cigarettes, to be done without question; and I did it. I was very obedient, and did everything he said.

It struck me nonetheless that I had now lost all physical desire for him. I could hear Arthur's voice – "I didn't like him – slimy, like a toad" – and now I tended to agree. There was a snake-like quality to

Orlando, a warm oily smoothness, a glittering sinuousness that at first had seemed attractive to me, and gradually grew to be repugnant. I sucked his cock without arousal, thinking about other things. Once when I was careless my shirt front took a glistening stain, and after that I took my upper garments off, and Orlando liked the idea and insisted upon complete nakedness. It excited him that I should be so as I helped him dress for dinner. He brought Jem and Francis round to watch this odd charade, and afterwards when he was ready to go out, he said that he would wait and watch me do the same for Jem and Francis, who certainly put up no resistance. First Francis, then Jem, I serviced both; and then Orlando made me pay them, which they found most amusing, and I did not.

"Oh," he said, certainly aroused by what he had just seen. "I'd like to fuck you now – but I have to go out to dinner. Wait here till I get back. I will not be more than three hours."

I waited alone in Orlando's rooms till he returned. I waited there amongst the furs and feathers and the ugly urns and the jungle sprays of tapering plants and the leering poster of Zabarov. To be sure I searched among his things for the papers he had stolen from me; I did not find them. When he had finished dining Orlando reappeared, took off his coat, and beaming with a childish delight in the joys of domination ordered me over a table, where, as the phrase has it, the act of sodomy took place.

Such was the unholy arrangement of my first week of servitude. And this was how things were when I attended Oscar's trial for the second day.

The day began with the questioning of Alfred Wood the black-mailer by Sir Edward Clarke, with interesting revelations upon the kind of fees that could be earned, as opposed to those of honest toil. I was surprised more people did not take up the profession. A waiter from the hotel at St. James' Place then verified that many young men of lowly station visited Oscar at his rooms there. The next witness was Freddy Atkins, of whom I shuddered to think I had come so close to becoming a victim. Orlando was bizarre but he was not yet sordid.

Oscar had taken Freddy Atkins to Paris, as his private secretary. Freddy had visited the Moulin Rouge. I knew the place myself; I had been there in the company of my dear friend Philippe D'Ourcelles on many a glad occasion. I marvelled at Oscar's audacity. And I thought with sudden envy: What fun they must have had! He's paying for it now – but what a merry life it must have been!

Sir Edward Clarke then easily discredited young Atkins as a blackmailer and a liar. He proved that Atkins had perjured himself and he reduced the youth to wriggling uneasiness. The judge ordered Freddy from the court.

The housekeeper at Freddy's lodgings, where Oscar regularly visited, took the stand to give her evidence concerning sheets stained in a peculiar way. I had the impression that this unpalatable detail had caught the imagination of the court; the information was received in a fascinated silence.

A very agreeable youth named Mavor was the next witness, a different class of person from the previous ones. We learnt during his testimony that Mr Wilde liked nice clean boys, and gave Mavor a silver cigarette case and a night at the Albemarle, during which nothing happened. The Albemarle had seen some to-ing and fro-ing one way and another, for the next witness also stayed there with Oscar, although he did protest too much about how vehemently he had rejected Oscar's advances. An unstable, sensitive youth, he had suffered much at his place of employment from the jibes of workmates who called him Mrs Wilde and Miss Oscar. Before the day was out, the owner of the Albemarle Hotel himself gave evidence, and admitted that because of the vast quantities of young men who visited his establishment when Oscar was in residence he had asked Oscar to leave.

We all left shortly after that, and I took cigarettes to Orlando.

That evening I was obliged to share with Orlando his penchant for the Gaiety nymphs, and I began to learn the limitless potential which the blackmailer, gradually perfecting his trade, has at his fingertips. I understood that he could effortlessly make my life a misery, intruding upon both my private and public domain.

The Gaiety revue was not my preferred form of entertainment but I could tolerate the frivolous music, the ranks of prancing girls upon the stage, the silly songs, the innuendo – I was, however, to partake of it in the company of Orlando and his current *belle amie* and to escort her friend Julia, a lemon-haired trollop whom I had to believe chosen for her exceptional capacity to irritate. The girls drew constant attention to themselves by squeals of laughter, seductive glances at all and sundry, coarse comment about young men in the audience, and were moreover tipsy before the evening started. To my intense embarrassment I encountered at the theatre several gentlemen of my acquaintance with similar nymphets about their person, who greeted me with noisy bonhomie and showed an obvious delight in my having joined the ranks of good fellows, and the winks and smirks I received as a result caused me to suppose

242

that I would soon be rumoured to be something of a womanizer. To add to my chagrin of course, I was the one who paid for the entertainment, and the drinks and ice creams and the sprays of orchids.

Afterwards we went to a cellar off the Strand, with red plush seats, stained mirrors and great swathes of plum-coloured drapes, where through a heavy fug of cigar smoke we watched a display of half-naked females on a dais. Much in the way that food is spread out on the sideboard for the guests at breakfast, the women, variously costumed, were arranged in poses likely to appeal. One was a slave-girl with a veil across her chest and a white cloth gathered round her hips; one a hussar with thigh boots and suspenders, a minuscule tunic and a plumed helmet; one a Bacchanalian extravaganza trailing bunches of grapes in a provocative fashion about the contours of her body.

I marvelled that women could behave with such abandonment of dignity and finesse, and gentlemen so easily cast off the social trappings to reveal themselves in their relentless voyeurism. I could not help but wonder what Claudia would make of it.

Again I saw amongst the guffawing throng some faces that I knew. Kennington was there and waved cheerily, and having caught my attention tapped his nose and frowned and grinned, an exhibition calculated to affirm that we were all having a good time and would not tell each other's wives.

Orlando called for more wine – and more and more, since I was to pay for it – and became rosy with merriment, indeed so far gone as to nudge me conspiratorially, boasting: "What d'you think of this then? Isn't it something? We'll soon have you back on the straight and narrow path, you'll see!"

"Is Algy always so gloomy?" Julia asked, twining her arms about my neck and tapping my lips with her fan to elicit a smile. "I hope he's going to be more fun later on!"

"You'll take Julia home, of course," Orlando told me.

"Of course."

Julia's dwelling was a dingy upstairs room in a tall house in one of those narrow sidestreets off Drury Lane. She giggled in the hansom cab, nibbled my ear, pouted, and slapped my wrist for unresponsiveness.

"You'll come upstairs now, Algy?"

"I think not."

"Orlando told me you would come upstairs."

We mounted an uncarpeted stairway to her room, every part of which was covered with an array of brightly coloured gowns, hats, furs, scattered shoes and artificial flowers; and here amongst this profusion she turned and faced me, not at all too drunk to make her standpoint known.

"Orlando says you are not likely to want favours; but he says that nonetheless I may ask you for anything I want. Is this so?"

"I suppose that it is."

"A hundred pounds?"

"Very well."

"Five hundred pounds?" she said, emboldened.

"But absolutely no more."

"All right. I ain't greedy. I want to leave the stage. I'm going to set up as a milliner. Have girls work for me. Five hundred'll start me off nicely. But I got this friend Felicity. I'll tell her about you. *She* knows Orlando an' all. You'll like her. She wants to leave the stage too . . ."

Julia watched me speculatively. She put her hand on her hip and jutted her bosom forward.

"Are you sure you don't want favours, Algy?"

"I must be going."

"Don't you find me pretty?"

"Yes, of course."

"Then kiss me."

She wound herself about me, hard and sinuous, her tongue in my mouth, her hips grinding against mine. I stood starch-stiff in her embrace. She drew back and laughed nastily.

"I pity your wife."

I turned to leave.

"I didn't want you anyway," she called after me. "You wait – you'll have more trouble with Felicity. She won't be put off. A man like you'll be a challenge to her. I wish I could be there to see the fun!"

I had caught glimpses in the courtroom of people that I knew; but on the third day of the proceedings I was surprised to notice Mr Joseph Pearson. He saw me and acknowledged my presence. I pondered over this during the course of the day, while a professor of massage at the Savoy said that he had seen a young man in Oscar's bed, and some chambermaids revealed that they had seen some more sheets stained in a Peculiar Way. Over the day the Crown concluded its case. As we emerged I accompanied Mr Pearson to the main doorway. To my utter astonishment he was with Willie Smith, and now I realised that he had been all the time. I had not recognised my one-time lover. True he had been in part obscured by the crowd. But that was not all.

"Willie!" I began amazed.

"Algy!" A spontaneous smile of pleasure was his first reaction.

Crowds milled about us, jostling. Mr Pearson looked vexed.

"After so long . . ." I murmured, marvelling at his changed appearance. "To meet *here* . . ."

"Oh, you haven't seen me since I dyed my hair," said Willie, looking suddenly amused. "I *wondered* what you were staring at."

I continued to stare. I couldn't help it. His lovely auburn hair, so beloved of artists and lovers – dyed to dull brown, an inconspicuous and unremarkable shade that did not flatter him at all. Oh, he was still good-looking – what would he be now, twenty-nine? – he would retain his natural beauty, with those high cheek bones and well shaped features. A little less elfin, harder round the jaw, stronger in expression – it could not have been easy for him, civilising the riff-raff of the streets. But to abandon his Moreau glory – ah! how could he!

"This is not the time nor place . . ." said Mr Pearson irritably.

It was true. We were shifty then, as if we had been caught in a compromising situation. *Why are you here? Why did you come? What does it mean to you?* None of this was spoken; but the eyes said it.

"You were away when I called to see you," I blurted out.

"Mr Pearson said you'd called."

"Mr Charles is dead. He wanted me to fetch you."

"Mr Charles? Oh," he said slowly. "How sad . . ." I felt a rush of sympathy as I watched Willie take the news – the same reaction as I had had – the surprise of remembered sweetness – confusion – the social front that clicked into place as he suppressed the inconvenient memories, the determination not to let the past disturb. "I'm sorry that I was not there."

"I too . . ."

"I was away, you see," he fidgeted. "But," he added firmly, "I came back. And it's been nice to see you, Algy."

"A dreadful business," muttered Mr Pearson. "And we have to get back now. Find out what a wreck Baines and Andrews have made of the place."

"We left the oldest boys in charge," grinned Willie. "Best be off now."

Mr Pearson uttered a polite goodbye, and they were gone. Nudged and pushed by the escaping throng I stumbled my way out. After all this time . . . to meet in the corridors of the Old Bailey . . . because of Oscar Wilde . . .

That night I slept in the dressing room. Some time in the middle of the night I woke in panic. A cold insistent voice was speaking to me saying: *You took the boy to a hotel – you had adjoining rooms – did any impropriety take place? – I ask you once again. Remember that you are in a court of law!*

"No!" I gasped to the empty air. "Nothing happened – I swear it." I looked about me, at the blank, still room. My heart was pounding. How I longed for Arthur – someone to hold. But I suppose that moment was the one when it finally burst through to me that I could not see him, possibly never again, for his own safety. Nothing was possible. I had been wrong. The symphony was wrong. The only security was in denial. No contact must be made, not by letter nor by visit, nothing. Time must pass. Let time pass, months and months of time, let all this be forgotten. Let Orlando tire of baiting me, relent and hand the stupid papers over, let the ghastly trial be long forgotten. Then in some bright dawn, perhaps . . .

I recalled poor Somerset, whose visits to the Cleveland Street brothel had been observed and whose indiscretions had led him to social disgrace and exile. The boy involved with him had been kept in police custody for weeks in order to testify against him – he swore he was not held against his will, but what else could he say? – while Somerset prowled disconsolately round Europe, awaiting arrest.

And how could I avoid this sure collision for myself? I could not live forever at Orlando's whim – I knew that sooner or later he would overstep the mark of what I could accept – what then? whatever could I do? Dare I call his bluff? The answer was no.

I flung back the sheets and sat upon the edge of the bed, my head in my hands.

Both Mr Pearson and Willie were present in the courtroom and I contrived to keep close by. Thus on the fourth day of the trial I found myself seated next to Mr Pearson. I had the impression that he intended keeping me from Willie; but such morbid imaginings may well have been the result of my very jittery state of mind. I should have stayed away. But no, I was impelled to be here; I could do nothing else.

Sir Edward Clarke I swear believed in Oscar's innocence. He first of all commented upon the conduct of the press, which had done immense damage to the possibility of a fair hearing; and he criticised the prosecution for their persistence in questioning his client about disgraceful works of literature which Oscar had not written. He maintained that by facing trial Oscar had revealed his undeniable good character. No one charged with such an offence would stay if he were guilty. And then Oscar himself was called to give evidence.

A palpable air of expectancy filled the room.

"Any doubts that still exist in the minds of the jury," Clarke predicted, "will be completely removed when Mr Wilde denies upon oath that there is any truth in any of the accusations."

"There is no truth in any one of them," said Oscar. "None whatsoever."

They cross-examined him upon the poetry of the day, that damaging side alley which always led to prejudice. He was invited to pass comment upon a poem by Lord Alfred Douglas in praise of Shame. However dare anyone write verse again, I reflected gloomily, when in a court of law the fancies of a moment could be held up to analysis and scorn, little wisps of chiffon to be tugged and torn and trampled underfoot? I was glad to notice there was sympathy for Oscar here. But Mr Gill was undeterred, and read a second poem, which ended with the line: *I am the Love that dare not speak its name.*

"Surely it is clear," said Mr Gill, "that the poem is referring to unnatural love?"

"No."

"What *is* the Love that dare not speak its name?" asked Gill.

It was, said Oscar, the affection of an elder for a younger man – as with David and Jonathan, as in the philosophy of Plato, the sonnets of Michelangelo and Shakespeare – deep and spiritual, pure and perfect, much misunderstood, so much so that in this century it had come to be called the Love that dare not speak its name. It was beautiful, fine and noble. It was not unnatural – it existed when the elder man had intellect and the younger the joy and hope and glamour of life. The world did not understand it, the world mocked at it, and on account of it put men in the pillory. It was why he stood before us now.

So elegantly and with such finely controlled emotion did Oscar speak the words that a burst of applause echoed round that crowded court – then some hisses – and the judge ordered no further displays of emotion. But there was one I noticed. Willie's hand and Mr Pearson's linked for a moment almost imperceptibly, and then withdrew; but I had seen, and what I understood from that filled me with joy and confusion. Had Willie all this time been Mr Pearson's lover? The idea was a revelation to me. I had always perceived Mr Pearson as severe and daunting, dedicated to his work, without the softer sentiments to weaken manly fortitude. In his business transactions with myself he had been brusque, ungracious. Indeed, I had felt sympathy for Willie, living with such a bear, and wondered how my jaunty rebellious friend could ever stand such domination. Similarly I had supposed that Mr Pearson would not have found Willie the easiest of assistants at his school; though I admired their work, I sometimes thought they were an unlikely pair to be in partnership – Willie had been on the streets at one stage in his life, and Mr Pearson always seemed strait-laced, respectable, one that would heartily disapprove of immorality, if only for its social implications.

This radical reshaping of my concept of their relationship blended like a bold thread within the unfolding scenario before my eyes.

Leaving behind the aery regions of Lord Alfred's rose red lips, the prosecution closed in upon those other youths, whose lips did not resemble flowers.

Did Oscar go to Alfred Taylor's rooms? Were they not in rather a rough neighbourhood?

"They were near the Houses of Parliament."

I winced. How well I remembered the night when I had paced the streets between Westminster Abbey and the tall impressive government building, tormented and alone, afraid to enter the Paradise of promise now so relentlessly revealed.

The cross-examination of Alfred Taylor now followed. He impressed us all, I believe, by admitting to having spent his way through an inheritance of £43,000 in just a few years. It was suggested that he had made a living since that time by procuring boys for rich gentlemen. He denied it.

We all retired to luncheon and Freddy Merton collared me and chattered on irrelevantly – irrelevantly, for the greatest relevance to me at that point was the discovery of my supposition that Willie and Mr Pearson were lovers. How wonderful and amazing to be able to live inconspicuously together, working side by side, preserving a professional exterior, but secretly at night to know a different world, the world of hidden love . . .

If this were so, there did remain yet hope . . . but not for me, not while Orlando dogged my footsteps.

All afternoon Sir Edward Clarke spoke passionately in Oscar Wilde's defence. He pointed out that by trying Wilde together with Alfred Taylor the former's case was much prejudiced by evidence which belonged to the latter – that the poetry upon which Oscar had been questioned had been written by another. His accusers were proven blackmailers, and if the Crown had knowledge of their true characters what business had they to offer them up as witnesses?

He urged the jury to try to disentangle truth from calumny. In a beautiful and impassioned speech he trusted that the result of their deliberation would be to clear Oscar's name and society itself from stain.

The courtroom buzzed with its approval. Some were visibly moved and there were bold calls of "Hear! hear!" and "I say, well done!" Such was the power of oration that I was convinced by it and believed in Oscar's total innocence, I who knew him to be guilty – guilty not of odious abominations, but of merely loving other men.

Oscar himself was patently affected by the speech and shed a tear, penning a note of thanks to Clarke, who nodded his reply.

Mr Grain then spoke up for Taylor; and Mr Gill then closed for the prosecution. His speech was grim and plain and stemmed the gathering euphoria, in which those of us who felt for Oscar's plight had been indulging.

Why should the witnesses have given false evidence, he asked? What could they possibly gain? Why should they accuse themselves of vile acts if it were not the truth? And it was true that Mr Wilde had given them presents, and such presents were always given after he had passed some time alone in the boys' company. Society may well regret the downfall of a prominent man, but if the sore at the centre of its heart were not removed, it would in time infect us all.

Leaving the courtroom in a most sober frame of mind I had hoped to speak to Willie. I do not know what I would have expected to say, but in the light of my new knowledge I wanted verification, with a look, a nuance or tone, of what I now suspected, indeed hoped. But both slipped away so pointedly, without any contact or remark, that I could not but suppose that they had chosen not to converse with me. I could imagine what was in their minds. The atmosphere was charged with tension and emotion. What could they have to say to me, a married man, respectable and wealthy, in no way threatened by the situation which to them pulsated with menace and despair? Yet I longed for their support – to tell them of my need, to share with them the knowledge of my love for Arthur – and I dared not.

It was possible that the gloom induced in me by the day's events suggested to Orlando that he might further steep himself into that crime in which he had so recently taken his first steps. He asked for details of the whole procedure and I told him what had happened.

"So tomorrow will be the last day of the trial," he said. "And things are looking pretty black for Oscar. Well," he said, "you shall celebrate the verdict, whatever it is, by inviting me to dinner at your house."

"I would prefer not."

"Your preference carries no weight whatsoever. We shall dine at your house, you and I, and you will see it is a proper little banquet, with your servants waiting on us. And afterwards, your carriage will take me home, as I am finding cabs so very common. Indeed, now I think of it, I'll come by carriage. You shall send it for me here. What time shall we say? At eight?"

"If you insist."

"I do," he sniggered. "So the Crown protects the blackmailers if they give evidence that'll get a conviction! That is a handy thing to know. What money have you with you at the moment?"

I told him.

"Give it to me. But I'll be generous," he chortled, "and give you back just enough money for the cab fare home."

The last day of the trial.

Willie was not present; Mr Pearson was, but kept his distance and I only saw him from afar. I sat next to Freddy, who sucked peppermints throughout. Mr Justice Charles, a beak-nosed gentleman with a long pointed chin and glinting spectacles, summed up the case. He pointed out what Edward Clarke had so often stressed already, that the hysterical press behaviour had made it impossible to view the case objectively.

At half past one the jury retired with a plentiful supply of food and drink – a long deliberation was expected.

At this point I lost my nerve and slunk off to Pall Mall. I passed a dreary afternoon there in the library. My spirits were not lifted by reading in the *Daily Mail* that the police had set a watch upon the houses of men who were suspected of having similar tastes to Oscar. I felt menaced on every side, like a deer in a thicket. I could settle to nothing. At about six thirty Freddy found me and explained that the jury had returned at five fifteen, unable to agree upon a verdict. There was to be a further trial at a later date, and in the meantime Oscar was expected to be released on bail.

The inconclusiveness of the result depressed me. I had hoped for some symbolic indication of my own position – either a ghastly and punitive thunderclap that would cause me to consider a visit to Philippe d'Ourcelles; or a beacon of hope and tolerance that would inspire and hearten – and there was neither. In the greatest gloom I betook myself back home, to await the arrival of Orlando, for whom I sent the carriage.

I was dismally aware of the contrasts within the "dome of many coloured glass" that made up my life, as I read stories to Perceval and Sophy in the nursery shortly before Orlando came to dinner. Here in the children's kingdom I was looked upon with affection and respect – yet the self who sat with infants on his knee and read the tales of mice and rabbits was the same at present held in thrall by a cynical young man who was growing daily more acquisitive. Where would his demands end? The foolish carnal triumphs would no doubt begin to pall and he would seek more dangerous proofs of his control. His trespass on my personal domain was a most

250

unwelcome encroachment and its imminence preyed upon my mind and spoiled my visit to the nursery.

"May I speak to you, sir?" murmured Emily, the children now tucked up in bed.

"I am a little pressed for time this evening . . ."

"I will be very brief, sir."

"Not a problem with the children, I hope?"

"A private matter."

Our conversation took place upon the landing outside the children's room. No longer the dark place of the winter months, this little corner yet retained its shadows.

"It is about Polette," said Emily gravely. "You may remember, sir, that while that unfortunate woman was in this house I struck up a friendship with her. Or perhaps you did not know that? When Mr Charles died she was taken under the protection of a certain gentleman."

I grew rapidly uneasy. What indelicate matters were we to have here? Ought Claudia to be a party to the conversation? I had never supposed that I would ever be obliged to discuss with Emily any other matter than the children's welfare.

"That gentleman," continued Emily, "has no further use for her."

"She was to be his model, was she not?"

"No sir!" Emily looked at me severely, as if I should know better than to play the innocent.

"Well, I know nothing of the arrangement."

"No, sir," she agreed politely, much in the tone of one who humours an idiot. "Whether or not you know that he has cast her out is immaterial, but the matter upon which I wish to speak concerns a package which she left here."

"She has been here?"

"She came to the servants' door. She recalled my friendship and she left some small belongings. She wished that they should be sent to her sister in France. I said that I would do that, sir, but I require some guidance, for some of the things are valuable."

"Indeed – of course I will look into the matter if you wish it. You say that she – has no home now?"

"The wife grew jealous and insisted that she left. The gentleman did not wish any scandal. It is an old story."

"Where will she go?"

"I think there is a man . . ."

"But she did not ask for help? We could have found her employment."

"I do not think," said Emily, curiously reprovingly, "that she wanted to be anybody's servant."

I had the impression that Emily held me in some way responsible, as if by being male and an acquaintance of Sir William Franklin I was part of the conspiracy that sent the world's Polettes to lives of degradation.

"And she left some things here? Why was that, do you suppose?"

"She trusted me. The possessions have a sentimental value. She considered them too precious to take with her on the life to which she knew that she is destined."

"Do you know where she can be found? Surely we can help her? There must be other paths open to her – all this is most upsetting."

"I fear there is little choice for her by now," said Emily, "and as for finding her, I do not think she wishes to be found."

"Very well," I said. "We will do as she wishes as regards her belongings; bring them to me tomorrow."

The gentleman did not wish any scandal, I thought angrily as I walked downstairs. Our society was composed of hypocrites and casualties, exploiters and victims. The trick was not to get found out. Arthur Somerset had been found out. Oscar had been found out. But all over London, there were Franklins, men who took their pleasures carefully and tossed the refuse to the gutter, having the fine knack of treading the delicate line that kept their name intact, their reputation unsmirched – circus artists all of them, knowing how to walk on eggshells.

"A lovely dinner!" said Orlando, leaning back. "I think the next time the girls would enjoy it too. I could bring Amelia, with Felicity for you. She's eager to meet you now I've told her all about you. You did us proud, I must say, Algy. And it's very gratifying to be sitting here in the best parts of your house with servants waiting on us hand and foot, and not to be stuffed upstairs like Charles was, in a poky little attic. This is the life for me! Good food, good surroundings, and you being so sweet and affable to me and to know that you're going to be sweeter in a moment."

"What do you mean?"

"Light me a cigarette; you should be good at that by now. You could go on the streets with all the practice you've had from me!" He chuckled nastily as he drew in the first smoke.

"What do you mean, sweeter?"

"I'm low on funds again. I don't know how I do it. Money drips through my hands like water. Just like water! You're so jittery, Algy. Don't worry," he patted my hand, "I won't tell your butler that you suck me off!"

"Come into the study. I can't stand to hear you talk like that in here."

252

"So tense and wary! What do you think I'm going to do – order you to strip in your own dining room? I told you I had class. Those cheap thrills are for the *poses plastiques*, and *we* are quality. We must be, sitting here. I say, Algy, or rather Lord Algernon, you must be very rich! It brings it home to me, sitting here and looking about. And there must be so much more that we can't see."

"Not so." I answered. "What you perceive obscurely as wealth is otherwise, being bound up in land tenure, inacessible and invisible."

"Not so invisible as that," Orlando corrected meaningfully, looking about him. "But by all means let us betake ourselves into the study. It sounds a more appropriate place for a business transaction."

Closing the door I told Meredith that we did not wish to be disturbed, and I resigned myself to the sight of Orlando sprawled upon the Chesterfield drinking my brandy and puffing the cigars which were my daily tribute. I sat stiffly upon a hard-backed chair and suffered the reproach from the steady-eyed gazes of the family photographs about the room. The brandy consequently tasted bitter and my feelings of revulsion towards my most unwelcome guest grew with increasing rapidity.

"Land, you say?" he murmured. "That's right – you have a house in the country, do you not? I would imagine that is a pleasant place. And in the summer a person likes to leave the dust and grime of city life. I might be interested to visit there."

"That is impossible," I said swiftly.

"There you are wrong," said Orlando. "All things are possible for a person who holds all the trump cards. I've heard about these country house parties – dukes and duchesses mingling with the great ones of society and the arts – beautiful women glittering with jewels – countesses from Europe – assignations in the conservatory. Have you a conservatory, Algy? A person of my talents might easily net an heiress in such circumstances. What do you think? I'm pretty, am I not? Do you not find me pretty, Algy?"

"Less so with every passing minute."

"Don't be bitchy, Algy. Well! So I shall visit you this summer and I shall need proper clothes. Summer suits and shirts and shoes and elegant underlinen. Does not that thought excite you? And before I leave this evening we must ratify our agreement more concisely. A hundred here and there is no bad thing, but a person needs security. You shall make me an allowance. What I have received so far is a pittance – and I reckon that the peace of mind you will receive by knowing I am happy is worth as much as a thousand – several times a year. Don't look so long-faced, Algy – you can afford it. And after all, what's the alternative? All your aristocratic friends get to hear that you're a sodomite, your lady wife petitions for divorce, your name is never mentioned in front of your little golden-haired children – oh, and did I forget the scenes at Bow Street, and the trial?"

"Very well, a thousand," I winced. "But after that leave me in peace, at least for a while. I cannot endure much more of this."

"Poor Algy," cooed Orlando. "Am I being rough? Well, you should not have been so foolish, should you, messing about with tarts and dirty literature and writing letters from Pall Mall? Not to mention all that could be discovered further if the detectives were to probe . . . it's always the families that suffer, isn't it? I would be so reluctant to bring sorrow to your lady wife. I don't believe that I have met her, Algy?"

"You certainly have not."

"What is she like? Good-looking, I daresay. Younger than you, perhaps?"

"I would prefer you did not speak of her."

"No doubt," he sneered. "However, I have a whim to meet her and be introduced. After all, she will be my gracious hostess during the summer months, so she should know me. And after all, it's not as if I'm unattractive. I'll be an ornament for her parties. Does she play the piano? We might sing some duets – did you know I sing in a fine tenor?"

"You would be insulting if you were not so grotesque."

"I mean it, Algy," said Orlando, narrowing his eyes. "I want to meet your wife. Get her for me."

"This does your cause no good, I warn you. I ought to have you thrown out . . ."

"But you dare not," said Orlando complacently. "So go and fetch your lady wife. What is her name? Don't glower at me, Algy. I said what is her name?"

"Claudia," I choked. "But do you promise to behave – ? Ah, what am I asking? I would not believe you if you gave your word."

"Nonetheless I give it. In front of her I will make no reference to the fact that I like to fuck you up the arse and that you dine with Gaiety girls. Now be a good boy and bring her. Bring her now."

I stood up, sickened and appalled. I went slowly up the stairs to the bedroom, where Claudia sat in the yellow chair with every appearance of greatest comfort, her feet up on the tapestried stool, her hair dishevelled, a book in her hand, and the clutter of her dinner tray upon the low table beside her.

"Has he gone?" she enquired, not looking up.

"Not yet," I fidgeted.

"Algy, I wish you would read this book," said Claudia. "I would be

254

so interested to discuss with you the issues which the author raises. Her name is Sarah Grand, a bold woman who has left her husband and now has become well known for her daring ideas. She is quite a sensation! She has so much to say upon the subject of men and women."

"Claudia . . ." I put a hand on her shoulder. "Would you do me the kindness of coming downstairs and meeting this visitor – only for a moment – he is about to leave – "

She put her book down and grimaced at me. "Oh Algy – I cannot. Must I? I am not properly dressed and my hair is such a mess. Why is it necessary?"

"Because I wish it," I mumbled. "Just as a favour to me, that's all."

"Who is he?" she frowned.

"Nobody – absolutely nobody." This unhelpful explanation obviously did not satisfy her. I ploughed on. "A young man . . . nephew of somebody at the club . . . hoping to take up a profession in the theatre . . . merely social . . . murmur a few pleasantries, that's all. It will only take a moment. Please, dear."

"Oh very well," she relented. "If I must." The ease and affability with which she acquiesced made me feel every kind of worm. To see her move about making herself presentable – for Orlando – humiliated me indescribably.

Within a little while she turned the finished effect towards me, smiling. "Will I do?"

"Immaculate."

We went downstairs together and entered the study. I introduced them. Both were charming, but Claudia's charm was innocent and well-meaning, born of a wish to please me and of her own natural attractiveness; Orlando's was entirely false and something of the quality of sugared oil. It oozed from him like treacle from a cake.

"My husband tells me that you are interested in the stage . . ."

"Yes. I once worked at the Hyperion as an assistant to a magician."

"How very interesting that must have been!"

"It was. But limited. I feel that I should like to stretch my talents. I feel I have a lot to offer."

I pursed my lips.

"Indeed?" said Claudia. "What particularly would you like to do?"

"Oh, Shakespeare, like they do at the Lyceum. Henry Irving is my ideal."

"Orlando would like to play Iago," I observed.

"No I wouldn't," complained Orlando, "Not at all. I'd like to play the leading man – Bassanio or Ferdinand, that sort of thing."

"I'm sure you'd play them very well!" Claudia assured him.

"Thank you, my lady. I think Lord Algernon is a little more dubious about my talents; but I am very grateful for your belief in me."

"I think Orlando is about to leave," I interposed. "I believe the carriage is ready for you now."

"Oh, must he go?" said Claudia politely.

"He must," I answered soberly, as much to myself as to anyone.

Orlando gave a dazzling smile. "Yes, I must be away now, but, as they say, parting is such sweet sorrow, and I shall surely see you both again."

I accompanied Orlando to the front door and we stood for a moment upon the steps while the carriage drew up in the street below.

Orlando nudged me. "Very nice, Algy, she's very nice. She's kept her looks well, hasn't she, considering that you have been married for some while. Still – I don't suppose you tired her very much with *your* demands in the bedroom, eh!"

"Get out," I muttered through my teeth.

"I will," he said obligingly. "But I'll see you tomorrow when you bring my cigarettes."

The door closed and I turned back into the house, the weight of all mankind upon my shoulders. Claudia was waiting on the stairs.

"Are we truly seeing him again, Algy?" she enquired. "*Who* did you say he was? I must admit I did not much take to him."

"Claudia . . ." I took her hand. My palm was icy cold, my lips were dry. "Let us go upstairs. I have something that I want to tell you."

CHAPTER TWENTY

I WAITED until Claudia and I were ready for bed before I embarked upon what I suspected was to be a very difficult and lonely monologue.

Claudia was sitting up in bed when I entered from the dressing room. With her hair down and brushed back she looked extremely young and fresh, reminding me of the delicate girl I married with the sworn intention of protecting her from life's nastier aspects, some of which I was now about to be the cause and outward expression. I was mildly irritated to notice the book in her hand. I doubted whether Sarah Grand, New Woman that she was, had much to offer in the present situation. I took a breath.

"What I have to tell you will be very painful for us both. This evening may in fact be the last time that you look at me with anything approaching love, respect or friendship. I am truly sorry to see the loss of these shared years, when we meant something to each other which we may not mean after tonight. But there is no other course open to me. I have to tell you. I have been living under unbearable strain, and if I do not unburden myself I fear that I shall certainly experience some kind of crisis in my health."

She said nothing, staring at me with expectation and some alarm. I continued: "That young man downstairs . . . it is true that he has some connection with the theatre; but everything else I told you was a lie. In fact that youth is blackmailing me, and he invited himself here to prove the extent of his power over me, and also to demand more money, and to threaten me with his continued presence, at Mortmayne. Of course, that could not be tolerated."

"Certainly not!" cried Claudia, utterly astonished. "And you must go to the police. It is your only course. But this is dreadful – I had no idea – I don't understand. Whatever could you have done to give him cause for blackmail? You never do anything wrong!"

"If only that were true . . ." I groaned.

"Well – just what *have* you done?" she asked in some exasperation, still so disbelieving that she was inclined not to take me entirely seriously.

"You remember Mr Charles," I began. I sat down on the yellow chair.

"I certainly do," she said darkly.

"Well, Charles interested himself in the erotic . . . collected it – as some people collect for instance – "

"Stuffed pheasants?" suggested Claudia briskly.

"Yes, why not?" I said gloomily. "In Charles' instance, drawings, writings . . . and unfortunately these fell into Orlando's hands."

"But so what?" Claudia demanded. "If they belonged to Mr Charles, what possible connection have they with you? How can blackmail enter into it? You simply have to deny all knowledge of them."

"No – 'simply' doesn't enter into it," I said ruefully. "The writings, of a purely private nature, were to be passed about, and any gentleman who so wished might add to it with revelations of his own. One foolish evening I wrote something, and therefore my handwriting appears in that unpleasant manuscript."

"I see . . ." she murmured thoughtfully.

I was awed by her equanimity. A woman who had just learned that her husband read and wrote pornography, and she had not raved and ranted! But perhaps she had not understood?

"You realise that I am talking about the kind of writing that no decent person countenances?" I said carefully.

"Algy – I am not quite the stranger to such matters as you suppose," admitted Claudia, to my surprise. "One of the ladies at the League brought specimens of such along to a meeting. Her husband was a regular visitor to Holywell Street. He kept his purchases in his wardrobe in a box under his shoes. She found it. She thought we would be interested to read what some men think of women. There were obscene pictures and horrid little stories, and an overall effect of hatred and ridicule. We were struck by the hypocrisy of our times, where superficially women are revered and called 'the angel of the house', yet at the same time obviously despised. Hannah said it was because men are afraid of women; but we did not generally see how this could be possible, since men hold all the powers."

"I had no idea that you talked about such things at the League," I said astonished.

"Why should you?" she returned. "You never ask about it, and your comments upon it are typically of a puerile nature. However, I mention this only to assure you that I do know the kind of thing to which you refer."

"But I did not write anything like that! I would never write anything scurrilous about a woman – the idea is disgraceful."

"But then what does that leave?" She looked blank for a moment. "I don't mean to pry. You do not have to tell me what you wrote."

We paused. She was quite right; I did not, nor had I intention of so doing.

"You say it was in your hand," she continued. "Did you sign it?"

"No."

"Then you are clear. Your writing is not so distinctive."

"This would be true," I began painfully, "but unfortunately Orlando has another document also, which I not only signed but which was written upon club notepaper. This writing connects me with the former, and in this instance I must take full blame. It is a letter."

"To whom?"

I ignored this very relevant question. "Oh!" I cried with a gesture of frustration. "The stupid part about it all is that I never even sent the letter. It was a crazy flight of fancy, the indulgence of a moment. I wrote it at the club, then realising that I dared not leave it in a waste basket or even cross the room to risk its contents left charred in the fireplace, I stuffed it in a pocket and brought it home. I placed it in my dressing table drawer and then forgot about it. Orlando stole it; and the contents are so open to misinterpretation that it would appear that I had sent the strange sentiments within to a real person – no one would believe otherwise – "

"Do you mean that he broke into our house?" said Claudia frowning and alert.

"I beg your pardon? Who?" I blinked.

"This vile Orlando."

I did not catch her drift, nor see my blunder.

"I fail to see how he gained access to the dressing room," said Claudia.

I daresay my face was a picture as I struggled to extricate myself from this one.

"Why – it must have been one of the times when he came to visit Charles . . . when you were in Ramsgate. He often visited – he was very fond of Charles – and I could not always be present and so he must have taken advantage of the situation. As Charles lay dying!" I added, hoping to throw her off the scent with the implications of reverence and solemnity that a reference to our mortality brings in its wake.

"But how revolting!" Claudia cried, more angry about this than about any part of the previous matter. "Prowling round my house – touching my possessions – how beastly of you to have left him to his own devices if you knew he was a bad lot! Your irresponsibility is beyond belief. Did he take anything else?"

"Of course not. He's not a burglar."

"I see – each crime has its limits, does it? One is either a blackmailer or a burglar – well, that is reassuring to know!"

This side-tracking had had the unfortunate effect of prejudicing her against me. Annoyance with my dismal stewardship of our domain lent a certain brittleness to her subsequent remarks.

"And so," she said, "our blackmailer-but-not-burglar stole a letter which you did not send and threatens you with it. To whom was it addressed?"

"There was no name."

"No name? Then how can it be incriminating? Or even a letter?"

"Come now," I winced. "There are ways of beginning a letter which necessitate no use of name. My darling . . . my dear . . ."

"Ah. So you begin with a Darling." Her gaze narrowed. She said carefully: "I believed you, Algy, when you told me that you had no mistress. This was not a letter to a woman?"

"Good Lord, no," I groaned. "I wish it were."

Illumination overtook my wife as patently as if a switch had pressed upon her consciousness.

"Ah! It was a letter to a man!"

"Exactly. It began My Dearest Boy; and in the content lay the kind of thing that would leave a reader in no doubt that the writer cherished inclinations which the law considers criminal. And now you see the full horror of my situation."

"But why did you write it?" Claudia sounded utterly confused.

"I don't know," I wailed. "I must have been out of my mind."

"I just don't understand. I just don't see why you should write a letter to an imaginary boy."

I sat there, calmer now. I toyed with a comb that lay upon the dressing table near my hand. An imaginary boy – how fortunate that she had somehow understood that to be the case.

"The fact remains, I did," I said.

"And Orlando thinks that you intended to send the letter and is attempting to blackmail you on the strength of it," she mused. "I suppose that the Oscar Wilde case put the idea into his head."

"I suppose it did."

"Of course," she nodded. "For Oscar Wilde sent letters. That one to Lord Alfred Douglas that caused all the fuss – the slim gilt soul and the rose red lips. Oh, surely, Algy, yours was not like that!"

"I am not a poet of his calibre," I said sarcastically. "Mine was couched in more everyday terms."

"I wish that you would tell me what it said."

"Oh Claudia, I cannot," I cringed. "It was – ramblings – "

"I only ask so that I understand what we are up against," she said with sympathy that embarrassed me beyond belief.

"It was not the kind of letter that I would relish hearing read out aloud by a barrister in court," I said bitterly. "That is enough."

"But what I'm trying to ascertain," she said, leaning forward eagerly, "is whether we can call his bluff. You say you never sent the letter. There is no name on it beside yours. A married man of social standing and impeccable reputation, what have you to fear for having played with an imaginative idea? The Oscar Wilde business is talked about everywhere – you idly wrote a letter of the kind that everyone has read in connection with the case. It was foolish – but amusing – you did it as a silly game – and of course I would be there to verify that you are not abnormal – you have children – why, we could surely laugh the whole thing off, and make Orlando seem a fool for thinking there was any truth in it."

"I would of course take that obvious course of action," I replied heavily, "if my conscience were perfectly clear."

She continued to stare at me, presumably understanding my meaning instantly, but disbelieving it, fighting against it, hoping she had misread me.

"You yourself referred to Oscar Wilde," I said. "Foolishly he decided to take the course of action that you recommend – he too is a married man with children – perhaps he assumed that no one would believe an artist to be capable of what society calls an unspeakable sin. And see where he is now, what he has endured, the dismal straits to which such action brought his wife and sons. If he had left the country when he had a chance, the grim result of his indiscretions would have been spared to the innocent. And that is the course that I propose to take, to save us all from any adverse repercussion."

"Wait – you go too fast – " said Claudia breathlessly. "You hurried over something rather startling. You said your conscience was not clear. What did you mean by that?"

I said nothing. I could not find appropriate words. I stood up and began to pace about. Her penetrating stare shone on me like a searchlight; I had to move out of its searing ray.

"Algy? *What*?"

I turned round swiftly. "Well, it's obvious, is it not? Must I be obliged to admit it word for word? Then you had better hear it. Some of the allegations against Oscar are such as could be brought against me if Orlando chose to make my foolish abberations known."

"You mean – renters?" she said faintly. "Is not that the term? You cannot mean that. What *do* you mean? In plain words, Algy, just what have you done?"

"I met some boys at Mr Charles' lodgings and I – " Here I floundered. I had never used those kind of words with Claudia. Love? I could not so degrade the word in connection with Jem and Francis. But how could I explain carnality?

"I'm waiting, Algy," she said mercilessly. "I believe that I am owed an explanation at this point."

"There were two boys who made a living out of prostitution, and I went with them," I mumbled looking anywhere but at my wife.

"Why?" she screeched.

"Well, why do you suppose?" I snapped.

"I cannot imagine," she said almost incoherently. "You never seemed – you always – I had thought – I thought you were not interested in that sort of thing – with me you are so reticent – unemotional – am I to suppose then that with them it is a different matter?" Her voice vibrated dangerously. I gripped the bed post, the whorls of its ornamentation a curious consolation, firm and steady.

"I believe that I may be one of those unfortunate men who seem to prefer their own kind," I said dully.

"How can you be?" she said dismissively. "They are supposed to be insane and degenerate. You manage the estate, and conduct yourself in every way with dignity – you are respected at the club and popular in society. I won't have you so denigrate yourself by that vile implication."

"Nevertheless," I continued with lowered eyes, "it seems to be the only explanation for my behaviour in the last few months."

"The last few months? These things do not come on so suddenly, do they? Is it possible to change from being sane and normal to such a degree that you pursue these street boys?"

"It isn't sudden. Before we married I had that kind of experience."

"Oh no!" she cried in horror.

"I went with some boys – in Greece and Italy – and here in London I – there was a particular boy with whom I fell in love. We caused each other some emotional distress and parted. I believe that my mother suspected, and she hurried me into marriage. Not that I did not wish to marry!" I assured her fervently. "I did, with all my heart. Our years together have been very dear to me. But I believe the germ was there all along, like a hidden seed that waits until the time is right and then begins to grow. It begins at school, you know. It's common there . . ."

"The time is right now, is it?" she said with horrible contempt.

"I believe it was to do with Charles . . . he stirred some kind of need I'd long suppressed."

"You did not go with *him*?" she said appalled.

"No! Good God – let us keep this in perspective." I relinquished the bed post and began to pace again.

"For Heaven's sake, sit down," she snapped.

I sat, hands clasped between my knees. With my head bent I stole a glance at her but her expression was quite chilling, and I looked away.

"So," she said, "Charles introduced you to two boys. Two, Algy! Was not that a little greedy?" As I winced beneath her sarcasm I could almost hear the whirrings of her intuition. I dreaded what must follow.

"I hope it was not they who visited Charles in this house?" she said. "I know he had visitors."

"Oh no," I lied quickly.

"And did Orlando visit here?" she followed.

She had only to ask Meredith. It would be worse, I reasoned, to be caught out through the evidence of my butler.

"Yes, Orlando visited," I said wearily. "And yes, the boys also visited, mostly to get money off him."

"And you permitted it," she said expressionlessly. "That is quite unforgiveable."

"Nothing happened! They only talked and took their money."

"Nothing happened," she repeated, flinging back the sheets. "Am I to feel grateful for that? Am I supposed to exonerate you because you did not take advantage of the moment to give vent to your baser urges? In my house? Ugh! I cannot sit here listening to this – it is one vile disclosure after another." She struggled into her robe; then hesitated – there was nowhere to go. She stood beside the dressing table and leaned there, breathing hard. "I was away in Ramsgate then," she murmured, thinking back. "A god-sent opportunity. I will assume that Charles' proximity to death was some slight hindrance to a full blown orgy; but after he died . . . there would have been a few days left to you . . . that's it, isn't it? Orlando did not need to break into the house – he was here already!"

"He wasn't living here! Lord knows what you are trying to imagine. It's true he stole the papers while he was still here. I left him alone, and he took advantage of my absence to pick the lock of the dressing table drawer."

"You let him into the dressing room?" she asked with a most unpleasant glint in her eyes. We were in some proximity now; she, standing, seemed alarmingly tall. "Is Orlando one of those – renters? The person whom you obliged me to meet earlier this evening?"

"No, he is not," I said warily, looking up at her. "I told you, he

263

works at the Alhambra. Or at least, he used to, till he began to live off me, a week or so ago. He has," I added wryly, "a private income now."

"Is he one of your lovers?" She was terrifying, like an avenging angel.

"Yes – but not for money – nothing sordid – with him it was because – "

"Because you wanted to!" she finished witheringly.

"Well, yes. I used to think that he was very attractive. But it's odd how physically repulsive a person grows when he is continually asking for money!"

"And in my absence you invited this one-time attractive youth into your dressing room. The dressing room, was it, Algy? I'd like to be sure. Our own bed here would have given you more room."

"Of course I did not take him into the bedroom!" I seethed.

"Some scruples do remain then," she said coldly. "How many times?"

"I beg your pardon?"

"The dressing room, how many times?"

"Only once."

"You made love? You call it that, do you? It's unbelievable," she marvelled to herself. "A month ago I would not have known just what it was that men may do with other men, but suddenly because of Oscar Wilde the whole of London knows the grossest details."

"With Orlando I did not call it making love," I answered soberly. "But I was lonely, and I found him comforting."

"I do not suppose, however," she said scathingly, "that comfort was confined to soothing words."

"No, there was a physical embrace. You would prefer me to be honest, would you not?"

"Why spare me?" she cried, her voice raised quiveringly. "I have read the newspapers. The playing with each other's privates – the putting it into each other's mouths – the fecal stains – these now are household terms! Did you do all those things with Orlando in the room next to our bedroom?"

"Not all of them," I answered evenly. "Do you suppose me superhuman?"

Her hand lashed out and slapped my face; and since I had no doubt merited it I sat with somewhat stinging cheek and waited for her fury to subside.

She sat down on a little chair and gazed ahead, her thoughtful silence eerie after so much venom.

"What do you want to do? I asked rather humbly.

"How do you mean?"

264

"In similar circumstances certain women have been known to petition for divorce."

"Why should I want to do that?" she answered strangely reasonably.

"I assume that you despise me."

"No, I don't despise you; I am not so arrogant. My feelings are confused, I must admit, but they are largely puzzlement, amazement."

"Amazement?"

"That you could live this secret life, and that living it you could behave so stupidly. You should have burned the papers. It seems to me that without the papers it would simply be your word against his. In which case, yours is the one that would be believed, society being what it is."

"Yes I know that. But there is no legal way of ridding myself of Orlando, and I refuse to stoop to further acts of criminal folly."

"What do you propose to do?"

"I thought that I would leave the country for a while, till Oscar's second trial is over, and allow the horrid atmosphere in London to disperse."

"Is that wise?"

"What else can I do? I'm driven mad by the prospect of Orlando's leeching. I am tormented when I read the newspapers concerning Oscar. I live in fear and dread. These past two and a half months – and that is all it's been, my dear, this secret life as you call it – have been a ghastly business, what with Charles' death and all. And I cannot suppose that you will be anything but relieved to see me gone . . . I realise that whatever good opinion you had of me once is quite destroyed . . . I am desolate for the pain I cause you by my despicable behaviour . . . I wish I was like other men – no trouble to you – I feel every kind of shame – "

"Don't grovel, Algy, please," said Claudia, sounding more like her usual self. "I've told you that I don't despise you, but I think you've been a fool. I hope," she added dubiously, "I hope that after you had been with the street boys you took baths?"

I squirmed. "I did."

"You can pick up diseases, you know, from whores," she told me seriously.

"Whatever happened to innocent wives?" I grumbled edgily. "Your League of Female Friends has much to answer for."

"Well, yes, we have discussed those topics," she replied. "And many others relevant to society today. Because of Oscar Wilde we have discussed the matter in question, and from what some of the other women said I gather that it is more prevalent than we are given to suppose. If I said bitter things to you it was because I was so taken by surprise and because you permitted *them* to enter the house. That was very wrong. But you are punished quite horribly for that mistake."

We sat in gloomy reverie.

"There is some confusion as to the nature of what you tell me you believe you are," said Claudia carefully. "It is supposed to be a form of madness. But you are living proof that that is not the case. Nor Oscar Wilde – for how could one write brilliant plays that must surely be remembered for their sparkling wit – and be insane? Or do you think that he is innocent?"

"Innocent of the kind of depravity some newspapers would have us believe. Guilty of an unusual form of love."

"You see, if you and Oscar Wilde are examples of this kind of person," she said seriously, "then this kind of person is hardly a monster or madman. Why, I read somewhere that a person of Oscar's type is comparable to Jack the Ripper, stealing forth to commit his crime by darkness and then returning, like a werewolf, to his ordinary life. Such accounts are no better than gibberish then. It is disgusting that anyone agrees to print them."

"You are being awfully fair to me," I murmured chastened.

"You are still yourself. Is it a question of hating the sin and caring about the sinner?"

"You think it is a sin then?" I said uneasily.

"I don't know; I'm no theologian," she said uncomfortably. "I don't believe it's natural. How can it be, when men and women are upon the earth to procreate?"

"But do you find it abhorrent?" I pressed.

"Well, yes, of course I do. To go with street boys – how could I not?"

"Oh – I meant the love of one man for another."

"But who was talking about love?" she shrugged.

"Yes, of course; nobody," I mumbled.

"I hate the business of prostitution," Claudia said. "We understand that young girls take to it for economic reasons. It is disgusting and immoral that this dreadful situation exists and I think it very wrong for married men to avail themselves of it."

"But if it had not been a prostitute," I asked her tremulously. "Is it understandable to you on any level – the love of a man for another man – such as Oscar Wilde described in court – Uranian Love?"

"Love is easier to understand," she admitted. "I have no sympathy for the idea of buying – that sort of thing is sordid. But yes, I can envisage that there could be love. Like David and Jonathan. But

266

Algy," she said bleakly, looking at me. "You give me a sorry tale of renters and blackmail; and that is something other. You do not love any of the persons that you mention, quite the converse, it would seem. If I thought that you intended to go with those boys again, then I would find you despicable and I would consider that we should begin to lead completely separate lives."

"As I told you, I intend to leave the country as soon as possible. I shall have nothing further to do with rent boys, and if I had my way I would never look upon Orlando again."

"Oh Algy . . ." she said dolefully. "It is one thing to discuss the matter of abnormal men with my friends at the League. It is quite another matter to suppose that you believe yourself to be one. Could you not be mistaken?"

"I don't know . . . I need to think, away from here. Whatever it has done, the discovery has not made me happy."

"I also need to think. Perhaps we should consider in the morning what is to be done."

"I suppose you wish me to use the dressing room tonight."

"Yes." She gave me an odd look. "I find I do not want you in my bed."

"I think," said Claudia as we took breakfast in the bedroom, "I think that you are suffering from nervous strain. I suspect that you have been a little unhinged by Mr Charles' reappearance in your life, his stirring of old memories and then his death. It is well known that shock causes strange repercussions. It may well be that you are not abnormal at all; and for this reason you are almost certainly right to go abroad, for in different surroundings the situation may seem clearer to you."

"I wish you would not keep saying 'abnormal'," I said irritably. "It makes me feel like a freak in a fairground."

"I don't know what else to call it," she said, reasonably enough.

"I believe the current term is the Love that Dare not Speak its Name," I said sourly.

"And as we agreed," returned Claudia briskly, "the term is not appropriate to renters."

"You sound cheerful enough," I commented. "At least the news has not laid you low and brought you to your bed."

"Did you expect it?" she said, buttering her toast.

"To be truthful, I had no idea what you would say or do."

"Naturally I spent a large part of the night reflecting upon the things you told me. Your confession would have shocked me more if you and I had been personally close. But we have not. I do not know, Algy, what it is like to be in harmony with someone, but I

267

know that you and I have never known it. If it is so that you are someone who seeks comfort with his own kind, then I understand why you could not do so with me; and rather than find this abhorrent I feel some relief. It means that whatever lack exists is not my fault . . . Algy, you never did ask me about what I did in Ramsgate. I told you that Hannah came to stay – you cannot believe that one person can so change one's outlook. We talked and talked; it was like a breath of fresh air in a darkened room. As a result of her friendship I have grown prepared to see everything more clearly, and to open up my mind to different influences. You must have noticed the books I read now – this is such an exciting time for women . . ."

"Is it?" I said, having noticed nothing.

"You jibe at me for being a so-called New Woman. But if I had not been, I might well have wrung my hands and called for my smelling salts as the ladies in the Mudie library books do. But real women are not like that. Different things are happening. For instance, we no longer take small deprivations for granted. Have you thought, how when a woman travels on a train, her luggage label tells the world whether she is Mrs or Miss – taken or available! – yet a man may keep his personal status as mysterious as he chooses? This is something that could easily be changed."

"I suppose so; I had not realised that women cared one way or the other."

"I mention it as an example. Sarah Grand says that men understand traditional women, which she calls the 'Cow Woman' or the 'Scum Woman'; whereas the 'New Woman' is a little above them. She will be the one to reach out a helping hand to them and lead them out of their moral infancy."

"I see! And this is what you propose to do for me?"

"Yes," she promised shamelessly. "For I think you need it."

"I do?"

"Part of your problem is that you have been too private, Algy. You should have spoken to me before. I could have helped you."

"In God's name how?"

"By sharing our thoughts. You are in trouble and you have been foolish. But you will find that I can be strong."

"Your new-found confidence is alarming. Do you propose to take up smoking also?"

"I suppose that it gives you some obscure pleasure to trivialise the things I find important," she sighed.

"But it is you that trivialises the situation in which we find ourselves! I confess to you a leaning towards what society considers crime and depravity, I tell you of my distress and loneliness, and you tell me about luggage labels."

She stared at me. "I was only trying to convey the background to my reaction. For months you have not spoken to me on a personal level, and meanwhile I have been changing and increasing my awareness also, in a kind of solitude, depending upon female companions for my mental liveliness, when if our marriage had been different I could have depended upon you. You criticise me now because my considered reaction to your news is unconventional – I have not gone into a decline. You should be proud of me!"

"Yes – " I began awkwardly. "But I wonder whether you fully understand. It still leaves us with the problem of my – my nature."

"But need it be a problem?"

"How do you mean?"

"You say you do not intend to visit street boys ever again. I am prepared for us to continue living the kind of life we do – husband and wife, without either making particular demands upon the other's privacy. I have long since accustomed myself to the fact that there will never be passion between us. So you, Algy, have merely to be strong, and come to terms with your personal trial: you cannot satisfy your preferred form of love, and you will have to learn to direct your thoughts elsewhere – there is much to be done with Mortmayne, for instance, or perhaps you could travel . . ."

"I see. So you would condemn me to some kind of sexual void – like a monk, perhaps, or a eunuch?"

"Whatever alternative is there for you?" she said utterly reasonably.

I had not the courage to suggest it. I felt that I had probably been fortunate this far.

"I'm going to help you all I can," she said. "I think that when you get away from London you'll begin to see the situation with detachment. It's simply a matter of time."

I smiled wanly. I appreciated such firmness. But I knew at heart that it was not so simple. She had not all the facts at her disposal, and this attitude of seeming strength was built on a delusion.

"It's *boys*, isn't it?" said my mother grimly. "That's what's behind this sudden visit to Philippe."

"It's true that I am in a spot of bother . . ."

"You should not go."

"Let me be the judge of that, please."

"You should stay and face the matter squarely. It never does any good to run away. The thing always catches up with you in the end."

"That may be so, but believe me, I need a breathing space."

"That was always your way, Algy. Run, run, run. Any difficulty in life – turn your back on it – avoid it. An honourable man would stay. Whatever he had done, an honourable man would face his challengers. And though Oscar Wilde in his personal life is despicable, yet by remaining here to take his punishment he shows himself an honourable man. *His* mother will be proud of *him*."

"I am sorry that I fill you with such shame. At least you will be able to say that my behaviour was consistent with the opinion of me you already hold."

"You are unfair to Algy, mamma," said Claudia.

"He knows my views," said my mother. "He also knows that I will of course declare to all and sundry that my son has gone to France to fulfil a long-standing engagement. I think it most unlikely that anybody will query the issue in my presence."

I discussed at length with Claudia the various problems likely to arise from my absence; but I had every confidence in her ability to deal with them.

"There is just one other thing," I added hesitantly.

"Yes?"

"Do you remember Arthur Hughes?"

"Of course I do."

"You may remember that I took him to a concert? I believe that Orlando may be jealous of him because of that, and may pester him in some way. You never know with blackmailers – they can be very disturbed people. If he should annoy young Arthur in any way I've asked Arthur to let you know, and you will inform me at Philippe's."

"Very well." She eyed me with a curious sideways glance. "Arthur Hughes? *He* isn't involved with all this business, is he?"

"Of course not!" I said sharply. Then I added with a reassuring smile: "No. Of course he isn't."

I said goodbye to Sophy and Perceval with great sadness. They did not want me to go and I did not want to leave them. I held them to me, weeping foolish tears. How dreadfully I had let them down by being who I was, behaving as I had! I was unworthy, racked by guilt and shame. Their innocence and affection tore afresh at my strained senses. It was best for all of us that I should go away.

Before I left, I put a couple of their books into my suitcase. One was *The Alphabet of Flowers* –

"N for Narcissus all white and gold
It tosses its head as it laughs at the cold."

Narcissus – he was the source of it – he was to blame for our misfortunes – poor slender flower, what chance did he stand against the snow's embrace?

I wrote a letter to Orlando, a short account of my immediate intention, enclosing enough money to keep him quiet for a while. I spent a day at Mortmayne overseeing things there and conferring closely with Wingate as to the business of the next couple of months. But there was another letter that I had to write and this one was no easy matter, for not only did it rather betray Claudia's kindness but it put me at risk a thousandfold more so than anything I had written before.

I wrote it at the study desk. The sunshine of early May played at a window, hinting of a different world, a warm light-hearted one of dancing leaves and children with their hoops and tops out in the square, one that was not accessible to me.

My dearest Arthur,

It will be apparent to you that by writing this letter to you I am putting myself entirely in your hands. But as we both know, there is nowhere else that I would rather be. In your heart perhaps, and in your bed.

You will have wondered why I have not been in touch since that exquisite Brahms concert, the last time that I was happy. The truth is that Orlando has been blackmailing me, and I dared not compromise you by a meeting or a letter. But now I have decided that the way out of my difficulties is to go abroad – not very far, only to France, and not for very long, maybe only for a month or so, till the trial is done with and the hounds cease baying.

I don't believe that you will be in any danger from Orlando. It's money he wants, and that is to be found with me, not you. But if he pesters you in any way all you have to do is let Claudia my wife know and she will write to me. I have not told her about our love, and so you will be perfectly safe from her.

And now a mad idea has occurred to me. What if you came to Paris with me? Oh, Arthur, do! Think what a Paradise it would be, you and I together in a city where it is permissible to walk freely, man and man, without the fear of the detective at one's elbow. In France the legal code is more enlightened. Naturally the expense need not trouble you – we could say you were my private secretary or my valet or anything you like, if you feel uncomfortable about simply going as my friend. Oscar has done a lot of damage for the concept of the older and the younger man, for all his beautiful speeches.

If you agree, you will need to decide pretty quickly, for I'm leaving on Thursday. I shall catch the boat train from Charing Cross station (here I gave him the details of the time and place).

Please be there, dearest Arthur; but if you think it foolish I will understand.

With greatest love, yours, Algernon.

P.S. I need not tell you, need I, that you must destroy this letter.

Yes, I could see the grim coincidence between my dealings with Arthur and my dealings with Willie, so long ago. I had persuaded Willie to come to Paris, and the sweet dear boy had burnt his boats and waited for me at the station. To my everlasting shame I had not come.

But this time was different. This time I was really going; and the afternoon found me there at Charing Cross station in plenty of time to receive my beloved if he should decide to dare join me.

Did I expect it? No, I think not. He would not wish to leave his mother, and his little income helped support her. But what if he agreed! That chance, that unbelievable chance that he longed to be with me as much as I with him – that love was stronger than fear – that risk was better than convention? If he came, it would be to strike a blow for hope, and dreams – for that small bright light that flickered in a grim oppressive darkness. It would be to say I love, I dare – when circumstances round about were hostile, dreary and forlorn. For that reason alone I prayed that he would come; and then for other reasons, like the need I had for his so cherished presence, the ache of loss I felt for him, the fear of what the future held, which only holding him could keep at bay.

Who would have supposed me a prey to such thoughts as I stood there on the platform, a solitary youthful-looking gentleman immaculately dressed, his fair hair ruffling in the gusts of steam, looking continually about him at the train close by, the milling throng, the porters pushing their luggage carts, the guard that shouted, almost hidden by the billows from the funnel? Down on the railway track lay a newly dead pigeon which had met its end beneath the train, every wind shift catching its wing feathers, curiously soft and grey and delicate; I could see it from the corner of my vision even when I looked away.

And Arthur did not come.

CHAPTER TWENTY-ONE

THERE WAS in Paris at that time a great vogue amongst the nobility for claim to ancient origin. The *nouveaux riches* and those who had acquired their titles by purchase were quite despised. An unbroken line back to the days of Louis IX was a treasure above rubies; similarly an ancestor who had made a name for himself at the Crusades. The d'Ourcelles had surpassed all these lesser boasts by claiming descent from a bear, when Paris was no more than a swamp. There was no evidence of this unusual progenitor among the members of Philippe's family, for they were all good-looking, elegant, and completely without fur, except the kind that trims one's hats and coats – of this they had abundance.

Philippe d'Ourcelles was tall and handsome, some ten years older than myself, with black-grey hair and bright brown eyes and a curious retention of youthful exuberance. I had known him many years and considered him an honorary cousin. His family house, where lived his parents and his wife Marguerite and those of his children who had not left home, was an elegant grey-stoned seventeenth-century mansion near the Bois de Boulogne, but he maintained a bachelor establishment on the Avenue de l'Opéra for himself; and an apartment on the Boulevard des Capucines for his mistress Léonie de Sarasine.

Entirely sympathetic to my situation he did everything possible for my welfare, from lending me his valet to providing me with constant entertainment and this of a highly dubious nature. On my first evening at the family residence, a place of marbled floors and panelled walls, with Louis Quinze gilt furniture, tapestries from Beauvais and heirlooms miraculously saved from the Revolution, he sent a boy up to my room, a nice young footman named Octave.

I was obliged to remind myself that Philippe's upbringing had been remarkably different from mine in matters sexual. At the age of seventeen he had been initiated into the rites of love by his mother's best friend, and this entirely with the connivance of his mother. Thus taught by a skilful and beautiful older woman Philippe embarked upon an adult life where love was of the greatest importance, indeed a fine art in itself; and of the acquaintances I met through Philippe I had no doubt but that each one lacked the crippling reticence and inhibition so typical of English marriages.

I turned from the window, whose distant vista of greenery had contrived to induce a curiously soothing melancholy, and faced the young intruder with every intention of sending him about his business with an avuncular reproof. But he was winsome and endearing and I could not but suppose that Arthur was now lost to me for ever. Octave was small and inclined to plumpness which suited him immensely and he had delicate hands and a gentle manner. His hair was fair and curly, his face oval, his eyes blue and honest, his lips playful; he had a habit of giving a cheeky little sideways glance after he had spoken.

"Monsieur Philippe thought you would like some company, milord."

"You are the young footman in the pretty livery whom I noticed as we dined."

"Yes milord. The uniforms are new. Did you think that pale blue suited me, perhaps?"

"Extremely well. But I cannot believe that your duties as footman extend to the comforting of lonely guests. Let Monsieur Philippe know that I am grateful for the gesture but I have no intention of taking advantage of your goodwill. Be off with you, Octave, and go to bed."

"I will go to bed, milord, but if you prefer it, with you."

He gave a smile that melted me.

"Sit down," I said. "Tell me about yourself."

There was nothing to tell, he assured me – a childhood in the Rue Mouffetard where they make the wine and the narrow streets are always noisy with the sound of horse-drawn wagons trundling to and from the warehouses. You get to hate the smell of wine, he told me, and anyone who manages to leave that place behind him thinks he's fortunate.

"I was fortunate and I know it," he confided. "I did all kinds of things before. Cleaning windows – odd jobs – and other things. Which Monsieur Philippe knows about," he added swiftly. "I did well to land here, and I've never been so clean!" he marvelled. "And so you see it could be very agreeable with us if you were willing."

He could see that I was weakening. He sidled towards me and held out his hands. I took them and we shared a tentative kiss. Cupid's bow lips, they parted sweetly, with every indication that the boy was no stranger to the ways of love. We moved towards the great four-postered bed and climbed between the sheets that without his company would have been cold indeed.

274

The small physical communion that occurred between us was merely a prelude to sleep, for Octave stayed with me till dawn. To reassure myself that I was no seducer I asked about his former lovers, and I learnt that he had known in the grimy courtyards of his youth the early experiences which made this night's encounter nothing new; he spoke of them without emotion. He promised me that he had come to my room completely willingly, that although M. Philippe had suggested it a personal desire had brought him hither, my interest seeming flattering to him.

"The only thing is don't let me oversleep, for I've my day's duties ahead of me."

"Are you happy in your work?"

"I certainly am. When I think how things were and how they are now – then, grime and cold and shabby clothes, and now a rich house and two suits of livery and a room of my own and money. Not much, but some. And I like to see the pretty people who come visiting; and then there are perks like this," he said, "when I can give pleasure to a nice English gentleman."

There was a curious mixture of the arch and the innocent in Octave's manner. I forbore to ask him what had been added to his wages for tonight's venture, particularly as he behaved as if the whole affair were his idea and of benefit to us both. There was no sophistication about him and he slept like a child or a puppy, curled up, snuffling, nuzzling into my shoulder. The uneasiness as to the morality of the incident which had plagued me at first, dispersed in the gratitude I felt towards him and towards Philippe for this unusual gesture of goodwill. I could not have slept alone in that great panelled room whose velvet curtains drawn were so thick that all light was excluded and all sound so muffled as to be non-existent. To my original despondency was added a peculiar sense of unreality and a bewildering supposition that I had imagined everything to do with Arthur, created him from fevered longings, a phantasm of the wayward brain.

I murmured my appreciation, and Octave said politely, like a well brought up infant: "*Y a pas d' quoi.*"

"Happy notes of music upon the octave?" enquired Philippe with delicate amusement.

"Thank you, yes, Philippe; but no more, now, eh?"

"Today you are to accompany Marguerite and see the shops."

I spent a brilliant and vacuous fortnight. On one of the days I attended the society wedding for which I was reputed to be here. The newspapers called it a glittering affair. With Marguerite, the most immaculately dressed woman I had ever encountered, I visited

275

the *grands magasins*, our open carriage, quilted with jade satin, gliding down the wide Boulevard Haussman where the omnibuses, the fiacres and the landaux bowled along and bicycles wove a tenuous path between, and the Mucha posters flapped a splash of colour on the advertisement columns on the pavements.

Marguerite wore a dress of pale grey silk patterned with coral roses, the sleeves elbow-length, frilled with bouffant lace, and lace at the high collar. Her long gloves were of grey, jewelled bracelets over the wrists. She wore a pale pink hat, curiously swept up into pink satin whorls, tied at the side of the throat with a tangle of ribbon. She carried a cream parasol, on its handle a rosy tassle which shifted rhythmically with the movement of the carriage.

The day was dull and heavy, lowering clouds that hung over the high rooftops, pressing a warmth down on to the road, and the air smelt of horse dung and fumes. We bought collars, gloves, high button boots; and in a milliner's in the Rue Royale we sat on red plush chairs while comely shop assistants paraded hats for us; then we took tea in a restaurant near the Place de la Madeleine.

"It is agreeable to come out with you, Algie," said Marguerite. "Even your silences are romantic."

"Was I silent? I do apologise."

"Not at all. An elegant milord with a tragic air is a most intriguing accessory to an excursion of commerce. How everyone will talk!"

We joined the ranks of the leisured throng on the Allée des Acacias in the Bois, and Marguerite discreetly pointed out which of the *demi-mondaines* sat in the next carriage, whether she had worn that dress last time, and which wretched young man was pining to death for love of her – "Would you believe it, that one began her life as a Russian Jew and now she calls herself Lucy Pearl – and that is the Comte de Rochemartel – last week his brother shot himself. And there is Marie Fernand the singer – you know she rose to fame by dancing on the tables at Maxim's and then lifting her skirts and planting her behind in a plate of ice cream. Ah, La Belle Zizine – now there's a lady if you like! Not a whiff of scandal to her name – pursued by dukes and princes, but the rumour goes that she'll have none of them – she sings at the Moulin Rouge . . ."

Polette's sister, Giselle, who was called La Belle Zizine! She's famous now, Polette said, she's a singer in Paris. I leaned forward, and the glimpse I caught of her showed me a Sarah Bernhardt profile, inclined away from the gentleman who sat beside her in the carriage – an orange hat with matching feathers and a yellow jacket, high-collared, with enormous leg o'mutton shoulders. Their carriage turned and she was gone from view.

276

"At last," Marguerite observed. "Something that has caught your interest."

One night there was a small dinner party at Philippe's family home, and I met Raoul de Girardin. We sat at a table whose white cloth shone like snow, and an immense explosion of luscious pink roses bloomed amongst the glittering silver. A row of liveried footmen lined the walls, Octave amongst them.

"Raoul de Girardin," said Philippe. "Never tell him, Algie, that he is the living epitome of Duc Jean Floressas des Esseintes – even more than poor Montesquiou-Fezensac is supposed to be – and neither of them relishes the suggestion."

"One prefers to suppose that one retains some flavour of one's own," murmured de Girardin. "And I protest I never owned a tortoise laden down with jewels."

"You throw us off the scent by tossing in my direction the literal interpretation of my remark. In tone and in intention you resemble Huysmans' pale and troubled hero."

"What do you think, Lord Algernon?"

"I do not know you well enough to judge."

"I hope that will be remedied."

I must admit I saw a physical similarity in the appearance of this gentleman before me and the image created in the sensuous pages of *A Rebours*. Of some thirty-five years of age, De Girardin was lean and angular, long-legged and tall. His hair was black, exceptionally smooth, and drawn back from a narrow brow and thin cheek bones that gave his face a pointed look. He had a fine black moustache, disguising somewhat the heavy lips beneath. The nose was Roman and the eyebrows quizzical; his eyes full of movement, a butterfly quickness that refused to hold your gaze. The texture of his exquisitely-cut suit gleamed; he wore a black silk loosely knotted tie, and in his buttonhole a yellow rose. His cheeks I suspected were lightly rouged; otherwise his look would seem to have been of an excessive pallor. His long nervous fingers were enclosed in white kid gloves.

"What news of Oscar Wilde?" he asked me, and I told him what I knew.

"The English press!" said Philippe's father with a noise of contempt. "In every sense ridiculous! Can there be another country so strait-laced, so moral on the surface, and so putrefied within!"

"Their treatment of the fellow is barbaric," Philippe said. "He was often in Paris, you know."

"It was his spiritual home," said Raoul expansively.

"Why, yes," said Philippe ironically. "Indeed, I often saw him at the Moulin Rouge."

"And always surrounded by a whirling circle of dedicated satellites," said Raoul. "Like an emperor from a strange land who draws all towards him by the magnetism of his presence."

"Our poets and writers find him most impressive," Philippe agreed. "And he has always been an incredible success with cultured ladies, foreign diplomats, and journalists of a provocative nature."

"And boulevard boys," said Raoul.

"Oh? I understood that, along with luggage and a floral buttonhole, he brought his own."

"Well, as with cigarettes, one has one's favourite kind," smiled Raoul indulgently. "A superb speaker. I heard him at a dinner party. Spontaneously he produced the kind of speech another would have laboured over for a month; yet to him such brilliance seemed as natural as the wind across the grass."

"What do you know of grass?" teased Philippe. "When did you last tread on anything but an Oriental carpet or a white fur rug?"

I found myself much disturbed by these reminiscences of Oscar. This man they spoke of – scintillating and successful, a sensation wherever he went – seemed to me the creation of a dream's extravagant disorders and bore no relation to the pale and haggard figure I had seen so recently standing in the dock, his hands behind him, his manner showing lassitude, indifference. This discrepancy much added to the sense of unreality that possessed me while I was living chez Philippe.

"I hear that you are in Paris . . . for your health?" Raoul said, his manner leaving me to understand that he knew my situation. I gave a silent acquiescence. "Paris," he said, "at this time, is particularly healthy, and I myself am known to be a physician."

"How rapidly he moves towards his prey!" expostulated Philippe with a laugh.

"Algie does not fear me," said de Girardin. "Now that he knows my house contains no jewelled tortoises, he has relaxed. But what a notion, eh, to take an ugly beast like that and weigh it down with chrysoberyls, peridots and turquoises, until it dies of luxury. Is that possible, do you suppose, to die of luxury?"

"I think it is more probable to die for lack of it."

"Oh let us have no dismal realism, Algie, not from one as beautiful as you. Do you not think Des Esseintes' philosophy possible in this hard mechanical world? I assure you there are many like him in Paris now, men who use their wealth to explore all manner of sensual delights."

"Sensual delights – well – every man with money is entitled to

278

make what best use of it he may," I said, "but as I recall, Des Esseintes' predilections do not cease there, but he actually sets out to corrupt. That is not, I think, a proper use of wealth."

"How English, Algie! How Puritan!"

"Come now, Raoul, we have philanthropists in France," put in Philippe.

"Philanthropy is dull, as all direct and uncomplicated notions tend to be," said Raoul. "Corruption as an experiment is ingenious and has as much to recommend it as any invention – one must ask oneself what use can be made of it for mankind?"

"You refer to the scene where he picks up a young man from the street and takes him to a brothel, to introduce him to the pleasures of female flesh," Philippe supposed.

"Yes; but not for the plain and simple wish to teach him debauchery – anyone could have done that – but for the exciting possibility that to give him those pleasures and then withdraw them, might lead the desperate and frustrated youth to kill for money. Corruption indeed, to be the cause of another's downward path!"

"Yet his intentions were supposedly well-meaning," said Philippe. "He wished to make a scoundrel, an enemy of society. For society was what he despised, believing that the governing classes were not worthy of respect, nor the lower classes worthy of pity. To do harm for reasons of good, it is the reasoning of the madman, the inversion of logical thinking."

"And anyway, it did not work," I added.

"Ah – so you think that it could not be done!" said Raoul, his eyes dartingly bright.

"I would not have thought it possible that an individual could so dictate another's will, unless the other had some inclination that way to begin with."

"You may be right," said Raoul, leaning back, and seeming to lose interest in the subject.

"What happened about that chambermaid?" Philippe's father asked unexpectedly.

"We lost a chambermaid," said Philippe to me apologetically, as if one might accuse him of having been less than vigilant.

"Lost?" said Philippe's father grumpily. "She ran away to join her lover, an anarchist who's living in the maquis behind Le Moulin de la Galette up on Montmartre. The rabble that secretes itself amongst those tumbledown shacks and rat holes is incredible, the scum of all Paris, every one a cut-throat or a pimp. The sooner they build a road through it the better."

"Well, in the meantime, no doubt, she will lead an interesting and colourful existence," remarked Philippe.

"Entirely wasted on a chambermaid," sighed Raoul shaking his head. "It's such a pity that life's thrills are always offered to those unable to appreciate them!"

"She's likely to be knifed within the week," shrugged Philippe's father. "Her kind of little dramas always end in violence."

"Will no one go after her and bring her back then?" I wondered.

"Why?" said Philippe reasonably. "We can always get another."

Philippe removed me to his bachelor apartment.

"Here," he said, "we shall be more comfortable, and from here we shall embark more easily for the places that will do you good."

This place was his retreat from the life of family and responsibility to "the essential things of the mind" as he called them, and in a heavily panelled room that overlooked L'Avenue de l'Opéra, that broad and noisy thoroughfare, he attempted to discover them. The walls each side of the fireplace were entirely composed of bookshelves stacked with books – massive tomes of medicine, biology and history; the works of Shakespeare and Dickens, ranks and ranks of poetry, the French Philosophers and a broad selection of the influences upon the modern writers till the present day – Stendahl, Flaubert, Balzac, Zola, Schwob, de Goncourt.

Here in the undeniable comfort of our surroundings we reminisced about the vagaries of our friendship – when was it exactly we last met? Last year when we had been to see *Lorenzaccio*, a long and turgid slowly unwinding play, but wonderfully *élevé* by the amazing Sarah Bernhardt looking like a darkly glorious boy; and what a marvellous time we shared six years ago at the Great Exhibition in the Champs de Mars.

"And to think I saw that tower emerge," said Philippe. "Huysmans called it a solitary suppository riddled with holes! Stage by stage it grew, like some bizarre and monstrous spider's web. I did not like it – I considered it an ugly heap – I winced to see it pointing up against the sky. But now I am converted – not only does it not offend me, but if it was suggested that it should go, I would protest most strongly. I would even say I have grown fond of it . . ."

Philippe brought me to meet his mistress Léonie de Sarasine. We took tea in her white apartment, with madeleines and savarins flavoured with rum. An impression of white – the carpets, curtains, cushions, walls, the lugubrious silent parrot on a silver perch, the rotund cat with one blue eye, one tawny, who, well fed and dignified, moved only from the cushion to the chair, and to the sliver of sunlight from the half-drawn shutter. Leonie herself also a study in white sat still and straight with her head tilted up, for if she did not sit so, her chin increased and showed she was no longer young. She had marvellous black hair piled high and wide, and a slim back ribbon round the throat. She admitted to a weakness for Chinese laquered furniture, and it could be clearly seen that all that was not white was black and gold.

All our conversation was of gossip – who had been seen together at Maxim's – how a certain duchess there had made such eyes at one of the Hungarian musicians that it had been truly *enervant* to watch – that a certain restaurant had opened for "ces dames de violettes" where no man was allowed to enter, and nude Burmese dancers performed to this gathering composed only of women. And was it true La Belle Zizine had turned down the King of Belgium? These consequential matters were picked over in fine detail; then we came away.

"We have now been together seven years," Philippe confided to me mournfully. "I know her every mood. I dare not leave her; our harmony is almost legal. Between she and Marguerite there is nothing to choose; yet I find myself unable to be faithful to either."

"You will find this interesting," Philippe said. "I will leave you here for an hour or so; my presence will inhibit you. I will be intrigued to hear your impressions."

Philippe directed us towards Rue Jacob, where amongst the narrow streets and seedy hotels around Rue des Beaux Arts he found the place he sought.

It was a bar with an English name – something ridiculous; I believe it was The Copper Kettle – and here I stayed for some two hours in strange company and setting. Strange, because the intention here was to recreate a scrap of England. Outside in the street were tall thin houses with their peeling paint, grey shutters, ranks of wrought-iron balconies smudged brightly with red and pink geraniums, and in the muggy air an ugly stench suggesting drains; curio shops selling Chinese trinkets; dark little bookshops – inside, the illusion of being back in London. There was much mahogany and several marble-topped tables, certain brands of bottled beer, notices irrespective of their function placed at random – This Way, Keep Out, Great Clearance Sale, Cadbury's Cocoa, and theatre programmes from Her Majesty's in glass cases, somewhat out of date, and of course a portrait of the Queen, the whole effect a stage-set scene. A beaming French barman welcomed me in my mother tongue, escorted me to a seat, with a patter which I swear he thought was Cockney, and which patently was not. The whole idea was so freakish that I could wonder that anyone should patronize the place, yet it was crammed with expatriates, as in some curious lapse of time, expatriates not from the present day, but three years back, five years back, ten years – indeed I saw at once Lord Kerwin, reading an old copy of *The Times*, who fell on me for news of the old country.

I sat down with him; we drank beer served by young waiters in long white aprons who spoke bad English and who seemed to show no aversion to having their bottoms pinched by bearded elderly gentlemen as they went past. The windows of this bar were frosted glass and so no glimpse of Paris showed beyond its portals, and the heavy wood and stalls made it Dickensianly dark. Of course the talk was much of Oscar and what they called in an affected way "sa pédérastie", and of the situation back in London; and it was clear enough that the clientele here were for the most part refugees from political scandals – much like myself, I thought appalled. Why, you could almost trace the history of impropriety over the last twenty years inside this place! I dreaded I would meet Lord Arthur Somerset, whom I believed had now made his home in Paris. Heatherington I felt sure would never frequent such a place; yet all the time I sat there I was most uneasy on that basis, for to be found here at all I felt sure was to admit that one was every kind of social deviant.

It was true that they talked of cricket in loud voices, that they asked about the credibility of Lord Rosebery and enquired if he were likely to resign – in spite of this there was an overriding sense of Lotus Eating here, as if this stagnant backwater would well suit to live out some half-life, necessitated by obscure sexual proclivities which once discovered put the genuine England out of bounds. They laughed and joked, ate beef joints laced with mustard, with apple pies and Cheddar cheese to follow; they passed the newspapers around and talked of Shaftesbury Avenue and the club, and as they laughed they eyed the waiters and the youth who came in to sell Woodbines from a tray. Nor was the ogling one way, for the waiters had been picked to please and flirted most obligingly.

Yet there was a most bizarre sense of taking part in a living museum. I noticed in one merry fellow's conversation from a nearby table that in a sentence otherwise much as one would naturally talk he used a couple of words that were long out of date, in vogue some ten or fifteen years ago. And when Lord Kerwin reminisced with me he spoke with fondness of his favourite haunts. "Ah, the Strand! I know every inch of it!" he declared warmly. And he began to list the restaurants which he frequented in his heyday, one by one, ticking them off on his fingers. But three of them had long since been shut down and one become a draper's. He knew it well indeed; but his familiar streets were those of 1888.

It was when one of the waiters sidled up to me and asked me if I'd like to buy the address of a madame who specialized in *le vice anglais* that I began to judge it best to leave. I said a polite farewell to Kerwin and I fled down to the broad and pleasant Boulevard St. Germain, where in some café opposite the church I sat and sipped chartreuse, to dispel a growing uneasiness.

We went that night to the Cirque Fernando, that marvellous extravaganza in the Boulevard Rochechouart, beneath whose garish tent-shaped dome we saw sights that would make mad the guilty and appal the free – a moustachioed American fellow in yellow tights who somersaulted through a hoop on the back of a horse; a demure female in frilly culottes who walked across a tight-rope twirling a parasol; a brute in a leotard who could lift a pyramid of his brethren; a series of athletic monkeys dressed as clowns racing on small piebald horses; and a wealth of beautiful supple young women on the high trapeze, their muscular pink haunches spread upon the swinging bar, their long hair flowing as they hung upside down. Gorgeous young equestriennes in spangled tights and wisps of chiffon waved and cavorted on their stunning steeds. Clowns with funny faces juggled and tumbled, and the fanfares deafened us as each new wonder was announced.

A horrid waft of homesickness came over me: I wished that my children were here with me. I mentioned it to my companion.

Philippe despaired. "But this is a refined sophistication. I have brought you here to stir carnality – look at the thighs of those young girls – and see where the buttocks tease with just a glimpse below the bouffant skirt – and surely as the acrobats hang down we hope to see a pretty breast break free from that low bodice! But never tell me that you were not highly moved by the female ringmaster in her long boots, cracking her whip so expressively – ah, Algie! A circus is no place to bring children!"

"It may be, Algie," said Philippe, "that your particular problem is not what you think, but merely a certain *ennui* caused by too long with the same partner. Now tell me, have you ever been unfaithful to Claudia – I mean with another woman?"

"Never."

Philippe tut-tutted disapprovingly. "On such slight evidence then, to assume a doubtful sex! Give me one chance, simply one, that's all, to test your true inclination. Come with me to a very nice place!"

"I'd rather not."

"Oh don't be so English, Algie."

"I can't help it – I *am* English."

"That's no excuse. Just the one time – I can assure you it is most select and clean; I promise you that you will not regret it. It is not everyone to whom I would offer this favour, the chance to sample my very favourite establishment."

"It would be pointless."

"Algie! A favour to a friend!"

Vaguely, distantly, I wondered whether there were any truth in what he suggested. Here in this brilliant city where adoration of the female sex was rampant, where on every boulevard visions of a perfection somehow rarely achieved in London glided by, and poster after poster showed the female form in every stage of colourful adornment, how could one not wonder about women, whose proximity gave one security, whose attentions cleared one of the imputation of perversion? And so I let Philippe persuade me and I went with him to an address not far from where he lived.

I knew that it was a mistake as soon as we were ushered inside. Not that it was anything less than the very highest quality. The décor was rich, lush, elegant – white gilt-panelled walls and glittering chandeliers, crimson carpets along corridors and stairs. From a wide foyer a straight staircase led upwards to a gallery; here at its base, curved red plush sofas scalloped the edges of the walls. Mirrors decorated with dancing Cupids gave our images back to us upon all sides.

Madame Lily was a charming female in plum-coloured silk, her silver-gold hair done in a series of little quiffs upon the forehead, and a pleasant low voice calculated to reassure the nervous and disperse all doubts. Like so many butterflies the girls at her disposal fluttered. I met Clémentine who wore a low-backed wasp-waisted dress of green and white stripes, with a jutting bustle and sleeve shoulders big as cushions, her ginger hair coiled up in an amazing jaunty bush; Aimée who had long black hair and lazy eyes and wore a tropical sarong, her arms and shoulders bare; and slender Gabrielle with hair like a frizzy yellow powder puff, and long black gloves, about her neck a white fur boa. Diane sat with her knees apart, a girl in a black dress whose skirt was a billow of frills, drawn slightly back to show black stockings, orange culottes bright as a sunset, threaded with black ribbon; and Adele was draped in a green gown that all but slid off her shoulders to show that she was naked to the waist, each breast quite visible, and her chestnut hair in finely curled tendrils caught to one side with a bunch of large white daisies.

We took a drink with these delightful people and discoursed enthusiastically about the weather and the traffic and the difficulty of acquiring orchids. How civilised we were!

A door up on the gallery opened, and a gentleman descended the staircase, a sprightly white-haired fellow, top hat gleaming, white moustaches curled to handlebars; he pulled on white kid gloves as he came down. After he had left, a girl strode down with petulant appearance, certainly annoyed. She swore heartily and flounced past, disappearing through a doorway; no one paid attention. She had been wearing a soldier's jacket tightly cut to fit her luscious curves; and slim black boots with heels so high a lesser mortal would have tottered. Between those garments she had not a stitch of clothing.

"Perhaps something like that?" Madame suggested, noticing the flicker of my eyes, and Philippe chuckled and said no.

I was a disappointment to Philippe, I knew, but he was far too well bred to make an issue of it, and in order to recompense the kind Madame Lily for her inconvenience, he himself made an assignation for later, with Clémentine.

"I have been a failure," Philippe admitted. "I have not made you happy. But what all else has not done, le Moulin Rouge will do."

Accounts of visits to this famous *boîte de nuit* are lavish in superlatives; but I daresay I was not the only one who felt like a spectre at the feast. There is nothing like mass gaiety to make one aware of gloom, solitude and mortality. Moreoever, it was raining hard, and the horse dung in the streets had been pounded to slime by the ferocity of the rain. Our fiacre took us north towards Montmartre — the narrow slope of Rue de la Rochefoucauld ("Moreau's house!" Philippe pointed out. "Your favourite painter, was he not? He must be seventy years old now!"), Place Pigalle, a mass of brightly-lit cafés; and so into the Boulevard de Clichy, that dim-lit broad way with its band of plane trees down the centre, an out-flung arm that bore in its crook Montmartre, like an overladen basket of fruits, luscious, ripe and rotten.

CHAPTER TWENTY-TWO

"AH, MONTMARTRE!" Philippe apostrophised. "A mound of Venus on a hill of gypsum! What is it but a vast pleasure dome where the mills that once ground flour now grind the lives of the satiated, desperate for just one gramme more of powdered pleasure! How it has changed ... The old innocence quite gone. Why, not so long ago, when Renoir sat and painted in the Moulin de la Galette, this was no more than a village – gardens, flour mills, chickens – ponderous washerwomen, pretty little *grisettes*, young lovers, urchin lads – all rustic and respectable. You came here on a Sunday to be pastoral, to dine and dance in the open air to the music of the accordion. And then you found the taverns and the cabarets – it seemed so daring: le Chat Noir with its monstrous décor, its stuffed owls, its china cat, its singers and its songs of love and politics, its clientele of rich folk rubbing shoulders with the poor, the picturesque, the poets, the painters whose work no one would buy. 'Come, you pimps, you whores,' they said to us (delightfully shocking, for we were an audience of the élite), 'come, forget yourselves, and sing and drink', and they passed around the wine, like wine of nowhere else in the world:

> *. . . le vin de Montmartre*
> *Qui en boit pinte en pisse quatre.*

"Yes I admit it," he continued, "I seek here the lost days of my youth – perhaps on some street corner I shall catch a glimpse, a whiff of that lost innocence, that gamin joy. Vain hope! Look all about us – in every *pissotière* along the boulevard a man and boy embrace, their feet in urine – in every doorway some young woman sells herself to an aged greybeard with a small fortune to spare, and the pimps wait with their menacing protection. Opium sellers leech into the skin of those they pretend to help and the fiends in the pay of the white slave trade prowl like jungle animals after maidenflesh. And if," added my companion with a swift self-mocking smirk, "we do not see examples of them all I shall return home feeling utterly disappointed! Ah, but no," he said, "my fears are not that innocence has been lost to sin and vice – at least that has the shudder of romance and degradation – no, we are losing innocence merely to Commerce. Very well, that brings in the money, but at what cost! Each evening omnibuses tip out on to the pavement outside le Moulin Rouge a horde of tourists eager to be shocked. They come to see the *chahut-cancan* – and why? To look up skirts, to see if it is true that the girls wear no culottes, or drawers with slits in them, just as the rumour goes. Is it not depressing the lengths to which the human male will go to peer at the hinges of the female thigh? They all know what is there, so none of them will be surprised at what they see if they catch a glimpse of something naughty – yet there they are, night after night, a fresh batch, then another; and they bang the tables and call out obscenities and the girls call back, eager participants in this curious ritual . . . sexual culture is bizarre, is it not? If it was decreed, for example, that the elbow was a wicked and mysterious spot, instead of that which is between the legs, the *cancan* would consist of ladies pulling up their sleeves . . ."

Sustained by his philosophy Philippe watched with equanimity the approach of the Place Blanche above whose little shops the red sails of the Moulin turned and all about whose pavements circled just as he had said, the omnibuses tipping out their loads of pleasure-seekers.

"I sometimes think," he said, "that one day the entire Butte will simply collapse upon itself. You know that it is merely a heap of alabaster hollowed out like a tooth cavity, with quarries and tunnels where they used to hold Satanic masses? The main entrance to the quarries used to be where that great unfinished basilica le Sacré Coeur now stands, like a surprised white mushroom. Once in the gardens of a merry little restaurant a wedding party was holding its celebration. Suddenly the musicians began to sink through the ground – then the bride and bridegroom – all the guests – all sank, all disappeared, all dancing . . ."

If Philippe had come here to rediscover *sa jeunesse* I had come to see La Belle Zizine. It was not my first visit to the famous cabaret and I did not much marvel at the cavernous dance hall, the reddish glow that pervaded the atmosphere, the glittering chandeliers, the fug of smoke, the mirrors and the distant stage ablaze with footlights and the bright ear-shattering cacophony from the demented orchestra.

We sat at a side table, drinking our way through several bottles of red wine: two painted females adopted us and twined themselves about us – "Don't worry," Philippe assured me, "I will pay what is required." This heroism seemed no hardship to him and I left all in his capable hands. It is true that I would have been disappointed not to have witnessed the celebrated dance of the *chahutoirs*; and I was entranced by its liveliness, its energy, the whirling petticoats and the lacy drawers, the high-kicking black stockings and the garters of pink ribbons. The girls' coiffures grew more and more dishevelled and their breasts bounced in their low cut bodices and the eager audience stood up and crowded round and clapped and yelled provocative suggestions. With their dancing partners, men who almost split their trousers as their legs cavorted higher than their shoulders, they raised a dust that powdered the tablecloths and drifted up the nostrils and settled on the surface of the wine. It was a spectacle, no doubt; but for me the highlight of the evening was the silence when the lights were dimmed to violet and La Belle Zizine stood before us. She was all in white, or rather she was in whatever dappled light and shade the play of colour from the footlights cast on her – mauve, grey, lilac, rose. Her long hair which seemed auburn was entwined with flowers. I thought her stunning. She sang songs of love and loneliness. Her voice was low and husky with a curious resonance on the sad sound of the word "jamais . . ."

"They say she is a virgin," Philippe commented.

"I don't believe it."

"No more do I; but it is true she has no lover."

"At least none that the world knows of."

"In Montmartre it comes to the same thing."

"And you, Philippe, do you find her attractive?"

"Her nose is too big. She rarely poses from the side, have you noticed? But personally I bless her – she is the only thing of all the gems I have cast at your feet that causes a little flicker of curiosity. Can it be that you begin to come alive at last?"

"But how dramatic you are, Philippe," I demurred.

"Why not pursue her, Algie?" he suggested. "Be the one."

We drove home through a vast nocturne – a sky of midnight black and turquoise, melting into indigo above the silhouettes of houses flecked with lights, and all the length of the wide streets the shimmering ribbons of the irridescences of restaurants seen through opalescent glass, the gas jets streaming trails of gold, and rainbows underfoot in every watersplash.

A most astonishing coincidence occurred the next morning.

I entered a *pâtisserie* on the Boulevard des Italiens, where I sat at a table looking out on to the bustling thoroughfare. The trees along the pavement were a mass of rustling green; a slow-moving stream of people flowed towards a green omnibus drawn by two grey horses. Upon the domed advertising column just outside, a poster showed a young girl in white fondling an oil lamp with a bouffant crimson shade: *Electricine – Eclairage de Luxe.*

A slim well-dressed young gentleman was sitting at the table next to mine, quite alone, and when he raised his eyes I saw that he was none other than Lord Alfred Douglas. I had no idea that he was in Paris though I had heard that he had fled to Calais at the start of the trial.

There was no way we could pretend we had not seen each other. Douglas looked as startled as a rabbit. Quickly recovering his composure he stood up and came across to me.

We told each other how pleased we were to see each other. A ridiculous conversation then took place.

"Paris looks so delicious at this time of year. I would be most distressed to miss the blossoming of the chestnut trees."

"Indeed it is a city which has much to delight the poetic temperament."

"Of course, I often come abroad . . ."

"I also . . . regularly."

"My mother has been most unwell. I came abroad to visit her."

"I trust she is recovered."

"Thank you, yes."

"I am here to attend a wedding."

"How perfectly lovely! And the weather has been very fine for weddings. On the whole, that is. Of course, it rained last night."

"But this morning it is very clement."

"I do hope that I shall see you again sometime."

"I profusely hope so."

With a charming smile he said goodbye and hurried out, and I lost sight of him.

Philippe and I took luncheon at his family home, with his wife and father. Afterwards he showed me the nature paintings which he had gathered over the past few years and which he had had framed and arranged the length of a gallery.

"I did not see Octave at dinner?" I remarked.

"Octave?"

"The boy . . . the footman."

"Ah yes. Well, I did not notice either. I'll ask my father."

We took a fiacre driving back to Philippe's rooms. As it brought us towards our destination Philippe said:

"Oh by the way, that footman you enquired about . . . my father gave him to Raoul de Girardin about a week ago."

"Gave?" I blanched.

"A footman's task is much the same in any house. Apparently Raoul lacked a footman, and when offered, asked specifically for

289

that one. Well! The boy made no objection."

"I see . . ."

I said nothing for a while. The news disturbed me. It stirred me as nothing had during that disembodied time when I had floated from one entertainment to another with as much involvement as an autumn leaf has with the branches of the tree amongst which it glides.

"Philippe . . . you will think it strange, I know, but I would like to hear from Raoul that Octave is well situated."

Philippe looked surprised. "Surely we must assume . . ."

"No; I cannot. I feel a little responsible for that boy and I was not impressed by Raoul's discourse upon the finer points of corruption."

"What would you have me do?"

"You, nothing."

We arrived at Philippe's door.

"De Girardin lives in Montmartre, I believe?"

"He does. He lives in the Rue Lepic near le Moulin de la Galette."

"Near to the maquis," I observed.

"Obviously."

"I cannot help it, Philippe – I must hear that all is well. I propose to take this fiacre now and find out."

"Ah – you are mad. All this for a footman!"

"Nevertheless," I answered, with a sudden lightening of the spirit. "You have looked after me long enough, I think. Now let me go my own way."

Rue Lepic wound up and round into Montmartre, a market street at first, with stalls of fruit and vegetables, then turning with many a devious curve past the great mound where the Moulin de la Galette jutted up, it climbed steeply towards higher regions, becoming secretive, and acquiring in spite of itself an inevitable picturesqueness. Behind it lay the No Man's Land of the maquis; and from time to time I passed some swarthy villainous-looking creatures who no doubt had their bolt-hole there.

Leaving the fiacre at the Rue des Abesses I went on foot to find the house of Raoul de Girardin; it was late afternoon. The oppressive muggy air that had characterised the last few days had been quite dispersed by the rain. A freshness sparkled. Over low garden walls hung lilacs, white and mauve, and for the first time since I had been away I was aware of the season. It was May; the Winter was well over, and the air was warm.

There was nothing of Bluebeard's castle about the exterior of de Girardin's house. A little wrought iron gate between a clump of tall trees opened on a narrow flight of old stone steps up to an attractive dwelling, a villa from a bygone age with shutters at each window and a trailing lemon-coloured shrub to one side of the house. Yet I did notice that each shutter was closed. There was an iron bell-pull at the door and when I rang it, to my surprise the man I sought opened it himself, dressed in a white suit with a dark blue floral waistcoat and a knotted neckerchief between his stiff lapels. He carried a white silk hat and gloves. He wore a perfume which I thought to be patchouli.

"But Algie!" he declared with every appearance of delight. "This is most charming . . ."

"I have come about the boy."

"I thought you would," he observed swiftly, almost as if he had scored a triumph by my presence.

"I hoped to reassure myself that all was well . . ."

"He is not here. But I will tell you where he is . . ."

"Yes?"

". . . if you do me the great pleasure to share the afternoon with me and dine afterwards. You see, I am just going out; but to a most intriguing place which you shall find an entertainment."

"I have come prepared for neither," I protested.

"It does not matter. With me convention has no place. So if you crave for details of the fair Octave, accompany me. I am going to a sale, and it is so nearby that we can walk there."

I found no reason to demur and so together we regained the street and made our way towards the Place du Tertre, a quiet square with one or two small cafés, a *pâtisserie*, some sapling trees in iron supports.

"Madeleine Roussel is dead!" he told me. "And the contents of her house are to be sold – and best of all, her personal effects, her jewellery and her clothes. She was a singer, Algie, and in later times a sad pathetic figure, thin as a bird in winter, living on absinthe, with cockroaches for company and her lovely voice a cracked discordant squawk. But she was a woman with a Past, for naturally she had been very beautiful in her heyday. Princes were her lovers – Russian counts – aristocrats from the very oldest families; and the rumours are about that there were many gifts – not merely jewels as we know them, but *les bijoux de fantaisie* – a parrot made of enormous rubies that dropped little rubies from its gilded beak, and ropes of diamonds thick as fishermen might use to drag a boat. But best of all, she was reputed to possess clothes, jewels, *objets d'art* from a hundred years ago – the days of elegance and decadence, the last great brilliant epoch, just before the Revolution. Every treasure from that time is tainted with a curious reproach – each jewel represents a thousand starving peasants, each frill and ribbon a cry of anguish and despair, each buckled shoe the hungry trodden underfoot. These jewels speak to me – these jewels bleed."

I found his sudden intensity out of place. I did not think the sale of goods belonging to an aged courtesan merited such display. I did not like the fellow; but I had agreed to keep him company and, as he promised, I was interested.

The sale was advertised upon the wall of a house, a poster bright and artistic as any in an exhibition; but I was growing used to seeing works of art that advertised objects banal as toothpaste and throat lozenges. A stream of people made its way through the tiny doorway of an ordinary house and down into the basement; we joined it. An eerie sensation, for the steps wound down into the very hill upon which Montmartre stood, and I recalled Philippe's lighthearted recounting of the disappearing wedding party with less carelessness than previously. The walls were cold, white and smooth, with jagged cracks haphazardly spaced, like a map of some enormous delta. Down in a cave-like space which must have been the wretched woman's home the eager throng was tightly pressed and a serious fellow with a brochure tried to exact authority and order.

I was in close proximity to a stout young man in formal attire, with well-cropped hair and neat concise features. His ears were dainty and his hands also in their white kid gloves holding up a length of tawdry silk brocade. He was with a pretty girl dressed very simply in a brown dress of medieval style, her long hair braided by a single wide ribbon across the crown of her head. She whispered to the youth and kissed his ear. Against me brushed a fellow with a painted clown's face, tapering black kohl eyelashes around his eyes and one black immobile tear dropping from those eyes, all on a face as white as flour, whose stiffness had dried into curious little crinkles wherever the skin had moved beneath. A buxom girl lounged beside me, shoulders bare, and almost every inch of skin a smudge of love bites, obliging one to wonder where she lay last night. There was an Arab, in his desert robes, severe, impassive, watching everything, immobile; and also a very fat man in a faded military uniform, his gold braid hanging by limp threads, his buttons unable to close over his pendulous stomach. Wisps of pale hair were combed across his pate and he snivelled silently throughout, his tears as steady as a leaking tap.

Two things became gradually apparent as I stood there – the first that there was great dissatisfaction and an ugly buzz of disappointment; the second that La Belle Zizine was there, in crimson, with a hat which was a fountain of flame-coloured feathers.

Leaving Raoul to carve a path towards such objects as he fancied I made my way towards the lady. Instantly I was accosted by an immense Amazon, a female of most alarming bulk and stature, with every intention of protecting Zizine from intrusion. I would not be thwarted.

"Tell her that I come from England; tell her I have news of her sister Polette, and keepsakes from her."

Most ungraciously the bodyguard relayed my message, and for a moment, beyond the hustle of the crowd, I met the langorous eyes of the lovely lady. I saw there a most tender expression.

"You are to come to her house tomorrow afternoon at three o'clock," said the Amazon; and she gave me the address, just nearby, in the Rue Cortot.

Elation thrilled me, and with just a passing glance at jewelled waistcoats, necklaces that hung from makeshift rails, and ostrich feathers, ribbons, laces, slung in generous profusion, I extricated myself from the close press and climbed back into the sunlight of the little square.

Out through the door came the white-faced clown, emotions safely hidden from the world by his self-imposed mask. Soon afterwards came the stout young man and his medieval sweetheart. As they walked away together hand in hand I suddenly understood that they were both women. I wondered what was their story.

Eventually Raoul joined me, peeved, gnawing his lips like a thwarted stage villain.

"They are fakes, Algie," he told me seriously disturbed. "Seed pearls and paste. The only genuine things were the ostrich feathers – well, who needs ostrich feathers except ostriches? I have been terribly cheated, terribly . . ."

I looked for some humour; there was none.

"She sold them, to keep herself in absinthe," I supposed.

"She had no business to do that. How could she get through that amount of money? They said she owned a palace in North Africa – they said she kept a cellar full of coffers, each one bursting with rare gems – "

"It is to be hoped the money bought her something which she valued more – some satisfaction of her own to be enjoyed before she died. Otherwise it would be such a waste."

"I have been terribly betrayed," he insisted. "I trusted in the living fantasy. She has betrayed me. The death of the woman, that is nothing. But the death of an illusion – that is everything – that is quite unforgiveable."

I did not particularly want to dine with him or be with him at all, but since it seemed to be a condition of acquiring news of Octave, about whom I felt increasing disquietude, I accepted his invitation and returned to his house with him.

I was astonished by what I discovered there.

The interior of his house was nothing but a staircase. I exaggerate – but on entering, one found oneself in an empty space, the central floors having been completely removed, and in the middle of the space a staircase, a wonderful staircase indeed, which cascaded like a waterfall down from some upper floor. The rail and steps were all of exquisitely wrought iron lightly touched with gilt, as was each stair. The underside of the stairs was coral pink, the same colour as the walls that surrounded it. I had never seen metal flow so gracefully; it spiralled like the flow of thought.

"It is true that I live alone, like Des Esseintes," he told me in an intimate tone. "But though I love the feel of precious things the similarity terminates there. I am always visited. Company comes to me. Some time I may tell you some of the things which have happened on that staircase."

He lived alone, yes, but he had a series of servants, all male, that flitted to and fro to minister to us, young men in costume of the eighteenth century, with billowing cravats, knee breeches and white stockings, buckled shoes, and little half-wigs powdered white. These servants seemed not to have been chosen for their beauty but their silence.

A library with every space of wall filled by de Girardin's immense collection contained works of history, and tomes from other ages. Amongst those volumes I saw books of incalculable worth, old manuscripts bound up in leather, clasped by ornate sealings. In glass cases he collected relics from medieval times; and in another room a wealth of costumes from the period he most cherished – shelves of *tricorne* hats with plumes, ranks of wigs on stands, cravats and shiny waistcoats, wonderful satin coats; ladies' dresses that shimmered and rustled to the touch, and feathered fans and buckled shoes and artificial flowers. The whole effect was curiously disturbing, for these garments were all genuine, and I believed the relish with which he regarded them stemmed from an unwholesome fascination with the ultimate fate of those who once had worn the clothes.

No daylight penetrated this house. Gas and electric light showed all that we saw of the interior. The shutters remained closed. The phenomenon did not overmuch surprise me: wealthy men who live alone are entitled to their eccentricities; moreover de Girardin being of a fastidious nature no doubt preferred to shut out the shabby Rue Lepic on one side and the maquis on the other, for surely I was not mistaken in supposing that the derelict and mysterious area bordered on the back of his house. How unsettling that must be for him; but maybe he found it exciting, to live cheek by jowl with villainy.

We dined near the foot of the staircase, waited on by his eighteenth-century servants. I noticed that around the walls were placed at intervals a series of glass aquaria in which coloured fish swam. De Girardin was carelessly pleased with these, explaining that bred originally from the Oriental goldfish all these fish were man-made; therefore an individual could create the fish that best expressed his character, just as he would choose his clothes. And sure enough, not one fish in those glasses was a natural shape. There were bulbous black ones, others with a head so top-heavy that they swam in a crooked line, some with sickening multi-coloured growths upon their backs, some without tails, instead a trail of wispy weed-like streamers; some blind, their eyelids hanging down in folds like curtains, some barely fish-shaped, more like blobs of aspic. Revolted, I looked away.

I was quite a dull companion at the meal, uneasy in the surround-ings, blunting my senses with excess of wine, quite unable to respond to my host's florid conversation. Considering that I had now fulfilled my part of the bargain I brought up the subject of Octave and awaited explanation.

"I am disappointed in you, Algie," said de Girardin. "I had hoped that proximity to the matters of the spirit such as you have seen within these walls would have caught the higher aspects of your imagination. Yet still you demean yourself with harping upon footmen."

"My concern for Octave was after all the reason why I agreed to dine with you. I cannot suppose it such a surprise that I now ask about the boy."

"Might I enquire your purpose? What is the boy to you?"

"Nothing at all. I simply feel a certain responsibility."

"Ah yes. You slept with him. He told me." De Girardin's face showed a leer of amusement. "He has a certain skill there, would you not say? I certainly thought so, in the short time that he was here with me."

"What has happened to him?"

"Come with me."

We stood up, and de Girardin led the way slowly up the staircase. He said: "Algie – what satisfactions – what exquisite pleasures could have been ours – two men of sensibility, of refinement – the loss of what might have been is the most poignant loss of all . . ."

At the top of the staircase was a black velvet curtain. Here we stood.

"What happened to him?" said de Girardin. "What do you suppose? This house has many delights to offer. I shared them with him. To debauchery he took quite readily. To cocaine a little more slowly, but he has grown to like it. It was our conversation about one person's ability to corrupt another that gave me the idea. You hinted that it could not be done. I am sure it can. But let us not be troubled over him. The drug is easily accessible in the taverns of Montmartre; he will be able to have as much as he needs. I introduced him to a man who has his own source; and as for money, Octave has the means to pay for his requirements – as I say, he took to debauchery with the ease of a virtuoso."

"But where is he now?"

De Girardin drew aside the curtain. A mass of darkness faced us, pinpointed with flickers of intermittent light.

"A man who lives in the maquis took him home. There it is, below us. That blight of tattered huts and filth and lean-to shacks where all the villains on Montmartre go to ground." He turned to me and smiled sardonically. "Will you go look for him?"

CHAPTER TWENTY-THREE

I DID not notice much about the small hotel room at the lower end of Rue Lepic where I booked a room for the remainder of the night.

I stumbled in there tipsy and despondent, very much oppressed by what I'd learnt, but there and then in no condition to accept de Girardin's contemptuous challenge. I was offered a small room on the second floor and here I awoke next morning to the street sounds and the authoritative tones of sunlight.

I lay and looked about me; the room was bare and shabby, dominated by a cumbersome wardrobe. The ceiling dipped a little, as if above it many other wardrobes all in the same position had contrived to press down one above the other till the weight of them had caused this curious curve. A burst of operatic singing surged suddenly up from the floor beneath; these small *hôtels de passe* were home to the artists at the Cirque Fernando and the little *café-cons* along the boulevard below. I washed in cold water from the washstand, dressed, and looked out over the little balcony to the street below.

A street market was in process of erection, stalls were rapidly massing, traders with busy lives were unloading fruit and vegetables, heaving buckets of flowers, stacking crockery, the colourful profusion covering the pavement, spilling on to the road. The sky was blue; the sun was warm and bright.

Downstairs in a small back room I drank coffee, paid for my room and left. I went out into the vibrant street, aware of the richness of the flowers. A man was carrying an orange amaryllis striped like a tiger, in a blue pot, his hand about it protectively as one would hold a butterfly; on the pavement in a green tub was a lily of the valley. At the corner of the street a door was open and a youth was taking paintings from the house to a waiting handcart, canvases on wood, almost as tall as he was, pictures of women, radiant splashes of paints and oils.

I went back to Philippe's apartment in the Avenue de l'Opéra to change my clothes and make myself presentable for my visit to La

Belle Zizine. Philippe was out. I would have liked to discuss with him the possibility of ordering the police to comb the maquis for Octave. I left a note explaining where I would be. Then I returned to Montmartre, where I paced the Boulevard de Clichy gloomily, on the offchance that I might encounter the hapless youth. There were a couple of painted fellows lounging in a doorway who smirked encouragingly as I stared; but I did not see Octave. I sat in a *pâtisserie* on the Place Clichy whose large windows had a clear view of the bustling square. A serious waitress in black with a long white apron and white cuffs upon her sleeves moved silently between the tables pouring wine. Against the counter comfortable women leaned in nodding hats, and a small boy in a sailor suit trailed sticky fingers thoughtfully along the counter's marbled edge. A man in a tall top hat was reading an English newspaper. It occurred to me that I had no idea what had been going on at home.

"You do not much resemble your sister Polette," I observed to La Belle Zizine as we sat in her garden drinking tea from porcelain cups painted with butterflies and sweet peas.

"I never did; she was a little older. This is so strange for me; I have not spoken her name for years; I no longer know anyone that used to know her. My real name is Giselle; please call me that – it brings back piquant memories."

We sat in secluded perfection. Passing through the concierge's lodge which housed no doddering old crone at her knitting, but a great muscular brute no stranger to the prize ring, one achieved a high walled garden with an intricate magnolia tree. Lilacs were everywhere in bloom, and yellow roses, and there were small stone urns from which trailed purple hearts' ease, and a trellis where a little later there would be a profusion of honeysuckle. Cats dozed on the warm paving stones. I sat in a cane chair; Giselle shaded by lilacs reclined upon a garden seat scattered round with grey silk cushions. Her lawn was long and wild and full of daisies. When sparrows darted from the trees she fed them; and the cats opened sleepy eyes and assessed the possibilities.

Giselle was pale of features, with a firm square chin, wide generous lips and hooded violet eyes with lashes that reminded me of Arthur's. Her auburn hair, somewhat of the colour that Willie's used to be, was arranged in gleaming coils, with tendrils at the temples, and a great bouffant fringe. She was excessively slim, angular, with a small waist and long tapering hands. She wore a dark blue skirt and a satin blouse striped black and gold, with a high neck edged with black lace, making her skin more ivory.

"You know," she said confidingly, "I would never have agreed to

298

see you if it had not been for the connection with my sister."

Before us on a little wicker table lay the things Polette had entrusted to Emily to give to Giselle – a strange little collection of photographs, pressed flowers, a square of silk, and jewellery and letters and other odds and ends. I felt amongst my pockets to see if I had forgotten anything, but the only thing remaining was Perceval's little book of flowers, which Giselle found interesting, and read thoughtfully, turning each foolish page as if it were important; and before I knew it we were talking about my children and my family life and how Polette had come to be there, and much more besides; and I daresay I gave much away.

We were not free of Giselle's other bodyguard, the statuesque virago, but she sat apart, impassive, in a rocking chair.

"I could not possibly manage without Hortense," Giselle said by way of explanation.

For myself I had never found a woman of such sweetness as Giselle. We talked all afternoon.

"Come; we will walk," she said. "We shall sit in one of my favourite places, and give the world something to talk about."

The street of flat cobbles, Rue Cortot, curved sharply down past an ancient buttressed wall. On the corner of the street below stood an old-fashioned tavern with rose-coloured walls and green shutters. It bore the sign of an ugly rabbit leaping from a pan, painted on its wall. A rustic fence enclosed a little forecourt with benches, and an old man sat, white-haired, leaning on a stick. We stayed there a while and sipped cognac in the warm sunshine.

"Have you visited the maquis?" she enquired – we could see it from where we sat.

"Does one visit the maquis?" I said startled.

"Why not?" she asked.

"I thought that it was dangerous."

"It *is* dangerous."

I told her about Octave. It came easily to tell her everything.

"I know someone there who can give you any news that exists. We have just time, before I must get ready for the evening."

In the company of Giselle I made the transition from the street to the maquis with perfect ease. True it was daylight now and the place had not the threat that nightfall brings; yet it was sinister – even Giselle admitted it.

The hill where the Moulin de la Galette etched its black sails against the sky was silhouetted behind us, with the irregular shapes of houses and the tufted clumps of trees. All over the slope between it and the long curved Rue Caulaincourt lay the maquis – a place of tumbledown shacks, dusty little steps, raggedy fences, patches of bright garden, big daisies, gracious lilacs hanging down broken walls. Lines of washing hung from sagging posts, and chickens pecked and scrabbled in the soil. Amongst scrap metal, tattered railings, heaps of crumbling bricks, grew stunted apple trees and iris. Children and cats played amongst the stones. Sullen-faced fellows watched us, hat brims pulled down low; and gaunt young women in black dresses, sitting in the open doorways of dilapidated houses. A dark-eyed Corsican slunk by us with a scowl, and an old tramp with a limping dog, who asked for money.

Giselle seemed wholly comfortable in this place, not simply because her prize-fighting concierge accompanied us, but obviously her nature felt at ease here. I remembered Polette's tales of a poor background and hard times till their circumstances changed, and the three children took their separate paths. She led the way, and I watched her, wondering why she so obsessed me, why of all the women I had seen, a strong attraction drew me to her – perhaps it was her slender boyish frame, for like Bernhardt she would certainly grace doublet and hose – but more likely it was her pale elusive beauty and her luscious auburn hair, her violet eyes, her low melodious voice, her kindness.

She took me to a gipsy caravan, which for lack of wheels was propped upon a bed of flat stones, giving it a jaunty and uneven stance, the more so for the crooked tin chimney at one end. An old Italian woman with a suntanned, wrinkled visage lived here, eyes like black beads, and about her head a faded crimson kerchief. She received us on the steps of her caravan. She seemed to think the world of Giselle, and from her we heard that a boy who might well have been Octave had been here some days ago "with Léon" but was here no longer, and she thought he worked the boulevards now.

"But we have other boys here," she suggested, looking at me with a total lack of any kind of condemnation. We thanked her for her trouble.

"Make her tell your fortune, Algie – then you can pay her with no shame."

Hesitantly I proferred my palm and silver, but though she studied what she saw with proper seriousness all she could promise for me were changes and a journey across water, which I understand are customary visions.

Slowly we regained the street and as we drew near to Giselle's house I asked if I could see her after the performance at the Moulin.

"I invite no one to my house," she answered. "I bring no one home. But I see you think that you have still something to learn from me. It may be so. Well. If you like, I can find you a little place to stay nearby and I will visit you there tomorrow. Only you must agree to have your portrait painted."

A thin cobbled alley between two blank walls led sharply down and veered to form a little street. On one side of this there was a studio shaped like an upturned boat, the roof composed of glass, upon which the evening sun purred warmly, showing a profusion of green leaves as within a greenhouse. Below, the windows at ground level were framed with tendrils of a luxuriant ivy, and underlined with window boxes full of pink geraniums.

In this place lived a bearded artist who was called Ivan because his real name was unpronounceable. He spoke French thickly with an accent as obscure as if he were speaking through treacle. His build was lumbering and heavy, and his clothes were smeared with a rainbow of oil-paint smudges. He lived in the top part of this shack, surrounded by canvases. He would lend a mattress to sleep on, yes, of course, he said, if I would promise to sit patiently while he painted, and if I would divest myself of the trappings which made me look *un milord anglais*, both terms which I was happy to accept. So I said *au revoir* to Giselle and settled to my new abode.

It was hot beneath the sloping glass amongst the ferns and fronds and stiff gleaming leaves. I sat, with my white shirt open to the waist, my hair dishevelled – clean and fresh, said Ivan, like a schoolboy – and he ruffled the shirt about to make me look, he said, like ordinary people.

"The only thing," he said, "you have to tell me that you don't look at the painting until I have finished it."

"And why is that?"

"Because you will not like it."

"Oh, how can you say that? How can you be so sure?"

"I not only say it – I promise it."

In the evening I went out, dressed as I was in my shirt sleeves, delighted to be living, sleeping here if only for a moment, with no pressure to take a cab back to the thunderous brilliance of the boulevards – a villager, like the man with the painted clown's face and the woman with cropped hair who seemed to be a man. I wandered around in the warm twilight, up and down dusty streets, past high stone walls over which hung thick and fragrant lilacs and streamers of laburnum.

I dined in the open air at a café whose tables spilled out into a cobbled forecourt, so high above the city that from my table I could see it all spread out below me beyond a slope of trees – rooftops, and the distant hazy shape of the Eiffel Tower. The turquoise sky moved imperceptibly to mauve and rose and a single star shone.

On my way back to the studio I went into a greasy bar, drawn by the sound of a piano playing. It was a small low hole with timbered beams, dark, smelling of sweat and wine. Every inch of wall was covered with posters, and the ceiling also, but posters stained and tattered, hanging like torn cloth. I had a cognac here and a blowsy woman sat beside me, recounting all that she could do for me and what it would cost. Someone had left a newspaper on the table and I read it; then the woman drifted off and leaned against the piano, where the pianist played songs for her to sing, with every word in argot and malicious if her face was anything to go by. In the dim glow I read that the trial of Oscar Wilde was to take place tomorrow – but the paper was already out of date – and that our brilliant Henri de Toulouse Lautrec had met him in London and sketched a portrait of the doomed man against a background of the River Thames, all in one sitting. It was sure to be a masterpiece.

Ivan had disappeared; I slept alone, sweltering under glass amongst the stiff immobile greenery. I slept badly because into my peculiar euphoria the insidious tentacles of the outside world had begun to penetrate.

Next day I bought a newspaper, feeling guilty about my irresponsibility.

I sat and read it in the morning sunshine on a bench beneath some flowering chestnut trees, in a little square with steps down to its lower level. To one side a ramshackle building was an artists' studio and an earnest young man with tousled hair was lifting easels in and out. Close beside me in the square a wrought iron fountain with green nymphs beneath a green dome filled the air with the sound of its trickling water. A youth sidled up to me and murmured the address of a place where I could get cocaine – "but just nearby, monsieur!" – and slipped as silently away.

I learned from the newspaper that M. Alfred Taylor had been tried first, tried and convicted, but no sentence passed as yet. I learned that young Edward Shelley whom I myself had seen giving evidence under a certain amount of stress, had not much improved since – "jeune homme fortement perturbé" – and had been called again for the prosecution. I read that Alfred Wood the blackmailer repeated all that he had said before. And this was all that had happened on the first day of the trial, and in the afternoon Giselle came to the studio and sat and played with a cat which she brought thence in a white wicker basket, while Ivan painted from behind his huge wide canvas.

"If you wonder why it needs to be so big," said he with a quirky little smile, "there are others on my picture besides you."

Giselle took me to eat at her favourite *auberge*, La Cour des Serins, where the painted sign of a perky yellow bird upon the peeling plaster of the outside wall and a shrill trilling from within indicated the nature of its inhabitants. You entered by a low archway and found a cobbled court with green wooden benches and tables in the centre and others against the surrounding walls, in little trellised arbours lush with laburnum which trailed a flowing golden curtain between each nook. From every possible part of the wooden framework and the intermittent branches of the slender trees hung bird cages full of canaries, whose excited caperings caused every cage to shake and shift, whose warblings filled the air with arch and frisky carolling.

Giselle looked like a Mucha poster in a long loose dress of tea-coloured muslin edged with innumerable turquoise beads, her long hair wound about with a scarf of purple Indian silk. She wandered from cage to cage talking to the birds in a low seductive voice, stroking them with her fingertip.

"Look, Algie, look at this one – see his face? ah *mon p'tit* how you have slung your seed about today; now see the mess you have to walk in – these two here are lovebirds, look, they're green and supercilious – always preening each other, but they will peck your hand to shreds – their nature is so vicious – yet how I love these two. You know, Algie," she said thoughtful, "it is only the males that sing, did you know that? And they sing best when they are not with females. Once they marry, they don't sing at all. Canaries learn to sing alone . . ." she laughed. "But now I am making myself sad! Tell me, how do you like Ivan? He's a big brute, isn't he! The women love him!"

He was certainly different from poor Charles, I thought, as I sat and watched the artist at work. He was all beard and hair, and that of a vibrant blackness, bushy, like a peasant in a scene from Russian rural life. His arms were muscular and hairy; he stooped somewhat, his neck was thick and sinewy. He hardly spoke; he grunted, and sometimes sang beneath his breath, or laughed; and then he'd put down his brush and say:

"Well. You need a pause. Be so good as to water my plants."

And he would make himself comfortable on the floor and take a swig of some obscure mid-European wine and suppose that it would benefit me to trail down to the tap in the yard below and fill a bucket of cold water for his jungle. The water was then poured into a delicate beaker with a long spout, and must be meticulously sprinkled to his direction, each plant of such a different nature that individual handling was required.

"Gently!" he growled from his beard. "Ah – clumsy – no, that's

303

better." And once he said, observing me: "Just a boy, that's all you are. I am sure you never lifted anything heavy in your life."

In the evening I went down the hill to the Boulevard Clichy and walked up and down hoping to meet Octave. I felt that I could save him. I felt I was in part to blame. I longed to meet him and take him back to Philippe. I saw other Boulevard Boys, more shameless than their fellows on the Dilly, but I did not see Octave.

Next day my pattern was repeated, and the newspaper I read up in the little square explained that Shelley's testimony had been much discounted and that grotesque revelations from short-sighted and forgetful servants had been offered by the prosecution. An angry paragraph headed "La Corruption!" spoke of suspected bribery of the witnesses – weekly payments to the boys by police officers throughout the course of the trials. It was a new experience for me to read descriptions of the events from a standpoint sympathetic to the victim. There was no ghastly moralizing here, but a controlled bewilderment as to the English legal process.

I spent the afternoon in Giselle's garden and we talked of our respective childhoods, but my thoughts were very much in London, with events that progressed even as we spoke. We dined again with the canaries and we talked of life in passionate clichés. Again at night I was alone, my dour companion out on mysterious business of his own; he lumbered in by morning and crashed down like a tree to sleep, while I brewed coffee on the blue-tiled charcoal stove, and went uneasily to buy a newspaper.

"Sir Edward Clarke claims that Oscar Wilde has been unfairly treated – accuses the Solicitor General of trying to procure a verdict by any means he may have – Mr Wilde is a broken man!" The third day of the trial made disquieting reading. Oscar questioned once again – his relationship with Lord Alfred – his sonnet – the nature of their rooms at the Savoy. Taylor's dark perfumed establishment – cigarette cases – dinners with boys – the Café Royal – the wretched bed linen. Then another noble speech by Sir Edward Clarke, and a powerful address by the prosecution following, unfinished as the third day ended.

In the garden of Giselle's house we spoke entirely about Oscar Wilde that day. Her utter sympathy prompted me to confess more than I ever had to any woman, the strange entanglements of my immediate past. I admitted all, in a way that I never could with Claudia, my love for Arthur and my loss. Around us, lilacs dipped and swayed in the breeze, and Giselle's cats patrolled the outer reaches of the grass. I felt sure that I had fallen in love with her.

"You don't know what it means to me," I told her passionately, "to speak so freely to a woman. It leads me to hope that my future may not be the dark thing I imagined."

"Oh Algie," she said sadly, "how mistaken you are in your conception of the world! You do not see it as it is. I can tell you more about yourself than you can, I who have known you only a few days. It is not I you love, but Arthur."

"But that is all over!" I protested painfully. "It *must* be."

"For you it is not over," she replied. "Your voice, your tone when you speak of him tells me so. Arthur, and your children, these are what you love. What are you doing wandering about Paris with their nursery book in your pocket? What are you doing in Paris at all?"

"I told you – I had to get away."

"Yes, perhaps."

"But certainly. I put Arthur from my mind; I had no choice."

"You cannot put love from your mind. It sneaks back, like a thief, to rob your peace of mind."

"But Arthur didn't come – he didn't dare – "

"Poor boy – then he must need you very much, to make him brave."

"I don't know why you say these things to me! I am doing my best to stamp out my true feelings, and you encourage them. It's irresponsible. Are you not pleased and flattered that in knowing you I start to think it could be possible for me truly to love a woman?"

"No my dear," she answered, and she came and knelt in the grass at my feet and reaching took my face between her hands. "Look at me closely, Algie. I have never permitted you so close to me. But look at me now; what do you see?"

"Your beautiful face."

"No compliments please. Have you not guessed my secret? I will share it with you now. I've watched you try to fall in love with me, supposing I might be your salvation. You cannot use people like that; you cannot give them such a measure of responsibility. I cannot feed your foolish hopes. A woman cannot solve your true condition, and certainly not I, even if I were one . . . Dear Algie, remember there were three of us, Polette, Giselle, Louis. Polette went to England, and Giselle – Giselle died. She was not famous then . . . a little singer in an unknown backstreet – but she had more chance of success than I did, and I dared to take that risk. Nothing is as it seems in this world, Algie, especially here in Montmartre – it is a painted place, a stage-set, with painted people playing out the parts society denies them."

I knew the truth a fragment of a second before she told me. It came as no surprise. It slipped as naturally into place as lips to lips,

305

an image which came easily as she and I embraced.

"I love you," I said, "more than ever now."

"Maybe you do," she answered kneeling, leaning on my knees. "But I have to be fair with you and tell you that nothing will come of it."

"Why not? It seems such a waste."

"My whole life is a waste," she shrugged. "I was never comfortable as the odd one out with my two sisters. I love the role I play. It pleases me. But it has a certain sadness, as all illusions do. No love that you could give me would be anything but sadness once again, because it would remind me that I could not love you as a woman does."

"Are you not afraid to trust me with a secret of such enormity?"

"Well, it is not such a secret," she smiled. "Most of them at the Moulin know. And if it were discovered and made public, nothing would change – I believe that I would become more celebrated, for on Montmartre all is distortion, so what is one more to the general sum? They come here to be shocked, to wriggle in the luxury of rented degradation. I am sorry that I cannot be what you want."

I accepted defeat gracefully. "What I want?" I said. "Whatever is that?"

Giselle accompanied me the short distance back to the studio, where we climbed the steps and found Ivan in jovial mood.

"Well, Algie, you are finished!" he declared, his beard streaked generously with ultramarine. "I am glad Giselle is with you, for you will slay me when you see the painting!"

But somehow he did not look at all apprehensive.

Giselle and I walked round the other side of his immense canvas and stared. She burst out laughing. "I suspected something like this," she said.

"You laugh," shrugged Ivan, unoffended. "I also expected something like that."

The finished picture was a brilliant mass of circles, triangles and spiralling shapes in every conceivable colour. I saw nothing in it which I could relate to human form. To me it seemed a flamboyant juxtaposition of fried eggs and peacocks' tails, whirling parasols and moons and stripes, in colours which had neither mood nor relevance.

"I cannot understand," I said, "why you needed me to sit there, while you pretended to convey my image on to your canvas."

"There you are at fault," said Ivan. "My intention is to create a crowd. Each person in it has been drawn from life. This is you; this one." His paintbrush jabbed a yellow shape, "and you continue

306

here, and here. You are white and gold and you exist in fragments. Believe me, you are here. I looked at you most carefully. I painted what I saw."

"You see with a distorted vision," I snapped. "Giselle says that that is how it is here on Montmartre.

"Who can say whose vision is correct and whose is not? Is yours so wonderful?"

"I understand the human form – the one that has been with us since the dawn of time and brought to life by every classical artist."

"Yes! Till we no longer see it; we only see that it is there."

"I find it preferable to your rainbow-coloured spillage."

"Well," shrugged Ivan modestly. "I am before my time."

That evening as I paced the Boulevard de Clichy I found Octave; or rather, he found me.

"Monsieur Algie! Are you looking for a boy?"

Two passing gentlemen looked at us and chuckled.

"Yes I am," I said severely. "You!"

"Ah!" he practically preened. "I am already booked immediately; but I could see you at eleven."

"You little fool, I don't want you for that! Is there somewhere we can talk?"

"But what about?" he pouted. It had only been a fortnight since I saw him last, but what a change was there! Whatever I had seen of innocence was quite dispersed. He had that hard and knowing look I recognised from Jem and Francis – he stood and walked much as one would expect from a Boulevard Boy, a horrible exaggerated suggestiveness and a penchant for curving one leg against the other. His face was heavily made up with rouge and lip gloss, kohl-rimmed eyes and silver-painted eyelids. From the scent that wafted from him you would have supposed him to have fallen into a vat of eau de Cologne.

"I was sorry to hear that you had left Monsieur Philippe's service," I began.

He shrugged. "Monsieur Philippe is very nice; I thought that I had landed well there. But what I do now pays better, much better."

"But – it is a bad life," I protested. "Not only is it wrong, but it is also dangerous; and short, because it lasts only as long as your good looks last. Have you thought ahead?"

He looked vague. "Nobody does."

"Ah, Octave – return to Monsieur Philippe," I urged. "He will take you back."

He shook his head. "No. He does not pay me well enough, you see, not for the things I want."

"You had enough before – for clothes, a place to live."

"No, no, you don't understand – the other thing, my other needs – the price is always high. I always need more money – the kind of money I make here." He turned a whinging beggar's gaze to me: "Ah, for old time's sake, Monsieur Algie, go with me. I'll give you all you want, better than I did before . . ."

"I knew a man once who had the same needs as you," I said soberly. "He died before his time, thin as a skeleton, subject to hallucinations, loss of memory . . ."

"Better than before, I tell you," Octave pleaded. "Anything you want to do – just come with me, eh?"

I gave him money; I daresay that was wrong. I told him to buy food with it; but I supposed that he would not. I left him and I turned up the Rue des Martyrs to make my way back up to Ivan's hide-out. On the way I bought two bottles of cheap wine, and lying on the mattress in the hot little room under the glass I drank my way through them, surrounded by the plants.

It was dark now, though a street light lit the room, and stiflingly hot, and I took off all my clothes and stretched out on the mattress. I felt light-headed from the wine, heavy of limb, and in no way cheered. My head began to ache, I slept and woke, and slept, and thus it was I half thought I was still asleep when I heard Ivan clomping home and barging about like a bear. Through a tipsy mist I was aware of him hauling his shirt over his head, and the irritation I had felt with him for that jest he called a painting came rushing back. I was surprised when he crouched down beside me, and more so to find his hirsute nudity within inches of my face, as he squatted there, elbows on knees, surveying me.

"You are very nice without your clothes," he said and laid his hand on me and rolled me over. "Yes; all nice. We should try a naked painting."

I intended a contemptuous laugh, but laughing hurt my head. He pushed the empty bottles to and fro.

"Drinking, huh?" he said astutely. "Well," he said, as one who has made up his mind. "That will make it easier for me."

He stood up, rooted about amongst his tubes and pots and padded back to me, then planted himself astride me like the engravings of the Colossus. Then with something of the sensation of a mountain toppling, he descended on me and mauled me somewhat, assessing me for any signs of resistance. There were some, but I was drunk and he had the build of a navvy. I lay on my front and suddenly there was half a bottle of linseed oil trickling down my balls. In the morning I would smell like a cricket bat. His paws wrenched my thighs apart, his fingers and thumbs dug between my buttocks.

"No – I don't want – " I mumbled into the mattress.

"Yes you do. You do want," he corrected firmly, and I felt his hard prick flop on to my arse. His hairy thighs brushed mine. With one hand underneath my belly he shoved me up to fit the angle of penetration. His cock pushed commandingly till my muscle gave, then drove in deep with one hard thrust. I yelled.

"Now don't pretend that hurt," he said, and settled himself upon me, grunting. I moaned and groaned; my writhings caused such pleasure that I paused amazed. He laughed and probed me savouringly.

"You like it," he said gloatingly. "You like it and you want it and you will tell it it to me before I let you go."

I felt too humiliated to reply.

"I wanted to do this before," he chatted comfortably, fucking me steadily. "But I knew you would say no and I would not get my painting finished. So I waited till I do my painting, and now I do you!"

He chuckled to himself at such a profound witticism and then his arousal grew and his rhythm more insistent. "Do as I say, boy, say you like it, now."

I did not, and he dealt me a punitive thrust and then another, till I told him what he wanted, many times, till he had had enough.

As I stood in the tiny yard behind the studio early in the morning, washing myself at the pump, the sun warm on my bare skin, and from behind the neighbouring wall a clump of white lilac nudging against my shoulder, I marvelled at the recollection of the night.

I hardly knew whether I felt most of embarrassment or delight. I was not blessed with the confusion of those who wonder whether something was all a dream, no, I had been aware of everything that had happened. A man whose name I did not know had been my lover – no, worse, had taken me whether I would or not, and I, like Oliver, had asked for more, and had been given better things than soup! We had slept, yes, but when I woke I had crawled across the floor to where Ivan snored on his own mattress and I'd woken him and wound myself around him and so stirred him that he grumbled up from slumber. He slung me on my back and towered over me and spread his hand on my face and shook my head about and told me I was greedy. Then he plunged and gave me what I wanted. In the heat our bodies became slippery with sweat; with my legs twined behind his back I abandoned myself to hedonism. Ridiculous the sense of freedom and release that night brought me – must it take a bearded nameless Russian of bizarre artistic talent to break down my self-control, to show me who I was and what was necessary to my personal well-being? For in spite of Jem and Francis, in spite indeed of Arthur, I had always felt that this aspect of my character could be suppressed, pushed to the back of my mind, even forgotten, as something that made me feel guilty and unhappy. But now I knew it was not so, that it was a vital and important part of me, and necessary to my health and happiness.

All the birds of Montmartre were singing in the lilacs, and I lifted up my arms to the morning, and relished that sweet moment of elation, carefully fending off the terror that must surely follow. Those clear mirrors – moments of revelation – that show you yourself are merciless, and make it clear that beyond the joy lie the pain and trouble of truth's responsibilities. I knew now that I must be in London, must find Arthur, must *confront* . . . In the sunshine I began to shiver.

Slowly, reluctant to leave that moment which had already passed, I went indoors, upstairs to brew coffee. Ivan, dressed, was going out. Seeing him by daylight I felt hesitant, uncertain how to treat him; but he soon reduced all to its proper perspective.

"Now don't stand looking at me with cow's eyes. I've other things to do than hang about fucking you. And water the plants, will you, huh?"

I walked to the little square beneath the chestnut trees and sat beside the fountain as was my custom, the newspaper beneath my arm. I was like one in a daze. I knew that I was free, and I was savouring the feeling. Clear of London society's hypocrisy and venom and the chains of its conformity, this strangely disembodied time in Paris had given me a respite and an understanding born of detachment. Montmartre was a fantasy I had been privileged to share, but it had shown me that I had no business here – the flitting and the running and the self-deceptions all must end. Oscar must have known these things – there must have been a curious relief to stand there finally and say *I am; do what you will.* They often wondered why it was he let himself be caught – I believe it was for this. And as for me, I had no intention of becoming one more Arthur Somerset, hiding out in an obscure Parisian backstreet, nor becoming one of the caricatures at The Copper Kettle, "old boys" growing older on their memories of England, mocked behind the hands of the servants who brought the roast beef to their tables.

Grimly I dreaded the difficulties to come, but the relief of facing up to everything was more than compensation. I knew now what I was; if that meant that I was mad, or beast-like, well then so be it; but it did not feel so to me – it felt sane and good and right, and I would hold on to this feeling in the days ahead. The thing to do now

310

was to find Arthur and challenge him and go on from there. I felt much as I suppose it feels to be upon a mountain peak – exhilarated, moved, cold, lonely and at peace.

Overwhelmed with an awareness of my own freedom it was through tears that I read the headline that danced before my eyes: "Condamné!"

Opposite me in a doorway two lads were kissing.

"Dirty brats, go home," a passing woman shouted entirely without rancour or concern. The four green nymphs continued guarding their Castalian Spring, and a sparrow took a dust bath at my feet. I tried to make sense of the words before me.

Two years' hard labour – and for what? For the life of me I could not see what was his crime. Who had been hurt by what he'd done? Yes, Constance had; but she would not require that kind of punishment meted out for her own private pain. The larger questions that the world would be asking later did not occur to me just then – why was not Lord Alfred Douglas tried? Why not the other gentlemen to whom the witnesses referred? How was it possible to condemn a man upon the testimony of rent boys in the pay of the police? Why were they to be allowed back on the streets? What could be said of the police's role at all? Where in the whole sorry tale was blind impartial justice? And who, in all the accusations of corruption, had been actually corrupted, if not perhaps the man of sensibility and strange naivety, through the bad company he kept?

The grisly account unrolled beneath my gaze.

The land must have been scoured for months to produce the most bigoted of beings possible to pass judgement on the case. His name was Mr Justice Wills. He said that it was useless for him to address the prisoners for they were beyond shame and dead to finer feelings. He said it was the worst case he had ever tried. Since it was without doubt that Taylor had kept a brothel and that Wilde had been a centre of hideous corruption amongst young men, he would be expected to pass the severest sentence possible. Yet even such a punishment, he felt, was not extreme enough for such a case as this.

I sat there snivelling into my fist in harmony with the unthinking fountain. Both the owner of the *pâtisserie* and his wife came darting out, surrounding me with palpable goodwill, shaking my hand and bringing me a cognac which I gratefully accepted.

"Monsieur knew poor Monsieur Wilde perhaps?"

"Only a little, alas."

"Ah, monsieur, it is terrible – accept our sympathies – the world is not just. Monsieur is on holiday? We noticed you each day, here with your newspaper . . ."

"On holiday, yes," I answered, pulling myself together with the assistance of the brandy. "But not any more."

There remained only my farewells to make, and these were easily done. I embraced Giselle in her garden and I thanked her for her friendship and I promised that I would come back again, with Arthur. Ivan my liberator barely looked up from his new painting as he wished me good luck.

Philippe and Marguerite were getting ready for a society ball to be held that evening, and so our parting took place in their splendid home in the Bois. They both agreed that the punishment of Oscar Wilde was barbarous, and gave directions to their bustling servants as to where the orchids should be placed and where the lilies. I warmly thanked Philippe for his tolerance of my previous indifference and I assured him that my time with him had been of the utmost benefit.

"So – did you sleep with La Belle Zizine?" he asked me when we were alone. "It is already widely rumoured that you have become her lover. And did you find the boy?"

"I found the boy; he works the boulevards now, alas. As for Zizine, she retains her mystery; and though I saw her garden I was not permitted to enter her house. But of course I fell in love with her."

"That is what one comes to Paris for," said Philippe lightly. "The romance of a memory."

"Well, I have one or two of those," I grinned.

Philippe expressed surprise at the suddenness of my proposed departure but did not burden me with questions; and we discussed at length his family's proposed visit to Mortmayne later in the year. I found I had no difficulty in treating this with perfect seriousness, even though I had no idea whether I would be in a position to receive him there, for I could conceive of any number of possibilities awaiting me on my return to England. How apt it was that it should have been in Montmartre, that hotbed of anarchy, that I should begin to develop my own transformation. I recalled the bedroom at Zabarov's house – what was it about Montmartre that sowed the seeds of social rebellion whose flowering would now begin to mean something actual to me?

I had been away for three weeks; next day I was at the Gare du Nord on my way home.

Considering my habitual vacillation, the decision to return had been perfectly easy to make. Although I was returning to a country which had just proved itself a den of bigotry and injustice and would henceforth be dangerous and hostile terrain to a man of my persuasion, I had no doubt whatsoever that it was the place where I should be.

CHAPTER TWENTY-FOUR

B UT THEY don't live here any more!"
I was standing at the front door of Arthur's house, astonished beyond measure to find myself in converse with a girl in gingham who knew nothing about Arthur's whereabouts and who was quite prepared to see the matter closed at that. I practically had to force my way into the vestibule in order for her to go in search of other tenants who might be of help. The redoubtable Miss Verrinder – she who was rumoured to have been in the house when I made love to Arthur in his room – was persuaded to emerge from her upstairs eyrie in order to volunteer the information that Mrs Hughes had married Mr Simmons and left to set up home above his shop.

I breathed again. Achieving against all odds the appearance of normality when heart and mind were in a turmoil, I made my way to Mr Simmons' shop. Fugitive still, for I had told nobody of my return from France, always one glance behind me as I walked, I turned down the alley, a gathering elation overtaking me as I hurried to the door.

It was early evening, warm and dry, the streets still crowded with their mess of omnibuses, carriages and carts, the pavement thronged. In the cobbled court a street pianola played a sentimental tune. Suddenly everything blended for me into an instant of great happiness. My indecisions over, I felt supremely confident that I could now persuade Arthur to overcome his fears. Lord knows to what purpose precisely, but my surge of optimism would admit no let or hindrance.

Mr Simmons, in the doorway of his shop, was preparing to close the shutters. When I explained my business was with Arthur, when I gave my name, his manner became uneasy, and he frowned and said we had better go indoors.

We went into an upstairs parlour where Arthur's mother sat knitting. It was a small room, impeccably tidy, with a disturbing juxtaposition of furniture and ornaments that I remembered from before, and others that had no relation to the place where Arthur used to live.

"Here is Lord Algernon Winterton, my dear – he says that he has come about Arthur. Won't you take a seat, your lordship?"

"Arthur? Have you heard something?" His mother sat upright, a look of dread upon her face. "Is it bad news?"

"Mrs Hughes – Mrs Simmons – you put me to confusion," I said, sitting down beside her. "I thought to find him here. You know that I have always been a friend most eager for his welfare. Do you mean to say he is away from home?"

The wretched woman cried into her handkerchief, and Mr Simmons drew up a stool to face me. "The plain truth is, my lord, we don't know where he is."

In the brief statement Mr Simmons conveyed much. I sensed vast irritation on his part that Arthur could so blight the marital happiness; moreover, that he himself was personally indifferent to the fate of Arthur I had no doubt.

"Since when?" I asked.

"Since the day that we were married."

I remembered then that Arthur had expressed his own dislike of Mr Simmons. If that day ever comes, he said, I shall certainly leave home.

"And you have no idea where he is? I can't believe that he would not let his mother know of his whereabouts."

"He sent some money in a letter. But there was no address."

"May I see the letter?" She handed it to me.

"It was not written by Arthur," Mr Simmons shrugged. "It says nothing, merely that he is well, no more."

"How very odd," I frowned. "He sent money – that surely means that he is in employment, does it not? That must be reassuring. You need not feel too troubled. He will have taken a place such as he had with Mr Simmons – some clerical position – something suited to his nature?"

His mother said in some despair: "Employment? Whoever will give work to somebody who cannot read or write?"

I stared at her. For a moment I was so taken aback that I could barely understand her meaning.

"Yes," she said, aware of my amazement. "Arthur cannot read or write and that was why he felt so grateful to Mr Simmons who gave him employment in spite of his disability."

"But how came he to have lacked these ordinary skills?"

"Well, all his early life," she said, "we only spoke our native tongue; then when we moved to Swansea it was all to do to learn to speak in English, and in all the rough and tumble of the classroom by the docklands somehow writing things down was not properly done, and as for reading he was somehow overlooked."

"I had no idea . . ."

I felt so sorry for him. I could barely imagine what a simple walk down a street must be for one to whom the letters of the hoardings must be merely a jumble.

"I wish he had told me," I declared.

"He never told anybody. He was too ashamed. He found he could get by."

My letter! The letter I had written to him, asking him to come to Paris with me, telling him of my love. He would not have been able to read it. And knowing it to be from me – for he had seen my name written in the book I gave him – he would know better than to take it to someone to decipher it. Whom could he trust? He would have burned it.

Appalled and agitated I quickly reassessed my judgement of the situation. Arthur had not rejected me at all, because he had not read my appeal. It was not that he was too afraid to come to Paris or that he had thought better of joining his life to mine – he had not even known that I had asked him to accompany me! With rapidly increasing horror I began to see how my behaviour would have appeared to Arthur. He knew nothing about Orlando blackmailing me, which I had explained in the letter – all he knew was that I had not visited him, and then as if that were not reprehensible enough, without explanation or farewell I had gone off to Paris. What a desertion that must have seemed! Maybe he thought that I had gone for good. Maybe he thought that for those with wealth the answer was always easy. I shuddered to imagine what he must be thinking of me, who had sworn to be his friend, protector, lover.

"Have you looked for him?" I blurted out. "Have you made any attempt to find him?"

"How could we?" Mr Simmons shrugged. "He patently has no wish to be found."

"He knows there is a home here for him," said his mother.

"That obviously means nothing to him at all," said Mr Simmons in a righteous tone. "What kind of a son would upset his mother so? What kind of a son?"

"I will initiate a search for him," I stated.

"We could not impose – " protested Mr Simmons.

"We do not deserve such kindness," said his tearful wife.

"I hope," began Mr Simmons fidgeting somewhat, "that you do not feel it necessary to involve the police – we would not wish to cause inconvenience – and so forth – "

"Good Lord, no, nothing was further from my mind," I assured him with some fervour. "No, no, leave it to me. Have you perhaps," I asked, "a photograph of Arthur which might help me in my search?"

Mrs Simmons hurried to procure one; her husband apologised for the trouble to which they put me. I fended off their gratitude, and I withdrew as soon as was politely possible.

In the streets outside I gazed my fill at the precious photograph. It was a good clear study, showing Arthur's beauty to its best advantage. I felt a surge of rage. What the devil did he mean by taking off like this?

Although the envelope of Arthur's letter bore an East End postmark I was not, however, so far gone from logic as not to take the obvious course of action. Having procured Ronald Grey's address from the Simmons' – who insisted that he knew nothing; they had asked him – I visited the youth at his lodgings near the viaduct, where he broke off from the earnest tome he studied to volunteer some information.

"Arthur made me promise not to tell them," he admitted. "But I was not at all comfortable in the deception. I'd be glad to help you, sir. Yes, I know where Arthur is. He's working for my brother as a clerk."

The initial elation I experienced was swiftly superceded by a certain wary caution. "As a clerk?"

"In fact he spent the first night of his leaving home upon that very sofa. He said he meant to find some work. I knew my brother needed clerks – he always does, he has an office in Leman Street in Aldgate – and so I accompanied Arthur there and introduced him to my brother. I left him there – I had to get back to work. But he'll be all right. I was very glad to help."

"You've seen him working there since?"

"No I haven't. I haven't been back. I've been too busy – I take my examinations in a week's time. But I will visit him, as soon as I'm able."

Why ever must Arthur go along with that charade, I thought impatiently; and guessed with resignation that having never let his secret slip he obviously had not had the heart to tell Ronald that his good intentions were in vain.

"When was that?"

"Two weeks ago, perhaps . . ."

In some despondency of spirit I took a cab to Aldgate in the gathering darkness. The office in Leman Street was closed, but Ronald's brother, working late in a small back room, was helpful enough to my urgent enquiries.

"Yes, I remember him. Ronald brought him as a clerk, but after Ronald left, the boy declared there was a misunderstanding – he did not want clerical work, but ordinary labour. So I sent him to The

Rose and Crown in Whitechapel Road – they're always glad of willing boys to wipe the tables and carry barrels. He seemed pleased enough. And there are any number of doss houses nearby where he could get a cheap bed for the night."

There was a curious little pause. The question shouted itself as loudly as ever spoken words might form the phrase: And what, sir, is your interest in the boy?

I hurried away.

It was dark now, a summer darkness of street markets packing up, of drunken lads at public house doorways, of carters going home. Whitechapel Road, which I traversed on foot, was a long and sordid street. The Rose and Crown, a seedy tavern, was not the kind of place I would have wished for Arthur. That he had sent money to his mother showed that he was in employ, but I dreaded that he had found some vile labour unfit for one as sensitive as he. Or worse, he might have come upon the money by dishonest means. Not that I believed that Arthur could be dishonest, but London is very much a place where a boy can make money easily if he so chooses. It was with the greatest apprehension that I began to make enquiries.

"Yes, that lad was 'ere," the barman told me, pocketing my proferred silver. "Ho ho! A prince in disguise, was he? I never knew such a one for attracting the interests of older gentlemen! You ain't the first to ask after 'im by any manner o' means! Seems I 'ad a treasure there if I'd but known it. Brandy, sir? You look as if you need one."

I did not disagree. "What can you tell me?"

"Well, your young man ain't the first I've seen picked up by those up to no good," the fellow said, his elbow on the counter, his grizzled face close to mine. "Young Arthur was here two evenings, wiping tables, clearing up. There's always those as come in here to look for lads, know what I mean, take 'em up west for one thing or another. Well, this bloke comes in, sees Arthur, sits 'im dahn and sells 'im Paradise – you can earn good money, he sez, not like this place, real money and I'm talkin' hundreds. You get to see the posh places of the town, he sez, you go in restaurants and big hotels and the gentlemen gives yer clothes and silver cigarette cases. A boy like you could make a fortune and all you has ter do is be obliging to the gentlemen. A boy like you could make a fortune! I heard the lot. Well, why not? I like to hear about the other half of the world, know what I mean? Well, Arthur's all polite and says no thank you – it did make me laugh – no thank you, just as if he was bein' offered a sip o' gin! And then this bloke he turns nasty like. You got such a pretty face, 'e sez to Arthur. It would be a pity if I had to spoil it. Think on what I said. I'll come back again. I'll come back for your answer."

"And did he?"

"Indeed he did – but Arthur had took off by then. Vanished. Well, he couldn't stay here, could he, with that sort of bother? Yeah, this bloke came back again and another feller with 'im an' all. But too late. And I couldn't help 'em – or wouldn't!" He chuckled. "I never wanted to see Arthur end up with the likes o' them. I liked 'im, see, and he never struck me as the sort of boy who'd be impressed by all that talk of posh hotels and restaurants and gents with money."

I nodded, gloomily agreeing.

"He didn't tell you where he planned to go?"

"He didn't, no. But he was staying at the Salvation Army Refuge. You might try there."

Tall and clean and smelling of disinfectant the Salvation Army Refuge shone like a beacon and radiated good intention.

A lassie in a uniform remembered Arthur.

"He only stayed one night. He left next morning, saying he had had enough of God. I did not think that I had preached," she said, a little hurt. "I tried to talk as naturally as possible. But it does come naturally for me to talk about God. I was sorry that I seemed to have driven him away. I told him where the nearest doss house was, but I warned him that he might not like it. He was a nice well-spoken boy, a little different from the sort we usually see."

I tried the doss house which the girl had pointed out, a horrid place off Mile End Road, but nobody there had seen him, and I came away feeling thoroughly infested. The hour was late and I was tired. I put up at a grimy little hotel. As I fell asleep I vowed to go through every public house and sleeping place in Whitechapel till I found him. The matter being fraught with the entirely unforeseen, however, I decided it was time that I explained the circumstances to my family.

I arrived at the quiet country station unannounced. The day was dull and heavy, and the sky – of which there always seems to be so much in Bedfordshire – was piled with billow upon billow of enormous grey-blue clouds. Rather than be recognised I took the track along the ridge that led to Mortmayne by an old drove way, and much shorter than the road's route. I saw no one as I walked, but every hedge was white with hawthorn bloom and a pest of a cuckoo sang his silly song. The track curved down behind the house and I saw I was in luck – Claudia and Emily and the children were by the lake. I hurried down the slope amongst the drooping bluebells, and emerged like some Royalist sneaking home from

318

Worcester with a price on his head.

"My God, it's Algy!" said Claudia in a bland well-bred voice.

"Papa! Papa!" cried my offspring with gratifying enthusiasm, running to me. I bent down and gathered them to me; we hugged. I wept a little. Whatever would the future hold for them?

"I can't stay," I said to Claudia over their heads. "I have to talk to you."

"Shall we go into the house?"

"No. Walk with me in the wood."

I greeted Emily then, and told her that Polette's remembrances had been safely delivered. If she ever saw Polette again she was to tell her that La Belle Zizine was well, and famous.

Emily thanked me; she did not think it likely, but she was glad that we had done our part.

Leaving Sophy and Perceval in Emily's capable hands, Claudia and I walked down the lane towards the wood. Past the gardeners' cottages we went, with all their secret memories.

"What is it, Algy?" Claudia asked touching my arm. "Whatever can be troubling you? You look awful." She frowned. "Is it Orlando? Has he made fresh demands?"

"No, no," I shook my head. "He doesn't know I'm back in England. No one does. Oh! How can I say it? I swore I'd tell you everything; but Lord it isn't easy."

We paused. We had entered the wood now, and the bluebells at our feet stretching away to a mist of blue-mauve gave off a sweet perfume. I took a breath.

"We talked once – dear Claudia – about my realisation that I was a person who loved my own kind – like Oscar – and you were tolerant, and I was grateful that you did not think I was a beast."

"Oh Algy," she smiled affectionately. "As if I would think that. And are you still persuaded of this condition after spending some time away?"

"Even more so!"

"You did not go with renters, did you?" she demanded.

"No. Nor will I, ever."

"Then your condition must remain a private matter, something you will have to learn to accept."

"It's not that simple, Claudia."

"Why is it not?"

"Because I love somebody!" I blurted out and looked her in the eyes.

"Whom?" she asked reasonably; and I admired with all my heart her steadfastness, her lack of hysteria and all those ranting qualities which women are supposed to show in the face of this kind of reality.

"Arthur Hughes," I answered.

She was utterly surprised. I watched her. "Does he *know*?" she asked.

"Oh my God, yes," I groaned.

"You mean you've told him?"

"Yes. I'm so ashamed, Claudia, for not having been entirely honest with you." I turned away. "What can I say? I fell in love with Arthur the first time I saw him, and I have loved him ever since."

"I think that I would like to sit down," said my wife pointedly.

We walked in silence to a rustic bench set by the path's edge; here we sat, not looking at each other. I continued. I poured out the tale in its entirety – Zabarov, my night in the hotel with Arthur, our time at Mortmayne.

"But whatever did the servants think?" gasped Claudia.

"Oh come now," I said testily. "They thought I'd given a week's solicitude to a deserving invalid. And so I had. We came back to London much refreshed. And I told him I loved him. You have to know this – you have to know it all – because I will not be forgiven or accepted under false pretences. This is, if you do forgive me," I added, stealing a sideways look; but she stared straight ahead.

"Did you sleep in the same bed?"

"Yes. And yes, I did love his body."

She turned her back on me.

"Don't shut me out; I need you, Claudia," I muttered.

"*What for*?" she said acidly.

"I can't put it into words. I need you to be what you always have been to me. Nothing has changed between us."

"There *was* nothing . . ."

"Yes there was!" I cried. "You are the mother of my children and my own dear wife. But if you have lost all feeling and respect for me," I added bleakly, "I do understand. I did expect it. But I didn't come here to abase myself; I came to explain my course of action. Will you listen?"

"Your course of action?" she murmured, half turning. "Whatever do you mean?"

I told her about my letter to Arthur and his silence – my return to England – my discoveries – my dreary search among the streets of Whitechapel – my unwillingness to have anything to do with the police.

"This is a matter for myself alone. In a previous life I would have called the police in to help; not now. If Arthur is by chance engaged in anything shady I would get him into trouble if I brought the police to him. But that is not the main reason. When a person has decided that love of his own kind is the right kind of love for him, then at one stroke it puts the police upon the other side. If Orlando has his way I shall be having much to do with them at some stage in my life, whether I will or no. And would I ever now from choice ally myself with men who had so treated Oscar Wilde! No, I shall leave the law alone."

"Then how do you propose to find the boy?" cried Claudia. "London is a large enough place in which to hide himself for someone who does not wish to be found."

"I shall simply keep looking."

"Alone, Algy? In Whitechapel?"

"How else?"

"I wish you would not. I am afraid it may be dangerous."

"It might; and this is why I came here, to let you know all this, in case anything happened to me."

"Is there no one who could accompany you?"

"No."

"I don't like it. It seems foolhardy."

"When I was in Paris," I replied, "Philippe's young footman took off into the scrubland of Montmartre, a place of ill repute where villains of all kinds hold out. I saw the place from a window – it was a great dark mass with little flickering lights. I didn't dare enter it to look for him. But by day it was not so bad; and it was clear enough that the greatest crime there was poverty. Here I see the same situation, only now the boy is Arthur, and that makes all the difference."

"Stay here tonight at least," insisted Claudia. "If only for the children's sake."

As I hesitated she reminded me: "There is always a tendency to fear the worst. But you must trust in Arthur's own integrity. He could after all be living in a pleasant rented room and working in a decent public house."

"In Whitechapel?" I said morosely; but I was half convinced, and stayed.

In the morning over breakfast, Claudia who certainly did her deepest contemplation during the hours of darkness, said to me: "I have been considering what you told me yesterday."

"Yes?" I said uncomfortably. "What have you decided?"

"Not what you think, from the look on your face!" she answered with a flicker of amusement. "Have you given any thought to the future, Algy?"

"It is a total blank to me."

"If you find Arthur . . ."

"If I am so fortunate . . ."

"I assume that you intend to pursue your friendship?"

"Again, if I am allowed to be so fortunate. I would suppose that we would be obliged to travel. That is what they do, the Englishmen who flee the country for reasons of this nature, and then they settle, usually in Paris."

"And is that what you want?"

"No! But at least I would be with him."

"I would have thought that there were ways in which you could achieve that state here at home."

"How could that be possible?"

"It would be possible if I permitted it."

We looked at each other across the coffee pot.

"Would you be prepared to be so generous?" I said cautiously.

"I was considering the alternatives – divorce or separation – you permanently abroad – "

"I in prison," I agreed morbidly.

"Now listen, Algy," said my wife. "All of those courses are to admit defeat and to capitulate to society's rules, all of which I accused Constance when she sat so unhappily at the Napiers'. Do you know that she intends for Oscar never to see his children again? She and they are to live in Switzerland and I believe that she intends to change her name. Of course it is very much worse for her, her situation being what it is, but even so that is not the decision which I would have taken. And I do not propose that we should embark upon any such course."

"Whatever could we do instead?"

"I do not want us to separate; do you?"

"No. I told you so. But I realise that in this business I am entirely in your hands. I've behaved badly towards you and I feel guilty as we discuss it. I cannot believe that you are suggesting even by implication that I could possibly achieve a situation which includes both you and Arthur."

"That is the only answer," Claudia said.

In the face of my bemused silence she declared: "Why should our children be deprived of a father? I won't have that. Why should you be obliged to live abroad and never see them, when you and they are so affectionate together? Yesterday, when you all played on the lake – whatever justification could I have for taking that from them and you? And why should we give up our life which both of us enjoy most of the time? No, I am not going to allow conformity to win. I refuse to sacrifice ourselves to an old-fashioned set of rules which make no provision for the individual."

"You are amazing," I said weakly. "If many of our acquaintance

322

had any idea of this they would confidently expect me to shoot myself in the head."

"Don't be obscene," she said dismissively. "Now listen to me. When you find Arthur you are to bring him to meet me."

"Oh really . . ." I said uneasily. "Is not that carrying the New Modernity too far?"

"We should look facts in the face," she answered firmly. "The ideal thing would be for him to be your private secretary," she mused. "Of course," she added with the nuance of a smile, "the fact that he is illiterate precludes that for the moment! We shall have to acquire a tutor for him. You had better suggest to him that he could be your valet. Would he consider that?"

"I've no idea. He did give me a shave once; it was very pleasant."

"As for the sleeping arrangements . . ." continued Claudia.

"Now you go too fast."

"You and I will never share a bed again and I shall have my private suite, where I shall entertain whomsoever I please without question on your part. Of course you can rely on me to be discreet in every way. I shall expect the same of you. Do you agree?"

"What do you mean, whomsoever you please?"

"Must I spell it out? I mean that I may take a lover."

"I see," I said faintly. "Well, I am hardly in a position to forbid it, am I?"

"No, you are not. Therefore in principle, do you agree?"

"I do."

"I do not see why such a way of life should not be possible, do you? If we are careful . . ."

We sat silently then, each in our own thoughts. Eventually I sighed: "I only have to find him, deep in Whitechapel's maze of back streets – and then convince him – and then deal with Orlando, who holds evidence enough to send me to prison."

CHAPTER TWENTY-FIVE

THE FOLLOWING few days were the dreariest of my whole life. From the small hotel in Aldgate which became my base I set out each day and paced the streets laboriously, enquiring at each public house, each doss house, each mean board and lodging place, showing Arthur's photograph to blank faces. I saw much of poverty and distress and much of filth and squalor. I entered barn-like refuges where men slept in rows of numbered boxes, like ranks and ranks of coffins; and in a warehouse with broken windows, dormitories of tightly packed iron bedsteads each covered with a thin grey blanket. I saw communal basement kitchens, where ragged folk cooked ghastly little meals on smoky stoves, and old men rooted in the straw for scraps, and children fought for cold potatoes. In boarding houses I saw overcrowded rooms where one bed throughout the day was rented out to different people who came in at separate times to sleep in it.

Between these places the streets themselves were a curious mixture of respectable back to back houses with yards and gates, up against vile alleys where it took all my courage simply to enter. There were dark low passages without any form of street lighting, indeed, my steps took me all over the ground already passing into legend as the streets where Jack the Ripper once plied his grisly trade. Seven years ago it was, and still he was not identified. It could not but cause a shudder to walk through the low arched alleyway of George Yard, where on a warm summer morning such as I now experienced, a policeman had discovered the first of the mutilated bodies; and my systematic peregrinations took me also along Buck Row and Hanbury Street where further mangled corpses had been found. Would the grim secret ever be revealed – were any of the strange outrageous rumours true?

Trailing my way up Brick Lane I passed pawnbrokers' shops and Jewish tailors', and innumerable public houses where all day long the drunkards spilled out on to the pavements and sat, feet in the gutter, calling out to passers-by with hoarse renditions of a snatch of song or an obscenity. There were street barrows laden with overripe fruit, black with buzzing flies; and ragged children who made no art of thieving, but grabbed whatever lay to hand and ran. Women handled heaps of musty-smelling clothes at a rag stall; an ancient crone sat on her doorstep stuffing straw into a mattress; a man lay underfoot sprawled upon his back, an empty bottle by his senseless fingers, while two urchins busily unlaced his boots; and in a dustbin down a sidestreet a wretched fellow foraged so deep inside you could not see his head. A many-flavoured stench hung in the air and through a muzzy haze of smoke the warm June sun shone down upon it all.

Possessing not at all the fortunate invisibility of a dream walker I had on my way encountered some hostility and some indifference – shrugs, stares, curses, some abuse, a threatened fist, and clumsy attempts by pint-sized ragamuffins to relieve me of my wallet. I had perhaps been lucky to have met nothing worse, but then, vile as the streets had been where I had so far journeyed, they were not the worst.

The heady whiffs of the smell from the brewery reminded me that I was not far from Goff Street and Mr Pearson's Boys' Home. A strong compulsion drew me towards it. What if by some freak of chance they had seen Arthur? Now I remembered it, Mr Pearson was accustomed to spend some of his time upon the streets in his quest for waifs and strays – the boys themselves perhaps, familiar with the sordid courts and narrow alleys, might throw some light on my depressing task. Already heartened, I made my way along dimly remembered streets and eventually after some unintentional meanderings I arrived at the place I sought. It was late afternoon.

I crossed the gravel and rang the bell-pull. As I stood there on the steps I suddenly realised just how tired I was. I had been tramping to and fro for several days with the accumulating exhaustion of depression, drawing a blank each day and returning disheartened to the hotel where I slept. My feet ached. I was glad to see the door open and Willie answer it.

"Blimey, Algy!" he remarked expressively.

"Can I come in?"

"Whatever's up? Is this a business call? Do you want Mr Pearson?"

"I simply want to sit down."

"Come in." He looked puzzled, as well he might, but led me down the hall to the big warm kitchen at the back. A broad bustling woman was peeling potatoes at the sink. The place was unbearably hot, from a variety of soups and stews that simmered on the range. Some young boys sat at a scrubbed pine table, chopping cabbages to shreds.

"I don't usually show visitors into the kitchen," Willie said. "But you look fagged out. I'm going to make you a mug of tea."

"Well, if you must . . ." I murmured looking hopefully and in vain for signs of anything stronger.

I sat down at the table, much aware of my weariness. My feet were boiling in my shoes. I watched him, with the great brown teapot, moving about the kitchen, the ridiculous dyed chestnut hair cut in a curiously civilised style instead of the long-haired fringed Renaissance page that I remembered; the slender well-shaped form, in close-fitting black trousers, with a brown shirt, sleeves rolled up, neck open, and a loose green gipsy waistcoat – I felt a pleasant surge of the old affection.

The woman at the sink – Mrs Potter – and the boys continued with their tasks in cheerful unconcern. From other rooms the clatter and chatter of boys rose and fell, and Mr Pearson's exquisitely stern tones achieving calm and order.

"I'd like to talk to you both," I murmured.

"Oh Lor', it ain't money, is it?" Willie paused, teapot in hand.

"No."

"Is it private, like?"

"Yes."

"We'll go in the study. We have a study now," Willie boasted. "It's where we Receive."

One of the bigger rooms downstairs had been partitioned off; this was the study. I liked the kitchen better. The study was cool and formal. It had a writing desk in the corner, shelves of papers of an official-looking nature, heavily framed engravings on the wall and a half-circle of stout chairs. I sat upon one, wielding my mug and gazing at the mezzotint of Salisbury Cathedral opposite me.

Willie returned with the daunting Mr Pearson whose presence always had an ill effect upon me, as it did now. I withdrew instinctively into a habitual and possibly haughty politeness.

"I am so sorry to trouble you, Mr Pearson . . ."

"How may we be of help?"

"I wonder whether you have seen this boy?" I proferred Arthur's photograph. "He may be lost in the vicinity of this place."

"Is he wanted by the police?"

"No!" I cried aggrieved.

"I beg your pardon. Why do you look for him here then? That is the usual reason for people who come here with photographs of missing persons."

"I thought you may have seen him."

"No," said Mr Pearson handing the photograph to Willie. Willie shook his head; but more sensitive to my condition than Mr Pearson he added: "Who is he, Algy?"

"His name is Arthur Hughes. I undertook to search for him – as a favour to his mother. Are you quite sure that you don't recognise him?" I asked despairingly. "I've been walking up and down – I've looked in the obvious places – public houses where he may be in employ, lodging houses, doss houses – "

"*You* have, Algy?" Willie asked with a little frown. "You went to doss houses?"

"Yes," I answered hurriedly. "The more respectable ones. I've still some others to see . . . I suppose you are in no position to help me in some way? You couldn't lend me a couple of boys to ask about? They must know the more obscure places – Arrow Court, for instance, just nearby – I should go there – and company would be a great help to me."

"Certainly not," said Mr Pearson stiffly. "The boys are entrusted to me for education, not to run messages. You must have plenty of servants of your own, Lord Algernon?"

I swallowed, justly rebuked.

"Couldn't we –?" began Willie hesitantly.

"No," said Mr Pearson firmly. "Lord Algernon, you should know better than to be alone on foot wandering round places of a questionable nature in this district. Whatever it is that you are doing here, it does not seem appropriate for you. For your own good, go home. The police are paid to do the work of search and find; hand over the photograph to them; they go about in twos and threes and know what they are about."

It was justified advice. I suppose I had given off the impression of a dilettante posing as an amateur detective. I felt burdened down with helplessness.

"This is a boy who – is special to me," I blurted out. "And there are – reasons – why I may not ask the police."

Willie glanced at Mr Pearson quickly but Mr Pearson kept a tight impassive expression. I gave a swift beseeching glance in Willie's direction: "I thought you might have special cause to help me."

There was an awkward pause. "No, we have not," said Willie looking down, and as he handed me the photograph he did not meet my eye.

"I see I was mistaken," I said stiffly, standing up. "I am sorry to have troubled you."

They ushered me politely to the door. The atmosphere was most uncomfortable. I daresay they were as glad to see me go as I was to get away. What a fool I had been to go there! How stupid of me to have thought that some mystic communion would bind us together, some shared ether that would let each know the other's secrets.

I was angry, weary, and more careless than I should have been. I strode off, paying no attention to the type of street down which I walked, which previously a natural caution led me to do. I was in a narrow court, more gutter than street, and I hurried through it; now in a little maze of alleys I attracted a swarm of ragged children who buzzed round me with questions – who are yer, mister? Wotcher doin' ere? Is 'e a toff? Course 'e is – oy, mister, wotcher after?

I arrived at a tawdry public house – The Rat and Shovel (Lord knows in what connection those two subjects joined!), the one that served these dingy passages. Its door was open and a couple of louts were sitting on the step. One stuck out a foot as I went in, but I sidestepped it. At the counter I produced the photograph again, and the barman having nothing better to do, passed it round amongst the lounging crew that leaned upon the bar, and played the comedian.

"We seen 'im, haint' we? Wasn't it 'im the perlece dragged orf in a Black Maria, just last night?"

"Nah, that was someone else. Nah, this was the one whose 'ead Charley cut open wiv 'is barber's knife – and then 'e pickled both 'is ears!"

"You ain't seen Charley's knife, 'ave yer, mister? Show 'im, Charley."

Charley, a lean gaunt fellow in a grey overcoat, with a head of tousled grey hair and a sharply etched frown drawing his brows together, lurched along the counter's edge towards me.

"Wotcher fink 'o this!"

He drew from deep within his sleeve a sheathed knife which he removed as gracefully as any violinist drawing bow. The long thin blade gleamed and he fingered it caressingly. "You know whose this was!" he hissed at me. "You know who gave me this!"

The others sniggered comfortably; they knew the answer and looked forward to the effect his revelation would produce.

"Go on – whose was it, Charley, tell us!" they encouraged.

"Jack the Ripper's!" Charley said, with all the relish of a show-man.

I pocketed the photograph and turned about. The two oafs on the step stood in my way; a third sloped up to join them.

"You didn't oughter be here," one remarked. I tended to agree. I hurried past. The other one was more intellectual. "Hey! Ain't you famous? Ain't I seen your face before?"

Suddenly my dusty clothes seemed startlingly indicative of wealth, my hair too glossy. As I made off down the alley light dawned upon the dim recollection of the man behind me.

"I know who you are – you're that yeller-mopped boy that Oscar

Wilde went buggering with."

My heart sank. Oh that wretched likeness! I could not get from this foul maze of side streets quickly enough. And literally this was so, for in my haste I'd taken a wrong turning, and as I heard boots upon the cobbles giving chase I ducked beneath a low archway and ran between two high black walls that led into a yard. Suggesting to each other in loud voices what should be done with Bosie Douglas, the three pursued. I ran. I saw a further low-arched passageway leading from the yard. I darted down it. It stank of piss. At its far end I could see a street, with people passing. Then I felt my jacket seized by the shoulder, I was jerked to a standstill and an elbow hooked my neck. Next thing I knew, a fist was driven in my guts, which blow, when the arm about my throat allowed it, doubled me over, and as I crumpled forward a fist grabbed me by the hair and lifted up my head and punched my face. My vision exploded. I was shoved to the ground and kicked about the shoulders; I lay hunched up, knees to chest, my hands about my head and face; boots trod on me as I was heaved about, my jacket wrenched off and its pockets emptied, and all this in daylight, two yards from a busy street.

"I'm not Alfred Douglas!" I protested thickly, furious even while I suffered.

"It don't matter," answered one. "You are his kind."

They ran off then. I could not straighten up for the burning in my stomach, and lay writhing, squinting at the slimy cobblestones through a wedge of matted bloodstained hair. I was desperate to reassure myself as to the condition of my face – my lips felt like rubber and I could not see clearly from one eye; my nose was bleeding heavily and my body throbbed. The children who had pestered me earlier now appeared and gathered round, staring with interest. This unnerving audience had some effect in spurring me to shift; I crawled to my hands and knees and inched my way to standing, every part of the unravelling a penance. I staggered to the end of the passage holding on to the wall. Anger was uppermost in my mind. Perversely it was all directed towards Willie, whom at that moment I held completely to blame, and also I was angry with the wretched nobleman who looked like me and who probably was even now in Paris dining out.

I saw that I was back in Brick Lane and I limped my painful way back towards Goff Street, nauseous and filthy. My shirt-front was spattered with blood and my sleeve hung off one shoulder. I must have presented a ghastly spectacle, yet if anyone stared at me I did not see it, and nobody stopped me and asked what had happened. I rather felt that I had let the side down by appearing in a public place dressed so and I was seething with rage at the indignity I had undergone; I was moreover terrified about what might have happened to my face. My eye was closing up. Everything was bleeding.

Clutching my stomach I crunched across the yard to Willie's door. I heaved on the bell-pull and the door opened. To Willie's startled face I said: "For God's sake get me a mirror!"

It occurred to me that in order to be made welcome at Mr Pearson's residence it helped if one was tattered, bloody and in difficulties. The contrast with my previous reception was marked. Now in the kitchen I had the personal attention of Joseph Pearson himself, my mumbled pleas of "couldn't Willie – ?" quite ignored. Mrs Potter was given the evening off, the shift of boys about to do the washing-up permitted to vanish, with whoops of glee. The kitchen door then firmly closed, amongst the piles of plates and bowls they gathered round me with most flattering concern.

"We never thought you'd go down Arrow Court!" said Willie, torn between distress and admiration.

"I said I would."

"Yes – but we thought you'd got your people with you . . . or that you'd go home. You never used to be so plucky, Algy!"

Sitting at the kitchen table before a big enamel bowl I writhed and winced as Mr Pearson cleaned my face. Blood plopped into the water. The mirror Willie obligingly brought me I turned face down, groaning at the sight therein.

"For Heaven's sake," Mr Pearson commented mildly. "Has no one ever punched you in the face before?"

"No! Well – at school . . ."

"I thought that Willie was vain – but *you* . . ."

"But what will happen to me? Look at my face!"

"Nothing. In a week you'll look as good as new. You were lucky not to lose your teeth!"

"The aristocracy," said Willie helpfully, "have teeth like horses'."

"But as for your black eye you'll have to sit there with a cold compress. We can't afford raw steak. Take off your shirt. It is repairable, I see; but *you* may wish to throw it away?" I noted of course the sarcasm here.

"I could never wear that again!"

"The trousers too . . . we can fit you out in something . . ."

I think that Mr Pearson took a plain delight in reducing me to the ranks and cladding me in what I would have described as work-house gear. He bathed the bruises on my back and shoulders – I could not see them properly, but Willie assured me they were purple. Then he found me a serviceable grey shirt, a coarse black jacket and some awful trousers; and then they gave me soup and listened to my tale.

"And so what is this boy to you?" asked Mr Pearson carefully.

"I love him!" I declared emotionally, determined to hold nothing back.

"We felt bad about not helping," Willie said. "But honestly, since Oscar we have been in such a state . . ."

"Do you appreciate this, Lord Algernon?" said Mr Pearson speaking low and passionately. "When you asked for our help you came as somebody with wealth and privilege – a man moreover known to be happily married, with children, and a position in society. I could not see what you thought that we could do for you that others better qualified could not do. You who had everything seemed to be expecting us to take a certain risk. You possibly don't understand what it's like – we daren't put a foot wrong, not one step. You know, I hope, that this Home for Poor Boys is my whole life. I know that we are doing good, filling a need that far from decreasing, daily grows more desperate. Yet all the good we do would count for absolutely nothing if the slightest hint of impropriety attached itself to us. With what ferocity the newspapers would clamp their jaws into a scandal at a boys' home – we have to live a daily life of a certain dishonesty, always on our guard. I could not possibly lend you any of our lads upon a paper chase for a good-looking boy upon a whim of yours."

"Of course I see that," I said soberly. "But you are quite wrong to suppose me what I seem. Although I have a family, and although my wife is an exceptional woman in every sense, my deepest feelings are towards Uranian Love, and Arthur in particular. Since that became clear to me it has been the dominant influence in my life, and I hope I am not ever called upon to deny it."

"You will be," Mr Pearson warned. "And though it is brave and beautiful to speak the truth, as far as I am concerned it is more important to do my work than to make statements about myself. If the one precludes the other then I choose my work. I will tell any lie that's necessary to make it possible for that work to continue. Which means, Lord Algernon, that just to suit your purposes and your high ideals I could not make admissions about my private life which might eventually cause some backlash to the situation here. I have suggested Willie ought to do the same." He looked severely at my friend.

"Well, I would do ordinarily," said Willie. "But it's different with Algy. I'm so pleased he's found someone to love."

"And lose!" I moaned.

"Algy knows that I have always felt that kind of love," said Willie, "and without committing you in any way then, Joseph, all I'll say is that I have found greatest happiness in the life I lead, and leave him to make of that what he may."

"Quite enough, I would have thought," grumbled Joseph. "You will of course stay here tonight, Lord Algy? I would like to say treat this place as your own; but as it is your own, that would be superfluous."

"Oh, Joseph, don't be such a bear," said Willie. "Don't mind Joseph, Algy, it's simply that he doesn't like you!"

"Willie!" Joseph snapped.

"And he gets most disgruntled every time he remembers that your money makes his life's work possible."

"What a little swine you are tonight," said Joseph. "Still at least you're *here*. You know, Lord Algernon, he disappears from time to time. The thing about Willie is that he simply doesn't like hard graft. And when it gets too much he takes off for a sojourn with his more disreputable cronies. That's where he was last time you dropped by."

"No I wasn't; I was at a political meeting."

"Oh yes, Algy, Willie has become quite a little anarchist in his spare time. Prince Kropotkin, Eleanor Marx – he knows them all."

"Not anarchist; radical," Willie corrected. "Society must be changed from the roots."

"You hear him? I believe he was the *éminence grise* behind the Dock Strike!"

"What does that mean?" Willie demanded. "Eminence what?"

"Algy will know; it's nice to have someone here who understands some culture."

"Yes, it is nice to have Algy here," said Willie aggressively. "He and I can talk about Old Times."

"Oh well, I'll certainly be in the way then," Joseph scowled and heaved the bowl towards the sink, tipping away the bloody water most expressively. "And now I have some work to do," he said with dignity; and left the room.

"He means he's going to write his Memoirs," Willie said loudly. "His Life in India. No one'll ever read it; it's awful dull. It isn't even useful, like my political meetings are. All about fevers and dysentery and how his district was administered, all the facts and figures supplied."

"I thought you said that you'd found greatest happiness!" I cried. "Are you two always so – so – ?"

"Bitchy? No," Willie grinned. He drew up a chair. "He didn't want me to tell you he's my lover. He didn't even want me to suggest it. He don't trust you. Why should he, I suppose, 'cause all he knows of you is not much in your favour, and, you see, at heart he's awful jealous of how you and me were once. And it's true he's sore about your money."

"What a shame. I intend giving more," I said drily.

"See, you're just as mischievous in your way," teased Willie. "Now, tell me all about Arthur – everything. Is he as good as me?"

Without answering that unworthy question I told all, all that had happened to me since last we were close – the intervening years of conformity and suppression, the return of Mr Charles to stir my stagnant lake, my forays into Soho, my dealings with Zabarov and Orlando, my growing love for Arthur. I recounted the idyllic week at Mortmayne, the dreadful atmosphere caused by the trials; the blackmailing and the flight to Paris; Ivan and Zizine, and my release from doubt and self-delusion; the unexpected support that I received from Claudia the New Woman in all her magnificence; and my long dreary search for Arthur.

"Ah, dear Algy," Willie said, his hand upon my arm. "You ain't alone. You have been, but not any more. We have to stick together, we that's different. Someone told me that once, a man who saved my life when he got me out of the reformatory. We have to help each other – it's the only way. Joseph might be sour to you, but you can trust him with your life. We'll find your lad for you, you'll see.

"It ain't been easy, Algy," he explained. "We've had some nasty moments. There was a policeman once who brought some boys to us and kept lookin' at me odd and sayin' 'Haven't I seen you somewhere before?' 'E must've known me when I was on the streets but he couldn't be quite sure. We was lucky there because he moved to a different patch soon after, but 'e was the reason I cut my hair and dyed it brown. I ain't so noticeable now; I merge. That's how we 'ave ter be ter carry on – unnoticeable. It's dreary, ain't it, but it's true. Fortunately Joseph never loved me just for my hair! He loves me," he grinned, "for my lovely personality."

"I don't doubt that," I answered warmly, for I was suddenly overcome to think that I was sitting here at all, with Willie, who had been my dearest love, and who was still my friend. Our hands touched, and I knew he felt the same.

"You'll stay here, wontcher?" he said practically. "A coupla boys can go and bring your luggage for yer. You probably want to wear your own posh clothes again, though far as I'm concerned you look good in what you're wearing. Even with your lip split and your eye swelled up!"

Mr Pearson wandered nonchalantly back into the kitchen.

"Tea, Joseph?" Willie offered, jumping up.

"Please."

"Algy's told me such a tale . . ."

"I hope you apologised for our bad behaviour."

"Algy understands."

"He will," said Mr Pearson enigmatically, "when he has known Arthur as long as I have known you."

"I ain't easy, am I?" Willie said complacently. "But you always knew that. He don't really mind my politics, Algy."

"It's not his politics as he calls them to which I object – after all, his views are the same as my own. It's the fact that after every meeting he attends he keeps us awake long into the night telling me what everybody said, and worst of all, what he thinks about it all. Willie's thoughts are a bottomless pit. Did he run on so when you knew him, Algy?"

"Yes," I remembered happily. "But then, so do I."

"He reminds me of that famous speech of his heroine Mrs Annie Besant in some radical newspaper, a very dramatic utterance: 'The People are Silent. I will be the Word of the People. I will be the bleeding mouth when the gag is snatched out. *I will say everything!*' That's Willie all over."

"Yeah," grinned Willie. "Get me on my favourite topic and I never shut me bleedin' mouth!"

Mr Pearson slung his arm around him and Willie nestled.

"I couldn't do without him, Algy," Joseph said.

I slept that night in a small room beneath the eaves. I envied them their situation. At night they had the top floor of the house to themselves, the boys in a dormitory below. A couple of the older boys helped with the organisation of the place; Mrs Potter and her daughter came in to cook and clean, but always with the aid of the lads. I saw that it was hard continuous work; but Willie and his lover were together. For all their difficulties, fears and personal discrepancies I thought that it must be a good life.

I was peeved next day to find that my inflamed midriff was a problem still and all my bruises ached. The idea of tramping the streets again depressed me.

"Don't worry; you won't have to," Willie promised.

"Why not? And what are you smirking at?"

"Your face, Algy; I can't help it. You've got such a grand black eye, and you was always such a peacock!"

"That's all I need, an idiot to snigger at me. Why don't I have to walk the streets?"

"Because you'll scare the passers-by! Ah no, that ain't the reason. I'm takin' you to meet my mate Harry. He's the one to help us now."

"Oh no!" groaned Joseph. "Must he be involved? The greatest undiscovered criminal of our time, with the morals of an alley cat!"

"Joseph don't like *him* either," Willie sniggered.

Years ago, in the house in Kensington, Willie caused an uproar when he instituted a soup kitchen for the poor without telling Franklin – even in those days a snob – what he was about. I helped him dish up soup. I was reminded of that time now, as he and I beside the kitchen sink washed up and dried some thirty plates and bowls and an endless stream of cutlery.

"I'll tell you about Harry," Willie said. "Do you remember when I took you round the streets where I grew up, and showed you just how horrible it was, and then we wandered up through Spitalfields and I showed you a worse place and I said I knew someone who lived there? Ah – you won't remember – you'll just remember how you couldn't wait to get away! When I was a nipper I got into bad ways. I met this feller, handsome as a gipsy prince, with coal black ringlets and the flashest clothes I'd ever seen. But he was a bad lot and if I'd stayed with him I'd have got into a heap of trouble. But I always had a soft spot for him, like, and he for me. Two of a kind we were, he reckoned, a cut above the rest!

"Well, years went by and I moved in with Joseph. You know he goes about the streets sometimes and finds our waifs and strays. I had a try a few times but one night I got beaten up. And afterwards I thought about it and I decided I was too easy to beat up and I should do something about it. And I remembered that the landlord at The Lamb near Harry's old house was a prize fighter, so I disappeared as Joseph calls it, and I asked Mr Vargiss if he would teach me some skills, and he said yes and so he set about to train me. I put up at Harry's house which lay empty and deserted, and I slept there, and Mr Vargiss taught me strengthening and how to throw. If someone comes at me now I can sling him over my shoulder. I'll show you when you're better," he promised temptingly.

"Well, one night who should come back but Harry. He'd been to The Lamb and heard I'd turned up, so he knew it was me, and we had quite a chat. Cor blimey, he was gorgeous! Even better looking than I had remembered! And would you believe, we still had fondness for each other after all that time, and we had some good times then, while I was learnin' throwin'. When I was able to throw Harry, then I knew I'd won; then I came home.

"Well, Joseph was livid with me for takin' off, and worse when I told him what Harry had been to me in the past – I mean a bad influence in my formative years. See, Harry's still a villain . . ."

"And what about his . . . sexual leanings?" I said jealously.

"Oh, he's a womanizer!" Willie laughed. "Oh yes! Back in them days you couldn't keep him from the tarts! He's what I call a Manly Man. He's done cockerel fighting, played the race tracks, knows the inside of every gambling den from here to up west and makes his livin' makin' deals. I don't ask him about that. He knows the kind of people who dump people in the river . . ."

"I think, like Joseph, that I shall not like him."

"Ah, but he's much reformed!" insisted Willie. "One night he met a poor sad girl who wasn't makin' a very good livin' on the streets, and he Saved her from her Fate. It turned out she had a baby and he took them both in and looked after them. That's the kind of man he is, all heart. Thizz her name is."

"Thizz?"

"Yeah, Thisbe. Anyway, he moved her from that hovel where he once hung out, where we'd had them good times, and bought a proper house in Stepney, and they have been together now for a coupla years. They got another baby, Catherine. I chose the name for 'em. It comes from *Wuthering Heights*. It's nice to see a person settle, ain't it? Their neighbours don't have no idea what Harry does for a living. Well, bleedin' hell, nobody does!"

"Why must we concern ourselves with Harry at all?" I said. "He sounds as if he could be trouble."

"Not a bit of it," said Willie stoutly. "He's my good mate. He'll help us. He's got contacts all over London. I think the world of him. We've had good times."

Exactly. In my mind I had no doubt what those good times might well have entailed, and I daresay Joseph thought the same. A womanizer he might well have been, but all alone with Willie in seductive mood and I did not give much for his chances.

"Sometimes," said Willie distantly, "I need to be out on the streets at night. I never do anything to let Joseph down, and it's not that I'm not happy – I love him something awful. But sometimes I just need to go and walk and see the lights that dance along the river; and be on my own."

Desperate to be pressing for news of Arthur I had to be patient as I waited at Goff Street while Willie went away to fix up a meeting with the famous Harry. Not that I had any time to kick my heels; Joseph was quite merciless.

"Here, Algy; you know how to read and write; see what you can do with these."

He sat me at the corner of the kitchen table, with a bunch of lads six or eight years old, and a collection of slates and chalk and writing paper and pencils, and a heap of reading books, and the only advice he gave me was that in the formation of letters one used broad downs and fine ups. Mrs Potter moved about preparing luncheon and I did what I could with five illiterates scrubbed clean, pathetically eager, whose home a week ago was a piece of board at the back of an alley.

When I considered Sophy, William and Perceval who had known an atmosphere of literacy and comfort from birth I felt much out of my depth here, for there was an abyss between us. These boys were terrified of me; as for me, I was so dreadfully moved by their appearance and situation that I could barely keep my composure. One had an empty look, as if he had long since withdrawn from life; one was all eyes, and they full of the reproach of centuries; one had a demeanour of total resignation, as if he had seen it all and expected nothing; and one was chattering and perky, with jug-ears and a cheery grin, nervous pattering humour, and so defiantly undaunted by his experiences that I felt quite humbled; and the one I could hardly bear to look at for the pain he somehow stirred in me – perhaps I saw in him what Willie must have been like as an urchin, for he was exceptionally beautiful, with enormous eyes and lovely features, but the indescribable hopelessness in the expression on his face would haunt me ever afterwards.

Together we formed a's and b's and looked at words and drew them in the air and then upon the slates. The smiles of achievement that I induced by the end of the morning were wealth to me.

When Joseph asked me later how we'd done and I described it, I could not help adding: "How do you bear it?"

He didn't answer, but said briskly: "I have a fresh batch for you for the afternoon. Those five are off to learn some carpentry. I don't think you would be so useful there!"

"Find out what they're good at," I said fervently. "There will be employment for them anywhere within my power."

"Thank you, Algy," Joseph said. "I'll take up your kind offer on their behalf. If only benevolence were the simple answer!"

Benevolence from a comfortable home had sent a bag of cast-off clothes; and Joseph knelt amongst them, sorting them.

"I understand from meeting you at the Old Bailey that you felt for Oscar Wilde," he added thoughtfully.

"He has been almost constantly in my mind these past few months," I nodded.

"Of course, you will have read *The Soul of Man Under Socialism*?"

"Indeed I have not," I remarked. "I am afraid that amongst the kind of people I know, that piece of writing was treated as a curious aberration on the part of a man who otherwise wrote entertaining dramas."

"I believe it is the best thing that he ever wrote," said Joseph. "I was pleased to find his talents so directed. It is wonderful to read a piece of socialist writing which is able to make its point so freshly and with humour. Such skill and brilliance turned to the matter of serious comment upon our miserable society was a revelation to me. Most social documents are very heavy going."

"I suppose you do not have a copy here?" I enquired with a certain resignation. "I believe it is quite a short work?"

"You will have no difficulty fitting it into your busy afternoon," said Joseph. "You can read it over your bread and cheese."

That evening, in a public house in Spitalfields, I met Harry; and not only he, but also Mr Vargiss the landlord who had taught Willie to throw.

Inoffensively christened The Lamb – possibly because it did a good line in chops – this place housed a motley collection of folk whom last week I would probably have crossed the road to avoid; indeed, I dreaded that the oafs I had encountered in Arrow Court would suddenly march in and join us. Against the counter leaned a throng of noisy ragged men and women, while children holding jugs and cups pushed through this impediment to get access to gin.

Mr Vargiss, an old man now, with a patent warm affection for Willie, came and took our order, chatting on to us as he bore trays and tankards. His hair was smoky white, his face a beefy red; he was in rolled-up shirt sleeves with a blue and white striped waistcoat. Even elderly he was immense. His huge hands were dark and discoloured from years of rubbing pickle into his skin to leather it up and lessen bleeding in the ring. One side of his jaw was uneven – with great relish he explained to me that a lump of bone had come loose, like a tooth, and they'd had to prize it out and sew the skin back up.

"Ah," he said, "the good old days, when the Fancy was legal, and enjoyed by royalty. Fist fighting, that's a manly sport, that is, but the villains took it over and the gentlemen backed off, and took up *boxing with gloves*," he cried contemptuously. "A pansy game with rules and regulations. All the fun's gone out of it. Ah, in the old days they'd go for the balls, they'd hammer a man's knuckles till they swam inside his fingers, they'd crush the lungs and rip the flesh off the cheek. Mint on your chops or plain?"

"Algy wants to learn to throw," said Willie mischievously.

"I'm the man ter teach yer," Mr Vargiss bellowed. "Look at this."

To my alarm he undid his waistcoat and off it came, and then his shirt. I was face to face with a monstrous rippling chest, somewhat past its days of glory but impressive nonetheless. A mat of curly grey hair covered the upper part, and he drew in his belly so that his great rib cage expanded. Here and there his skin was puckered with old white scars.

"Hurt me," he offered comfortably.

I stood up and gave him a flat-handed blow; I had not even been brilliant at the despised glove boxing. It was like hitting a wall. I laid into his belly with both fists; he didn't even budge. I straightened my hair, which had flopped forward.

"Miraculous!" I gasped. "How do you do it?"

Pleasantly gratified he showed me a slim club and he whacked it against his guts time and again, his flesh resounding with the slaps and no effect of pain at all.

"Like that," he said. "For months on end. The sides of my hands are the same."

"He can slice the necks off bottles!" Willie told me in thrilling tones.

"Yeah," said Mr Vargiss, "and I'll teach anyone who cares to learn. I taught this young scrap here. When I'm through with you, I said, you'll be able to throw a bloke about like a bolster. Then as he topples, you can swipe the back of his neck. A light blow'll confuse him. A heavy one'll snap it. Yeah, I taught Willie. But Harry I never had to teach!"

His voice glowed with admiration, and the object of it, Harry, drew on his cigarette, and commanded another round of stout.

A viciously handsome fellow Harry, with dark brows and an easy arrogant manner. He had jet black ringlets streaked with iron grey. He wore black trousers very straight and stylish and a dark brown velvet jacket, and his shirt was black and brown striped, with a crimson neckerchief at the throat. Upon his curls he wore a black corduroy cap slung askew, the angle so perfectly arranged that I suspected it took an hour to fix. He must have been nearing forty, I guessed, lithe and wiry, with long slender hands, wicked eyes, and a slow sardonic smile. If Willie had told me that he had not attempted to get Harry into his bed at some time or other in their years of "good times" I would not have believed him.

"You should have gone into the ring!" said Mr Vargiss. "I could have made you a hero."

"Go in the ring?" cried Harry. "'Ave me beauty spoiled wiv a punch in the mahf? You must be jokin'."

"You done some trainin' though, ain't yer? You got a good set o' muscles there."

"I might 'ave 'ad a little mingle with the swells in some fancy games room or other," said Harry airily. "I gets arahnd."

Willie grinned at me during the ensuing conversation about horse races, sharps and bookies, lynching welshers, dog fights, rat pits, ferrets, broken necks and trophies.

"Harry has wide interests," he reminded me.

"Ah, Willie," Harry said with smouldering eyes. "When are you goin' ter leave that bleedin' Good Shepherd you took up wiv and come and work for me?"

"Work – you don't know what that means!" said Willie. "How you manage to stay clear of the Law all of these years it's a bleedin' miracle."

"It's called bein' slippery," Harry decided. "Some people when yer grabs 'em they slithers aht yer hand. Quicksilver, that's it. That's what I am."

With Mr Vargiss back behind the counter, Willie, Harry and I dined on chops and stout and talked about the matter dearest to my heart.

"I heard a bit abaht yer from Willie," Harry said. "Whyever you should so come dahn in the world as to be mates with such a little tart as 'im is quite beyond me; but I see you are and that's enough for me. Money I respect; it's abaht the only thing I do respect, but money I does, and I can tell you come from a good stable, even in them 'orrible cloes!"

"In my own clothes I look like Alfred Douglas and risk the wrath of curiously moral idiots."

"Yeah, Willie told me. Tough, ain't it, to be done over for someone else's crimes! Still, why pick an' choose – blood'll taste the same whoever knocks it dahn yer froat and no matter what the reason is they done it for."

"I have to ask it, Harry," I said. "Have I not seen you before? I have a memory of someone in the Café Royal . . ."

"Yeah, I go there. I'm often up west."

"I'm sure that it was you. Some men were playing dominoes, and you made them leave – someone was waiting outside, and they were pretty scared."

"I wonder who it could have been?" said Harry innocently.

"I was impressed by your authority."

"Ah, was yer? Ta," said Harry modestly. "Right then, let's have a look at this 'ere photograph."

The crumpled picture gazed up balefully from the beer-puddled table top. My heart ached.

"And what's 'is name?"

"Arthur Hughes."

"Never mind," snorted Harry. "Arf a Hughes is better than none!" Then he questioned me closely about the trail I'd followed, and about what Arthur was like in character and habit, and with which places he was familiar.

"Mind if I take it?" Harry said briskly.

"No," I lied. "I'm desperate to find him," I murmured. "Do you think there is a chance?"

"Oh yeah," shrugged Harry. "Just a question of how long it takes and what it's worth." He named a price and I accepted. We solemnly shook hands. "I'll find 'im for yer, Lord Algy, I got ferrets everywhere."

There was a fair in Commercial Street as Willie and I made our way home. It was night-time, and the music from the barrel organs blared, the street lamps streamed their trails of light. At the open stalls upon the pavement they were making toffee over boiling pans, and pouring liquid peppermint on to a marble slab to cut up into chunks. Willie bought some, and we strolled back munching, past the fortune teller and the performing fleas, the parrots on perches trained to pick up your lucky card, and the man who ate broken glass, the girls from the Salvation Army calling us to God.

"What d'you think of him?" said Willie proudly.

"Stunning," I agreed reluctantly.

"Ain't he just? He took to you an' all. And," he added, "something I'm really pleased about. Joseph says he was wrong about you."

"Oh? In what way?"

"He says you ain't the Pompous Shallow Autocrat he thought you were!" Willie grinned.

"Oh does he!" I replied. "But he is every particle as pompous – more so. And as for autocratic – why, he practically held me by the nose to force *The Soul of Man Under Socialism* down my throat!"

"I wish I'd seen that," Willie sniggered. "So did you read it?"

"I did not dare refuse."

Willie flung his arms wide between the sweet stalls.

"Man is Made for Something Better than Disturbing Dirt!"

"Course 'e is, dear," said the woman selling peppermints.

I felt suddenly happy – full of love. I never thought that I could feel so comfortable on the streets of Spitalfields. I was with Willie; and his way of life showed me that it was possible to live together with the man you loved. Not easy – but possible. Hope, that's what we needed. Harry would find Arthur for me; and true love would finally be mine.

The warm air wafted treacle and beer, the naphtha flared, the barrel organ played *Ta Ra Ra Boom Der Ay*. The moon shone overhead beyond black chimneys that gushed forth a sea of silver-streaked illuminated smoke.

We made our slow way homeward.

Early next evening, Harry called in to Goff Street Boys' Home to bring this piece of news:

"We got a lead, Algy, on yer Lost Boy. He was washin' tables in The Mitre. Then a gentleman came in and said a boy like him was fit for better things. And he took him up west."

CHAPTER TWENTY-SIX

ALL MY old dreads and apprehensions returned a thousand-fold on hearing Harry's tidings. Had Arthur finally given in? Did he go willingly – and to what grim future? The spectre of Octave – if such a plump boy could be so described – lurked in my consciousness, reminding me that once a good-looking youth lands on the streets, he is very much at risk.

"Up west ..." I blanched, recalling Piccadilly and the painted boys that walked its pavements, elusive moths in the pursuit of a light.

"Calm yourself, Algy," Joseph said. "It may not mean what you think."

But Willie looked grave and said: "We had better waste no time."

"No reason to be downhearted," Harry declared. "West or East, it makes no difference how we go abaht it. No problem!"

"For me there is a problem," I interposed. "I cannot sit by and wait while you search. But if I were to venture anywhere near Piccadilly I am certain to encounter someone who is blackmailing me; he lives in Half Moon Street and frequents the Alhambra and the Gaiety; we would be bound to meet."

"Hey, Algy, you got a blackmailer on yer?" Harry asked with interest. "What's his hold?"

"He stole some papers from me."

"Papers!" grinned Harry expressively. "What a multitude of sins that word covers! What a deal of trouble we would save if we had never learnt to read and write!"

"Be that as it may, the wretched youth has fleeced me out of a tidy sum, and will again if he supposed I was in London."

"D'you want him nobbled?" Harry offered.

I stared, torn between the civilised man's dislike of menace, and a very primitive desire to discuss the matter further.

"Come on, Alge, don't look so mealy-mouthed!" Harry encouraged. "Does yer or not?"

"Well – what could you do?" I said hesitantly.

"You tell me what you want doin' and I tell you whether it's what I do, or whether I mention the business to Others."

"All I want is the papers returned to me! I don't wish the fellow ill – well, not much. I was indeed a little fond of him at one time. But he quite betrayed my trust. As long as he possesses those wretched papers I am at his mercy."

"So it's the papers then that are the trouble. The bloke himself ain't the bother?"

"No, because without the papers it would simply be his word against mine and I would deny his accusations. He has no proof and no corroboration. Without the papers in his clutches no line of enquiry could be pursued. He is an actor of sorts and has no standing. Much as I hate to mention this in this hotbed of Socialism, my name and situation would incline the law to take my part. But truly I do not think that he would pester me without the trump he holds."

"Then it looks to me," said Harry, "as if the next thing to be done is get this feller off your back."

Willie sniggered.

"Oh Gawd!" groaned Harry. "He ain't one o' *those*? Am I the only decent ordinary law-abiding bloke 'ere?"

In a state of tightly controlled excitement I met Harry as arranged, in the street where Orlando lived on the north side of Piccadilly.

Some three hours had passed since our conversation. How Harry had spent the intervening time I did not know, but I had divested myself of the borrowed homespun garments which I had been wearing and returned to a mode of dressing to which I was more accustomed and one which, for all Willie's approbation, I felt suited me better. My face was a little recovered and I was able to approach the mirror with something akin to equanimity. Walking a short way in the direction of the city I was able to acquire a cab and make my way along the night-time streets to our destination.

Not only Harry, but also Mr Vargiss and two others were lurking in respective doorways. Silently they emerged; we entered the building by illegal means, and climbed the carpeted stairs to Orlando's apartment, which again we had no difficulty entering. The place was in darkness and we settled ourselves to wait. It was a strange sensation for me, to be seated in this room for which my money paid and which held sour memories for me of the straits to which a gentleman may fall when he takes a wrong track.

We heard Orlando approaching long before he opened the door. He had Amelia with him, and they were both very merry; we heard their boisterous passage up the stairs. They entered, and the light was turned up and then the door was quickly closed and their retreat cut off.

Harry's companions were of ghastly proportion and appearance. Both were big brawny men, so horrible in mien and feature that I could not but suppose they had been chosen for their ability to terrify without raising a finger. One, shaven-headed, bulldog-jowled, leering like a man desperate to be considered for the role of Attila, guarded the door; the other so hirsute about the face that Blackbeard the Pirate would have envied him, and bearing the black eye patch that further identified him with the robbers of the deep, loomed up to bar Orlando's way.

My fair-haired one-time lover looked appalled, as well he might, and Amelia clung to him, a mass of wayward curls and ribbons and a trailing feather boa.

I remained seated; Harry and Mr Vargiss sloped towards the petrified pair like panthers on the prowl.

"Is this your friend, Lord Algy?" Harry asked, his fingers lightly resting on the lapels of his corduroy coat. "The one what treated you so bad?"

"Orlando, we meet again," said I; the scene was so theatrical that the well-worn phrase was nothing out of place.

"Who are these people, Algy?" said Orlando looking very pale. "Get off me, Amelia – I can't protect you."

The quivering girl moved aside, hands clasped, eyes wide and lashes fluttering.

I stood up. "I've no wish to see you harmed, Orlando," I declared. "But you have lived for long enough at my expense."

"So you found some heavies to do your dirty work for you!"

"What other choice had I? I could not live how you would have me live."

"Don't waste yer breath, Algy," Harry intervened. "We came here to do a striping. I finds," he added reflectively, "that the ones with pretty faces always minds a striping most. But just to show him we mean business we begin with action. Don't we, gentlemen?"

I knew well enough that further demonstration was needless; but Mr Vargiss had no intention of coming so far for nothing, and I could not but admire his skill as he neatly hurtled Orlando over his head and threw the hapless youth to the ground. Amelia shrieked, then froze, silenced with a growl from Blackbeard. Attila then produced a razor and began to sharpen it. The display was totally convincing. Orlando stared up glazed-eyed from the carpet.

"They wouldn't, Algy?"

"Get Algy the papers, sharpish," Harry ordered.

Orlando scuttled crab-like across the floor. Damn me, he had hidden the wretched things in the elephant's foot – it had a detachable base – and therein lay the heap of Charles' pornography, instantly recognisable. I crouched down beside Orlando turning the pages carefully, trying not to let my elation cloud my judgement; every page must be accounted for.

"And the letter?"

"Here. It's all here. I'd have given them back in the end, Algy. You know I would."

Harry lunged across and seized Orlando by the hair. Attila and his razor hovered over him.

"Remember," Harry glowered. "This is always waitin' for yer, pretty boy. Any time you steps athter line. Algy don't want to hear no more from you. Algy got some very powerful friends."

"All right!" cried Orlando. "I gave them back – you saw me do it. God, Algy, where did you pick up these people?"

"Are they all there, Alge?" said Harry solicitously.

"Yes."

"Burn 'em; do it now."

Harry and I crossed over to the fireplace, weaving our way through the exotica and together burned the stuff out of existence.

"That's it, then, Algy?" said Orlando querulously. "All even now? They aren't coming back? Fair's fair, eh? I've done what you want."

"As far as I'm concerned," I stood up. "There is no need for you to meet any of these gentlemen again nor for you and I ever to cross paths further. I shall of course no longer pay your rent; but with your not inconsiderable talents I have no doubt that you will make your way."

"I daresay you're right," said Orlando. "I shall use the experience which I have gained with you."

"Right then," Harry declared briskly. "Business concluded."

Was I over-imaginative, or did I sense a palpable air of disappointment as Attila put away his razor? Without further ado my companions and I made our way out of the building and into the summer darkness of the street.

Emotionally I thanked these Myrmidons, clasping their hands, assuring them of my deep appreciation; nor did they lack financially for a night's work that had not proved an excessively demanding trial of their own particular skills.

"I cannot tell you, Harry, what this means to me," I said as we stood together on the corner of the street. "The shadow of fear and dread that has been at my elbow – at one blow removed – the lifting of a cloud – the indescribable relief – and yet," I sighed, "if only – "

"The boy," said Harry. "You think he's on the Dilly."

"I don't know what to think. But everything I do think merely conspires to fill me with a monstrous gloom. I have seen how easily the vulnerable fall prey to corruption."

"My mates an' me'll run our eyes over all the tarts in Soho for yer," Harry promised. "If he's there we'll find him."

"I must come with you."

"Ho no," laughed Harry. "Are you crazy? I gets you aht o' one mess and you wants ter jump head first into another! You think a gentleman like you can do the rounds of all the street boys' hideouts and no one bat an eyelid? You got ter keep your reputation very pure now, Lord Algy. You won't keep gettin' second chances."

"Cannot I help? There must be something I can do."

"Not with me; you would be very much in the way. You're too emotional, Alge. There's no place on the streets for Hearts an' Flahs. Go home ter bed. I'll meet you in the morning."

"Take luncheon with me at the Café Royal."

"I will take a meal there, yes, but not with you. You got ter think abaht appearances. You'll see me there, but I'll sit with me cronies and you sit with yours. If I get news I'll pass it on. Go home nah. Thank your lucky stars your friend back there was such a push-over."

In Willie's kitchen I sat disconsolately drinking tea. It was past midnight; Joseph was abed; and Willie, having waited up for me, leaned against the sink, hands in the pockets of his corduroy trousers, silent for the moment while I voiced my despair.

"It's not knowing, the possibility that he could be anywhere – in bad company – in danger – a boy alone so easily becomes the victim of – and he has a propensity to drift towards what is not good for him when he's depressed. Ironically all is falling into place for me – Orlando dealt with – Claudia compliant – but all this counts for nothing while Arthur is still out there, left to his own devices – and I can do nothing. Harry said go home – keep off the streets – but I am in this torment – "

"Why should you do what Harry says, huh?" said Willie sharply.

"What? What do you mean?" I raised my head.

"You'd feel better doin' somethin', wouldn't yer?"

"Well, yes, I would. But what?"

"Lookin' for Arthur. I'll come wiv yer. Get yer 'at."

I blanched. "But where would we begin?"

"At The Mitre, stupid, where he was last seen. Don't you know anythin' about detective work? Go to the starting point. Don't you never read Sherlock Holmes?"

Speechless with gratitude and excitement I watched Willie leave a note for Joseph, penned in his exquisite copperplate: "Gone to find Arthur. May be late for breakfast."

"Joseph'll kill me when I get back," he added guiltily. Looking cheery enough at the prospect of the slaughter Willie arranged his black cap carefully aslant his brow and we came away.

It was a tidy walk down to The Mitre, through the dark and shadowed streets.

"You don't need to fear nothin'," said Willie observing my glances about. "Walk bold, that's the secret. Remember I'm a champion thrower. And I daresay even you could be some help in some way," he sniggered cheekily.

"I daresay I could," I agreed and thumped him.

"We're in Hanbury Street here, see," Willie commented. "And that's Christ Church Hall where Annie Besant held her meetings. You remember the match girls' strike seven years ago, it was really good down here them days. The whole East End rose up. We had public meetings and we wrote letters to newspapers, and money came in from all over the country, from people who cared about the way these girls had been exploited. Passers-by stopped and cheered us, on our marches. The employers had to give in. The girls got their wages raised and formed a trades union. And after that, other downtrodden workers got inspired to rise up too, and Mrs Besant helped them an' all to shake off their chains. It was glorious. And it's still goin' on – you got to be always vigilant against the rich – sorry, Algy, I don't mean to be personal . . ."

"Not at all," I murmured. "I don't dispute Mrs Besant's capabilities. Hanbury Street – isn't that where one of the prostitutes was murdered?"

"Oh there you go," said Willie irritably. "This fascination about Jack the Ripper. Everyone who don't live here has it. We get foreign tourists coming here in groups to have a look, and nobs from the West End pokin' abaht, goin' 'Yes! This is where they found her!' And they gasp a bit and have a little shiver and then hop back in their hansoms and go home to pheasant and claret. Do you want me to take you to the spot?" he challenged.

We stood staring, hostile.

"No!" I cried. "You quite misjudge me. I can't help it if the only connection I've ever heard with Hanbury Street is that of the unfortunate woman. Please don't be offended."

"It's just that so much else goes on in these streets," Willie muttered sulkily. "So much political and social things – events and changes – things against our horrible society – all for the good – and all that people know about is Jack the Ripper."

Chastened I fell silent as we walked. We turned into Commercial Street, breathing fuggy air that smelt of beer and dung and richly rotted fruit.

"Wait – I've got an idea," said Willie. "Maybe your Arthur's sleepin' in Itchy Park."

The ornate pale pillars of Christ Church, Spitalfields, now rose above us, unashamed baroque elegance jutting up from the squalor beneath. Amongst the trees beside it I now saw that people were asleep. On tombstones, steps and paving stones they lay, dead to the world, sad ragged heaps of humanity, too poor to buy a bed in a doss house, men and women both, and children too, thin scraps of hopelessness too weary even to wonder at our presence, too tired to lift a hand. I looked at Willie, stricken, feeling much like Scrooge faced with his conscience-pricking visitation.

"Search, Algy," Willie said implacable.

"But Harry said a gentleman took him away . . ."

"If he refused the gentleman he could be here. It ain't far from The Mitre."

We moved amongst the desolate that lay there, obliged to look closely to be sure that Arthur was not here. I knew that after that grim search I never would again be able to refer to "the poor" as if it were a distant and intangible aspect of society. I had considered myself something of a philanthropist and now I felt ashamed. Arthur was not here, but I would put my money to more practical use henceforth.

Willie understood, and squeezed my arm.

"Not far now to The Mitre. We'll find it closed; but I can get us in."

We crossed Bell Lane and Houndsditch, finally arriving at a dingy little courtyard where, winding between beer barrels in a pitchblack yard, we found a small back door and knocked upon it. As we waited, Willie nudged me and whispered wickedly: "Take yer to see where Catherine Eddowes was murdered, gov. Right there!"

The landlord of The Mitre sat and munched his way through a sizzling dish of chops and carrots while he spoke to us of Arthur. Bald-headed, beaky-nosed and affable, he had the air of one whom life had long since ceased to startle. A very old woman half asleep sat silent in a rocking chair, hair white and wispy, beneath a lacy cap, her face a mass of wrinkles, her cheeks hanging down in folds beneath her hollowed eyes.

"Like I told Harry," said the landlord, spitting out a blob of gristle, "Arthur worked here for a day or so. But he wasn't happy. I could see as he were down. What could I do? I ain't a charitable institution, am I, mother? You got to make yer own good cheer, I say, not wait for someone else ter do it for you. Yer needs a laughin' way o' lookin' at the world. How else can yer deal with it? Ain't that so, mother? Young Arthur was a sad 'un. Cheer up, lad, I used ter tell 'im, it may never happen! And he'd raise a smile, and lose it straightway after."

"He don't sound like much fun," said Willie tartly. I scowled at him.

"Then this bloke came in."

"A gentleman," I prompted.

"Well, he wasn't a proper gentleman," our landlord said. "Not like yourself, sir. Oh, he was respectable and clean, but not a toff. And they got chattin'. He bought Arthur a beer, like Arthur was his guest. He had a very pleasant manner. I could see that Arthur liked him."

"Arthur liked him?" I said staring.

"Oh yes. They was gettin' on like a house on fire."

Willie shot a sideways glance at me.

"This man," I frowned. "What was he like? Elderly perhaps? Wizened even?" Willie snorted.

"Well, no, he wasn't that old," the landlord answered, pausing with his mouth full. "And he seemed a very pleasant sort of chap. Like a do-gooder. Like them teachers as comes dahn here and help the kids. Yeah, now I come to think of it, he said something abaht reading. Didn't he mother? And Arthur said 'Yes, I'd like that very much'."

Now this development I had not foreseen. Arthur in the clutches of a seducer, Arthur forced into a life of crime – how readily I had succumbed to fears like these! But Arthur finding a saviour – Arthur in the hands of a decent benefactor, one who might help him, care for him, *love* him – this idea was in every way as threatening as the former. More so! One nearer to his station in life – one with whom there would be no problems of adjustment, of adapting to an unfamiliar life – one unencumbered by a wife and children – now my fancy raced and now my heart sank like a bucket in a well, down to the chill dark depths.

"Did you hear any of their conversation?" I asked unhappily.

"Shelton Street!" cried the landlord, putting down both knife and fork. "Shelton Street. That's what he said – something about Shelton Street."

"Wherever is that?" I asked.

"It's up west," Willie answered. "I know it very well. It's just near Covent Garden. I once had a room near there."

"But this is wonderful," I marvelled. "An unexpected break-through."

"Why didn't you remember this when Harry asked you?" Willie asked the landlord cynically.

"Well, you know Harry," shrugged the landlord wrily. "Barges in – gimme a gin, mate – 'ave yer seen this boy? Flashes a photograph. Yeah I seen 'im, went up west with a gemmun. Ta, mate; off he goes. He never sat dahn like you two did and probed, like, and started me off thinkin'. Did he, mother? But since I saw Harry I daresay I been mullin' the matter over in my mind, like, and so nah when you two come and asks me I remembers more, as that's the way of things, I reckon – when you starts to thinkin', who knows what you set in motion? Ain't that likely, mother?"

"Shelton Street then, Algy?"

"Shelton Street."

Outside in the dim-lit streets once more, we paused.

"You are not suggesting we should walk?" I said.

"Why not? I used to, as a nipper. We thought nothing of stompin' through the city on foot. Why, I remember nights . . ."

"Yes, I believe you told me," I said curtly. "I suggest we bear towards civilisation with our eyes peeled for a cab rank."

We picked up a hansom in Cornhill and settled gratefully into its welcoming interior. Willie sighed ecstatically and I warmed to him, remembering his love of these sleek conveyances. Our thighs touched; neither shifted his position. We sped westwards, towards Covent Garden.

"You think he's gone with Another?" Willie said with sympathy.

"He thinks I fled to France without him. He thinks I've abandoned him and saved myself. That does entitle him to believe the worst of me, and it would not be inconceivable that taking up with someone else would follow. Who'd blame him?"

"But when he sees you . . . when you explain . . ."

"I can but hope." I paused. "Willie . . . I waited for him at the railway station, and he didn't come. Just like with you and me. Heaven deals out its justice very fairly, wouldn't you say?"

"Oh," Willie said awkwardly. "That was long ago. We were all different then."

"In some ways we were. In others . . ."

I stole a glance at his profile, framed as the passing street lights caught the silhouette. He turned to me, his lips a little apart, remembered kisses almost visible upon them.

"Willie – "

"I know, Algy."

"You still love me."

"Yeah, and you love me an' all."

"I do."

Our hands met, intertwined. Streets laced with memories whirled about us, his life and mine, an intersecting web of pain and beauty binding us together, giving credence to this timeless yet all too transitory moment.

" 'Ere we are, guv," called our driver. "Shelton Street."

Standing there, we felt bereft, angels from a heavenly chariot set down upon that darkling plain. We looked about us.

"If he was any kind of gent," said Willie caustically, "he must have fallen upon very hard times to have brought Arthur here."

It was a dark and narrow street, two carts' width and some forty houses long. A single glance sufficed to show that it was a place of rented rooms and vile at that, for on this warm night many doors hung open to let air into the squalid maze beyond, and from the passages within the stench of choked untended privies spewed forth upon already fetid air. We heard a donkey bray: a costermonger's cart stood by the wall, its jutting shafts padlocked to a door handle.

"Should we knock, at random?" I suggested dismally.

"Nah. I reckon we should shout."

"Shout?"

"Yeah. Start at one end of the street, walk to the other, shouting."

Cupping both palms round his mouth and standing in the middle of the street Willie bellowed: "Arthur!"

Reaction certainly we achieved. All up and down the street windows opened, slammed, and angry voices cried reply:

"Oy! Wotcher fink yer doin'?"

"Bugger orf!"

"Stop that row or I'll be dahn and kick yer teef in!"

From the rancid doorways dark and tattered figures tumbled, all aggressive, most half asleep, surrounding us in curiosity, accompanying us on our dreary round.

"Who's Arthur, mister?"

"He don't live 'ere. Go home."

"Arthur! Arthur!" we persisted.

"Arthur! Arthur!" yelled some of those about us, and one wit added: "Arthur pahnd a tuppeny rice, Arthur pahnd a treacle!"

"Frederick!" Willie shouted suddenly.

"Frederick?" several of us echoed.

"Yeah," grinned Willie. "We ain't havin' no luck with Arthur, and for all we know there might be dozens of nice lads inside who'd come out if we knew what names to call."

The costermonger, rising like a genie from a bottle, big, immense and brawny, burst forth from his doorway and reduced us all to proper seriousness.

"Nah, what's all this abaht? Disturbing people's peace. I gotter be up in half an ah. You want Arthur? I'll get Arthur for yer." And he brandished a handbell and majestically strode the length and breadth of Shelton Street clanging his bell and crying "Arthur!" like the knell of doom. No Arthur could have slept through that; and no Arthur emerged. Several objects were thrown from windows and a fight broke out, and nothing was achieved except a certain pandemonium and a rapidly descending gloom for me.

"Nah, bugger orf," the costermonger told us, and we slunk away.

"Oh Willie," I groaned. "What now? a dead end – a pure dead end."

"I think we need a change of tactic," said Willie. "We'll walk up to Goodge Street – it ain't far. I got some friends there. We'll have a rest and something to eat. We'll plan what to do next."

"What friends?"

"Friends Joseph don't like much. Anarchists."

"True anarchists? You mean they throw bombs and such?"

"They don't, and only as a last resort, and only in pillar boxes," said Willie inconsistently. "You got a narrow view of anarchy."

"It means chaos, doesn't it?"

"Not always," Willie answered. "In its purest form it means that everybody takes responsibility for himself – no government or law. No property and no man earnin' more than anybody else. A society without classes. Now what is wrong with that?"

"Only that it is an established fact that in our time anarchists have been known to attempt to achieve their ends through violence. Blowing up railway stations, flinging bombs into a crowd. There can be no justification for the maiming of the innocent."

"Oh I agree. But our society is so awful and so wrong that sometimes frustration breaks through when gentle words have no effect."

"Willie – should you be bringing me to meet them?"

Willie grinned. "Afraid they'll beat you up? You should be used to that now, bein' the victim of political aggression!"

"If you mean those oafs in Arrow Court! Political aggression!"

"Yes it was. They were strikin' a blow against the upper classes!"

"A blow? Three or four! I can still feel it when I bend."

"Don't worry. You wouldn't know these were anarchists if I hadn't told you. They're just ordinary people. We're only goin' there to get some respite."

"But I'm so patently on the other side . . ."

"They live in the real world, Algy, they know aristocrats exist."

"Aren't you afraid I'll give them away to the police?"

"The police know all about them. They are what is called 'known'. It means that they can't be politically active. They're all very nice people."

Nice people! Willie's friends in Goodge Street functioned like the characters upon a stage set. For a start, they all met in a cellar. Whatever joys the upper storeys of the house held we saw none of them; we were ushered down a rickety stair, and in the cellar by the flickering glow of an oil lamp we sat upon makeshift seats and ancient sofas, while Willie exchanged news of a political nature with those anarchists then present – a curiously well-groomed young man with sleeked-down hair and gleaming teeth, and an attractive youth who had a look of having stepped out of *The Pirates of Penzance*, a knotted handkerchief about the head, one gold ear ring, and a striped sash about his otherwise conventional attire. I was exhausted by depression and took no part in any of the conversation, merely sitting back against the plastered brickwork and drinking gratefully the wine with which they plied us, an obscure Balkan beverage and very potent.

It was good to be off the streets and for a moment cease the turmoil of my racing thoughts, for truly I had no idea what to do next. I had counted upon Shelton Street and it had proved a farce. If I were not so crazed with worry about never seeing Arthur more I would have marvelled at the weird turns that my life was taking. As it was, I closed my eyes and hoped to lose myself in the nepenthes of the wine. Distantly I heard that Paul was expected. I sensed the excitement – obviously Paul was of some importance and his visit something of a coup. I paid the information scant regard but I eventually heard him heavily descend the staircase and I opened my eyes. I stared. I found myself looking at Zabarov's butler.

It was not an instant recognition. There could have been no one further from my mind and I had always tended to compartmentalize my nefarious encounters, as if each could be contained within a mental box, the only link myself. Willie would have told me otherwise, that the Underworld's fluidity brought all its driftwood to uneasy proximity with one another sooner or later.

I looked at him then, Paul Picard, man of Montmartre, veteran of the bloody aftermath of the Commune, who knew the Taverne du Bagne where its glory was remembered, and the winding byways of La Butte; who knew perhaps the little square with the green fountain where I had sat and read of Oscar Wilde. Maudlin with wine for his connection with Montmartre where I had found my freedom, I warmed to him. I wondered how his life had been – his true connection with Zabarov – and did he remember Arthur?

"Monsieur," he inclined his head to me, the recognition mutual.

Willie's friends, at ease in the French language, spoke to him of generalities – the political stance of Europe at the time – and Willie whose French, unless there had been a marvellous sea-change, amounted to "I am an Englishman and I do not understand", read

353

his way through a pamphlet on agricultural reform, the lamplight illuminating his beauty and his lack of sleep.

"I am surprised to find you here, monsieur," said Picard, on his own territory here and at ease.

"Believe me, I am merely a visitor. I am with my friend there."

"Ah." I saw at once that he assumed some sexual commerce. One more pederast English milord. I winced. It was a fair assumption; he had seen me with Orlando.

"I have seen your other friend," he commented.

"Orlando?"

"No, the other one. The dark-haired one whom Count Zabarov made his servant."

"My God!" I blanched, propelled from my wine-glaze with rapidity. "Where? When?"

"What is this?" There was a little sneer, a certain sardonic amusement here. "Have you lost him so soon?"

"Oh monsieur, if you have news of him I beg you tell it me. I have been tramping the streets in search of him. I would give anything to know where he is. Name your price – I am desperate. In God's name, where?"

He shrugged. "Prepare yourself for a little disappointment, monsieur. You will not find him now. He has returned to his former master. Count Zabarov has claimed him as before."

"But Zabarov is abroad," I stammered.

"He has been in London secretly, this last month."

"But I don't understand," I gasped. "How could he find Arthur? We heard that Arthur was with a friend, a protector. Why should he go back to Zabarov?"

"Who can comprehend the mysteries of the dark places of the mind? Once in bondage, always in bondage. The weak, like your Arthur, will always need a master, and Zabarov knows it. He took the opportunity chance offered to him. He stretched out his hand," said Picard, so doing, "and drew the little fish back into the net."

"Where are they now?" I demanded, enraged, confused, and eager to pursue.

"Already gone," said Picard. "They spoke of leaving the country. They were to take the boat train."

"When did you see them last?"

"That was already two days ago. They will be gone by now."

"But to where?" I cried with a sinking heart.

"Who knows? The Count has many castles and central Europe many mountains, many forests. You will not find them now."

"Willie," I said weakly, turning to my friend. "We have to leave."

"Of course," said Willie, mystified.

"Excuse me," said Picard, with a little crooked smile. "I thought I was to be offered money for my information."

I was obliged to keep my word and pay him for so strangling all my hopes. I felt humiliated; I could not wait to get away.

Up in the street I blurted out what I had learnt. I had some crazy notion I would find Zabarov, Arthur with him, at the house in Fitzroy Street, not far from where we were. I strode in that direction, Willie following, never pausing till I stood outside the house. The light of dawn dispersed the darkness now. We stared at the closed windows and drawn curtains. Images of the strange bedroom, the occult symbols and the fiendish décor whirled about my brain. I saw Zabarov's visage, leering and triumphant, his hand on Arthur's neck. I was in torment.

"We must break in," I said.

"Oh Algy, are you out of your mind?" groaned Willie. "You don't know what you're saying."

"There's a way round the back, a servants' door . . ."

My loyal and protesting friend helped me unlatch a door that led into a long back yard. As burglars we were in the lowest league, for we stumbled on some garden tools which clattered in a heap about us, and instantly brought a query of "What is it, Jack?" and the answer from a manservant then appearing beside us, "Prowlers, sir, prowlers!"

"Act drunk," hissed Willie. "Oh, we ain't half sorry to trouble yer, mister – it's his lordship – wined and dined all night and don't know where he's goin'. We don't mean no harm; we mistook the house – when he's like this I can't do nothin' wiv 'im. Let me take him home."

The portly fellow at his house door in his dressing gown, his burly manservant at his side, so patently epitomised respectability, so little the occult, that my behaviour must indeed have seemed the ravings of a drunkard to him.

"Do you know Count Zabarov? Do you know where he has gone? Who lived in this house prior to yourselves? Did they leave an address?"

"Oh, humour him, sir," Willie begged. "He can talk of nothing else but this Count Zabarov."

"I cannot help him," said the fellow, blinking and bemused, delightfully equable about having been disturbed by lunatics at five o'clock in the morning. "I know of no Zabarov. I have no idea who rented these rooms previously. I suggest you take his lordship home, my man, before he harms himself."

"I'll do that, sir, and thank you. Come on, my lord. You've had enough for one night, ain't yer?"

Deemed harmless, we were ushered from the premises.

"Let's go home," said Willie.

"Home?" I said blankly.

"Yes, to Joseph."

"That's your home, not mine."

"It's yours, you know it, any time you want."

"I don't think I could bear it, seeing you and Joseph – it's all right for you – you've been so fortunate – you have all you need for happiness – it's easy for you now – let the world do as it pleases, you and he will be together."

"Yeah, but – "

"For me it's over. I won him from Zabarov once. I can't do it again; I'm too tired. It wasn't meant to be."

"You'll feel better when you've had a good night's sleep. Tomorrow you can make enquiries at the shipping offices . . ."

I smiled wanly, unconvinced.

We walked, bearing southward. By some chance we saw no passing cab, nor had we any clear direction then, and we skirted the edges of Soho towards Piccadilly, silent, in a cloud of gloom and inconclusiveness.

"I think I'll go to Pall Mall," I declared. "Now that I'm liberated from Orlando there is no reason why I should not go to my club. I'm tired and drained. You go home. I'll meet you later."

"I'd rather not leave you. You've gone all clipped and strained; you're shutting me out."

"You've been wonderful. But there's no more to be done. I'll see you into a cab in Piccadilly."

At the entrance to Glasshouse Street we caught a glimpse of the straggling line of those without employment, who hung about at the back of the Café Royal waiting for a chance to work in the kitchens.

"Dammit," I murmured. "I've arranged to meet Harry there at midday. He's to bring me news." I laughed brittlely. "Poor man. He was to spend the night searching brothels. And all for nothing. Would you like to join us? I suppose that I had better go through with it."

"Eat there? No fear!" said Willie fervently. "I wouldn't touch the Café Royal with a barge pole. That's a place as represents a lot of what's wrong with our society. Have yer seen what they charge for a dinner? And people are sleepin' on benches in rags!"

When we reached Piccadilly and the row of waiting cabs, Willie hesitated. "I'll stay with you."

"Go home," I said. "There's nothing you can do. I'd rather be alone. I'll be all right."

Within sight of Eros, the dancing boy with the arrows of love, I

356

saw Willie safely ensconced into a hansom. "Eat with us tonight, won't yer?" he insisted.

"I will."

"Promise. I gotta know you're all right."

"I promise. I'll be there."

"Till tonight then, Algy."

"Till tonight."

Willie leaned around the edge of the cab, waving violently. I watched him and his hansom out of sight.

CHAPTER TWENTY-SEVEN

I T WAS almost as if the trials of Oscar Wilde had never been. The newspapers in the smoking room were full of politics and the daily expectation of the fall of the Liberal Government with the possibility of Rosebery's resignation. The rumours were that he would be glad to go. One could not help but wonder whether for him also these past few months had been a time of dread and apprehension. It was said that he could not sleep. No one would ever know how close our nation may have come to a vast political scandal which now, with Oscar dealt with and removed, was safely averted.

"We have decided," Willoughby remarked to me, "to put it all behind us. When Oscar was condemned some spoke up for him; most thought the sentence lenient. In order to prevent bad feeling we agreed not to refer to it again. I would advise you, Algy, to do the same."

"Pretend it never happened?" I said, with a curl of the lip.

"Exactly. It would be deuced bad form to stir it up again and would do no good at all. I say!" he added warmly. "I'm damned glad that you came back from France. Some of the fellows started talking – your absence was so sudden – and Heatherington is still away, you know. One draws one's own conclusions. I suppose you did not see him in Paris?"

"I did not. As I told you, I merely attended a wedding."

"Quite. It's good to see you back. The fellows will be glad. Let's get together sometime – and how is Claudia?"

Indeed, the general opinion confirmed Willoughby's assessment of the situation. Everyone received me with effusive welcome, patently relieved that some unnamed private *faux pas* had not obliged me to remain in France and so besmirch the honour of the club. What hypocrites we were, each one of us, supporting one another in the creation of a monstrous edifice of seeming strength and permanence, perhaps suspecting in his heart its insubstantiality, a house of cards, no more.

The habitual lightening of spirit which previously always overtook me upon entering the Café Royal was not present with me that day.

I took up my remembered place in the Domino Room, sitting upon the red plush seat, looking about me once again at the extravagant décor. The long mirrors flung back images – the glittering chandeliers, the dark pillars with their golden vine leaves, the flamboyant ceiling and the luxuriant caryatids. I saw it all with indifference.

I could not believe that I would ever feel happiness again. Arthur was lost to me. The future seemed an unremitting blank of empty days and desolate nights, laced with a certain evil irony – Orlando silenced, Claudia supportive, and all to no purpose, all that pain and confusion for nothing at all. Moreover, how could one disentangle the presence of Oscar from the Café Royal? Its most notorious luminary was now gone, disgraced, the void a tangible shadow. A way of life was over.

Harry was there; but he was right – we would have made an ill-matched pair, and he looked comfortable and regal with a crowd of sporting types in loud checks, puffing big cigars in every manner redolent of the race track and the gambling world. I caught his eye. His quizzical frown told me nothing about his last night's exploits. All the same, I was glad to see him. I called to mind our night-time sortie and his villainous confederates, and all the devious byways of the past few weeks. It had been a strange interlude in my life. It was over now, but I would not regret a moment.

The young waiter who brought me my drink was one that I remembered, in the stylish black outfit and the long white starched apron worn by such at this establishment.

"Lord Algernon!" he observed with a smile. "For a moment I thought it was Lord Alfred Douglas come back amongst us! My heart skipped a beat, it did. He'd never dare, I thought, not now!"

"Oh really," I grumbled. "This is too much. Douglas is a little weed. I have always been far better looking."

"I know it," he assured me cheerfully. "It is the hair, that's what it is. You both have such smooth golden hair, you can't deny that. But as you say, you have the advantage."

He disappeared, and I sat thoughtfully and sipped my Amontillado.

The waiter had returned; I was aware of him beside me, and I raised my eyes with careless unconcern.

I found that I was staring at the kind of mirage which men half dead through lack of water are said to see as clearly as if the sight were true. I believe that thirst causes them to see what they most long for – lakes, rivers, waterfalls. The same was so in my case: I saw

Arthur.

"Take your order, sir?" he said.

"What are you doing here?" I gasped.

"I'm a kitchen worker. Your waiter came and told me he thought he had seen a ghost, Lord Alfred Douglas, but it was another gentleman. I asked if he knew which gentleman it was; he said he did, it was yourself, and now he thought of it, you were not at all alike. I pretended that I was interested in this supposed likeness, and he allowed me to borrow his outfit and come up to have a look."

"It is the first time that the comparison with Bosie Douglas has worked in my favour," I said faintly.

"I had to see you, to explain about the letter – "

"Hang the letter! What about Zabarov?"

"Eh?"

"Are you not with him?"

"No, of course I am not. You know that. He went abroad. You know he did."

I gaped like an idiot. Then my bewildered mind took in the truth. Why ever had I been so foolish as to believe what Paul Picard, Zabarov's friend, had so glibly told me? No doubt indeed he had seen Arthur, as he said, most likely waiting at the back door of the Café Royal – why, I too must have passed within yards of Arthur myself early that morning as I trailed past miserably with Willie – and the malicious lie that Picard told me was a sweet revenge upon me for the trouble I had caused him when he lost the haven of Zabarov's home. In my relief I laughed out loud, stood up, seized Arthur by the arms and shook him.

"Give in your notice this instant!"

"Algy – people are looking – " he murmured.

"The Café Royal has seen worse incidents than one of its frequenters losing his wits," I answered.

"Even so – "

"You're leaving with me, Arthur. Now."

"Well – I am supposed to wash up from luncheon. I shall have to explain that I have gone. I will never be allowed to work here again if I sneak off."

"You never will work here again! Explain your departure if you must, and then meet me immediately on the steps outside. I will wait for you there. You are not, I hope, in hiding from me, as well as from your mother?"

"No," he said sheepishly. "Very well. I'll meet you on the steps."

I stared after him. Was I a fool to allow him from my sight? What if I never saw him again? Could I trust him to reappear, this miracle created out of longing?

Instantly Harry was at my side, some kind of racing tip between his fingers, the kind of communication quite acceptable between our different spheres.

"Him, ain't it!" he marvelled. "Workin' here."

"In the kitchens," I murmured.

"I never thought of anywhere so obvious!" Harry said. "I must be losin' me touch. You know what it is, dontcher? Too much closeness to crime and you get so's you see crime where crime is not. To think I spent 'alf the night in converse wiv a crahd o' painted tarts wiv slits cut in their britches! And you was just as bad, to put the idea in my head!"

"I admit it . . . and I'll make it up to you."

"You will an' all," he promised. "But I don't deserve it, since I never found 'im."

"That doesn't matter now. As far as I'm concerned, for last night's escapade I am forever in your debt."

"Bring 'im rahnd ter Willie's – they'll be pleased as punch."

From the steps of the Café Royal, Arthur and I walked slowly through the midday crowds that thronged the Haymarket.

Our wanderings had brought us to Trafalgar Square and here we sat upon a bench. In the august company of the great naval hero and his lions we revealed our thoughts.

"I was told you'd gone off with a gentleman! I was told he'd taken you up west!"

"Ah yes – he wasn't exactly a gentleman, Algy, but he did bring me up west. Mr Williams. He comes from Cardiff; he recognised my accent; he thought I needed looking after! The English are very untrustworthy, he said. I could not help but agree in part – some of them go rushing off to Paris on their own, don't they? Anyway, it was he who suggested I might find work at the Café Royal. I reckon it's the most elegant kind of kitchen folk that anyone could wish for – retired professors fallen on hard times, writers and painters whose work nobody buys – I met some very nice people there; and one of them gave me a place to stay, a little attic room; I have been very cosy there."

"You little swine – I tramped the streets in search of you! And what about Shelton Street?"

"Shelton Street?"

"Didn't you live there?"

"No. Why should you think that?"

"The landlord of The Mitre heard it mentioned."

"Ah I know what that might mean. Mr Williams used to live there. Shelton Street, he said, don't ever make the mistake of taking a room there. It's a dreadful place!"

"When I think how I have suffered on your behalf while you were living in your cosy attic! I was attacked! I was left bruised and bleeding!"

"I didn't like to ask! I hoped you'd merely walked into a door."

"I walked into a fist! And all for you! And you tell me you were very cosy!"

"I'm sorry, Algy. I had no idea you were even in England . . . Ronald said you'd gone to France."

"Orlando began to blackmail me; it became intolerable. I decided to go abroad. But I wrote to you, explaining all. I hoped that you might join me."

"I did receive your letter."

"Yes; your mother told me."

"You went to see her!"

"The first thing that I did on my return was to come looking for you. Of course I was concerned and sad when you ignored my letter, as I thought. But your mother let me know the situation."

"Ah . . ."

"I wish that you'd told me! It wouldn't have made any difference. It isn't your fault."

"You don't know what it's like. It's so shaming. People would think I was stupid if they knew."

"They wouldn't."

"They do, Algy. I know. I wouldn't keep it secret if it was not so. It was a rough and crowded shack where I went to school; it was all they could do to teach us English speaking; there was never time to teach us all to read and write. Some learnt, but I did not, and then I found that I could get by, and after that we never had the money to pay a tutor, and once I worked for Simmons I did not need it, since he paid me."

"You'd like to learn, though, would you not?"

"Of course I would. But how can I?"

"Well, easily now, because I shall undertake it. You shall have a tutor and do it correctly, like a good little schoolboy."

"And then? What then?"

"Well – what would you like to happen?"

"I would like to use the reading and writing skills I'd learned; that must be wonderful."

"Would you like to be my private secretary?"

Arthur sniggered. "Aren't we being a little ambitious here?"

"I have become a convert to anarchy lately! It would be a way of being together all the time. You do want us to be together? I know I do."

"Oh Algy – how could it ever be?" said Arthur with a look of hopelessness.

"It must be, that's all," I answered. "There's no other alternative."

"But you have a family, a wife. What if she were to find out?"

"I have told her something of our situation."

"Lord!"

"Claudia is a very unusual person, Arthur. She's very sure of herself, her ideas – forthright. She and I have had no personal closeness for a long time – it suits us that way. I don't believe we are so strange. I know that under certain circumstances she would tolerate you being with me. She would like to meet you. She suggested you should be my valet."

"Oh did she? Well, I won't be that, and you can tell her so. It's one thing to shave your face for fun like we did in the cottage. But I'm not going to wait on you, Algy, or be your servant."

"No, of course not. I wasn't happy about the suggestion either. But the other – the secretary – you'd consider that?"

"Let's take it slowly," said Arthur. "Teach me to read and write. Then I will be my own man and I can do what I want and go where I choose."

"What do you mean? You surely want to be with me?" I asked alarmed.

"But not as your dependent. At least, no more than the other people with limited wealth who are connected to you who have so much."

"I see! You want me to give you the means to attain economic independence, so that you can leave me if you choose!" I accused.

"Yes, that's right. Then there will be a kind of equality between us, and not the giving from you and the receiving from me which has happened up till now. I am completely at a disadvantage. Oh Algy – I felt so bad about not being able to respond to your letter. I knew that it was about something important, for you to write to me at all. But I dared not ask anyone to read it for me. I saw that it contained the word Love, and so I knew that it was dangerous. And so I burned it."

I sat silently deep in thought. What kind of a society did we live in, I reflected soberly, when the word Love was dangerous?

"There was love in my letter, yes," I said. "But that doesn't matter now. All that matters is what we say today. I love you."

"I love you too," said Arthur.

Had other lovers plighted troth here in this bustling square, I wondered, in the heart of a city that provided them with both refuge and condemnation? I wished that I could take him in my arms. Of course, I did not. We sat, our thighs lightly touching, while the pigeons pecked about our feet.

"I'd like you to come and dine with some friends of mine tonight," I offered somewhat shyly.

"Oh no – not with toffs – I'd hate it."

"These aren't toffs at all. Quite the converse. You remember I told you about Willie Smith . . ."

"Yes."

"He helped me look for you."

"He was your lover, wasn't he?"

"Long ago. Now he's my good friend."

"But are you sure it's me you want, not him?"

"Entirely sure, my sweet. I love Willie dearly, but the briars and prickles of his socialist principles stand forever between us. More to the point, he has a true love of his own. You'll come and meet them, won't you? There is so much to say – "

"Oh yes, of course I will," said Arthur warmly. "I'd like that."

I was as close to Heaven upon Earth as I could ever be. Full of determination now, eager to tackle the future, I turned to practicalities.

"Can you not read at all?" I wondered.

"I know some letters. I know your name. I know obvious things – This Way – Gentlemen – Treasure Island – things like that."

From out of my pocket I brought the crumpled *Alphabet of Flowers*, which I had carried around with me for so long, a sentimental talisman.

"What can you read here?"

"A . . ."

"For Anemone."

"B . . ."

"For Bluebell."

And N for Narcissus. It seemed to me that Narcissus had much for which to answer. The past few months of my life had been littered with the casualties of his philosophy, the cult of aestheticism – from Charles to Octave, culminating in the greatest of them all, whose self-love and the adoration of the beautiful and the belief in a mode of existence dedicated to love and joy and individualism, in the face of society's cold harsh dictates of conformity and rigidity, had cost him dear.

I believed that by teaching Arthur the self-reliance of the written word I would give him the wherewithal to make his own way. It seemed a realistic, honest thing to do. There was corruption and exploitation in the way of Narcissus; and selfishness also. By giving him his education I would be giving him the means to move away from me if he so chose. I hoped he would not so choose; but he must have the craft to make the choice.

With the book open before us I put my hand on his, and together we traced a slow and thoughtful way between the flowers.

Also by Chris Hunt
STREET LAVENDER

If you enjoyed *N for Narcissus* you will want to read the story of Willie Smith's first meeting with Algy. In the busy West End streets of 1880s London, young Willie quickly learns to use his youth and beauty as a means of escaping the grinding poverty of his East End background.

"I read all 343 pages in two compulsive sittings... Both a funny study of a young gay's mounting consciousness and a voyeur's guide to the seamy side of Victoriana" -- Patrick Gale, *Gay Times*

"The rhythm of salvation and perdition -- from reformatory to male brothel to good works among the teeming poor, via a superb episode in Bohemian Kensington -- is fearlessly sustained. The effect of this harlot's progress with a silver lining is irresistible" -- Jonathan Keates, *Observer*

"A gem of a book. Chris Hunt's done a marvellous job intertwining a solid narrative full of good humour and wit with a message of real social conscience and insight... Really, you haven't had so much fun reading a gay-themed novel in years" -- John Preston, *Gay Chicago*

ISBN 0 85449 035 3   UK £7.95 / US $12.95 / AUS $22.95

MIGNON

The glittering Paris court of Henri III provides Marc with ample chance to advance his fortunes, as a *mignon*, one of the king's pet boys. But when a threat is made on his life, he flees his native France to seek refuge in the England of Elizabeth I. Here life proves just as dangerous, when he encounters a celebrated new playwright by the name of Christopher Marlowe.

"Finely researched, deeply detailed. You will find no better novel (certainly in the gay genre) which deals with this particular piece of English literary history" -- *Frontiers*

"A rattling good read which adroitly mixes an entertaining plot with plenty of authentic historical background" -- *Gay Times*

ISBN 0 85449 066 3   UK £6.95 / US $10.95 / AUS $19.95

THORNAPPLE

A renegade monk; a scheming lady of the manor; a mysterious old woman and a beautiful boy guarding magical secrets -- these are just some of the intriguing characters encountered by a young pedlar as he journeys through the east of England in 1204. Their stories intertwine to form a fast-moving tale of romance, murder and witchcraft.

"A romantic epic as any historical romance is... Hunt has once again created a historical novel from a homosexual standpoint. Writes a mean page-turning tale" - *Gay Times*

"In a language rich and lavish (it) carries you along, moving quickly from start to finish. Compelling and highly enjoyable"
-- *Northwest Gay and Lesbian Reader, USA*

ISBN 0 85449 104 X   UK £6.95 / US $10.95 / AUS $19.95

GMP books can be ordered from any bookshop in the UK, and from specialised bookshops overseas. If you prefer to order by mail, please send full retail price plus £1.50 for postage and packing to:

GMP Publishers Ltd (GB),
P O Box 247, London N17 9QR.
For payment by Access/Eurocard/Mastercard/American Express/Visa,
please give number and signature.
A comprehensive mail-order catalogue is also available.

In North America order from Alyson Publications Inc.,
40 Plympton St, Boston, MA 02118, USA.

In Australia order from Stilone Pty Ltd,
P O Box 155, Broadway, NSW 2007, Australia.

Name and Address in block letters please:

Name _____

Address _____

_____

_____